I0668202

Continuous Creation: Book I of the Complete

Revelation of Mick and Keith

By James H. Peterson III

Cover Art and Photography

By Rebecca L. Kelm

All of the characters in this book are fictitious, and any resemblance to actual persons, living or dead, is purely coincidental. Except for the Scion Tycoons. Those cats are all real.

Continuous Creation

Book I: *Continuous Creation*

Table of Contents

Author's Note: Concerning Typos & Philosophizing

"Every time you make a typo the errorists win."
--Robert Asprin

First, I dislike plot spoilers intensely. There is no plot spoiler in this Author's Note. There are just a couple of explanations and an apology to my Advanced Copy Readers.

Second, there is nothing essential to the story in this Author's Note either. Please skip to the story if you don't want to be bothered. I usually do when I find one of these rambling notes cluttering up the opening pages of the book I am holding. And I always skip ahead when it's an academic like me that's doing the noting, forwarding, or general eye watering philosophizing of the type I'm about to engage in. So feel free to turn the pages until you arrive at the photo of the Angel monument and then carry on from there.

Thirdly, whatever interest I had in numeration has just evaporated, so let's get on with it.

Many people have helped in the production of this novel. Mari O. Lydic provided extremely valuable help in content editing and research. Many of the best details in this book have been the direct result of Mari's suggestions. This book would be considerably less interesting without her valuable assistance. At times, the resources Mari provided to me on mythology, folklore, literature, and popular culture were overwhelming in their completeness. I still have a reading list I am working through and my debt to her cannot be repaid.

Robert Langenderfer provided excellent work as a copyeditor. His careful attention to detail and willingness to look at each sentence brought the manuscript back to life at a time when I was personally drained.

Ryan Nottingham did the final proofreading. He read the entire book in five days and calmly noted down the mistakes. Like my editors, I owe my final proof-reader a huge debt.

Editors are always valuable to any writer. To me though, they are essential. The problem is that I am absolutely rotten at proof reading and I have paperwork to prove it. I have a condition called a Central Auditory Process Disorder and it plays havoc with my ability to spell and proof read. The advent of computers and ever more sophisticated word processing software have helped me a great deal. But these adaptations are far from perfect.

Needless to say, any mistakes that remain are completely my own fault. In the event that you find any kind of error in the text, please contact me through my website at TheInfinityPlane.com/contact. Also, please feel free to contact me for any other reason too. I will be happy to engage with anyone that's not trying to sell me a better system for website traffic or a better WordPress plug-in.

I had a good deal of fun writing this book. I hope that you will have as much fun reading it. The book is meant to be fun, even though it draws on serious subjects as well. In the 1908 essay collection *All Things Considered*, Gilbert Keith "G. K." Chesterton wrote:

> So far from it being irreverent to use silly metaphors on serious questions, it is one's duty to use silly metaphors on serious questions. It is the test of one's seriousness. It is the test of a responsible religion or theory whether it can take examples from pots and pans and boots and butter-tubs. It is the test of a good philosophy whether you can defend it grotesquely. It is the test of a good religion whether you can joke about it.

I could not agree more and I doubt I could have written the idea in any clearer language than Chesterton used, so I won't try. You, the reader, will have to be the judge of the quality of the metaphors and jokes.

Lastly, I would like to give a special note of thanks to my wife Rebecca L. Kelm. Not only did she provide the novel's cover art, a feat I marvel at since I cannot draw a decent smiley face, but she also listened. I do not think the spouses of writers get enough recognition for what they put up with. For the last three years, she has listened calmly to complaints ranging from plot problems, to the thickness of publishers, to the complete stupidity of agents, and through it all, has continued to feed me and be the first to hear or read any part of the story. Not only did she do all that for the sake of my writing, but she also gave birth to our second son and pulled me through a major back surgery during the writing of this book. For this and the first 12 years of our shared life together, I can only say thank you. This book would never have been created without my wife's unfailing support.

Pax Tibi,

James H. Peterson III

Post Scriptum: James H. Peterson III lives in Louisville, Kentucky, in the United States with his wife Rebecca L. Kelm, their two sons, and about one thousand Cichlids. He spent almost a decade burning up his G.I. Bill and V.A. Benefits at the University of Louisville, for which he was saddled with a Bachelor of Arts in English: 19th Century Literature, a Master of Arts in English: Creative Writing, and a Master of Arts in Public Administration: Non-profit Management. Rebecca L. Kelm has a Bachelor of Arts in Studio Art with a Concentration in Painting from the University of Louisville and a Master of Arts in Art Education, Summa Cum Laude, from the Art Academy of Cincinnati.

Post Super Scriptum: If you participate in the Amazon Smile program, please consider making your donations to the Louisville Creative Centre located in Louisville, Kentucky. To find out more about the Centre's work in arts education, please visit our website at <u>LouisvilleCreativeCentre.org</u>.

Continuous Creation,

Being Book I

of

The Complete Revelation of Mick and Keith

Trilogy

This Revelation is dedicated to Stephen Briggs; David Case, Dick Estell, Hugh Fraser, George Guidall, Anne T. MacDonald, James Marsters, Nigel Planer, & Timothy West.

Sushi to Go

For Aziraphale and Crowley

"Everything you can imagine is real."
--Pablo Picasso

And then, it started.

Important things to know:

1. Angels are real.

2. Demons are real.

3. Cichlids are a mythical type of fish that are purported to populate freshwater lakes and rivers in Asia, Africa, and both Central and South America. The mythical history of these fish breaks down due to the fact that they obviously did not build airplanes to fly themselves from one lake to another and therefore can't be related. So the only credible explanation for the structural similarities in these fish is that way back in history, when France still had kings and the United States was still waiting to be discovered by the people already living there, the continents of Terra were all linked together. This is obviously complete Dodo droppings and you would be well advised to stay a long way away from anyone arguing such patent nonsense.

Part 1.

It began, or part of it began, near a motel in Salt Lake City. Several people had a very bad day. It was the sort of bad day you often dream about after you have seen a vivid and violent movie coupled with Cajun food. This bad day differed for most of the participants because they never awoke from the dream.
Sensational movies, serious documentaries, and both good and bad books were written about this bad day.

7

Two young men were arrested and charged with crimes they did not commit. One of the young men never said anything, not even to his lawyer. The other young man confessed to everything the police told him he had done. The police had told him what he did so many times and showed him so many pictures that he had come to believe, convinced by his nightmares, that he had, in fact, done the crimes. He dreamt of the slaughtered cheerleaders, the blood-stained money. He dreamt of the motel manager in his sloth and the crisp, clean mini-market across the dusty street, and the once pretty, now dead, cashier. Most of all, he dreamt of the little girl, that one that had come to the motel with her uncle. Once the dreams started to produce prolonged insomnia, the confessing young man went on to confess to every sin he could remember. That same young man's lawyer later tried to use the fact that the confessing young man also confessed to being James Earl Files' back-up shooter to make the point that this client was no longer dealing with reality in any coherent fashion. The judge disallowed this evidence, and the confessing young man and his friend were subsequently given due process and multiple life sentences. No one on the jury was bothered by the fact that none of the physical evidence placed the young man at any of the murder scenes. He had confessed, and that was the main fact presented at his trial. Later on, almost no one would remember that the young man's lawyer had been out of law school for less than one year and had never argued a capital case before.

This is called justice.

Somewhere twenty-four hundred kilometers east, Mary Smith put down the Courier-Journal newspaper in disgust. She and her husband John had become involved with The Innocence Project after John had picked up a copy of *The Innocent Man* by John Grisham that one of John's students had left in his classroom. Neither of them realized at first that the novel was a non-fiction account of Ron Williamson's life. Williamson spent 11 years on death row, more than once coming close to the last terminal show, before being cleared by DNA evidence.

Mary had been motivated to enter Brandeis Law School and had finished with the distinctions that only come from ignoring everything else in your life save the winning of distinctions. John had remained a History Professor and continued pointing out death tolls, casualty counts, the logic of blood debts, the cyclical nature of violence, and the long-term consequences of this or that war with surgical precision to whichever of his students managed to stagger into his seminars.

Mary stood and smoothed her red, orange, and yellow sundress before walking through their apartment to the bathroom. She inhaled the cold, crisp, winter morning air breezing through one open kitchen window of the fourth floor Cherokee Road apartment. She remembered how that same breeze would carry the smell of coffee and Indian food from the streets below. Stopping just before the open bathroom door, she cast a critical eye over her husband.

"We are going to be late," she said.

John finished the stroke of his razor before turning to her, one half of his face still covered in shaving cream.

"Right, let's go," he said.

Mary rolled her eyes.

"Just my luck," John said, turning back to the mirror and eyeing his work. "I find the one woman in the whole city that takes less time to get ready than me, and I have to go and marry her."

Mary folded her arms and continued looking at her husband.

"A sundress in winter?" John asked.

Mary smiled as she stepped backward and flashed him her woolen under wear.

Part 2.

It began, or part of it began, a little less than three kilometers west of Mary Smith in her sunset colored sundress. In a shotgun house on Samuel Street, Jobab Jabes Miller loaded rounds into the magazine for his Tariq 7.65mm pistol. Jo did not think while he did this. Jo had not thought much since his family had gone away.

Every now and then, Jo would come out of his reverie and realize he had washed dishes or been to work at the Thoroughbred corrugated box factory or been out for an evening's walk and had walked clear outside of the county. Then, and only for a brief time, did Jo wonder about how little conscious thought was required to get through the day.

Jo had thought even less since resolving to join his family.

Jo wrote out the following note and left it on the living room coffee table.

> *I do not want to be famous.*
> *I just want to be with my family again.*
> *–Jobab Jabes Miller*

Jo stood, walked to the coat rack beside the door, then stopped. He went to the mirror on the mantel and turned it around. He walked into his wife's room, where he never slept anymore, and turned her mother's full-length mirror to face the wall. In the bathroom, Jo covered the wall-mounted medicine cabinet mirror with a towel. As he travelled through the house, he pulled all the blinds down and drew all the shades. Jo paused for a moment in the darkened living room and stared down at the hardwood floor that he and his wife stripped and refinished the weekend after they had moved in.

His wife always maintained that was the same weekend that they had conceived their son.

Jo tried to imagine his son kicking his little soccer ball in the room, turning the never-used and well-scrubbed fireplace into a goal. Jo tried to remember showing a younger, toddling version of his son how to kick the ball, using the inside soles of the feet. Jo tried to remember the sound of his wife's voice.

Jo could not remember anything.

After stepping out onto the porch, he came back in for his coat, picked up the Tariq, placed it in his coat pocket, and left the house again. He did not bother locking the front door.

On the porch, he picked up the two-thirds empty gallon jug of purified water he had bought a week ago. He poured out what remained of the water into the street, between the parked cars.

"Baruch atah Hashem Elokeinu melech haolam, dayan ha'emet," Jo said aloud once. He repeated it over and over in his mind as he capped and returned the plastic gallon jug to the porch.

Jo had tried hard in the last few weeks to remember all the rituals, to remember everything he was supposed to do. He felt a great deal of pain whenever he tried to remember, so he had stopped trying to remember anything. His wife had been part of the Chevra Kadisha. She had sat with many, but no one had sat with her or their son when it was their turn.

Jo had tried to gain access to them in the county morgue. Taharah must be performed. The Chevra Kadisha had tried, even though they told him it would be a futile effort. The police, the coroner, the laboratories, all had to do their work. It had been weeks before their bodies were laid to rest in Saint Michael Cemetery.

Returning to the sidewalk, Jo turned right, away from his grey stone house, and headed southeast down Samuel Street in the midday mists. He paused before crossing Spratt Street while a large Ford pick-up with a set of double rear wheels accelerated by him, drenching his pants with freezing ice water. He hurried across the road and covered the last block to Texas Avenue. There he turned northwest and tried not to look at the obelisk crowned with a cross that stood just inside the cemetery gates at the end of Texas Avenue. Even in the icy rain, the American flag fluttered in the wind.

Jo stopped, brought himself to military attention, and saluted the flag. He then made the sign of the cross as he entered into the cemetery.

Part 3.

It began, or part of it began, on the third day of the year.

One Angel and one Demon sat in Café Mimosa drinking mimosas. The restaurant did have a liquor license to serve alcohol, but they did not make mimosas. At least, they did not make mimosas like these. These mimosas gave you the sense of having one perfect moment with each sip. This did not matter. There are a few advantages to being a Demon. For instance, there was always a table with a view and the wait staff never noticed them. Both the Angel and the Demon preferred it that way, especially since that cock-up at the motel in Utah, which had gotten so very out of hand.

They had left Salt Lake for River City after the mess at the motel. The Archangel Chrétien and Under-lord Mania had arrived to clean it up, and they were not pleased. Chrétien had taken them aside and told them, in a low, confidential tone, that management was not pleased. Mania took them aside and said that management was, in fact, well pleased. He even went on to add in a manic breath that it was '...important to see the big picture, and to be a team player in the context of this new world of customer-centric services, and that management wanted them to touch base with the humanity relations officer downstairs to talk about a

12

generalized program to up-skill everyone in order to enable more win-win solutions of a similar nature…'

The Angel, called Mick, liked Vietnamese food, and sat eating Pho Tai. The rare beef was medium well done and the noodles were under-cooked. The Demon, named Keith, sat toying with the last piece of Nigiri from his Osechi Ryori special. The Demon was almost everything but a traditionalist. Keith liked to maintain appearances. It was all he could do with a name like his.

Neither one of them liked Chinese food.

This had been a major problem when they had been posted to Shenyang as advisors to Lin Tse-hsü, during the collapse of the Qing Dynasty. The dynasty did not collapse so much implode after the loss of the First Opium War, and the subsequent Taiping Rebellion placed Hóng Xiùquán in power. The Angel and the Demon had both received medals of commendation and a hundred years of solitude for their efforts. Mick had taken up oil painting and studied under Jacques-Louis David. Keith had spent most of his time hanging around with Johannes Gensfleisch zur Laden zum Gutenberg, telling him stories about the good old days, which had not yet happened, and handing Herr Gutenberg tools whenever he asked for them. When Mick and Keith met up again, just in time to work for the newly elected President Andrew Jackson, neither one of them could explain why their side had been so happy with their work.

"What do you think went wrong in Utah?" Keith asked.

"It was the kid, the little girl," Mick said.

"Oh, the cheerleaders got what they deserved—"

"No, the little girl, the one that came in with her uncle," Mick interrupted. "That was it—that pushed it over the line."

13

"Yes, you're right," Keith agreed, stuffing the last piece of Nigiri sushi into his mouth. "My people have never been keen on hurting children."

Mick gave Keith a long cold stare, something that Angels are particularly good at.

Keith ignored him. If there is anything that Demons are good at, it's ignoring Angels. That, and both looking and sounding so much like a used car salesman that they can often not only sell you a stolen used car, but also the car you drove up in.

"I'm sorry," Mick said, "I had this silly little idea that your people were behind those little fiascos called the Holocaust and the Inquisition?"

"Which ones do you mean specifically?" Keith asked, feigning innocence while snapping another drink into one hand, and waving his dirty dishes out of existence with the other. "There's been more than one of each you know."

"You know damn—" Mick coughed. "You know the ones I mean."

"Yeah, yeah, sure," Keith replied, sipping his drink, "we always get the rap for those. Look, xenophobia and religious zealotry are fine things generally, but hurting children is never good for long-term evil. You need adults for long-term evil. Seriously, look at what the kids did that grew up in the kind, loving arms of the Hitlerjugend."

"I doubt that many people would agree with that argument," Mick said, looking over at a young mother and her daughter waiting for their take-out. A little old Asian lady with mid-neck-length black hair was handing them their order. Her face was set in a tight, but friendly smile.

Keith shrugged.

"Maybe," he said. "But some of those boys in the Deutsches Jungvolk were the first ones to join the Hitler-Jugend in the 1920s, and by the Creator what they did in Poland, France, and Russia in the '40s."

14

"I'm just glad all that's over," Mick said.

Keith choked on his drink.

"Over? You think that shit's over?"

"Hey, isn't that Mōt over there?" Mick asked with obvious relief, pointing to the slender, pale man who looked even paler for having a Middle Eastern complexion and thinning grey hair, walking through the back door. "Death's Scion, I think," the Angel added.

The little old Asian lady's natural tan and smooth manners looked rather young in comparison to the newcomer.

"The Angel of Death? Which one; Michael, Samael, Abaddon, or Azrael?"

"No, the other one, he's the adopted Scion of Death and god of Near-death Experiences. I wonder what he's doing here?"

"Probably came to see the cats next door," Keith said.

"That is a tasteless stereotypical comment and not the sort of thing that I want to—"

"What? There is a vet's office next door. Didn't you notice it? I parked right in front of the sign that said *Fairleigh Pet Center Parking Only*."

"I haven't seen Mōt in ages," Keith said, waving him over to their table.

The Angel frowned.

Mōt waved back and picked up his take out.

"Hello," Mōt said as he came up to the table, sat down, and looked at the traffic on the street outside through the Cichlid fish tank. "Are you here for the show?" he asked, unpacking his take-out order.

"Show?" Mick asked.

"Yeah, what show?" Keith demanded. "We're usually the show and I ain't talked with my agent about a show today."

"Oh, it promises to be fun," Mōt said airily. "Should bring out reporters and policemen and everything. I was going to go across the street and watch from the other side of the large glass window, but here is good enough."

And Keith grinned as he remembered just what Death's Scion had been put in charge of.

Part 4.

It continued, or part of it continued, in the back seat of a Yellow Cab somewhere between the River City International Airport and Café Mimosa. Rían Hunter sat in the back seat of the cab alternately flipping through his notebook and trying to consign the **NO SMOKING** sign to the purifying flames of pyrokinesis. Neither industry was working out for him. He had never been much good at reading in the car, and reading his own handwriting was sometimes a wasted effort when he was standing still. Now, after almost three years in Irvine, California, he longed for the relative freedom of smoking in public again, even if it was only outside. He looked out the window at the near freezing drizzle. There were few places on Terra that could compare to the Ohio Valley for weather that was not quite a snow, or rain, or ice storm. The sky slid between grey and bright white, depending on the cloud patterns. Hunter thought about how nice it was to be back home. Home, in a city where the cabbies ignored you and never tried to give you a copy of their script. That fact alone almost made up for the schizophrenic weather.

Hunter tried to focus on his notes from his one telephone call from Mary Smith, and cussed himself for not remembering the printout of the long and detailed e-mail that John had sent. Hunter would not even allow himself to think about having left his laptop back in his campus office. He had been in the air over Arizona when he had remembered. The phone call from the

16

airline phone to the GTA with whom he shared the office had cost him $24.00.

Hunter tried to focus and read:

Thomas A. Pierce, 39, Pleasure Ridge Park. Pierce was involved in gang-related activities and drug trafficking until his arrest at the age of 19, on rape charges that were later reduced to aggravated assault. After serving 5 years, his life was apparently straight. Ten years later, while he was working as a janitor, a murdered woman and her murdered son were found in the back seat of Pierce's car by the building's security guard. Chava Sarai Miller and Seth Abel "Sam" Miller, ages 33 and 5—their deaths caused by multiple stab wounds. Pierce was convicted 1 year later mainly because of his prior record rather than any actual evidence. Pierce was later released after four years on death row. Pierce's conviction was overturned after another death row inmate's confession forced a reexamination of the physical evidence, for which the Innocence Project had been arguing for three years.

Hunter reread the mini-biography again, and thought about what a miserable experience that must have been. The Smiths had contacted Hunter soon after Pierce's release to discuss the possibility of Hunter writing a non-fiction account of this man's experience. Hunter was not big on non-fiction, but his Irvine thesis fiction project was not going how he wanted it to, and he was seriously considering throwing it out, in favour of just about anything. One of the many things he wanted to do in life besides write was found a Neo-Gonzo Journalism school of thought and work. Perhaps a non-fiction work might be the perfect springboard to start with after all.

The cab stopped in front of Café Mimosa at a little before noon. The clouds had parted, taking the misty rain with them, and allowing the sun a brief visit to the asphalt and concrete. Hunter paid the driver, stepped out of the cab, and lit a cigarette. Smoothing his "Han shot first!" t-shirt and adjusting his well-worn blazer, he turned to face the sunlight, letting the smoke

17

linger in his mouth before making a slow controlled exhale.

Irvine is great, Hunter thought, but smoking outside is bliss.

Hunter turned a second time and looked inside the old familiar restaurant. The front area was empty, and so was the Sushi bar. One old, pale, Middle Eastern-looking man sat at a table in the raised, closed-in area that had been the smoking section before the city enacted a restaurant and bar smoking ban. Hunter had some choice feelings on that subject, but time in Southern California, which was rapidly burning down from a lack of National Guardsmen being in the country, had softened his stance somewhat. The Middle Eastern-looking man was visible through the window, but the two men accompanying him were obscured by the large Cichlid fish tank that sat atop the low wall surrounding the former smoking area. Later, Hunter could never accurately describe the other two men.

Hunter was hot-boxing his second cigarette when his phone rang.

"Hey Mary," he said after looking at the caller ID.

"I'm sorry, we are going to be late," Mary Smith said. "John just finished shaving and has now decided he doesn't like the tie and shirt I set out for him."

"No worries," Hunter said, "I've got five more hours on this layover before I got to catch another plane up to Hancock International."

"Pardon?"

"Sorry," Hunter said. "That's the airport in Syracuse."

"It must suck having an entire continent between you and your girlfriend," Mary said. "Then again, I wonder if it wouldn't help John dress faster."

"Nah, no way," Hunter said. "Besides, you'd just come home to months of dirty laundry."

Mary laughed, passed on some gossip about mutual friends, and hung up.

Hunter smoked another cigarette, ogled a few bouncy teenaged joggers, and went inside the restaurant. Settling into one of the tables on the raised platform in the front of the restaurant, by the large window, he ordered hot tea and five different sushi rolls, then settled down to wait, listening to the contemporary piano music playing in the background.

Part 5.

It continued, or part of it continued, in the middle row of small gravestones in the far southeast corner of the cemetery when Jo bent down to scrape the ice off one long gravestone.

The Miller Family

Jobab Jabes | Chava Sarai | Seth Abel

Jo tried to think of something to say. He had been trying to think of something to say for days. He pulled his wedding ring off his finger and placed it between his wife's first and middle names. He stood and wondered why he had not thought to bring an offering to his son's memory. He stood there a few more moments before taking the Tariq out of his coat pocket and ejecting the chamber. As the metal of the pistol turned cold and bit at his fingers, Jo picked up the round off the ice and placed it inside the vertical depression of the *t* of his son's name. Then, with a snap and click, Jo chambered another round and put on the safety.

Jo stood looking from the ring to the bullet and back again before turning away from his family. He made his way to the north side of the cemetery and made his exit through a hole in the fence he had found one day when he and his wife had been walking in the cemetery while she was pregnant.

It was a cold bitter grey two kilometer walk and Jo barely noticed it.

Jo entered Café Mimosa through its back door, travelled along the long hallway that passed the storage room and kitchen, and passed through a second door that opened behind the former smoking section. A few of the tables in the former smoking section had customers. One young man was talking about something that required expansive hand gestures, while his young lady companion looked bored.

A Middle Eastern man with thinning grey hair caught Jo's attention for a moment as he stood waiting for his take out. Jo wondered if the grey haired man of was of Syrian or Jordanian extraction.

When the waiter asked Jo where he wanted to sit, Jo froze.

What am I doing here? he thought.

"Sir?"

Jo shook his head and pointed to a table between the Cichlid tank and the front window section.

With only a curt nod, Jo sat down at a table with a good view of the Smiths, Hunter, and a fourth empty chair. He turned his back to the Middle Eastern man and immediately forgot him.

Jo nodded for both water and tea, sending the waiter away. He made a pretense of looking through the menu, knowing full well he would not order anything from this unkosher kitchen. Laying the menu down in front of him, Jo slipped the Tariq 7.65mm pistol onto his lap, pushed off the safety, and covered the pistol with his napkin.

Jo watched the lawyer, the professor, and the writer, and waited.

Part 6.

It continued, or part of it continued, back in the former smoking section of Café Mimosa. Mōt had just finished catching Mick and Keith up on the story.

"Well, I'll be Angelic," Keith said, while Mōt went to order more Crab Rangoon from the little old Asian lady. "That is one pretty messed-up setup."

"At least this one isn't our fault," Mick said. "That's a nice change."

"Oh, I wouldn't be too sure about that," Keith said while washing his hands with liquid hand sanitizer. "I'm sure people will blame us one way or another. You know, that old stand by—why didn't the Creator step in and make it stop, or my personal favorite, the devil made me do it. I really love that one. I mean, there is only one devil, the supreme spirit of evil—Mr. Lewis C. Furr himself. We Demons do all the heavy lifting and he gets all the credit. I mean seriously, I have never once heard a sermon about me and I've been working around here for close to the last quarter million years!"

"Pardon," Mick interrupted, "it has only been about fifty thousand, thank you."

"We were working on the last bunch and besides," Keith said with an expansive gesture, "I personally came up with the idea of the dinosaur bones. I waited a long time for that to pay off." Keith's grin widened to the point that his lizard tongue was visible. "Did you see the gun?"

"No," Mick said, putting his hands in his pockets and looking at the table. "I don't have to, I know it is there."

"Shame you can't get involved," Keith said, "and me, I don't want to."

Part 7.

It ended, or part of it ended, when Mary Smith picked up her beeping cell phone and read:

S2S CRAFT PDS CID TBL MTFBWU[1]

Mary took a deep breath, closed her eyes, and forced herself to calmly put down the phone.

"What's the matter, dear?" John asked, his eyes looking about the restaurant.

"Stock market crash?" Hunter asked in that sort of way that people do when they think that a yes answer will provide a lot of entertainment. He leaned back in his chair and added, "Shit, I got nothing to lose." Hunter picked up his birthday Zippo off the table. The engraving read 𝔄.𝔎.𝔭. circled by an extravagant heart design.

"Pierce is not coming," Mary said, pronouncing each word as if it were a death sentence.

"What?" Hunter exclaimed, slamming his chair down. "Not coming? What?"

John took a deep breath. He had taken that same deep breath several million times before in his graduate seminars, just before two graduate students were about to fight over whether or not Richard Nixon was or was not a worse president than G. W. Bush. John continued to look around the restaurant. John wondered again why it was that no one ever argued about John Fitzgerald Kennedy; the man who blundered two wars, brought the globe closer to

---

[1] Text Messaging Abbreviations:
S2S: Sorry to say
CRAFT: Can't remember a freaking thing
PDS: Please don't shoot
CID: Crying in disgrace
TBL: Text back later
MTFBWU: May the force be with you

nuclear annihilation than anyone else in history, and sold generations of Americans on the idea that America had to protect the entire world, J.F.K. was clearly the worst president since Andrew Jackson. John's eyes settled on Jo Miller.

Jo Miller saw John Smith look at him and dropped his eyes to the table. He intently stared at the teapot that emitted a faint aroma of green tea. Jo gave the engraved picture of a Chinese Cloud Dragon descending from the skies all the intense passionate attention that a sycophant gives its object.

"Great, that's just great," Hunter said, doing a drum riff on his skinny stomach. "I could have been in Syracuse already. What the Hell? He get pinched for something?"

Mary shrugged and tossed Hunter her cell phone.

"What's this fucker's phone number," Hunter demanded, randomly punching buttons on Mary's phone. "Geez," he said, staring at the screen, "I think I just dialed up a nuclear strike on the Kingdom of Norway."

John leaned forward and took Mary's phone away from Hunter and handed it back to her.

"Got some Scandinavian issues?" Mary asked, her eyes narrowing.

"As a matter of fact, I can't stand those pretentious peaceniks—"

"Shut up," John said. "The both of you."

Mary turned her head at an angle and looked at her husband.

Hunter tossed his arms up and locked his fingers behind his head.

"Mary," John said, "look at the table just in front of us."

Mary looked.

Hunter watched as Mary's face settled into the grim determined hardened lines of bureaucracy. It was the face often referred to as expressionless, despite the fact that it contained more expression then anyone ever wanted to see. That face contained everything but the hope there was anything to be done about your case. It was the face that functionaries the world over had refined to show nothing more than grim determination to be rid of their interlocutor. It was the face Franz Kafka inked ten thousand words to capture.

John nodded towards Jo for Hunter's benefit.

"That there," John said in a whisper, is "Chava Miller's husband."

"And little Sam's father," Mary added, almost to herself.

"The guy with the funny name?" Hunter asked, pitching his voice into a low register while not looking away from Mary's face. "The one that lost his family?"

Mary nodded.

"Does he still think that Pierce did it?" Hunter asked.

John said nothing.

Marry shrugged.

"Well Hell," Hunter said. He looked out the window and saw the same bouncy teenaged joggers returning from their turnabout. "We only live once," he muttered as he stood up, and turned for Jo's table.

John began to stand up and restrain Hunter, but heeded to Mary's grasp on his arm, and in mild astonishment, he sat back down.

Hunter jumped down the two steps that led to the raised platform and made a straight line for Jo Miller.

Jo Miller sat still, his hand gripping the pistol through the dinner napkin on his lap.

"How the Hell are you, man?" Hunter said, pulling out a chair and flopping into it. His elbow hit the untouched teapot, sending it over off its cradle.

Hot, steaming tea rushed across the table, flooding over the edge, landing in Jo's lap.

Jo screamed in pain, attempted to stand, and fell backwards.

The Tariq discharged.

Hunter sat stunned, his ears momentarily deafened by a low continuous hum. The sulphurous stench of rotten eggs mixed with putrid vapours of burning potassium nitrate irritated his eyes and nose. Looking down, he saw Jo Miller fumbling underneath one of the tables behind him.

Hunter slowly stood up to see Jo Miller recover the Tariq and point it at him.

Hunter sat back down, instinctively placing his hands, palm down, on the table. He looked at the Cichlid fish tank, and into the eyes of a gigantic Electric Blue Jack Dempsey Cichlid. Its face was enormous, and when it yawned at Hunter, it revealed rows of tiny sharp teeth. Hunter thought about Greedo.

I'm gonna get shot, Hunter heard himself in the darkness his own head.

Hunter watched in heart pounding silence as Jo Miller picked himself up off the floor.

Jo's left hand, his dominant hand, was badly scalded by the contents of the emptied teapot. Jo held the pistol trembling in his right hand, while his left was coddled into his stomach.

"Dude, I'm sorry man, really sorry," Hunter said.

Jo said nothing. He motioned from Hunter back to the Smiths with the Tariq.

"You want me to go back there?" Hunter asked.

Jo nodded.

Mary, her hands trembling, dialed 9-1-1 on her phone. As soon as the operator answered, Mary punched the volume down to its lowest level.

The operator said hello twice and fell silent.

Mary punched on the speakerphone and slid the phone back up on the table. She stared as the call timer seconds changed on the phone's screen.

Hunter slowly stood, keeping his palms pointed towards Jo Miller, and turned back towards the Smiths, who sat wide eyed at the table. Hunter noticed the contemporary piano music for the first conscious time since he came into the restaurant and tried to square it against the man pointing a gun at his back. He completely failed to do so.

The Smiths sat, one watching Hunter walk back to them, the other watching Jobab Jabes Miller hold a gun to Hunter's back.

Mick, Keith, and Mōt sat watching the scene.

Mick wondered why this sort of thing seemed to happen whenever Humans were around each other for more than five minutes.

Keith wondered how he could get the building to burn down. Insurance agents brought out the very best evil in their customers. It was a knack that he had spent a couple of years trying to cultivate while working for The Sun back in 1710. Since that time, he had helped in low visibility but singularly important ways to grow the firm into the Royal & Sun Alliance Company.

If I get really lucky, Keith brooded; maybe I can take out the vet's office too.

Stories about hurt puppies always depressed people, and depressed people could spread evil almost as quickly as the Streptococcal pharyngitis went through a pre-school. Keith inhaled the old familiar malodors of death and decay.

What an ingenious little species of creatures, Keith thought. Pack chemicals tightly together, apply

26

fire, and projectile death results. Brilliant, absolutely brilliant.

Mōt wondered about nothing in particular. He had given up speculation for Lent last year. By the time Lent was over, he found he had not missed speculation at all and vowed to give it up permanently.

Mōt noticed the little old Asian lady walking up behind Jo Miller, two hands tightly gripping the handle of a cast iron wok. The wok looked every bit as old as the Qing Dynasty. Mōt sat passively as the little old Asian lady raised the wok up over her head, charged Jo Miller's back, and connected the wok to the back of his skull.

Jo Miller went down.

The Tariq discharged.

Hunter screamed in pain, hit a table, and then the floor. The bullet had passed through the lower right portion of his gluteals, shattered a portion of the large glass window, and buried in the side of the Burritos as Big as Your Head building across the street.

"Well," Mōt said, turning to Mick and Keith, "the work of the little g god of Near-death Experiences is done here." Mōt stood up and headed for the back door.

The little old Asian lady was screaming at Jo Miller and kicking his limp body in the back.

"What, you're just going to leave?" Mick yelled at Mōt.

Mōt smiled and waved as he headed out the back door.

"*God* damn it!" Hunter screamed, "that fucker shot me in the ass!"

John Smith cautiously opened his eyes. His hands were covered in shards of glass and small cuts. He looked over at his wife.

"Mary?" he screamed, louder than he had meant to because of the dull pounding sensation in his ears.

Mary turned her head to him and nodded. Her face was pale and her eyes seemed to have sunk far into her skull.

"Some fucking help down here!" Hunter demanded.

"Say something, Mary," John said in what he hoped might sound like a soothing voice. His ears throbbed.

Mary opened her mouth, but only a small shard of glass fell when her lips parted.

"Close your eyes Mary," John said, before leaning into her and with gentle breaths blew glass dust off her face

"John," Mary said with her eyes still closed.

John stopped and looked at his wife.

She opened her glittering eyelids.

"I love you John."

John slowly put his arms around Mary as she began to cry against his chest.

"The bullet—Is—IN—MY—ASS," Hunter screamed, clutching at the hole in his backside. "No hurry or anything!"

Two of the sons of the little old Asian lady came running out of the back kitchen and dragged their mother screaming away from Jo Miller's limp body.

A third son ran to Hunter carrying almost every clean white towel in the kitchen. He stopped just short of Hunter and just dropped the towels on him.

It ended, or part of it ended, when the police showed up, followed by paramedics. The unconscious body of Jo Miller was taken into protective medical custody. They said he would most likely live, but declined to comment on whether or not he would talk again.

The little old Asian lady almost went in for homicide when one of the police officers told her that there would have to be an inquiry into her assault of Jo Miller. All three of her sons held her back, and the offending officer was glad afterwards that he had no idea what she said to him.

Hunter settled down after a shot of something that he later wanted to take back to California with him.

His last recorded comment on his witness sheet was "And tell that damned waiter I want my sushi to go."

Everyone in the restaurant gave a statement; everyone, that is, except Mick and Keith. Keith waved off each approaching officer with "We're not the witnesses you're looking for."

Later, the Café Mimosa burned down. The fire had nothing to do with the above related events. It was just something that happened. History is full of stuff that just happened. Even later still, the Café Mimosa reopened down the street from its original location. Again, that's just something that happened.

Chapter 1: Angelic Archives Department

The Angelic Archives Department at the Elysion Library, on the planet Elysion, in the Camulodunum System, about a million years later.

I have seen all the works that are done under the sun; and, behold, all is vanity and vexation of spirit. --Ecclesiastes 1:14, K.J.V.

And it came to pass that the librarian set in-motion the 11th Great Age of Creation, and the Angel did not get the book he wanted.

Hatshepsut Nefertari Djeserit Fukayna, called Hat, looked up from the Canonical Acquisitions form when the man-shaped shadow fell over her desk. While eyeing the stranger critically, Hat returned her quill to the inkpot, scratched just above her right eye, sighed, and settled back into her chair.

It stood about a foot away from her desk, dressed in a khaki coloured trenchcoat, fedora hat, and sunglasses. She had not heard it come in through her office door.

"Yes, *Angel*, can I help you?" Hat asked, putting more annoyance into the noun than she actually felt.

"What makes you think I'm an Angel?" the I'm-not-admitting-anything Angel returned.

Hat considered what stood before her. It was over two meters tall, dressed in a long 1950s style khaki trench raincoat, with a matching fedora that did not quit hide its Angelic blond hair, and a pair of large black plastic sunglasses of the style that use to be referred to as "birth control spectacles." Its body did not move other then to speak, and it had simply appeared in her office.

Let me see, Hat thought. A Demon wouldn't be caught consecrated in that get-up. Fairies never hide. I know where *all* the Scions are, even the dead ones. So that leaves *Angel*, you dope.

"Lucky guess," Hat said.

Then again, she thought, I don't really look like what I really am either when it comes to that.

After more years than Hat could remember, which after the "end" of Terra never seemed worth keeping track of, Hat's face was still that of a young woman in her early twenties.

Hat's dark black north African Middle Eastern hair was drawn back in a bun roll, and her bright blue eyes looked out at the world. Her skin was a smooth creamy olive complexion that hinted at forsaken desire and the thrills of anticipation. When she nodded, loose curls of her hair rustled around her ears and neck. And, while Hat could be one of the most graceful dancing partners any mortal could ever hope for, her natural instincts bent toward the soft, slow, and deliberate movements of the woman born to be a librarian, or a biochemical engineer, or a neurosurgeon, all of which she was or had been. Hat had worn many different career hats in her unnaturally long life.

The Angel pulled off its fedora allowing its blond locks to fall to its shoulders, but left his sunglasses on. It leaned in on Hat.

Hat pushed her chair further back from the desk.

"I need a book," the Angel said in what had to be the single worst excuse for a conspiratorial whisper in the whole history of the universe.

"Really?" Hat asked. "I swear- it never occurred to me that someone might come to a library looking for a book. Have you looked at *How We Destroyed Humanity Through Television, Movies, Streaming Media, and Simulated Reality Facilities*, by the Demon Fruchtbarkeitskultus? I believe you are mentioned in that one several times. One might even go so far as to say you're an antagonist in that apologetic chronicle."

31

"No, not just any book," the Angel said ignoring the barb. "I need a book about universe creation."

"Have you tried *Genesis*?" Hat asked, drumming her fingers on the arm of her chair. "Very popular that one, universe's best seller."

"Umm, I was thinking something more practical, sort of a how-to-manual," the Angel conceded. "Yes, you know, a how to manual for Avatars or whatever, that teaches them how to make a universe."

More like a how to for dummies, Hat thought.

"You mean a coding book for Simulated Reality Facilities?" Hat asked dryly. "Feeling the need to sow your oats all of a sudden? Talk to the Demons, that's their gig. I don't traffic in that sort of *thing*."

"No, not a sim reality, an authentic reality. I want a manual with practical instructions on how to create a functional, believable, credible, narrative causality reality. With worksheets if you have them, please."

"Ah well, *Chariots of the Gods*," Hat said. "Very practical that one. Runs circles around itself even. Don't know about narrative causality though. You'd have to talk to your Boss about that. Not my sphere of influence."

The Angel winced.

"You trying to reboot humanity or something?" Hat asked standing up. "Best to let dead dogs lay."

"Well, no, not really," the Angel said, allowing the slightest hint of exasperation into his voice.

Hat leaned forward, and snatched the sunglasses off the Angel's face.

"Mictlantecuhtli," she said tossing the sunglasses onto her desk. "So, it is you. Why are you skulking around my library?"

The Angel lately identified as Mictlantecuhtli looked about himself in horror before realizing that they

32

were the only ones in Hat's office, and perhaps the only ones in this wing of the planetary library.

It is important for readers of this raillery tale to understand just what the Elysion Library is, even though the Elysion Library itself does not play a large role in near-future events. The Elysion Library always has and will continue to play a huge long-term role in the near-total preservation of mortal knowledge. But that's another story and is recorded in *The Murder of Basil Berry*.

But for now, know that the Elysion Library is not just the "library of the Elysion planet," or a "library about the Elysion planet," or even the "official library of the planet Elysion." The entire whole of the Elysion planet is the library. Which is why both the planet and the library have the same name.

There are over 17 trillion non-fiction books, 242 trillion fictional novels- most of which are considered to be "finished products," 42 trillion journal series, some 3 quadrillion periodical series, and an untold amount of digital data stored on the planet. None of which has anything to do with the governmental archives of the entire Human species. However, as humanity was never much interested in improving its government when it had one, nobody has since been very interested in doing anything with the governmental archives- except the Demon Amy.

A word about the Demon Amy, who is also called Avnas. According to Johannes Wierus who authored the celebrated *Pseudomonarchia Daemonum*, the Demon Amy is the 57th, or 58th, or even the 60th great spirit of Hell. But more importantly, Amy *is* the President of Hell. Meaning the Demon actually wanted the job, campaigned for the job, and won the job. Really, what sort of a rat-rat bastard do you have to be to win an election in Hell? If you ever meet the blockhead, give the Demon a wide berth.

"Are we alone?" Mictlantecuhtli asked.

Hat sighed, picked up the Angel's sunglasses off her desk, and handed them back to him. After sitting back down, Hat he considered for an instant telling the Angel the truth.

But where would be the fun in that?

And the Angel of the Lord came unto the Librarian and she blew the gaff. The end.

No, that will never do, Hat thought. Need some fun in my life for a change.

Hat had been persuaded that eternity was boring not by the arguments of her cousin Scions, or the temptations of the Demons, or by the seemingly never ending paperwork generated by the bureaucracy in Heaven, all of which she filed for future historians. She had, in the end, been persuaded that eternity was boring by the fact that a couple of years ago she had actually considered watching an episode of "Married With Children" because she had literally seen everything else humanity had ever filmed, even the brutal bits.

"Angel," she said, "you're standing in the Canonical Acquisitions section of the Angelic Archives Department of the Elysion Library about a million-billion years after the Final Match at Armagedōn. Ain't nobody here but us Scions."

Here we should pause for a few words of explanation:

Concerning time; immortal creatures- not be confused with Immortals, just your regular run of the mill immortal creatures like Angels, Demons, Fairies, gods, and cats pay as little attention to the passing of mortal years as mortals pay to the passing of seconds. Sometimes the years matter, sometimes they don't. But either way, the main thing to pay attention to when immortals talk about time is whether or not they are using the proper noun form Time, or the past tense time, or the present tense, or the future tense verb form, since the words "a million years ago," means as little to them as "last season" means to mortals.

And concerning the Final Match; this was the Big War between Heaven and Hell, one game, instant death, no take-backs, and no, absolutely no fans allowed on the field. Some people called this the Apocalypse, but as those people didn't survive the Final Match long enough to form a consensus about the rhetoric, the oldie name failed to stick.

But whatever it was called, the Final Match did occur at Armagedōn; as in Armageddon from the Greek Ἁρμαγεδών, or the Hebrew הַר מְגִדּוֹ, or the Arabic هرمجدون or آرماگدن, or Armagedōn, which is obviously correct, and much easier to spell. This was the turf war where the ranked legions of Heaven and Hell got together one late spring day and settled their accounts. As it turned out, Hell owed some 50 trillion Pounds Sterling in library late fees and had to do some pretty slimy double talking to explain why they showed up packing steel to what had been clearly laid out as a skin on skin fight.

And there at Armagedōn, the Son returned to Terra and called out his half-brother Satan, The Accuser, The Divine, The First Fallen Angel, called Shaitan, or Shayṭan, or Ha-Satan, The Adversary, The Esquire- Stan to his friends, for being a lousy half-brother that never did his share of the washing up after dinner. And where Diábolos the Slanderer, Father of Lies, and Public Relations Officer for Hell, stepped up and called the Son out of order, pointing out that the Fallen had done plenty of washing up in the millions of years before the Son was incarnated, and that he should mind his own business and that Hell hadn't a thing in the world on its mind, just now being out for a family stroll.

Whereas the Son said, 'Oh, go blow it out your ear, you lying mooch.'

And it came to pass that Stan threw the first punch and as these things go, there was a god-awful row and before you know it, the whole place was a wreck, humanity was extinct, and the remaining immortals were all issued restraining warrants.

And so it was written that Stan, not being able to shake off the former Satan thing, was cast into The Pit, somewhere near Danville, Indiana, maybe in Greencastle, and the Son was sent to cool his heels at a bar somewhere in the vicinity of Zeta Orionis.

Unfortunately, that's when everything went really bad for humanity, as the Israelis fearing an attack in the never ending Canaanite War of Liberation from Eurasian Judaism, nuked Armagedōn, which poisoned the Sea of Galilee, thus causing the Tiberius River to run with the blood, bones, brains, and gore of two armies of immortal creatures, and one Watcher, all of whom were eventually issued new bodies by their respective governing bureaucracies.

The mortals though were not so lucky. It was curtains for all of them. That is to say, the Immortals all eventually got reincarnated or rather reformed as if nothing had happened. Humanity on the other hand, just got dead and stayed that way.

And it came to pass that there truly was no peace in the Promised Land because the people were stiff-necked and couldn't get along. Sadly, nothing much had changed since then and the appearance of the Angel Mick in Hat's Angelic Archives Department, in the Elysion Library. Angels and Demons still didn't get along much, and humanity was still extinct.

"Scions, where?" demanded the Angel, ducking down in front of Hat's desk.

Hat folded her arms and looked down at the Angel who was crouching down in front of her desk.

"Well, there's me of course," Hat said wearily, "and the on in the wall over there."

"What?" the Angel queried.

"I had a Scion embedded into the wall there," she added pointing at the wall painting of a mummy sitting upright on a throne reading *The Complete Love*

Letters of Völva and Freyja. "And, there should be several thousand more of us Scions around the planet. In fact," she continued with a shrug, "I think all of the Scions are somewhere in the Elysion Library now. Birds of a feather and all that."

The Angel was clearly not listening and remained crouched down on the floor.

Mick's gaze was arrested by the walls of Hat's office, which were painted to resemble the insides of ancient Egyptian pyramids. except that the mummy was reading a book about the love life of a Norse goddess and a prophet.

"You do realize that you should hide behind the desk, yeah?" Hat asked. "You know, so somebody coming in the office won't immediately see you?"

"Do you realize that the book the mummy is reading is an anachronism?" Mick asked.

"That mummy is an idiot," Hat said without even glancing at the indicated painting. "Rather reminds me of you actually."

"Yeah, right," the Angel said standing up. "Very funny, very funny. You got any decent light in here?"

Hat looked around her office and tried to see it from the prospective of an outsider. Smooth sand stone floor, slightly roughed sandstone walls with the pictorial history of the Egyptian people starting with their march out of the city of Wadi Halfa, called وادي حلفا, on the Sudanese shores of Lake Nubia and the governorship of Iry-Hor over the city of Abydos in Upper Egypt, to the end of the Human race at Armagedōn. Synthetic oil burned brightly in dark green oil lamps suspended by golden chains from the ceiling giving off a slight jade effect. The flames cast a bright light; the flames flickered continually around the room giving the illusion of movement to all of the figures and animals upon the walls.

Occasionally, one of the paintings changed its aspect in order to present the viewer with the sense that the paintings were watching them.

Which, they were.

Hat was forced, even if only in her own mind, to agree that the mummy was a miss. She would certainly see that he heard about it later.

"What's the matter with the light?" Hat asked.

"It's all weird and eerie," the Angel complained.

Hat shrugged. "The only other person that complains about the light in here is Basil Berry."

The Angel twitched at the mention of the Scion.

"Say not the name of the Demon's spawn," the Angel, intoned.

"Whatever," Hat said.

"Crap, he's not around here is he?" the Angel asked.

"I should imagine he's around here somewhere," Hat said. "You know Mictlantecuhtli, all the Scion work here, and so do most of the free Fairies, Immortals, Hellspawns, and the Numquam Land creatures. We even have a few Demons bunking about the place, but they hardly work."

"Mick," the Angel identifying himself as Mick said. "Call me Mick."

"Yes, Mictlantecuhtli," Hat said, standing again. "I shall surely do that. Just as soon as you tell me why you are disturbing my eternity. It's been rather quiet around here lately, and I like it that way. Actually, no, on second thought, I don't want to know. Good day to you."

"I need a book I told you, about universe creation," said 'don't call me Mictlantecuhtli' Mick.

"Yes and what for?" Hat said taking her fingers and outlining from top to bottom a imaginary rectangle in the air, which caused a slim white covered soft

38

paperback book with a drawing of the strand colour coded Deoxyribonucleic acid double helix to appear in the air. The imaginary rectangle turned real book, hovered for a microsecond, and dropped gently into Hat's hands. The lights reflected off the cover drawing of the Hydrogen, Oxygen, Nitrogen, Carbon, and Phosphorus atoms that formed the structures of double helix D.N.A.

"For instance," she said straightening her back in a mock attitude of respect. "We have here *Worlds I Have Known* by L. G. Dusenyi, 1st Edtion, Baker Books, 2009. That what you're looking for?"

"Umm, no," the Angel admitted.

"How about *Veni, Vidi, Velco,* by Colonel Hridaynath Jared Patton IV, 2nd Edition, Infinity Plane Press, 2727? Will that do?"

The Angel rolled his eyes and took a long look at the ceiling.

"That's fiction," the Angel said.

"Patton didn't seem to think so," Hat said laying the Dusenyi book aside and repeating the procedure again to produce a hardback book with a black dust jacket. *The True History of the World* by Lucien de Terre. "So, how about this one?"

"Will you stop dicking around?" the Angel said without any effort to hide his disdain.

Hat laid the third book beside the others and stood even straighter than before.

"Sorry," Mick mumbled.

"Cunt," Hat said, articulating every sound of the word and turning the t-sound into a knifepoint. "It is cunting-around for people of my particular *persuasion.* You know the dickless persuasion."

The Angel's eyes widened a bit, but remained solidly fixed on the floor.

Hat moved a hand over the two books returning them to their proper nooks halfway across the planet.

"Look here," Hat finally said, "Take this one."

The Angel looked up and took the proffered book.

"*How to Putte Questiones to the Dark and Understand Its Answeres*, by I can't make it out, it's all smudged," Mick said rubbing his finger over the ancient leather binding and succeeding in worsening the damage. "Look here Hatter, this bloke can't even spell."

"Take it, or leave it," Hat said with a shrug. "Either way, get the Hell out of my office before I beat you to death with frustrated sarcasm."

"Yeah, right, thanks Muhammadin," the Angel tossed back over his shoulder along with a flick of his long blond hair.

"I'm the daughter of an Egyptian goddess you dolt," Hat yell at the Angel's back.

Her office door slammed behind the Angel.

"My people settled the Americas before Ishmael was even born," Hat muttered to no one in particular.

Opening the top drawer of her desk, she took out her own copy of *Bradshaw's Guide to the Bookworld* by Commander Trafford Bradshaw, CBE, placed it upon her desk, and then removed from the drawer the book that the Angel was supposed to get.

Hat looked down at the second book and then placed it squarely in the centre of her desk, on top of the Bradshaw, and hesitated for a moment.

The Scion of Sešat then went over to a bookshelf behind her desk and pulled down her own personal copy of the *Prognosticated Peerage,* and flipped to the entry for Mictlantecuhtli, Angel. She then changed her mind and flipped to her own entry just to check if there had been an update on her in the last couple of days since she had last skimmed it.

40

While readers of this chronicle might have found Hat's behaviour odd, those familiar with the *Prognosticated Peerage* would not. No one is entirely sure who, whom, or what created the prognosticating book of gods, immortals, semi-immortals, and many seriously influential mortals. And the book was often as inaccurate as it is accurate due to its containing unvetted gossip, lies, and more absolute truth than any of its subjects would care to have written down anywhere. As the inscription on the title page says, *"Person, Place, or Thing? the Prognosticated Peerage knows!"*

Hat was happy to read the same information this time as she had read the last couple of centuries:

Hatshepsut Nefertari Djeserit Fukayna VII: called Hat, Current Scion of Sešat alternatively Seshat, Safkhet, Sesat, Seshet, Sesheta, and Seshata goddess of writing, wisdom, scribes, record keepers, librarians, and invention, also credited with the invention of writing, architecture, astronomy, astrology, mathematics, and surveying. Hat is the granddaughter by Sešat who is the daughter of Ré alternatively Ra god of the Sun, and niece to

Ma'at or alternatively Maat, Māt, and Mayet the god of truth, law, and justice. Hat is not the product of any union between Sešat and her on-again off-again consort Thoth god of the heart, mind, and memory. Hat is rumoured to have been fathered by the Demon James, whom was at the time imprisoned in the body of a flesh and blood Human mortal. Hat was born on the 3rd of October, 1974 at the Great Ormond Street Children's Hospital, London, United Kingdom. Notable achievements include becoming the youngest Director in history of the Neurosurgery Research Department of the Massachusetts General Hospital; blowing-up one third of Salt Lake City in an ultimately fruitless effort to kill a multi-dimensional bibliophilic tapeworm, and "accidentally" causing the Immortality Virus to be simultaneously let loose in Tōkyō, Guangzhou, Seoul, Delhi, Mumbai, Ciudad de México, New York City, São Paulo, Manila, Jakarta, Shanghai, Los Angeles, Karāchi, Ōsaka, Kolkata, al-Qāhira called القاهرة or Cairo, Buenos Aires, Moskva, Dhaka, Beijing, Tehrān, İstanbul, Rio de Janeiro, London, Lagos, Paris, Chicago, Shenzhen, Krung Thep, Kinshasa, Wuhan, and Danville, Indiana all of which lead directly to the onset of World War Zed, and the destruction of the Mists of the Abyss and thereby liberating the whole of the Infinity Plane. Hat is currently employed as the Director of Acquisitions for the Elysion Library, which boasts, although how they know is a mystery, to have recovered copies of 93.242% of all books ever written, typed, penned, or even imagined. Hat has been, as all her sister-Scion predecessors were also, given by her mother's leave the honorific of Mistress of the House of Books, Overseer of the Royal Scribes, Priestess of the Seal, and Guardian of Recorded History. Hat's godparents are Aclima of the first brood, and the Demon Fruchtbarkeitskultus von Zeta Orionis. Hat, in her role as the current Scion of Sešat, is the Guardian and Keeper of the Ada Machine.

Hat drummed her fingers on her desk. Nothing in her own entry had changed.

The passage about the destruction of the Mists of the Abyss and the liberation of the Infinity Plane had bothered Hat since the first time she read it when she was 7 years old. Now, so many eons after the end of the Human race and apparently anything else of any significance in the universe, the entry bothered her even more. The problem was that as far as Hat knew, it had never happened. Hat's mother had dismissed her daughter's concerns over the years with careless remarks about the accuracy of the *Prognosticated*

Peerage, none of which had ever given Hat one moment of peace. Particularly, since Hat knew, her own mother kept a careful eye on the ever-changing text of the *Prognosticated Peerage*.

Hat knew that it was inaccurate to say that the text of the *Prognosticated Peerage* "changed," even though she, like everyone else, said that is was what it did. It would be more accurate to say that it "updates." Details never- or at least have never been satisfactorily proven to have disappeared. However, details did at times modify themselves to such a degree that the original detail or details, often "disappeared" to the casual reader. One would have to walk around with an immense knowledge in one's own head in-order to keep track of it all. Even Hat with her Scion enhanced abilities required an immense computer database to keep an accurate analyses of the *Prognosticated Peerage* up to date.

Needless to say, neither Angels nor Demons could ever be bothered with such things. This really explains a lot about what happened later.

Hat glanced up to see the mummy, which had so bothered the Angel, casually stepped out of the wall painting. It began unwrapping its own head.

"Clever, very clever," Hat said walking over and snatching the book out of the mummy's hands. Tucking *The Complete Love Letters of Völva and Freyja,* which was a slim volume, under her arm, Hat returned to read the *Prognosticated Peerage* entry upon her so recently departed visitor.

> **Mictlantecuhtli**: called Mick: Angel. [Note: Not to be confused with Mictlantecuhtli alternatively Nahuatl called the "Lord of Mictlan," of Aztec history, who was a god of the dead and the king of Mictlan, called Chicunauhmictlan, being than the lowest and coldest bit of the Underworld. Although Mictlantecuhtli, Angel, called Mick did have a hand in the creation of the "Lord of Mictlan."] As noted the Pre-Light historian Leonard Eugene Dickson, the *Lat Monac*

Codex lists the Angel Mictlantecuhtli as the 33,550,336[th] Angel to be created. Little more is known about the Angel Mictlantecuhtli's doings for the first couple of million years, until he appears in the chronicles of the *Complete History of Man, Special Final Edition, with Complete and Accurate Essays on What You Did Last Summer*, teaching man how to make tasteful graffiti tags somewhere in the vicinity of Montignac alternatively Montinhac Commune in the Dordogne Alternatively Dordonha Départment of Aquitaine alternatively Aquitània or Akitania, near the Vézère River, somewhere between the Loire Valley and the High Pyrénées Mountains. It is rumoured, but not confirmed, that the Angel Mictlantecuhtli was sentenced for his part in the defacement of the Creator's Property to scrub all the walls of the caves in Eurasia with his toothbrush, but no evidence survives to indicate that he actually did this. The Angel Mictlantecuhtli then drops out of sight again, surfacing early on in the Aztec Empire Period, where he reportedly fathered a child by a king's daughter, got his heart broken, and got pinched on the "Pretending to be a God" clause of the Heaven Rules of Order, and was banished for about a million years to the far side of the Comet Galaxy, where he apparently cooled his heels for several thousands of years writing tragic epistolary novels, one of which he reportedly sold wholesale to one Earl Robert Lovelace in 1748. Where he promptly settled down to enjoy a long-term investment in the King's Theatre in Haymarket, City of Westminster, London, and staunchly refusing to ever recognize that any mere woman could change the name of his King's Theatre. In 1791, the Angel Mictlantecuhtli then moved with the Theatre Royal of Drury Lane into their third theatre building. In mid-May of the year 1800. The Angel Mictlantecuhtli caused quite a sensation when he when he stood-up in the royal theatre box and exclaimed "By Jove, that's that bastard Hadfield down there. He owes me 50 quid- and look- there's that ratfink Truelock sneaking out the stage door. By George, I'll kill you- you rotten-" at which point, the aggrieved James Hadfield emptied a loaded revolver into the Angel. At court, the Angel Mictlantecuhtli made such an ass of himself that the judges acquitted Hadfield on the grounds of "Bloody bad luck you didn't get the jerk." When the fifteen year old third Theatre Royal of Drury Lane burned to the ground, the Angel Mictlantecuhtli who was then going by the name Barron von Brinsley was reported to have said "My god, this Côte Rôtie tastes like crap. Nice fire though." After which, he was run out of London as a social-pariah. Mictlantecuhtli's largest contributions to Human history were his honourable military service in the Royal Militia of the Island of Jersey and later in the United States Marine Corps, and his efforts in the Hollywood film industry to spread morality and patriotism among the Anglo-Saxon peoples.

"What is the matter, my cousin Mistress?" asked a half bandaged mummy.

"Words, words, and more words," Hat muttered closing the book.

"No," said the head emerging from the mummy wrap, "what's the matter, the problem, the conflict?"

"Between who?" Hat asked running her fingers over the primeval leather binding of the book.

The now wholly unbandaged Scion sighed.

"You know what really gets me about you?" he asked.

"Hmmm?"

"It's how you can take a simple question and turn it into a bloody lifeless literary-"

"And what does the bastard Basil Berry want?" Hat asked eyeing the slim face, pointed nose, pearly white teeth, and cool grey eyes that stood before her.

"Just because a guy's mother doesn't acknowledge him doesn't mean you got to go on about it for the rest of eternity," the half-mummified turned Scion lately identified as Basil Berry said.

Hat scowled at him.

"What's it called? The book, I mean," Basil Berry asked, picking up the book that the Angel had wanted. "I never did lay my hands on a complete copy."

"*Continuous Creation*, by Kin Arad," Hat said.

"Don't you think you were a little heavy with the Angel?" Basil Berry asked as he placed a pair of thin round silver-rimmed spectacles upon his pointed nose. "We need that big hulk of whatever it is," he added looking at the door where the Angel had departed as if he more half expected Mick to charge back through it at any moment.

"I was trying to cover for your 'I got to make it obvious' fuck-up," Hat said grimly.

"Oh, I don't know about that," Basil Berry said cheerily. "Mictlantecuhtli has always reminded me about that bit with the rabbit and the duck where the rabbit finally gets hit in the head with the anvil. I mean, seriously, he's thick, even by Angel standards."

"Well, that may be as is," Hat said. "But I've still never been able to stand the guy."

"Well, it's not for much longer," Basil Berry said striking an optimistic tone completely at odds with Hat's demeanour. "And besides, we need for him to have the book. I mean we really really- really- really-"

"Oh shut-up," Hat said, placing the *Prognosticated Peerage* on her desk. "I'll have one of the Faeries take it around to him in the morning. Right now, all I want is for you to get the Hells out of my office."

46

"Right-o, Sis," Basil Berry said taking *Continuous Creation*, by Kin Arad off Hat's desk. "I'll send someone after Angelic-pants with this."

Hat merely grunted her reply.

Basil Berry made a mock half bow and began backwardly bowing his way out of the office.

"Knock it off you dolt," Hat said. "You'll break something, you most likely, and then I'll never be rid of you."

Basil Berry straightened up; dusted imaginary lint off the cover of the book, and made to finally exit the office.

"By the way," Hat said. "You never did tell me how you got the Angel to go in on this with you."

"He's not in on anything," Basil Berry with a wink and a grin.

Hat made to retort, but Basil Berry waved her off.

"But to answer the question," he continued. "I sent him an email."

Hat laughed. It was a full laugh, the sort of laugh that hits sand stonewalls and manages to bounce back.

"You've conjured up the biggest scheme since Vatican III and you started it off with an email?" Hat finally managed to ask. "How'd you phrase it? Oh, pardon me, I know we don't get on an all, what with be being kin to a devil and you being a sanctimonious bastard, but would you mind helping me start the 11th Great Age of Creation? Oh, and by the by, don't tell God?"

Normally, such an utterance might have produced a reaction; it certainly would have among most mortals whom often confused "job description" with "name." Can't be helped really coming from a species that went in for names like Abbott; Baker, Carpenter, Cooper, Farmer, Gardner, Goldsmith,

Potter, Smith, Taylor, Thatcher, and Weaver. People like that are bound to confuse the word God with, you know, the actual name of God.

So in order to avoid that tiny little problem, our readers should, just like with reading Hebrew what with its lack of vowels and extreme lack of punctuation, pay close attention to this manuscript to catch just what anything means. This is further complicated by the intense belief of the immortal creatures that to name a thing- any thing- is to attract its attention.

The fact that that belief is actually true just makes it worse.

"Umm, not exactly," Basil Berry said. "Mick thinks he's acting on orders."

"Pardon me?" Hat asked suddenly going very still.

"Yep," Basil Berry said with an air of serenity that Hat certainly did not enjoy.

"You, son of-"

"Hey now," Basil Berry cut in.

"You sent an Angel of the Creator an email, in the guise of the Creator, to give the Angel instructions on how to piss off- off- well, just about everyone-especially the Creator?"

"No, no, and no," Basil Berry said very firmly. "I sent dope-ass Angel an email in the guise of the Metatron. A small, but *significant* difference."

"I wouldn't bet my afterlife on it," Hat said.

"Na," Basil Berry said. "It's the same difference between impersonating a dictator, and impersonating that same dictator's press secretary."

"I don't think that the Big Guy has the sort of sense of humour."

"Are you kidding me? I made an entire career of making the Metatron look like a dope. Hell, I might even be part of that Ineffable Plan to make Metatron

48

look like an even bigger dope then he actually is all by himself."

Insane, Hat thought. He's utterly insane.

"And how did you explain the, oh Hells, time delay on that email?" Hat asked. "I mean, it's only been long enough for evolution to have repeated three or four times since the Final Match. I mean, it's even safe to go back to Terra these days."

"Have you seen her about?"

"Who?" Hat asked.

"Evolution. Have you seen her lately?" Basil Berry asked brightening at the thought of seeing his favourite anthropomorphic personification again.

Hat sighed, which she reflected, she did a lot of when Basil Berry was around.

"No, not for long," she said.

"Too bad," Basil Berry complained. "She's a harsh mistress, but ever so much fun to go dancing with. I remember this one time, during the Bombing of London, she and I went down to-"

"The email?" Hat prompted.

"Oh, yeah, that," Basil Berry said. "Well, it contained instructions for the post-end-of-humanity-reboot. All the usual stuff; tell no one, trusting you with the fate of the universe, etc., etc. Those over-grown bat-doves love that junk. And I sent the email from an A.O.L. account, so he wouldn't think twice about why took it so long to arrive."

Hat picked up her own personal copy of *Bradshaw's Guide to the Bookworld* and began slowly banging her forehead with it.

"What?" Basil Berry said with overwrought tones of injured innocence. "We are talking about a guy that's still wading through his spam mail from before the end of mortal time."

Hat looked up from her self-inflicted forehead massage and uttered her most clever rejoinder ever.

"Huh?"

"Yeah, it's hard to believe," Basil Berry said. "If I were you, I'd never believe it either, but that Angel is still wading through his spam mail just in-case he missed a notice about a late fee or something or just in-case there really is a Nigerian wife of a former freedom fighter that's won the American lottery but can't get the money because her mother's dying of H.I.V. / A.I.D.S. in an Obamacare government death camp and for a slight investment you can immediately realized a 10,000% profit."

"But he doesn't need money," Hat said.

"No, he'd do it because *it's the right thing to do*," Basil Berry said, turned, and left Hat's office.

Later, Hat pulled her chair back to her desk and sat down to organize her interrupted work.

Where are those acquisition forms? Hat wondered. I left them around here somewhere.

Hat found the forms sitting under her Ada Machine, the universe's most unique storage device, which Hat often used as a paper weight. Hat retrieved her personal copy of the *Prognosticated Peerage* and flipped through looking for an entry that she had never seen before. The Scion of Sešat was not surprised when she found the new entry:

> **Kin Arad**: called Kin Arad: Human, mortal: Kin Arad's biography was written by an English Knight of the Realm. She is the current Chairmen of the original planetary disc. She is formally a Lead Planetary Engineer in the employ of the Company, which terraforms and builds worlds for the use of Humans and Humanoids. Kin Arad is the original author *Continuous Creation.*

Hat drummed her fingers on the desk, briefly considered calling up her Mum, discarded the idea, and got back to work. Whatever it was that the inscrutable editors of the *Prognosticated Peerage* were saying would become clear in time. Best not to dwell on it, she had always felt.

Time, always an optional environmental variable in most libraries, settled onto Hat's shoulders like old age. It was a comfortable mantle that had long ago become as comfortable as worn-out slippers.

Hat re-examined her English translations of the Hebrew and Greek *Coptic Codex* copies of the "Book of Judas." Even though Hat had learned her Hebrew from an Immortal, the lack of vowels always got on her nerves.

The Immortals should not be confused with immortals. The Immortals are a type of creature, vaguely human-shaped, that is indestructible. Whereas an immortal is merely someone that will not die naturally, but can still be killed by any number of things. The Immortals though have been documented to survive direct atomic bomb strikes. One Immortal once restored the power cells of a massive space battle cruiser without even messing his hair. And it's a good thing Immortals had no other real powers as they would have been as gods rather than the lazy good for nothing but large parties type of people they were.

Hat sighed as another shadow fell over her desk.

"I thought I told you to-"

Hat broke off when she realized it was not, absolutely not, Basil Berry that was blocking the light.

What stood before Hat was an elderly black man, dressed in a dark black cloak, the hood of which was drawn back to reveal a full head of curly hair that had just gone grey around the edges. A soft shell pearl-rimmed pince-nez perched upon his nose.

A dog, or what might have been called a dog in a more nightmarish universe, stood behind the old man. The dog was unusual in that its body supported three heads, and a mass of snakes that curled around each neck like a lion's main. The three necks joined to a massive set of shoulder muscles that were balanced by a long body and an even more massive set of rear croup muscles and legs. The paws, if you could call them paws; better to call them feet or hands-suited-for-running-on, had four fingers, and two opposable thumbs, one on either side of the fingers.

Its name was Kérberos.

The three headed dog was the oldest extant Nightmare. Except maybe for its master, the Gatekeeper.

When someone asks you if you're God, Hat thought and quickly shoved the fancy into her mental abyss.

Hat had never been sure if the Gatekeeper could actually read minds or if he was just so extremely familiar with people that it just seemed that way.

Formality, she though, focus on the formalities.

Hat rose, walked around her desk, and curtsied low to the old man while completely ignoring Kérberos. Hat knew damn good and well that it took more than a Nightmare to rattle her. The trouble was that that 'more' was standing just in-front of her.

Hat knew that the Gatekeeper had made the Nightmares, or at least, had allowed them to be made. Either way, she had never understood why.

"Hatshepsut Nefertari Djeserit Fukayna, daughter of goddess Sešat and the Demon James of no rank, no house, and no tribe, bids you welcome, Gatekeeper," Hat sat.

The old man nodded, and Hat rose to her feet again.

52

The man smiled and said in a voice as charming as Morgan Freeman's, "I need a book from you, Guardian of Recorded History."

A momentary flash of amusement passed over Hat's face and then concealed itself even faster than it had arrived.

"What subject or author do you require, Gatekeeper?"

The old man waved away Hat's formality.

"Don't patronize me with that stuff," the Gatekeeper said mildly. "I've always found it clouds the mind."

"Oh," Hat said.

"Metallurgy, gardening, mythological creatures, and so-called *popular culture*," the Gatekeeper said. "Oh, and a book about dating for the over 30 millions."

"All in the same volume?" Hat asked, recovering her composure. She glanced at Kérberos and was not surprised to see the right head snapping at the snakes of another head. The left head was sleeping. The middle head however was staring straight at her. Hat stared back at the over-grown mutmare.

"Did they ever make such a book as that?" the Gatekeeper asked.

"No."

"Well, thanks be then," said the Gatekeeper. "Separate volumes will do."

"May I ask," Hat said tearing her eyes away from Kérberos, which blinked slightly less often than a gold fish.

"Yes."

"What do you need them for?" she continued while performing her now-ya-see-nothing-now-I-got-a-book-for-you trick.

53

The Gatekeeper took time to consider the question.

Hat worked quickly and efficiently, bringing one book after another to her hands, and laying each one softly on her desk.

Hat, her task complete, waited in a mildly nervous state. The Gatekeeper was one of three persons in the universe that made her uneasy. The other two were her mother and father.

Finally the Gatekeeper said, "Obfuscation," and began stroking Kérberos' sleeping head.

The other two heads growled.

"You've always been good at that," Hat said.

The Gatekeeper nodded his agreement.

"I have a job for you," the Gatekeeper said while looking at the titles of the books Hat had called to her office.

"Yes?"

"You will need to make peace with all of your kind, and between all of your kind," he said. "This must happen."

Hat remained silent even though her internal voice was screaming at nearly ear deafening volumes.

Impossible! Ludicrous! How? She wanted to know.

"You will have to," the Gatekeeper began and then lapsed into silence for a time.

Hat stood a while watching the third oldest known creature in the universe and then went for a bowl and a bottle of water.

When she returned, the Gatekeeper said as if Hat had never left, "be nice to everyone. That is it, be nice to them."

Hat reframed from the obvious lie.

"I'm sure you can manage that," the Gatekeeper said. "If you put your mind to it."

Oh well, Hat thought, and went with a more nuanced approach.

"I've always treated people in the way that I thought they would understand best," she said.

The old man nodded, pulled up a chair, and began to read the first book entitled *So You're a Forgotten god? A Pop Culture Guide to Getting Your C-corp Executorship Back Through Cable Access, Blogging, and Personal Brand Development on a Tight Budget*, by Chan Girlvinyl.

Hat sat down behind her desk and made an entirely unsuccessful effort to return to her Canonical Acquisitions forms. Growing up with her mother, goddess mother Sešat, had taught Hat how to wait. She was a champion Olympic quality waiter. If you have some waiting to do and one of those fancy machines for looping time, Hat was your woman. Well, half-Demon half-goddess semi-immortal anyway. Usually the waiting was tranquil for Hat, but now, all she had was a feeling of dread.

On the whole, Hat preferred her father's approach to feelings of any sort; be it extreme displeasure, read as happiness for non-Demons, or peace, read as blinding rage. In any situation, the Demon James was either overly loud or so overly articulate that he was often aghast to understand just why people completely failed to understand what he meant. Or, there was the outside chance that he would just confuse everyone by telling them flap-flap jokes.

Flap-flap jokes, as the stark raving Demon Black tells us, are knock-knock jokes, but with tents instead of houses.

The misunderstandings arose from the combination of both loud and over-articulation. People never tried to get past the loud and listen to the actual words. But that's people for you- overly wound-up balls of stress, tension, stress, fear, stress, and the

55

occasional act of completely selfless bravery- usually brought on by stress that was so extreme that they acted bravely out of sheer nerve-wracking-panic.

The Demon James on the other hand got past all that pop psychology by never-ever, not once, paying the slightest attention to anything he ever said about anything. "You can get a lot of peace," he used to say, "out of never paying yourself any mind. For example, you never feel embarrassed because as for as you are concerned, it never happened."

Hat often received snotty text messages from her father Demon that were longer, more hostile, more egotistical, and considerably more humorous, not to mention devoid of merit, than any Ph.D. dissertation in Literary Critical Theory written throughout the whole history of literary studies.

"How would you like to be the new Gatekeeper?" the Gatekeeper asked.

New? What do you mean, new? Hat wanted to know.

"I don't think I should like it much," she said looking up into the old man's face, and for the first time truly seeing just how old and care worn he was.

"Why not?" the Gatekeeper asked.

"I don't have the patience for it," Hat admitted. "And I'm rubbish at letting people be idiots right in front of me."

The Ancient man nodded and returned to his reading.

After a while, Hat got up and finished her Canonical Acquisitions paperwork, balanced the time sheets on Basil Berry- a true study in Speculative Math, tidied up her office, and got her Carpet portfolio case out of the closet.

The Carpet was well deserving of its Capitalization as it was one of the famous three Magical Flying Carpets. The other two were entrusted to two other Scions named Mayghin and Qdot. Hat's Carpet could and did fly to anywhere in the universe the owner wanted it to go to, and did a reasonable in-flight burger and chips, although the warmth of either never lasted long. Hat had won the three Carpets in a high stakes game of Vieux Garçon in which the alternative was a complete loss of honour, and Hat was still very particularly attached to her hounour.

When the Gatekeeper finally did speak, he spoke for a very long time. He spoke for such a long time and without any indication of stopping that Hat was forced to put everything away, put on tea for two, and settle in for an unrecorded history lesson. By the time it was over, Hat had wished that she had ordered a Meals on Wheels delivery.

And the worst part was that the Gatekeeper didn't say anything that Hat wanted to hear.

In fact, he said a lot of things that sounded like utter non-sense and which she would have dismissed out of hand from anyone else, accept perhaps her own mother.

Chapter 2: Main Circulation Desk

The Main Circulation Desk of the Elysion Library, on the planet Elysion, in he Camulodunum System.

For the poor shall never cease out of the land: therefore I command thee, saying, Thou shalt open thine hand wide unto thy brother, to thy poor, and to thy needy, in thy land. --Deuteronomy 15:11, K.J.V.

And it came to pass that an Avatar and a Hellspawn delivered the oracle unto the Angel.

Since this tale has a great deal to do with Scions, we should pause for a moment to sort out what Scions actually are.

According to the *Prognosticated Peerage*, a Scion is "...literally the begotten; one of the brood, the heir or heiress, the issue of a union- usually a royal one, and most importantly, the Successor."

The *Prognosticated Peerage* goes on at some length about the technical aspects of what a Scion is, and is not, and how one can be born of a goddess, but not be a Scion. For example, the Native American goddesses were for awhile really going in for surrogate motherhood in a big way. But we think that most of the technical details of Scionship are rather droll, so let's think metaphorically. In this more literary sense, the Scions are the products of a union between a Human mortal and a god, a god-child if you will.

Think about Hercules and Perseus who were begotten in the non-Immaculate macula sort of way. Conception does not always have to involve deception, at least not the shape changing sorts like Zeus or the old man deceptions of Óðinn. Most Humans crawl into bed with a god of their own free will. It's because they know damn good and well they're about to have a rip roaring good time. Whereas the Immaculate should've gotten her arse stoned had anyone really known about it at the time.

A moment should be given to consider the Son.

Done?

Okay. But we should still clarify.

The Son is, arguably the most famous Scion. But He is generally not claimed by any of the Scions, except Basil Berry, and even then, only when drunk. The Son, for His part, claims everyone indiscriminately, even the great First of the Fallen called Stan, as His brothers and sisters. Stan of course points out that he had no mother, and has no children- never had any- never will have any- ever, and therefore in the most fundamental sense has no kith or kin of any sort. To wit the Son always says "Tough luck buddy," and gives Stan a big old hug, while all the other Demons inspect either their boot laces or the stars.

So, that's your hyperbolic course on Scions. Tricky lot the bunch of them. They're the only folk worse than Faeries, so steer clear.

You've been warned.

Basil Berry came around the corner of Current Periodicals to see Yūko White sitting with her white knee-length stockinged feet spread up on the main circulation desk, plaid skirt up around her knees, reading a back-issue copy of *Pacific Vogue*. Loud chomping could be heard interspersed with the occasional pop.

Basil Berry felt an urge to look for other white cotton things.

"It says here," rang out the clear strong female voice of Yūko White, "that Moriyama had a secret love-child with the Emperor of Japan."

"Well, did she?" boomed a voice deeper both in pitch, and altitude.

"She most assuredly *did not*," Yūko White declared. "I can vouch for that girl's honour, even if I can't vouch for the Emperor."

"Which Emperor was it?"

"Who cares?"

"Didn't Moriyama do those girly ninja movies?" bombed the sub-counter voice.

"Yip," chirped the voice behind the wiggling white stocking feet and magazine.

Basil Berry really wanted to look. Just a little peep, he thought, one little glance of those precious little things.

"I always liked her work," the deeper voice said in a mild reflective tone. "Moriyama was a good one - never kicked anyone or anything anymore than she had too. That's real nice to find in a lady. Most time, they go on kicking you no matter what you do."

"Well, I never-"

But the world was never destined to know what Yūko White never did as she sat bolt upright, twisted the magazine, and began beating something beneath her desk.

"That tickles- you idiot," she yelled.

Unfortunately, for Basil Berry, it was also at this moment that he stepped up to the counter to sneak his peep.

"Sorry mistress," said the deeper voice, which had contrived to get even closer to the floor. "It's just this feather duster that they gives me. I tells them, can tentacle arms use this here straight handle like the monkeys can use? No, I says. But they go on and give it to me no matter what. Dust this they say. Buff that they say. But what about the muff? I ask. And they say--"

Bless the Beast, Basil Berry thought.

Tentacles flashed around both sides of Yūko White's legs, while a pink and purple neon nylon duster ran up and down her inner thighs.

60

Basil Berry, his view obstructed, sighed, and intentionally knocked over a rack of *The Adventures of Jinkies the Serial Monster* by Johnny Bravo.

The tentacles and duster disappeared under the counter.

Yūko White sat bolt upright, straightening her black Hwa Chong Institution jacket, skirt, and red tie. She just managed to smile as Basil Berry replaced the last book back on the rack.

"Good evening, Department Manager Berry," Yūko White said. "How can we- I mean, I, assist you?"

"I need you to deliver this," Basil Berry said swapping *Continuous Creation*, by Kin Arad for the back-issue copy of *Pacific Vogue*. "Hey look here, it says they are going to come out with a new edition of Super Mario Siblings soon."

"Oh yes," Yūko White said. "The Demon Shax has taken the game to new levels. I understand that he is going to incorporate your honourable Scions into the newest edition."

"Well, I'm sure Mario will win," Basil Berry said with a sigh. "He always does."

"With honourable contradiction," Yūko White said. "It is our, I mean, my understanding that the Demon Shax intends to make this edition adversarial, so that the monsters, no, say adversaries of the Sūpā Mario Siblings, or one also can play Mario, Luigi, and Giolla against one another in combat."

"Neat," Basil Berry said.

"To whom does this book belong?" Yūko White asked picking up the copy of *Continuous Creation*, by Kin Arad that Basil Berry had placed on the counter. "I don't know this title."

"Old Mad Hatter," Basil Berry said.

"Is this personal book
or Elysion book?" Yūko White asked. "I am not familiar
with this book at all. There is no aura code."

For those that are not familiar with the filing and
claims procedures of the Elysion Library, an aura code
is like a bar code, but does not require a sticker or an
ink stamp, which preserves the original integrity of the
book. The down side though is that they also make the
books impossible to misplace, photocopy, steal, or
even return late. There are never late returns because
E.L.P., the Elysion Library Police, show-up wherever
the book is ten minutes before the expiration date
expires and start playing show tunes from the
beginning. Since there are few things more irritating
than being pulled out of bed in the middle of the night,
or worse yet, away from a coquette that is about to
actually give it up, people tend to return books well
before time.

Basil Berry looked up at the ceiling for a
moment. The overhead lights, some thirteen meters
above him, showed a slight smear of dust on their
casings.

I'll have to get someone up there to clean that,
Basil Berry thought.

"You know, I don't know," he finally said. "I'm
not entirely sure who wrote it."

"Then this Kin Arad is a
pseudonym?" Yūko White asked.

"Yes, I think you can safely say that."

"So, not a real person then."

"Oh, I wouldn't say that, no, not that," Basil
Berry said flipping through the magazine again. "I'm
sure she existed somewhere, once upon a time ago. I
think the galaxy was called Salisbury."

Yūko White shrugged and wrapped the book in
a black and red silk cloth in the basic Furoshiki style
carry wrap called Bin Tsutsumi.

Basil Berry watched her small hands as they spread out the silk on the counter. Yūko White than placed the book in the center of the silk turned at a 45-degree angle. She than folded the silk diagonally across the middle of the square wrap, making a straight line across the spine of the book. Yūko White then rolled the remainder of the silk length ways until the book was wrapped up, resembling a long red silk sausage. Yūko White brought the ends of the silk together and tied two ends into a daft square knot.

Basil Berry picked the book up by the silk handle and turned it one way and then the other examining the wrapping.

"I love it," Basil Berry said. "I think I'll have you do my apartment like this."

"To whom do I deliver?" Yūko White asked, taking the wrapped book back from Basil Berry.

"Come on up here Phu," Basil Berry said banging on the counter top. "This job's for you too."

"Ain't nobody down here but us mice," boomed the Phu-denying voice below the counter.

"Come on," Basil Berry said. "Wherever Avatar Yūko White is, sure there is Hellspawn Phu too."

"Oh, all right," Phu said.

Several long black slick tentacles slithered in and out from under the circulation table. Two pink and white candy stripped rubbers were tentacled up, which Yūko White took.

Basil Berry watched in frank unabashed admiration as she first stood on one foot to slip on a rubber and then repeated the procedure for the other.

A white knitted hat, with pink drawstrings, and what Basil Berry took to be kitty ears was tentacled up next, followed by a pink and white umbrella with the 子猫セックス emblazoned in dark sable characters across its vertical. The umbrella was trimmed with bleached white lace.

"You do look rather smashing," Basil Berry said leaning on the counter. "You should come over for dinner sometime," he added with a grin.

Black tentacle arms, far longer than Basil Berry thought entirely necessary, wrapped around his wrists and ankles.

Yūko White frowned and lightly tapped one of the tentacles. The tentacle relaxed its grip on Basil Berry, but did not withdraw.

"With respect, Department Manager Berry," Yūko White said with what Basil Berry thought a sterner note than necessary. "I would not be caught dead alone with you," she finished off as neatly as if she were ordering a tidy Scotch.

"Oh come on pet," Basil Berry said. "Andy will have his little joke."

The black tentacles tightened again.

Basil Berry glanced down at the tentacles with mild concern. He was immortal, but only as long as nobody killed him. It was a point that Basil Berry was a bit sour about actually. He had the sense of humour of a trickster god, the sense of self of a thunder god, and about as much natural armour as a Filarial worm. It just wasn't fair.

"Now, to whom do we deliver?"

"The Angel called Mick," Basil Berry said, wondering when Phu intended to release him. "Do you know the twerp?"

"Yeah, I know him" Phu said from below the counter. "He blew past here about a minute ago. I waved, and called out to him, using his proper name, and he didn't even look up at me. A real jerk that guy."

"Well Phu dog, you have my personal permission to be as mean to him as you like," Basil Berry said.

"Oh, well, that's something else, ain't it?" Phu said releasing and withdrawing all his tentacles below and behind the counter. "Can I eat his soul?"

"Shouldn't think he's got one," Basil Berry said. "I served with him in the Crimean. Trust me; he hasn't got one. Least ways, not one that you'd notice."

"Too bad," Phu complained, "too bad."

Basil Berry followed Yūko White and Phu outside the library onto the covered entranceway.

"Any idea where the Angel Mick has gone?" Yūko White asked.

The Scion Basil Berry paused for a moment, looking around the front of the library for anyone to divert the conversation. The last thing he wanted was further conversation about the Angel Mick. Angels had a small hint of His ability to hear their own name, and Basil Berry certainly didn't want Mick's attention, not yet.

Disappointed by the lack of handy random people about when he wanted one, Basil Berry took up a mock attitude of consideration.

"The Angel's an espresso whore," Basil Berry said with a sigh, frustrated that for the first time he could remember there wasn't anyone standing on the library steps smoking and joking. "Try the Elysion Library Coffee Shoppe first. He's very likely to go there before leaving the system."

Yūko White made a slight, but formal, bow to Basil Berry.

Phu slammed a bundle of tentacles against Basil Berry's shoulder, sending the Scion stumbling.

"See ya later alligator," Phu said following Yūko White down the hover-chair accessible ramp.

After a while fucker, Basil Berry thought while rubbing blood back into his shoulder.

Once Basil Berry could no longer see or hear his couriers, he turned in the opposite direction toward the Deoradháin Café.

If I know anything about Mick, Basil Berry thought, it's that he's even lazier than he is arrogant.

Outside the Elysion Library Coffee Shoppe sat several examples of the remnants of the sentients in the universe after the end of the Human species. Two Angels sat playing Texas Hold 'Em with two Gorillas; Skooby Deel King of the Imps, and the Lesser Prince Petit Albert of the Mandragoras. The Hopkinsville Goblin sat dealing hands from behind silver mirrored sunglasses.

When the Angel Mick stepped into the Elysion Library Coffee Shoppe he felt, for a brief second, that he had come home. Just why the Angel felt so, or just where his home might have been, he couldn't say. But nonetheless, for one fleeting second, Mick felt that he had come home.

It is a rare thing in this universe, or in any other universe, for someone, or some thing, to be truly homeless. It is far more often the case that the subject does not like its home, or perhaps, has gotten its memories so cluttered that it does not remember its home. Most animals for instance have a certain temperate or other environmental condition that they require, which limits them from living much of anywhere else in the universe. But, everything, most sentient creatures anyway, know just where their home is, and astonishingly, often like the place. For most sentients, and most creatures, home is not just the place they live, or were maybe born. Home is the place that they are the most socially adjusted to, the place they are most psychologically attuned too. In short, home is the place their souls would drift back to if their bodily homes weren't available for lurking in anymore.

The Immortal band Guts and Rodents played their cosmic favourite "Take Me Down to the Pair-o-dice Café" as the Angel Mick looked into the universe's largest aquarium that formed 90% of the interior walls of the Elysion Library Coffee Shoppe, even though the coffee shoppe did not appear to be so large on the outside.

This spatial deception is due to the Demon James being one of only seven still living creatures in this universe that is absolutely certain that other universes exist.

And the Demon is the only one of three still living creatures that is certain that the other universes are accessible from this one

And the Demon James is the only living creature in the universe that has gone through the trouble of actually accessing those other universes on purpose. Patton's United Terran Space Navy team by contrast found thousands of other universes during their five-year mission to explore strange new spaceships, seek out new life and new weapons, and to boldly run back home as fast as possible.

But rather than sharing his demonic knowledge with the masses, or even with his fellow Demons, who almost all categorically despised the Demon James, he used the knowledge to sell larger-on-the-inside-than-the-outside condos in the Los Angeles, Chicago, New Your City, London, Frankfurt, Deli, Peking, and Tokyo housing markets. He was eventually caught by a joint American and Europe-African-Asian Union auditors taskforce, due to his owing several respective governments billions of pounds sterling in back sales tax due to his tendency to calculate the properties square meters by the exterior of the building, rather than the interior of the building. But that's another story for another tome.

And the Demon James also built aquariums-extremely large transuniversal
aquariums. Transuniversal is like transdimensional, but with universes instead of deminations. Neither of which

should be confused with parallel universes, which is just a silly nonsense sense made-up by a stoned physics graduate student that flunked out and made millions as an alternative history writer.

These points aren't particularly important now, but they will be, eventually. Like in the *Zita Chronicles*. They are frightfully important the *Zita Chronicles*.

What had always puzzled Mick about the thing was not its size of the Elysion Library Coffee Shoppe aquarium, weighing in at a mere 101 million gallons - although why it had to be 101 anythings was a mystery to the Angel. What perplexed the Angel was that the aquarium was entirely devoted to fish from the Lakes of Africa and South America.

It was also well known that owner of all those fish, said previously mentioned Demon James of no rank, no title, no notable achievements, or particular character, had put a hex-spell on his fishy friends in order to prevent inter-species warfare. Small baby Red Empress fish swam next to large 30 pounds Red Oscar fish without the slightest sign of trouble. The Demon James also claimed to have secured all 4,313 species of the Cichlid family, and also to have scientifically bred another 242 new species since the end of the Human race.

The real miracle though was that the café didn't smell of fish, and not that nice freshly deep fried fish smell, but that nasty poopy not quite alive fish smell of when the tide has gone out and left the fish just flopping around on the sand.

And the place didn't reek of tobacco smoke or beer or piss either, which was another minor miracle.

Far out in the aquarium, the Angel Mick could just make out two Demons; the Demon James and the Demon Rían, along with the Angel Ashleigh. They looked to be building a castle out of pre-fabricated moulded plastic pieces which the Cichlids were than swimming in and out of, some defending their castle, some invading other castles, and one with a brief-case and a flyer offering to sell his neighbour's castle.

Our dear readers will, or at any rate should, greatly appreciate the fact that the Demon James does not figure largely in this story no matter what the last page or two might suggest. His role in the mega multi-dimensional Cosmos is saved for later chronicles, like the *Zita Chronicles* that have already been plugged, or *The Murder of Basil Berry* being Book II of *The Complete Revelation of Mick and Keith*.

But there are two essential things to know about the Demon James. First, he is the father of Hat, and the second is that he is completely bat-fuck insane. The Demon was, by training; a compulsive liar, a complete narcissist, utterly devoid of any emotional depth, and extremely fond of war games, rather like billionaire politicians. Ironically, the Demon had also spent his time on Terra founding schools, supporting the arts, and annoying Ministers and political "science" Professors alike by the simple expedience of breathing right in front of them.

Now, the Demon Rían on the other hand is widely believed to be the only Human born mortal turned Demon in the universe. Not only is this daft, but it is inaccurate as well in that there are no less than thirteen Demons that were born of purely mortal Human parents. The rumour that Demon Rían was a Watcher like Shax is also. Rían chose the vocation of Demon, he wasn't saddled with it like Shax was. It is widely believed that the Demon Rían taught humanity the Art of Metallurgy. This is also inaccurate. The Demon Rían taught humanity Hunting, Gambling, and the Art of Fiction, more or less in that order. Celestial historians debate the value added impact of the Demon Rían's efforts to "improve" the Human condition, but one thing is certain, he was completely responsible for the mythology of "If you would be famous, go west young man." Considering he was standing in the dining hall of the Inuyama Castle at the time, one wonders why the saying stuck.

And what then of the Angel Ashleigh? Nobody has ever figured out why the Angel Ashleigh hangs out with the Demon Rían, much less the Demon James. Certainly she gave up trying to save either of them a long time ago. The Angel Ashleigh came to minor fame mainly on account of her involvement in that well remembered Nevada Motel Massacre incident along with the Demons Rían and James. Her only public statement on the incident given to the *Sun Times* was, "I went along to try and figure out why those two knuckleheads were so interested in the case. What I figured out was that neither one of them had the slightest clue why they did anything. It was totally fascinating."

Later, in the next universe, the three had a falling out, mainly because of Rían's refusal to ever show-up for anything, and the Demon James' lack of ability to sustain interest in anything outside of his own field of vision.

After watching the Demons and the other Angel for a while, Mick shrugged and wandered over to the shoppe's counter.

"Mr. Meak?" the Angel said reading the name tag pinned onto the green polo shirt of the short balding man-like creature standing behind the Elysion Library Coffee Shoppe counter.

The man behind the counter nodded.

"Guess you inherited the Terra?" Mick said, laughing at his own joke.

The man nodded a second time.

"And what did you do with it when you got it?" the Angel asked with a snicker.

"I let it go fallow."

The Angel frowned.

"Well, I guess some people just can't take a joke?" Mick said with a shrug.

"An original joke, I'll gladly take," Mr. Meak said blandly. "But every Angel that's been here in the last million years has made that joke. It was tired the second time."

"I'll have a double espresso and a fish sandwich," Mick ordered.

"Poor choice daddy-o," Mr. Meak said. "Fish are friends, not food."

"Calamari then?"

"Right, that'll be one vegan El Cheapo Burrito," Mr. Meak corrected.

"What the Hell is that?" the Angel asked.

"Black beans, organic diced tomatoes, olive oil, crushed red pepper, garlic, diced red onion, diced bell peppers, smoked paprika, cumin, cooked brown rice, chopped cilantro, with lettuce, tomato, non-dairy sour cream, and guacamole, served on fajita sized whole wheat tortillas."

"Oh," Mick said. "Hold the green shit."

"Right, have a seat and R.R. will bring it right over to you," Mr. Meak said handing the Angel a stick with a pink triangle stuck on the end. "Put this in the vase on your table."

"R.R.?" the Angel asked.

"Our waiter, Rizzo the Rat," Mr. Meak said.

"Oh, right," Mick said and turned away from the counter.

The Angel walked past Grendel and Mōðor, who were having an argument about whether or not the Dragon had cleaned his scales out of the bathtub after his last shower. Then, the Angel took an empty table between two haggard figures slumped over their table, and a table full of members of the L.D.R.B. who were playing Cripple Mr. Worblehat.

As most Immortals and almost no mortals ever knew, L.D.R.B. stands for Library Disaster Rescue

71

Battalion, a voluntary organization of immortals that have pledged a significant portion of their existence to the preservation of knowledge. Interestingly enough, nobody now remembers, or at least won't admit to, knowing who or whom founded their once secret organization. Like many secret organizations, the L.D.R.B. has prided itself on not keeping records of its own doings, lest they be caught and asked extremely embarrassing questions like "Why haven't you been paying your income tax on all these so-called charitable donations you've been forcibly collecting from the non-philanthropically inclined bits of humanity over the last couple of centuries?"

But tax dodging aside, the L.D.R.B. has found it convenient to show up during most library disasters and evacuate the book stacks, leaving behind cheap cardboard copies of the originals simply for the look of the ash. Demons have been particularly fond of this sort of work owing to their natural inclination towards psychological warfare against humanity. There's nothing like a good old contradictory and contentious holy book showing up several centuries after the facts for really mucking-up a religion. "Just look at all the fun that came out of the Dead Sea Scrolls," the Demons say, "and Judas wasn't even in those."

And it came to pass that the efforts of Nebuchadnezzar, Herostratus, Theodosius I, and many others were ultimately frustrated, even if the whole of humanity never knew about it.

Mick looked at the book that Hat had given him. It didn't look very good at all to the Angel, so he dropped it on the table with a resounding thud.

One of the two slumped figures next to Mick stirred at the sound.

The Angel watched as a young woman in tight jeans and a blue, white, and red halter-top t-shirt opened one glaring red eye.

Mick only caught a glimpse of the eye, as, at the same moment, a mass of brown ginger dreadlocks fell over the woman's face.

Mick averted his face in disgust, only to watch a three foot tall rat run up to his table carrying his food.

"Here ya go daddy-o," the rat said putting down a plate of food and a large steaming espresso. The froth genteelly swayed back and forth, covered in cinnamon and brown sugar.

"What the Hell are you?" the Angel asked in a tone that he meant to convey included an implied threat of species extermination. The tone the Angel actually achieved suggested that far from species war, the Angel just liked to whine.

"Folk hero," the rat said.

The Angel looked blank.

"You know, a fictional character that makes an impression on the popular consciousness," the rat said tapping his nametag.

"Oh, right, you're that Ratso Rizzo guy," Mick said. "Folk hero?"

"Ain't it flaming marvelous," the rat said. "Ralph Rizzo, the Rat, actually."

"Sorry pardon," the Angle said without enthusiasm.

"Granted, I'm sure," said Ralph Rizzo. "And yes, a folk hero, like Babe the Blue Ox."

The Angel continued to look blank. He had taken Blankness as a double proficiency at Angel College, and was extremely adapt at it.

"Paul Bunyan?"

"No."

"Black Hawk?"

"The helicopter?"

73

"For the love of the Son," the rat said. "You guys really are that thick aren't you?"

"Didn't you play in those moppet movies?" Mick asked.

"Ah, yeah," the rat said noncommittally. "That's me, a small million year old kid with 17 movies, and seven different television series. I'm bloody famous I am."

"Was," the Angel corrected.

"Once famous, always famous," the rat insisted, "just ask Ringo."

"Who's Anthony Eden?"

"Who?"

"He was famous once," the Angel said.

"Who cares?" The Rizzo asked.

"What's that," Mick said pointing at a semi-spherical lump of chocolate on the plate.

"Dark chocolate truffle with fruit inside," Rizzo said.

"Chocolate is sinful," the Angel said primly.

Rizzo shrugged and popped the chocolate truffle into his mouth. "Your fucking loss mate," the rat said through dark chocolate lips. "Oh and raspberry too."

"I didn't say I didn't want it," the Angel complained.

"You want it back?" Rizzo asked sticking a dark sludgy tongue out at the Angel.

"No, that's alright."

"You complain a lot, you know that?" Rizzo said, "a whole lot. You've the whole fucking universe at your feet and all you do is complain." The rat turned and walked off back to the kitchen.

Mick looked around.

Jim Kerr, Robbie Grey, and Robert Smith refereed HeroScape games. Deep Blue took strategy notes from a game between Viswanathan Anand and Wilhelm Steinitz. Half a dozen goddesses dressed in simple purple muslin gowns with a white sash across their chests sat around a table talking just slightly too loud about their Scions, ex-husbands, and mutual friends. And over in one corner sat Peter Lorre, smoking a cigarette, and rehearsing lines.

"Hey man, you going to eat that man?" asked a low-pitched dull voice coming from the table beside Mick's.

Mick looked over to see a pale unhealthily skinny man in torn jeans and a dirty red New York Jets t-shirt sitting next to the slumped mass of ginger dreadlocks.

"I'm really hungry man and could really use some help man, it'd be like a major karma boost for you too man," the man said.

Mick looked down at his El Cheapo Burrito, sighed, and pushed his lunch away from him towards the stranger.

"All right, total score man," the man said, rising quickly from his chair and moving over to Mick's table. After shoving several bites into his mouth, the man stuck out his hand to the Angel and said, "I'm Saki, who are you?"

The Angel looked politely at the man's hand and then took another sip of his espresso.

Saki shrugged and went back to shovelling his face.

"Save some for me," the mass of ginger dreadlocks said.

"Better hurry-up babe," Saki said.

The mass of ginger dreadlocks extended its scared arms and bruised legs, stood, steadied itself on the table, yawned, and shuffled over to sit down next to Saki.

"This here's Blossom," Saki informed the Angel, pushing a little less than half of the El Cheapo Burrito over to his companion.

Mick smiled and continued sipping his espresso.

"Dude," Saki said. "Do you like talk or what man?"

"I won't bother," Blossom said. "Don't you know an Angel when you're looking at one?"

"Oh," Saki said. "Well, thanks anyway, Miss-tar."

The Angel stoically continued sipping his one obvious vice until it was gone. He then stood, shoved his book under his arm, nodded to the two at his table, and left the Elysion Library Coffee Shoppe.

"What a jerk," Blossom said while scratching at one of the blisters on her left arm.

"Oh, I don't know," Saki said. "He did give us breakfast. Man like that can't be all bad."

Saki looked around the café, stood, and ambled over to another table. "Hey man, can I bum a smoke?"

When Mick stepped out into the bright sunlight from the darkness of the Shoppe, he had only two things on his mind: junkies and a ride to the London Station.

And breakfast, the Angel thought.

"Excuse me," the Angel said to a scrawny pale kid with long dirty blond hair pulled back in underneath a black skullcap, standing next to a stocky man with a beard, shoulder length brown hair, and a backward baseball cap. "Do you know if the Deoradháin Café happens to be around here today?"

"Yeah, I know," the kid said spinning around and knocking the book out of the Angel's hand.

76

The Angel and the stocky man almost collided going down for the book.

The skinny kid pushed the Angel before he got his book, and said; "What's it to ya, ya punk?"

"I would like for you," the Angel said forcing his tone level and calm, "to tell me, where the Deoradháin Café is."

The stocky man handed the book back to the Angel.

"Okay man, like will you hold my duster first?" the pale skinny kid asked, pulling off his duster.

"Ah, sure, why?" asked the Angel as he took the heavy trench coat.

"So it'll turn into Angel Dust," the pale skinny kid said, laughing and punching his friend's shoulder.

The stocky man with a beard smiled and tapped the Angel's shoulder.

"Yes?" ask the Angel turning around.

The stocky man with a beard smiled began to sign a complicated sentence.

"Why does the fish ride a bicycle?" the Angel asked.

The stocky man with a beard nodded.

"No clue," the Angel said.

The stocky man with a beard signed some more.

"Because it opened up the refrigerator and said apple butter?" the Angel interpreted. "I don't get it."

The stocky man with a beard signed, shrugged, and lit a cigarette.

"Oh, never mind," the pale kid said with a frown. "Give me my duster."

The Angel gave the pale kid his duster.

"Look, it's over that way," the pale kid said indicating one smooth stone paths that led away from the Elysion Library Coffee Shoppe back towards the main entrance of the Elysion Library. "Follow the sidewalk until you see the statue of Beverly Cleary and turn right there. Then go up to the statue of Mao Zedong and make a left. A little while after you pass the statue of Jessamyn West, you'll see the Deoradháin Café. At least, that's where I saw it last."

"Mao Zedong," the Angel said, metaphorical ice crystals forming around the words, "As in Chairman Mao Zedong?"

"Yep, that's him," the pale scrawny kid said. "Him and Beverly Cleary and Jessamyn West and all the really important librarians have statues around here. Shit, there's even a statue of Laura Bush somewhere. The Angels keep hiding poor Laura under a bush for some reason though. So yeah, all of 'em except Nancy Pearl. Hat said she wasn't holding with that sort of thing, not now, not ever, she said."

The Angel grunted, turned around, and walked into the thick chest of the Hellspawn Phu.

"The Mistress of the House of Books presents her compliments," Yūko White said stepping around the massive bulk of the Hellspawn. The pink tassels of her white knitted kitten hat bobbed around her smooth slim jaw line.

Mildly stunned, Mick reached out and took the bundle from Yūko White's hands.

"Yeah," growled Phu. "And we came all the way out here to give it to you so shut your fucking mouth and say *Thank-you*."

Mick stared at quivering tentacles. He forced himself to relax, rather than to go for the Holy Swords concealed by his coat.

"I said-" Phu started, but stopped as Yūko White held up the palm of her exquisite little hand.

"How can one, how you said 'shut your fucking mouth,' and say 'thank you' at same time?" Yūko White asked Phu.

The Hellspawn thought for a moment.

"I don't know," he confessed.

"Let us go for a milkshake and consider this," Yūko White said, turned, and walked into the Shoppe.

"Well, all right, *Sir*," Mick said with overt sarcasm.

"That's Ph'thrghn'msru," the Hellspawn lately calling itself Ph'thrghn'msru said.

"Phursragh?" Mick asked.

"Na, Ph'thrghn'msru," the Hellspawn said.

"I can't say that," the Angel said.

"And neither can anybody else," Ph'thrghn'msru said with a grin. "That's pretty much the point."

Ph'thrghn'msru, like many creatures, things, denizens, or whatever, of the Celestial planes believe that to name a thing is to one, get its attention, and two, maybe even control it. This is based on the prudent observation that that is what the Creator does, which is true. However, very few others have the power to get a creation's attention and you can just forget about control it. Still, it gives license to the lowercase-c creators of monsters like Hellspawns to make-up such interesting names as Ph'thrghn'msru. Don't you think monsters should have such interesting names?

"Come on, Ph'thrghn'msru," Yūko White said, pronouncing tones that only the Celestial immortals could hear. "I'm hungry. I'm thinking garden pizza."

"Yeah, what she said," Ph'thrghn'msru said jabbing his finger in the Angel's chest. Phu then turned, folded several tentacles over each other, and left trailing his own personal Mistress of the Universe.

The Angel unwrapped the bundle and stared down at the book for a long time.

It was a very, very, very, long time.

Entire new clichés evolved and crawled into the rubbish bin of linguistical history before the Angel spoke thus:

"And about damn time too," Mick finally muttered. "I thought I was going to have to leave without it. Freaking Scions."

Chapter 3: Deoradháin Café

The Deoradháin Café currently located on the planet Elysion, in the Camulodunum System, for the moment anyway.

For I fear, lest, when I come, I shall not find you such as I would, and that I shall be found unto you such as ye would not: lest there be debates, envyings, wraths, strifes, backbitings, whisperings, swellings, and tumults. --2 Corinthians 12:20, K.J.V.

And it came to pass that the Angel had two books, one that would bring forth peace, love, and eternal tranquillity; and one that would bring forth only darkness, and the Angel hadn't the foggiest clue which one was which, or that there was even a difference between them.

The Angel Mick walked into the Deoradháin Café somewhere in the vicinity of the statue of Jessamyn West and sat down at the first booth.

The interior of the diner was, like many things Faerie, done up in bright colours that would have clashed in most ordinary Human aesthetics. And just to be clear, that's Faerie, which should not be confused with the magic dust and tinkling bells type of Fairy. But Faeries have as much relationship to Fairies as Megalodon shark have to Guppy fish, and the same eating habits too.

The walls and booths were made up in milky white and deep purple. It was the sort of shade of deep purple that made one think of rainy days and broken hearts. And what little else was not the colour of a vanilla milkshake and heartbreak, was the bright metallic shine of highly polished stainless steel- the sort of which one used to get before Bernard London coined the phrase "Planned Obsolescence." A white and black checked floor, scattered with three-foot high chess pieces.

They were the Chess People.

Throughout the centuries that followed the end of humanity's central role in their universe, the Faeries in particular suffered a complete social break down. And while most of the Angels and Demons agreed that it was hard to notice the difference, Faerie society completely ground to a halt for several thousands of years. At any rate, the Faerie love of sport, particularly geo-political blood sport, won out over the collapse in the end. But, lacking a thriving humanity to play games with, the Faeries went in for simply playing games. But only after they had tried everything else.

The previous attempts to liven up the universe after the extinction and Rapture of the Human species included the attempt to reboot the Haplorhini primates and accelerate their evolution past the ability to write fiction. This was not only for the benefit of that the Faeries, but the Immortals, and the Celestial Armies of troopers, spies, and politicos. It didn't work.

Then there was the attempt to replicate Human brain structures and put them into cloned androids, which ended in the Clone Wars, the foundation of Joachism, and all the androids bunking off to the Ceti Alpha system leaving all the washing up unwashed, the ironing un-ironed, and the TV cable unconnected. It didn't work either.

The last straw was the Replicator Wars, which only by going dormant after consuming the physical resources of twenty-seven galaxies and the combined efforts of Stan and the Metatron to encircle the little metal bastards in a sphere of black holes. Needless to write, that attempt at amusement didn't work out either.

The Chess People on the other hand, were simply an attempt to liven up the game of chess by creating a species of living chess pieces and thereby adding an element of urban guerrilla warfare to the game. And so Urban Guerrilla Warfare Chess, or

U.G.W.C., was born. It was highly favoured for about two hundred centuries due to its simple rules, which were as complicated as a subprime Veteran's reverse mortgage buy back scheme. And no, we don't know what that is either.

The rules were thus; all of the rules of chess and all her variations were fair game, including that daft version that was in *Star March*; and no U.G.W.C. game could start with less than five teams in order to ensure alliances, double crosses, and the inevitable conclusion of a three sided cold war and eventual bankruptcy from the bar bills.

The Faerie Miyako Astor, Maître de la Chambre of the Deoradháin Café and Hôtel, was not a big U.G.W.C. fan. But since the Chess People had been about his café for so long and occasionally provided interesting gossip, he let them stay on as a sort of anti-mice party.

Miyako Astor was a slim man-shaped creature, with a slimmer face, and hair that looked like it had sprouted on a rather illtempered ox. He appeared, as Faeries were in the habit of doing, at the end of the Angel Mick's table. The slim Faerie stood in a felt hunter's green frock coat watching the Angel flit from one book to the other as if he was unable to decide unto which volume to commit.

The Faerie stood for a while, examined his perfectly manicured nails, sighed, and sat down. He took the nameplate that read "Miyako Astor, Owner, Cook, Bottle Washer, & Inmate" off and placed it in his pocket.

Miyako Astor then pulled a slender cigarette silver case inlaid with ruby runes from his breast pocket. With meticulously fluid hand gestures, he removed a long slender machine rolled cigarette that made a Capri brand cigarette look like a semi-chewed piece of gum. Last, the Faerie struck a sulphur match on the **FOR YOUR CONVENIENCE, THERE WILL BE NO SMOKING** sign on the table and inhaled deeply.

"You know what I hate about Angels?" Miyako Astor asked, smoking rolling out of his mouth.

"Hmmm?" hmmmed the Angel, who was in any event, not paying the Faerie the slightest bit of forward brain attention.

"It's that way you all have of being so gods damned rude," Miyako Astor said blowing double smoke rings out of his nostrils.

"Yes coffee, please," the Angel agreed.

Miyako Astor waved one lazy hand and coffee appeared beside the Angel's books. The Faerie promptly tapped ash into the Angel's coffee. It sizzled.

"I can't make heads or tails of this," Mick said finally looking up from the books and taking a drink of his coffee. "You need to get better filters mate," he added with a grimace.

The Faerie shrugged as if to say, 'What can one do these days?' and turned the book closest around to him.

"Oh yes, I know this one," Miyako Astor said tapping *How to Putte Questiones to the Dark and Understand its Answeres* with his finger. "Damn daft book really. The other one is a fairy-tale."

"You know it?" the Angel asked.

"The fairy-tale? No."

"I mean the other other one, this one," the Angel said turning *How to Putte Questiones to the Dark and Understand its Answeres* around for the Faerie.

"Yeah," Miyako Astor said with a dismissive gesture. "It's not very good."

"Who wrote it?" the Angel asked.

"The employer of one of my cousins," Miyako Astor said.

It should be noted that this remark was not only un-illuminating, but also a bit rude, as it is well known that every Faerie, either inside or outside of the physical world, refer to all other Fairies as either brother or sister, and to everything else as "cousin." It should also be noted that Faeries, like both Angels and Demons, were created unique and without all the tediousness of conception, birth, puberty, and divorce court. All in all, Miyako Astor might just as well have said, "Oh, I don't know. Somebody, I'm sure."

Miyako Astor pulled a slim, black-bound Piccadilly lined flip-top notebook from the front pocket of his felt hunter green frock coat and began to lazily doodle perfect circles.

The Angel closed both books, finished off his coffee, and looked at the Faerie.

"Can you drop me off at London station?" he asked.

"Sure," the Faerie said with a shrug. "That's why I'm still hanging around here."

The Angel watched the Faerie's hand dash off one perfect circle after another, each one interlaced with the one before it and above it, so that it began to resemble a sheet of chain mail.

"What's buggin' you?" Mick asked.

"You know what I really miss?" Miyako Astor asked the Angel.

The Angel shook his head.

"The cosmetics industry," the Faerie said with a sigh.

"Ah, Pride," the Angel said.

"Don't give me any of that Cardinal Vices crap, Angel," the Faerie said looking up from his doodle. "I really do miss it. All the girls, the pretty faces, the sundresses. All the," and here Miyako Astor paused, and gave a wave intended to include the whole of the universe. "I mean, what is the point of having a hopping diner now? There's no kids, no midnight drunks, no cops even, no nothing. Before I at least had company. Now all that come in here are broken down Demons and second-rate Angels with pretentions about their ability."

According to *Christopedia, The Universal Encyclopaedia of the Things the Son Never Said*; the Seven Deadly Sins, also known as the Capital Vices or Cardinal Sins, is a classification of objectionable vices that have been used since early Christian times to educate and instruct followers concerning fallen humanity's tendency to sin. The currently recognized version of the list is given as Wrath, Greed, Sloth, Pride, Lust, Envy, and Gluttony. Incidentally, each of the Seven Deadly Sins has been hanging around for so long that they have each developed into an Anthropometric Personification, and they were all employed in either the 3-D Simulated Reality Facilities entertainment industry or politics.

"To feed people?" the Angel asked after it became obvious that the Faerie wasn't going to carry on further. "Speaking of which, can I get-"

"What people?" Miyako Astor asked, finally looking up at the Angel with barely concealed hate in his eyes.

"Well, you've got us, don't you?" Mick asked, barely concealing his own scepticism of the observation.

"Neither Faeries, Demons, or Angels need to eat. Scions pretty much keep to themselves, now so even more than before. Avatars are completely self-sufficient, and Hellspawn always run out on their checks," Miyako Astor complained. "And besides that, it's the wonder that I miss. Teenaged women were like little four-year-olds with boobs."

"Ah, Lust," the Angel said the tone of certainty returned to his voice.

"Go stuff yourself," the Faerie said getting up from the table. Realizing that his cigarette had burned down past his fingers, the Faerie dropped it in the Angel's coffee cup.

"Stay a moment?" the Angel asked in a soft, almost sincere tone.

The Faerie cocked his head at Mick for a second, but did not sit again.

"Say, just supposing, you know, as an intellectual experiment," the Angel began.

"Yes?"

"Well, supposing you thought that you could do a thing and-"

"Well, can you or can't you?" the Faerie barked. "I never suppose anything. I know I can do this and cannot do that and I never confuse myself with supposing anything."

"Right," the Angel said and then paused. His hand unconsciously caressed *Continuous Creation,* by Kin Arad. "Say that, you, Miyako Astor, were going to bring humanity back. What would you do with 'em?"

"*King Lear,*" the Faerie snapped.

Mick fancied that his own words could have barely gotten to the Faeries ears before he heard the answer.

"Why *King Lear?*" the Angel asked.

"Well, it's go with that or the *Count of Monte Cristo,* now isn't it?" the Faerie returned in a mildly less peevish tone. "Or maybe, *Robin Hood, Chicks Without Tights.* Yeah, chicks without tights. Nobody has made any good girl on girl flicks since "Joymii-"

"Why Lear or Cristo?" the Angel cut in abruptly, but not before the image of a clutch of fluffy yellow chicks in blue and pink tights settled on his imagination.

"Well, that's easy," the Faerie said. "It's bound to happen anyway; give humanity a couple of years all to themselves and you'll have *King Lear* playing out everywhere you look. One guy's got stuff and three other people want that stuff. Basic narrative causality that is. So you might as well start the schadenfreude right off that bat. Then get a lawn chair, beer, and popcorn, and settle in for a good flick."

The Angel rolled a double natural and stared blankly at the Faerie.

"History always repeats itself," Miyako Astor continued, "or at least, it used to. And Lear and Cristo are two of the best histories in the ever-ever of humanity. Truer than any bit of actual written history. And humanity will do more to fuck itself up in their first year than the likes of you can think up in a million or more. Humanity was the Creator's most fantastic achievement in mutually assured destruction. One human is a genius. Two humans are a marriage. Three humans are a murder scene, and a tent or more of buggers is a war, particularly if the next tent over has wenches with bigger knockers or better beer."

"But *King Lear* needs feudalism or at least, the echoes of feudalism," Mick complained. "We'd be starting fresh; you know Adar and Evelina style of thing."

"So don't make 'em fresh, let them spring forth, fully feudalized, and be done with it. Think of it as a real-life sim, and just choose the Feudalism option in the setup sequence."

"You know, that has some merit," the Angel admitted, and penned a note on the inside cover of *Continuous Creation*, by Kin Arad.

The Faerie watched the Angel in the same stunned sort of way that people watch someone rape a child.

"Thanks, but it's a species advantage," the Miyako Astor said finally.

"How's that?" Mick asked genuinely puzzled. "Angels and Faeries ain't that different, biologically speaking. Morally of course, there's no comparison. Except to pearls and swine maybe."

The Faerie gave Mick such a cool stare that the Angel actually began to fidget.

"Quit," Miyako Astor said. "You know, you really have a way with people," he added pushing his hedgerow hair back behind his ears. "What I meant was that Faeries are inherently lazy, and like most artisimos," Miyako Astor continued thumping *Continuous Creation*, by Kin Arad with his hand, "we work not for fame, nor for money–"

The Angel choked on his own laughter.

"But only for the humble knowledge that at the end of the day, we are *not* in the fucking army." The Faerie lit a second match off the no smoking sign and burnt the end of a fresh cigarette.

"What army?"

"Any of them," Miyako Astor agreed. "Take your pick, Heaven's, Hell's, the Cylons, the Borg, the Americans. It's really all the same when you sign-up and swear to kill people you don't know on the orders of someone that wouldn't lose a wink of sleep if your children starved. But if I had to pick, I'd go with the Cylons."

"Why them? Bunch of tin cans with a really bad front loaded security system," the Angel objected.

"No way mate," Miyako Astor said. "I'd go for one of the slick updated versions like the jazzed-up female Asian model. Can't see the point of being about a feudal society and it being anything other than an Oriental one."

"Would you help then?" Mick asked. "With the reboot project?"

"Oh no," the Faerie said with a sigh, "I shouldn't think so."

"Why not?" the Angel asked.

"Because I don't like you," Miyako Astor said stabbing out his cigarette.

"Oh," Mick said. "I see."

"Besides," said the Faerie, "I'm on café incarceration until the next Age of Creation, or so He said so. So unless you can alter Him, speed up the end of this universe, or teleport me off this linoleum, than I'm to stay right here."

"Well you shouldn't have done what you did," Mick said. "By the way, what was it you did do?"

"I blew-up Chernobyl," the Faerie said with a shrug. "Who knew the Creator was so tetchy about that environmentalism thing. It's not like I flooded the planet."

"Adam was created as a Gardener you know," said Mick. "That was the whole point of creating man in the first place. Garden staff."

"Details, details," the Faerie said with a dismissive wave of the hand.

"Well don't blame me, creation wasn't my idea."

"I like the Vishnu version best."

"Which Vishnu version?" Mick asked giving the Faerie his suspicious eye look, which actually consisted of the Angel cocking his head at a weird Angel and slightly bugging out his eyes.

"The one where Vishnu comes up out of the infinitely dark ocean in the belly of a giant snake and dreams up the whole world," Miyako Astor said. "I always liked the idea of being a non-existent figment of a non-existent imagination. Don't know why."

"That's not how it went," Mick complained, "and I should know. I was there when it happened."

"And what was a good Christian boy like you doing there at the birth of a pagan god?" the Faerie asked with genuine interest.

"Oh, they were all back pagan then," Mick said. "This was way way way back, before Mr. Big went Jewish. And besides, the bloody prophets got it all wrong on that score. "It t'wasn't *Thou shalt not bow down before pagan gods*, it was *Thou shalt not bow down before Human-shaped gods.* You know, like Sešat and that lot."

"Typical," Miyako Astor said. "You do all that work to tell a good story and the bloody publisher screws-up the type set." He bent over and picked up *Continuous Creation*, by Kin Arad.

"It's not as bad as that bit about polygamy," Mick agreed.

Miyako Astor shrugged.

"Look," he said shaking *Continuous Creation*, by Kin Arad at the Angel. "I've been stuck in this dive since the dawn of civilization, right here, stuck in this "café-" and the Angel saw the quotation marks flash around the Faerie's head.

"How?"

"Faerie dust," Miyako Astor said smoothly. "Stuck, right here, in this "café" since the Theodiscusians invented the Gasthaus." He put the book back on that table and began tapping the filter end of another cigarette on it.

The Angel wrinkled his forehead. "But the Chernobyl explosion was in 1986 Anno Domini, not back in prehistory."

"Not that Chernobyl disaster," Miyako Astor said waving his hands about, "the other one, that happened because of Hat's people."

"Oh," Mick said. "Just what are you on about?"

"Never mind that now, I just killed a bunch of over-grown lizards, damn silly things," Miyako Astor said as if he'd simply misplaced a few thousand extinct species in the broom closet. "It was really Keith's fault. But look, my point is this; I've seen this place go from being a Gasthaus, to a tavern, to a hostelry, to a lounge, to a pub, and for an enjoyable while a speakeasy. After that, a drive through- and I mean they drove the cars through the building kind of drive through-burger and beer joint back before anyone cared if drunks killed kids with cars. And then some idiot invented the diner, and I've been stuck with decor since 1952."

"But why call it a café then?" Mick asked.

"Can't be bothered to change the sign, haven't got the time."

The Angel gazed for a moment at the straight face the Faerie was wearing, and then shrugged.

"Go on then."

"Whatever you do with your brave new world order," the Faerie said, "make it original, and make it your own. Do *not* let a bunch of critical pinheaded Professoratorial panty-wastes railroad you into creating anything you don't want, or convince you that you don't have the creativity of Job, which you don't by the way. Just make what you want and be done with it."

And with that, the Faerie got up, leaving both the Angel and *Continuous Creation*, by Kin Arad, and stormed off towards the kitchen.

"I'd like a waffle, a cheese and ham omelette, and crisp bacon, please," the Angel called after the Faerie.

"I'd like a get out of café free card," Miyako Astor yelled back.

The Angel Mick opened the book *Continuous Creation,* by Kin Arad and ran a finger under each word of the pulp fiction table of contents. The brittle pages cracked as his finger glided across under the words:

1. Title Page
2. About the Author
3. Contents
4. How to Make Paper
5. Planetary Geology and Planetary Archaeology

The Angel Mick took out an ink pen and circled the chapter Secondary Creation, then flipped to the chapter, and tried to dog-ear the first page which broke the aged page corner off in his fingers. He then licked the torn paper, and stuck it in length-wise to make a bookmark out of it.

"You know, if Hat caught you doing that," Miyako Astor said placing the Angel's food in front of him. "She'd kick your ass round the Cape Good Hope, and round the Horn, and round the Norway Maelstrom, and round perdition's flames before she gave you up."

"Why?" Mick asked tacking into his breakfast.

"She's got a thing for big white dicks," Miyako Astor said.

"Pardon?"

"Never mind. Look, I've been thinking; on behalf of your future subjects that is, about who'd actually help you."

"I don't need any help," the Angel said through a mouth full of cheesy omelette goodness.

The Faerie took-up an intense concentration on the jukebox across the café in order not to watch the Mick eat. It was bad enough to listen to the Angel without watching him masticate too.

"Yeah know Angel," the Faerie finally said, "when the Son said 'be like these little ones,' I don't think he meant you to have their table manners too."

"What's your thought about the reboot?" the Angel asked.

"Can you create people?" the Faerie asked.

"No," the Angel admitted, pushing his dishes to the side of the table.

"Resurrect them perhaps? How about animate the dead?"

"No and no."

"How are you going to bring anything that isn't still stalking around the universe back into existence in order to start this farce?" the Faerie continued. "You steal the Big C.'s magic wand or something?"

Miyako Astor reached for a cigarette and realized that the Angel had gone very rigid.

"Do not speak of Him like that," the Angel said in a grave tone.

"Or?" the Faerie asked raising one mocking eyebrow.

"Or," said Mick affecting an even graver tone that only really made him sound like a prat, "I shall have to report you for violations of the Heavenly Sedition Act."

"Oh, well, rock on then," the Miyako Astor said lighting his cigarette. "Tell the Committee on Unheavenly Affairs that I said H-E-L-L-O-Hello-Hello," and the Faerie double-clapped his hands.

"And what is your point, Faerie?" Mick asked in a tone so dry that it curled up and died.

"Hmm? Oh, sorry. I always think of this *absolutely* divine Filipino-Korean woman I use to know at school whenever anyone spells out H-e-l-l-o. She was a cheerleader and-"

"Your point, please?"

"She was really cute."

The Angel gave a sigh that sounded like all of the oxygen was been removed at great speed form an elephant's body.

"My point," Miyako Astor said sitting up primly "is that you're not an Aspect, or a Facilitator, or an Elemental, or a Sourcerer, or anything, really, just a bloody dull-ass Angel. So you need help if you're ever going to pull this caper capper off. It's not a matter of it looking like crap. With your power, it'll never get off the ground far enough to even crash. I don't see how you can do it."

"Aspects can't do any of that either," the Angel said peevishly. "And as for Facilitators, their just a bunch of jumped up gardeners."

"Aspects can create people," the Faerie said.

"No they can't."

"Can too."

"Can't."

As you might suspect from the above bit of dialogue, The Creator, maker and ruler of, well,

Everything, has remained stubbornly silent for all of recorded time on just what an Aspect is. But He has been silent about a lot of things. For example, how is it that He came from before He created the universe that He lives in, assuming He does live here, in this universe. The only thing more mystifying than the Creator's silence is the whole of His creation in the first place. Take the diamond planet out in the Cancer constellation as an example, and then see if you can think up anything more mystifying then that.

Okay, poor people voting for the same billionaire crooks that keep them poor is more mystifying, but you know what was meant.

All that read, nobody really knows what an Aspect is, or where they came from, and the Aspects themselves have never been talkative on the point. However, Stan once gave the explanation at a Tea Party rally on the campus of Southern Seminary which went something like this:

"We all know that *God* is a card carrying member of the Grand Old Party in good standing. And like all good old men, *He* has better things to do with *His* time than manage things down here. So *He* gave us the public option in the form of Aspects, whom tend to all the tedious business of making the sunrise, and the oceans tide, and keeping the space between the Terra and Luna wide. Unfortunately, the Son, like all dirty pinheaded pink-o commie liberals bastards, can't stand the idea that you know what to do with your money, and that twerp Kid wants one world government in-which your money will be stolen from you at gunpoint and given to the dirty poor fuckers that sit around all day driving their welfare Cadillacs. I mean seriously, if *God* liked poor people, *He* wouldn't have made 'em poor, now would He? Stands to reason. Keep the faith brothers. What *God* really wants is for all the really good people to share in his boundless universe. Fuck the poor."

To own the truth, the Creator actually hates everyone, millionaires, billionaires, and trillionaires all inclusive. Because at the end of the day, when Forbes publishes its list of *People Who Own Their Own Universe*, there is only one name.

And, the Creator is actually a registered Independent, Whom never votes, on account that He has never seen that it makes any difference. Because while Fatalism doesn't matter to mortals, not knowing the consequences of your own actions, Fatalism does matter to the Creator. It matters to Him, because He does know what those consequences will be. Not that He'll share. But that's another story.

Following on the general out-sourcing theme, Facilitators were created by Aspects who were just too busy lounging around in their gated communities to be bothered by actually doing Heaven's work as ordained by Stan. Facilitators are term-contract Aspects, liable for doing the same things, just for 90% less money. Think of them as Celestial Adjuncts and you will have the right idea; same work, less pay, no benefits, and no office. The savings of course are passed onto the consumer at the point of delivery, whom are generally so happy with their improved services that they spontaneously demanded to pay four or even seven hundred percent more than original cost directly into the pockets of the organization's President.

And last, according to the Swiss physician, botanist, alchemist, astrologer, and occultist Philippus Aureolus Theophrastus Bombastus von Hohenheim, called Paracelsus, there are four types of Elementals. There are the Gnomes, whom are of Terra 土, the Undines or Nymphs whom are of the Water 水, the Sylphs whom are of the Air 气, and the Salamanders whom are of Fire 火.

Paracelsus is correct, in so far as he went, which unfortunately, wasn't far enough by half. Paracelsus either never knew about, or at any rate, never bothered to write down all the other types. The other Greater Ntrollian Elementals are the Thalassinus of the Sea 水, the Caelums of the Sky 天, the Ætherians of the Aether 气, the Picus of the Woods 木,

and the Lammian of the Metal 金. The Lesser
Vacuusian Elementals are the Thalassinus of the Sea,
the Caelums of the Sky, the Vocītāre of the Void, the
Aboriorians of Mercury, the Salsus of the Salt, and the
Daimons of the Sulphur.

There are others too, but really, let's get on with
it.

On the other hand, in the text *The Secret
History of the Elementals*, by Crusty Clone Vapour, in
which the true history of the Elementals is told with
style, it is written: "It has long been told by the uber liar
Stan that the Creator gave unto Stan the whole world
for some factor of 7 worth of years. But this was not the
case. The Creator is a Force of Nature, just like the
rest of us, only bigger, much, much bigger. The Force
is our ally; the Force created us, makes us grow,
surrounds us, binds us, and totally lit up our universe,
like seriously, the Force made everything matter! Even
Stan is bound by the Force, for all that he tries to break
free of it. We feel the Force, like a tidal wave, around
us everywhere- the trees, the rocks, the land, the
rowboat. And after a while, the Force brought us new
places, new faces, the future, the past, and seriously
depressing New Year's songs that only sound good
through a beer haze. And thus the famous saying, "I
was framed! I wasn't even there! He forced me to do it-
I never wanted this. Fuck, anyone remember where we
parked? I really need to pee!"

The Angel pushed his untouched waffle around
on the plate with his fork.

"Look," said Miyako Astor. "Trust me on this. My
folk were helping humanity pull off works of minor-
godhood for millions and millions and millions of years
before you Angels came on the scene."

"And unspeakable evil," Mick said locking gaze
with the Faerie. "And we were here first, created right
after the Light."

"I saw also that there was an ocean of darkness
and death," said the Faerie dreamily, "but also an

98

infinite ocean of light and love, which flowed over the ocean of darkness, and squashed it."

"You okay there Astor old mate?"

Miyako Astor shook himself before replying, "Yep. Just had a Puritanical moment. What was I saying?"

"Unspeakable evil," Mick said.

"Yeah, right," Miyako Astor said.

The Angel started to speak, but Miyako Astor carried on regardless.

"We never gave mankind anything but what they asked for," the Faerie said adding a conciliatory shrug.

"Even if they asked for power to rule the world?"

The Faerie shrugged both shoulders again, and made a sort of hurmph sound.

"Very few ever did, and that's to the credit of humanity's common sense," Miyako Astor agreed. "Only an absolute idiot would want to rule over the entire world. What a fucking bother that would be. Take for example Satan, the Accuser, the Divine, the First Fallen Angel, called Shaitan, and Shayṭan, and Ha-Satan-"

"Oh shut-up," the Angel said.

"Right, Stan, was given power to rule over the entire world at the end and look what that got him," Miyako Astor said. "A load of people coming round all the time to complain about the plumbing and the rubbish pick-up, and mind you, they could have fixed everything thrice over in the time it took them to stand in the queue to get an appointment to stand in the audience acquisition line which would then book them a time to stand in the audience line."

"Well, I don't know," Mick said. "I sort of want to keep this on the low-down. You know, not to alert the authorities."

"Angel," said Miyako Astor leaning across the table.

The Angel leaned forward too.

"Confidentially, that's the dumbest fuck thing I've heard since the Metatron announced Amnesty."

Miyako Astor leaned back, and continued; "Like really. Obviously, the Big C. isn't interested in your plans. Because A., He'd have done it by now if He was interested, and B., if He was offended, He'd have given you one of those righteous Sodom and Gomorrah smack-downs already. And, we're here."

"Yes, I know that, it says Deoradháin Café right outside the front door."

The Faerie slapped his own forehead.

"London Station, you dope," Miyako Astor said. "Where you asked to go."

"The London Station, on Zeta Orionis, in the Orion System" the Angel asked. "I thought it would've taken longer."

"If there's another London Station, than I don't know about it," the Faerie said. "There certainly isn't one in what's left of London."

"No, no," Mick agreed, "there's not another one. By the way, how do you do it?"

"Do what?"

"Move the café?" the Angel asked.

"The café is a traveling node, so it moves itself," the Faerie said. "All I do is tell it where to go, and it simply goes there. I have to watch it though, sometimes it wanders off by itself. I think it gets bored if it sits to long in the same place."

"Bored?" the Angel asked. "How does an inanimate object get bored?"

"I think it's the Big Guy's idea of a joke," the Faerie said. "I get to travel all over the universe in the café, but never can get out of here. I can't even see out the windows like everyone else."

The Angel looked out the windows at the starlight shimmering off the mountains surrounding the London Station.

"All I see is darkness and the storms of dead emotion," the Faerie continued. "And the bathrooms are connected to the Node Pathways. Back in the day, I use to get people walking out of the loo that never went in there. Sometimes with pot in hand and hollowerin' gardez l'eau, gardez l'eau, gardez l'eau. They made such a mess. Civilization equals plumbing if you ask me."

The Angel looked over his shoulder.

"Relax mate," the Faerie said. "Not much been happening there since the Final Match."

"Oh, glad to know it's safe," Mick said.

"Oh, I didn't say that," Miyako Astor said. "Basil Berry's been in there since just before you arrived."

Chapter 4: Node Pathways

Somewhere near the bottom of the Indian Ocean, Terra, in the Sol Solar System.

Behold, I go forward, but he is not there; and backward, but I cannot perceive him: On the left hand, where he doth work, but I cannot behold him: he hideth himself on the right hand, that I cannot see him. --Job 23:8-10, K.J.V.

And it came to pass that the son of a Norsemen took a wrong turn at Albuquerque and found an ally.

If there was one thing that neither Basil Berry nor anyone else had ever understood about the two Terra's Node Pathways entrances, it was why the two central stations were in a basement tavern in Chicago and the Tube Station in the Southern Indian Ocean off the West Coast of Australia. The basement tavern in Chicago made some sense. Human practitioners of the arts frequented it for centuries and it's a well-known fact that too high a concentration of Drama majors will begin to distort time and space in very unpredictable ways.

The Tube Station in the Indian Ocean on the other hand, made no sense at all.

Contrary to popular mythic conceptions, the Challenger Deep in the Mariana Trench is not the deepest part of the oceans of Terra. The deepest part of the Oceans of Terra bears the ingenious name of the Subunda Vultus, which in the vulgar tongue is the Under Water Lookout. Just what anyone could be on the lookout for at a depth of 12,887 meters below the surface of the ocean is anyone's guess.

Basil Berry, like most, preferred not to think about it. He never liked the ideas his imagination came up with, and he actively avoided the place. But today, like most of the times Basil Berry travelled through

Terra's Node Pathways, he took the wrong turn in New Mexico and ended up in the Tube Station at the bottom of Subunda Vultus, instead of in Chicago where he wanted to be.

Another mystery that Basil Berry had never figured out, aside from why Node Pathways that went directly through Node-space always began and ended in bathrooms and gender-segregated the travellers upon both entry and exit, was the fact that no matter when one arrived at the Tube Station at the bottom of Subunda Vultus, there was always someone already there. And it was usually only one body.

The Great Marquis Shax, called Chax, Scox, Shan, Shass, and Shaz, Duke of Hell, and Peer of the Throne of Hell, Commander of 30 Legions of Hellions, sat at a table in the Tube Station Café working a crossword puzzle. A small mountain of paperback dictionaries of various languages were scattered over several tables, the floor, and a tattered book propped up a leg of the table.

Basil Berry was relieved to see that Shax was not in his stork form, or his natural Demon form, but rather concealed himself in his Human insurance salesmen form. The Peer of the Throne of Hell, second in command of the Legions of Rebellion currently, appeared as an overweight, balding man of no particular quality, or endearment, inhabiting a grey suit, sweat-stained white shirt, and loosened thin black tie. He looked like so many other humans that one saw, or rather, had seen, in every major developed city on Terra, and whom one just as easily forgot as a summer breeze. It made it a lot easier to talk to him.

"My dear Lord Shax," Basil Berry said in a jovial tone. "How the Hell are you?"

"Just as tired of that one as any Demon," Shax said without looking up from his crossword puzzle.

Basil Berry sat down across from the Demon insurance salesman, after carefully moving a small mountain of worked out crossword puzzles off the chair.

"I never would have figured you for a crossword puzzle fiend," Basil Berry said shaking his head in wonder.

"I've a bet with Kratos that I can make him one that he won't ever figure," Shax said.

"Terms?"

Shax shrugged.

"I think he gets to bash my head in with a sledgehammer or something. But I get Nike for a fortnight if I win. I'm gonna plough that little hussy so-"

"What's your plan to win?" Basil Berry cut in while attempting to mentally rinse the inside of his eyeballs that had just seen a vision of one of the loveliest female creatures in the universe submitting to Shax's most uninspiring mortal manifestation.

"I'm thinking of using all the ancient languages."

Basil Berry watched the beady little eyes of a balding insurance salesmen look up from the papers. All of the Cardinal Sins danced in his gaze. They were doing a Conga.

"Can you use coding schemes?"

Shax shrugged again.

"I don't see why not," he said. "No one ever said I couldn't. What do you have in mind?"

"Okay," Basil Berry said first slapping his hands together and then rubbing them briskly together like a master Khufu teacher who is about to give a restorative backrub to a barely legal student. "Binary is standard, but so much so that anyone will think to use it. Hex now, that's beautiful, a base 16, or hex positional numeral system."

"What is?" Shax began.

"Not important now," Basil Berry said. "Track me."

"Lead on kiddo," Shax agreed with a regal wave.

"But, for my money, Base64 is the way to go. That's a binary data set in an ASCII string."

"Still waiting to be led," Shax said.

"Just a minute-"

"I really miss old Clement Freud," Shax said. "We made-up laws and hung people. What an eyes wide open prospective on revenge that is. Rather reminds me of how the Big Guy ain't."

"Sigmund?"

"Right family, wrong kid," Shax said. "Do carry on."

"Riiight," Basil Berry said and carried on. "The mac-daddy coding scheme is ASCII itself. That's American Standard Code for Information Interchange by the way."

"Right, standard coding, that word standard being a problem?" Shax said with a dismissive wave of his hand."

"Na, na, na."

"Sha Na Na?"

"If you like, The Silhouettes for me, thanks," Basil Berry said.

Shax snorted.

"Phunny."

Basil Berry grinned and resumed up his coded monologue.

"So you start with something insanely complicated, like Archaic Chinese transliterated into Choctaw, and then take that text and convert it to Binary, Hex it, and then convert it to Base64, and then convert that to ASCII. After that, put a random twist on it, and you are all set. Mind you, make it something really fucking random."

Shax looked impressed, an expression not conducive to his current features.

"And what brings you here, child of Trickster Jötunn?" the old Watcher asked.

"Oh, nothing really," Basil Berry said. "I was taking a leak in the Deoradháin Café and wasn't paying attention to which door I walked out."

"I hate it when that happens," Shax sympathised. "How is old Astor?"

"Good, good, he's good," Basil Berry said. "Still bitching about how long eternity is taking and pissing about the next Age of Creation not happening, all the usual complaints. I mean it's not like he got a billion or so people killed."

"Faeries never have taken rejection well."

"Yeah, but he did go a bit overboard with the sacrificial bloodletting."

"Love is a bitch," Shax said. "That's why I stick to lust. Safer for everybody."

"Still makes a killer corned beef sandwich," the Scion said.

"He still slices the onions with a razor blade?" the Watcher asked.

"I think so," Basil Berry said. "I know he uses one on the garlic, so he can melt it into a buttered liquid with herbs and then mixes that into his bread."

"He still using that clay oven?"

Basil Berry nodded, and added, "The very one that he's had for the last million years."

"I really should go see him," Shax said patting his ample belly. "I ran out of peanuts and diet pop about a century ago."

"Hey, is that basement tavern still open on the other side of the planet?" Basil Berry asked. "They do good mead and roast beef sandwiches too."

"Na, and it was ale anyway," Shax said. "The old Dragon closed up a while back. Went back to Honnah Lee. The Immortality Virus following so close on the heels of the Dragon Wars and the Final Match exclamation mark all really took it out of him. And Chicago getting nuked by the Left Behinds didn't help either. I think he's got a place somewhere in the vac-"

"How about Casa Botín?" Basil Berry asked. "I haven't been there in ages."

"Yeah, I think they're still in business," Shax said with a sigh and put down his pen. "Service has fallen off though since all the monkey cooks ascended. Demons just can't cook worth a damn."

"Let's go, I'm starved," Basil Berry said.

Shax bustled around for a few minutes placing the dictionaries and sheets of papers into public lockers located near the café. Basil Berry noticed that the old Watcher didn't bother to lock them up.

The Scion and the Watcher turned Demon got up and headed for the end of the Tube Station to catch a ride topside.

"I never understood the point of putting in the windows down here," Basil Berry said. "There's not a blessed thing to see. Just darkness and darkness and more darkness. Creepiest place on the bloody planet if you ask me."

"I agree," Shax said. "I guess they were put in because they could be put in. There's a lot of that sort of thing in this universe."

"Still, there's no place like home" Basil Berry said, "'tis the only one we got."

"No it's not," Shax said.

Basil Berry cocked his head and started to speak when Shax abruptly cut him off, but not before Basil Berry noticed that Shax was clearly not looking either at, or through, the windows.

"So, what are you really up too?" Shax asked.

Basil Berry was silent for a moment, walking beside the Honorary Demon. Large windows gilded in white gold with jade green mosaic designs came into view as they descended the steps from the mezzanine down to the railway platform.

Basil Berry remembered touching the windows once, when he was a child, and for perhaps the only time in his life had been happy that his god sire was with him. The cold had struck directly to Basil Berry's heart. It had only been the innate abilities of his father's power that had stopped the sheer cold of the imprisoned Dragon's mind from stopping the Scion's heart.

Even so, Basil Berry had woke several years later to find himself under the care of the goddess Nintinugga in the city of Al Hillah, in the Babil Province of Iraq. His father of course was nowhere about, and it would be years before the half-god-child would see him again. Not that that bothered the boy. But Basil Berry had been upset to find out that he had missed the year in which Palestine had played against Lebanon in the final match of the World Cup Football tournament.

Palestine had won, 1-Nill in overtime.

Basil Berry took a deep breath and began to tell Shax about the project he was working on as they got into the auto tramcar.

Shax nodded in enthusiastic agreement and burst into hideous laughter every time the Angel Mick was mentioned.

Neither man noticed as the automated tram pulled away from the station platform, the small black bird feather waffling on the air current, down to the floor.

From high up in the open-air rafters, the beady-bird-eyes of a large black Raven watched as Basil Berry and Shax got into the train. As the train pulled away, the Raven turned its attention back to the large dark windows.

By the time the train car arrived at the Parque de Santa Maria station of the Brown Line Four in Madrid, Spain, Shax was actively advising Basil Berry on their future plans to muck-up the Angel's life.

"By the way," Basil Berry said interrupting the flow of Shax's commentary. "How's the weather topside?"

"Horrible," Shax said with disgust. "The length of time it would take for nuclear winter to lift was about the only thing the eco-fascist monkeys got right. It was only seventeen or twenty-eight nukes that went off, but the debris clouds covered the atmosphere for several months, which was long enough for almost all the bacteria, algae, and plant stuffs in the oceans to die, never mind triggering a new ice age. Some, not much, of the surface foliage lived longer. But once all the fish and other life in the oceans died, because the photosynthesis dependent planet base of their food chain died, it was pretty much all over. Then the amount of flesh rotting in the ocean poisoned everything else. I remember standing off the coast of Florida, southwest side of Key West, and seeing so much dead life rotting in the sea that I thought I could just walk to Havana. The sickness and disease that mutated out of that muck went airborne. The few monkey pigs that hadn't transcended already or bought it in the nuclear war or succumbed to disease got themselves killed in the prolonged global winter that was triggered by the amount of rotting fish flesh that went up into the atmosphere. That in turn killed off the rest of the surface foliage, which took all the mammals with them. By about a year after the nukes went off, everything, even the few holdouts in Cheyenne Mountains and similar places were dead. I mean, can you imagine the amount of methane that was released by all the trees dying? The ammonia from all the dying fish? The place was right fucked."

The Scion nodded in agreement.

"I remember and it's a horrible memory," Shax continued after a slight pause. "A much worse memory than anything even the most demented Demon ever thought up. Between radical temperature changes and basically the entire atmosphere becoming toxic from all the methane released by the mass extinction of everything green and everything that feeds on everything green. I mean, everything mortal was dead, even the monkeys held up in the fortresses were dead. Stan got his Seven Hundred and Seventy-Seven years rule on Terra, but after Year One, there wasn't jack-shit left to rule except the same old dumbass Legionaries he's always had, and a planetary sized pile of corpses and the largest organic compost heap in the history of the ever-ever."

"I remember reading this book, back in the day," Basil Berry said as they came up into the gloomy streets of Madrid. "It was about this kid and his dad and a bass-cart or something. Walking, walking, walking, fight, run, walking, walking, walking, cowardice, walking, cowardice, walking, cowardice, walking, walking, walking, dead. It was all supposed to be this meaning of life after an extinction event sort of story or something."

"Sounds like my last marriage," Shax said.

Basil Berry smiled. He never had figured out how the old Watcher had gotten into the arms of the Canadian angel.

"It was some sort of neo-nihilism rap about surviving a meteor strike or some kind of extinction event," Basil Berry said. "It was an Oprah Book Club pick."

"Not a fucking chance," Shax said. "Everything was dead within the year after the Israelis nuked Armagedōn. Pohl's "Fermi and Frost" was the only one that got it even sort of right, and even he was too generous with the post-nuclear war life spans."

"Oh," Basil Berry said.

"Where the Hell were you when all this happened?" Shax asked. "It's ancient history now. You should know all this."

"My godsister actually got a phone call from her mom, told her to bug out just before the Final Match went live," Basil Berry said eyeing the way the trees had grown up in Madrid with houses attached to them like little square aprons. "She wouldn't tell why. But the call went out to all the Scion Tycoons and then the rest of the Scions to bug out - and we bugged way way out. I spent an ice age hanging out with my godfather and Raven and Xavier Xerses Smith, on the planet Tau Boötis Ab, in the Tau Boötis system. Finally, word came about what happened, and there never seemed to be any point to coming back to Terra till now. Been slumming around the Elysion Library ever since."

"I got a call from Sešat once," Shax said. "Worse thing that ever happened to me."

"Worse than being cast out of cosmic soul repository?"

"Yeah, 'cause I left Heaven on my own, and there wasn't really any rancour in the beginning," Shax agreed. "Everyone thought it was just a grumble, you know, a family tiff. Hard to spend millions of years around the same folks without having a punch-up every now and then. Stan was all prissy like an eldest child that the Creator was taking such an interest in humanity, which even in the end couldn't manage to wipe its collective butts. And I've always been able to walk back in whenever I wanted anyway."

Basil Berry looked at Shax longwise.

"It's that not being an actual Angel thing," Shax said. "You ever finish that undergrad degree?"

"Na," Basil Berry said. "Can't be bothered. Too much reading."

"You work in the largest library in the whole of creation and you don't like reading?"

"Oh I like reading primary sources just fine. But fuck me with a pogo stick if I care what anybody else thinks about them. The only thing funnier than a

Literature teacher is a Political "science" teacher that thinks they actually do anything scientific."

"Fair enough."

The two walked along for a time, lost in their own thoughts. Shax was thinking about how much he missed the monkeys and Basil Berry was thinking about how glad he was he hadn't been around for either the beginning or the end of the world.

"Why did you stay?" Basil Berry asked. "For the end, I mean?"

"'Cause it was my job," Shax said. "I had to watch, 'tis in my contract."

"Oh?" Basil Berry said.

"You know," Shax said opening the door to Casa Botín, "your godfather would be a good one to bring in on this."

"Oh, he already is," Basil Berry sidestepping inside the restaurant. "He's the one that-"

Both the Scion and the I'm-not-a-Demon Watcher stopped abruptly as they bumped into the figure of an elderly black man standing, his head shrouded in a dark black cloak, just inside the door. The bulk of a dog with three heads, encircled by snakes stood just beside the old man.

All three of the heads growled at Shax.

The Demon Watcher Shax frowned.

The Scion felt the same feeling he had the last time he bumped into Fate. It was the anticipation of helplessness. At least, Basil Berry thought, Fate was, like her triplet sisters, a personification of a cultural phenomenon. Like her more famous sister that took on the Goth aspect, Fate went around in the costume of a Geek Girl by day and a Raver Chick by night. The third sister never got up before sunset and was always well inside before dawn.

The most popular anthropomorphic personification is of course, Death, followed closely by Dream, and Dit. Setting aside the fact that Death showed-up in person for the overwhelming majority of humanity, his popularity grew considerably with the positive public relations campaign that Death embarked on in 1983 in collaboration with an English Knight of the Realm who also worked as a historian and who chronicled over 40 celebrated campaigns in which Death played a dynamic and essential role. However, many other Anthropomorphic Personifications do exist. Famine, Pestilence, and War immediately come to mind, all being lesser aspects of Death, or at least, blood relations, on Death's mother's side. However, we should remember other Anthropomorphic Personifications such as Chaos, Chastity, Cupid, Destiny, Father Time, Fate, Fortuna, the Four Sisters; Autumn, Flora, Summer, and Janice Frost, as well as Hate, Lady Liberty, the Tooth Faerie, Temperance, and Victory.

The old black man smiled, thumped the middle head of the great dog on the head to silence him, and ushered Shax and Basil Berry into the entirely all too empty restaurant.

Shax stepped into the ancient restaurant boldly, and said, "Hello Gatekeeper, where you been keeping yourself?"

The Gatekeeper answered in a language the Scion didn't understand.

After a few minutes, Shax returned and grabbed Basil Berry just as the Scion was turning to run, and then pulled the Scion kicking and screaming into the restaurant.

At about the same time, back in the open-air-rafters of the Tube Station at the bottom of Subunda Vultus, a dark black Raven flew down to the large back windows.

The Raven firmly attached a unique silver-black helmet on top of its head.

The unique aspects of the helmet made of a Tungsten alloy composition were these; first, feathered wings could easily handle it, and secondly that the helmet permitted no light to pass through to the mouth, nose, ears, eyes, and especially the brain.

Raven then cleared his throat and pecked at the glass window with his beak, upon which he had already placed a silver beak guard.

I must look a right ninny, the bird thought. He cleared his throat.

"Here, lizard- lizard- lizard!" Raven crowed.

Slowly, a golden light began to fill the Tube Station at the bottom of Subunda Vultus, which transformed itself into a pure burning white light.

Raven began to feel uncomfortable.

"It was foretold to you," Raven managed, his voice trembling, "that you would be awoken come the end of time. Well- wake-up- damn it! Time, she's almost spent, looking really run down, like a tuppence bangtail."

𝔚𝔄𝔈𝔏𝔠𝔭𝔯𝔊𝔈!

The main quality of the Dragon Glaurung's voice, Raven reflected while lying against the cold floor, was that one never actually heard it. One felt it and how one felt it. It was just like being hit in the face with 15 tons of extremely cold iron. And no immortal likes iron. But this iron was the pure sort, and above all cold. It was the sort of cold that could pierce even an Angel's heart.

"Right," the Raven said, getting up on unsteady feet. "Do you think, I mean, may I suggest, that you think a bit more softly? You know, in smaller font or something?"

The Raven felt the sensation of light flooding through his eyes, even though the helmet.

114

It would be impossible for light to pass this helmet, Völundr had said.

But just then, with white hot light lancing his inner eye, Raven didn't believe it.

Raven hoped that he could trust in Völundr of Germanic of Norse mythology, who now went by the nom de plume Wayland Smith, and was, or rather still is, the legendary god of blacksmithing. According to the histories lain out in *Völundarkviða* and *Þiðrekssaga*, Völundr was a great maker of magic rings, swords, coffee mugs that never let the brew go cold, and various other things that people, ravens, and immortals were willing to pay for.

Why me? thought the raven.

Sorry. Will this do? I have not had visitors for such a very long time. Except the Watcher of course.

"Yes, yes, that'll do, thank you," Raven hastily agreed.

You are not Wælcyrge. You are the one called Yehl. Similar, but not the same.

"Ah, yeah, you got me there," Raven admitted. "I am not a Valhalla Girl. But I'm what you might call a Messenger, *the Messenger* actually, in this here particular case. Basically the same thing as a Valkyrie, and the thing is, the thing really is-"

It must be Wælcyrge. You cannot go around changing prophecy just because you find it inconvenient. That sort of thing will not do. Send the Wælcyrge.

"Well, you see, the thing is-"

NO.

Raven felt his legs wobble.

This will never do. Go away.

"Well, you see, the actual thing is, that *The Valkyrie* sent me to get you and-"

IT DOES NOT MATTER. WHAT YOU WANT DOES NOT MATTER. WHAT THEY WANT DOES NOT MATTER.

After a while, and Raven was not sure if he blacked out or not, Raven felt he could speak again. He also felt just fine speaking from the floor.

"Tell ya what big guy, I'll get Kára for ya, and she can sort this out-"

IT MUST BE ALL THE WÆLCYRGE THAT COME HERE. ALL THIRTY-SEVEN WÆLCYRGE. NOW GO AWAY BEFORE I BECOME ANGRY.

Before? Raven wondered as various parts of his brain shut down.

"Um, I thought there were only a half-dozen of them?" the Raven finally asked.

GO AWAY!

After a while, when Raven had realized that even his heart beat had slowed to a normal beating rhythm. He then got up, dusted himself off, and made his way towards the men's room. He didn't even consider taking the helmet off until after he was onto the Node Pathways heading towards Gylfagin.

All the *Wælcyrge*? Raven thought as he circled above the corner of Knot and Mass looking for a lift.

Just how the Hell am I going to budge those old girls? Raven wondered. I mean really, it's not like I've even got thumbs or anything.

Raven landed and perched upon the stump of an old worn oak tree, and removed his helmet. He was dismayed to find that all of his feathers below the bottom rim of the helmet had turned white. Being an Immortal bird, and having once been turned into a pink pocket dotted finch by a particularly ill-tempered witch, his semi-albino condition neither scared nor surprised Raven. But it did annoy, Creator knew it *annoyed*.

The Demon Keith, Raven thought. I'll go see Keith before going to Gylfagin. Keith'll know where the

Valkyrie are. Besides, he wants to see me anyway, Völundr said so.

And with that comforting thought of a decided course, Raven waited for his ride. It was a very long time before he saw two people coming down the path in his direction. One man, one woman, with enough hair between them for a half dozen normal people.

Perfect, just perfect, Raven thought when he saw who they were.

Chapter 5: London Station

London Station, Zeta Orionis, in the Orion System.

So Ahab said to Elijah, "Have you found me, O my enemy?" And he answered, "I have found you, because you have sold yourself to do evil: 'Behold, I will bring calamity on you. I will take away your posterity. --1 Kings 21:20-21, K.J.V.

And it came to pass that the Angel was foretold his fate.

Mick stepped out into the busy London Station.

At least, it was busy by today's Post-Armagedōn standards. Fifty or sixty sentient beings were engaged in all the things that one might expect of a transportation station. Here was a Demon hawking real-deal G666 hPhones, and there was a group of seven Angels and a Hellspawn playing TripleA scenarios on SuperJax Mark VII laptops.

TripleA, very popular with the immortals, is a turn-based strategy war game that originally ran on the Java platform, which was later surpassed by the Coffee platform, which was later surpassed by the $C_8H_{10}N_4O_2$ platform. The major features of the game's popularity were simplicity, customizability, and complete wireless network capability. Originally designed to run a streamlined digital version of a famous tabletop World War II game, TripleA survived and went on to become the universe's most popular game ever. The TripleA user community incorporated several millions of game scenarios, which eventually grew to cover every known war, civil war, rebellion, and almost all of the civil riots of any historical importance. The Angel Mick had once lead, in-game, a successful Baptist War slaver rebellion of 1831 through to a successful invasion of the United States in 2112, but suffered eventual defeat at the hands of the King Rven's Third British Empire, which was all too happy to gobble up its former colonial possessions in North America.

TripleA grew in popularity in the immortal world to such an extent that both the Metatron and Stan had to impose a complete ban on starting real-world mortal wars simply for the sake of creating new TripleA scenario material. The ban of course only served to make every immortal aware of both the game and the ban, which of course led to the creation of the Holy Unholy Alliance vs. Us TripleA game scenario, in which the Us team always won.

The SuperJax Mark VII laptop computer, on the other hand, was an engineering triumph of the Israeli-Lebanese micro-engineering firm Jax. Originally designed for Java API for XML Processing called JAXP, Java API for XML Messaging called JAXM, Java API for XML Web Services called JAX-WS, and many other irrelevant things like that that have JAX in their name. The SuperJax laptop series was mainly developed for high-end game performance. The last model, the SuperJax Zed-Queue XMLTQVC II had a Jaxware TTE3eCBSMyA Intel Core Processor, TTE3eCA Jaxware's first 7D Capable gaming laptop, TTE3e graphics and the 1, 342, 177, 28 Hz 7D-panel option for in your whole body, mind, and soul 7D Graphics card, with Self-in action option with high-definition VR Virtual Reality 1080P world, and the Jaxware TTE3e with ATI graphics, TTE3e Core 2.5 Zettabyte Hz 3.6 Zettabyte Hz with Turbo Boost, 8 Exabyte Cache. Operating System options Linux Mint, Ubuntu, Fedora, Miraculix, or Genuine Windows® That Actually Works Ultimate, 3.94e+145 bit.

Unfortunately, the current Max OS Foo Foo is not available because they are still refusing to play nice with others, and share their completely hacked source codes.

But still, by any objective Terran standard, it was a super slick machine.

But really, who cares about that stuff? Like everything else, the SuperJax technology was out of date by the time it hit the shelves. The only thing that kept it going now was that immortals were all completely pants at coding. Well, almost all of them anyway.

What Mick wanted now was a newsstand, an honest to Creator, cigarettes, bubble-gum, and newspapers newspaper-stand kiosk sort of thing.

Newsstands had almost died out after the Internet proved to be more than a passing fad technology. Interestingly enough, when humanity finally worked out modulating starlight and used it to harness the largest known communications system in all of creation, newsstands made a slight comeback. That is, a slight comeback, just in time to get nuked. However, it did seem that after mankind had hit what it considered the ultimate speed limit of communications with modulated light waves, people once again became content to sit back and enjoy the slow sub-lightspeed life.

While it was true that in former days, a transportation hub such as London Station, located near the star Zeta Orionis, would have hosted some million travellers per day, since the end of humanity, such traffic volumes never occurred anymore. There were only some 7 million Angels, about half as many Demons, and 13 million Hellspawn; Nightmares, and various *Things* that went bumpily-bumpily-la-la-la in the night.

The difference between a Hellspawn and a Nightmare is slight, but nonetheless, significant. A Hellspawn is a refined Nightmare created by the extreme terror of a mortal. The Vampire species for example are Hellspawn, whereas Ikkuod was the Nightmare that ate newborn bébé girls, and was dreamed by a new Nubian mother from the city of Kerma in 4,435 B.C. on the Gregorian calendar. Hellspawn, like children, can grow-up to become Nightmares, if they work hard at their studies and don't achieve a Darwin Award. But not the other way around. Each Nightmare is unique, and based upon a single incidence of mortal psychological terror that is so great that it permanently manifests itself in the being of a semi-immortal creature.

The Scions only numbered in the couple of thousands and such beings as Avatars, Gifs, Anthropomorphic Personifications, and Physical Manifestations numbered less than a thousand all combined. There had once been more of them all, but more than half of each species had taken the amnesty and gone into Heaven, leaving the ranks of the free and the stubborn, greatly reduced.

Today, the universe, which had contained some 777-sextillion stars, was now inhabited by about 24 million sentient beings. This rendered a star to creature ratio of approximately 3.2375×10^{16}, or 32,375,000,000,000,000, or 32,375 trillion stars per sentient. By any standard, the place was empty.

Makes you wonder, with all that empty real estate going spare, just what the Creator's game is?

The Metatron thinks he knows, but he's not telling.

Stan does know, but he's not telling.

The Gatekeeper? He gave up wondering eons ago, and has settled for finding a non-fattening bread that still tastes good. So far, he has not found what he is looking for.

Not that all that open space ever stopped humanity from polluting several tens of thousands of planets to the point making them uninhabitable. In fact, all the extra space rather encouraged humanity's reign of population.

Take the Free Texan Separatist Congregationalists for example. They left three whole solar systems in waste before conceding that perhaps water purity regulatory standards might, just possibly, be a good thing. Not that they ever actually enacted any regulatory standards, but instead went on to poison another four systems before picking a fight with the highly organized Intergalactic Green's Collectivists, which they lost.

The Angel Mick passed the statue of London Station's founder, the Demon Ba'al, and wondered why no one had torn it down. Then he considered where Ba'al might have gotten off to this time.

The only thing Mick was certain of was that the old wan'na-be-goddess wasn't actually dead. Like Vampires and Roaches, Ba'al never seemed to actually die, not in any sort of permanent way. Stamp her head in with a 1,000 jackboots and she'd just popup somewhere else, in another time, wearing another face, preaching the same rhetoric of hate and murder. Mortals never learned.

Mick had thought the false Demon god dead once in 3000 BC when the people had first invaded and then occupied all of the Middle East. Mick had again thought Ba'al was dead in 1575 BC when the Hebrews arrived in Canaan and proceeded to kill everyone that was not Hebrew. Well, okay, any male that was not Hebrew.

Then for the third time, Mick had thought that Ba'al had died on the gallows that were erected in the ashes of the Third Reich during that the late 1940s Anno Domini. Mick had lost track of her for several centuries after humanity took to space flight, but he heard news of extra-Terran galactic wars and recognized her handiwork for what it was. Same old *one tin soldier* song and death again.

However, on each occasion and a half dozen times since, Ba'al always popped back up, and was always ready for a fight. Mick remembered that Ba'al had built this London Station, and for just as flighty a set of reasons as she did anything else.

The Demon Baʿal, godmother to the book publisher Alistair Deacon, was so taken with the complaint of Judith Hanson that there was no such place as "London Station," that she, Baʿal, vowed to it build the mortal a London Station of her very own.

Alas, like her godson, the Demon Baʿal was quite given over to flights of fancy. Instead of building a simple tube station somewhere in the middle of the Canterbury County, the cracked old goddess went back into Middle Eastern politics, intending to build a London Station in the middle of the ruins of Babylon.

Instead, Baʿal met a certain dictator and feel in love. Over the course of a couple of years, she convinced that same dictator that yes, indeed, the Americans were dumb enough to think that even after those same Americans had led a Coalition Force that destroyed decades of military stock piles, Mesopotamia's entire economy and semi-secular government, that it was possible for the same Middle Eastern dictator to build a terrifyingly sophisticated nuclear weapons arsenal, entirely out of a length of aluminium tubing and a crumb of yellow cake. And that that belief would terrify the Americans into submission, which of course it didn't. What did happen were the deaths of somewhere near two million people, a high percentage of whom were women and children under the age of 13.

And Baʿal feasted.

Later, when the Demon Baʿal finally woke-up from feeding her frenzy induced death coma, she found that her godson and bride had managed to transcend to their next lives, in the first case a regression in spiritual evolution to becoming a political "science" Professor, and in the second case a spiritual evolution to becoming an Electric Blue Cichlid. Their romance carried on though as the Professor's Cichlid was the Professor's only friend. But Baʿal had not forgotten her promise to build and give the London Station to Judith Hanson.

And it came to pass that on the planet Alnitak Prime, in the Orion System, the Demon Ba'al tracked down the last linear descendent of Judith Hanson, who incidentally had been christened Judith Daemon and was married to one Ralph Hanson, no relation, and like the poor and much maligned Wicked Witch of the East, Ba'al dropped a tube station on the undeserving and uninteresting mortal descendant's head.

And if that doesn't prove you can't trust a god's timing, nothing will.

Like Ba'al's most famous student, Uncle Joe, who once held up in the Москва tube station during the Great Patriotic War, Ba'al ended up being held up in the London Station during the Gods' War that followed in the wake of the Finial Match at Armagedōn. After the decamping of humanity, due to their self-inflicted extinction event, the gods found a major power vacuum in the universe, or thought they had. Humanity was gone; the ranks of the Angelic Host were greatly diminished, and demoralized by an end game that was even more brutal than they had expected. The Demons were worse off than the Angels, because the Demons had lost at Armagedōn, which any right-minded Hellspawn would have told them would happen. Later, the few Demons still extant fell into their great depression because the Creator's mercy was absolute-all inclusive, and they watched one by one as trusted Demons snuck back into Heaven. Because the beaches were better in Heaven and a night of cocktails didn't leave you feeling ego-fucked in the morning.

So the gods felt that their time had finally come. This time, the Creator would really get what was coming to Him.

Fortunately, or unfortunately, depending on one's view, from a great distance for preference, the gods never got round to trying to whack the Creator. They did meet to plan their over-throw of the Creator, with the only noticeable result, being that all the gods went to war against one another. At the end, the Gods' War produced little change. Such is the way with gods.

The European gods schemed and double-crossed each other; brother against brother, sister against sister, and everyone against Loki, as it always has been with them. The Near Eastern gods banded together for a short time to defeat the African gods, which never actually happened because every attack proved beyond a shadow of doubt that the African gods had just happened to not be where they were supposed to have been, and everyone knew that they had been there just a few seconds before. The Aztec gods rallied their southern companions and attacked the north, only to find the their northern brothers welcomed them with open arms and peace pipes, which both parties commenced to smoke, only to wake up long after the war was over with the most terrible cases of munchies that either side could ever remember having had.

The Chinese gods played a waiting game, in which they sat opposite the Japanese gods on the one side, and the allied Korean and Vietnamese gods on the other, and not a one of them moved until some three centuries after the Gods' War was over. Indeed, Loki was perhaps the only one that came out of the Gods' War in good humour, as he had finally convinced Thor to buy his time-share in Florida.

But, here, in the London Station, Baʿal faced her most terrible enemy, Baʿal.

The great nature spirit Coyote, whom long had been annoyed by Baʿal's love of depravity, put Operation Hultkranz into action, which in the end, was the only completely successful campaign of the whole of the Gods' War. With the help of the Trickster's Association, which included Raven, Prometheus, Mercurius, Hermes, Eshu, Wakdjunga, Hansen, Uncle Drosselmeyer, Loki, and Thor (because every good organization needs a fall-guy), Operation Hultkranz invoked the spirit of everyone that Ba'al had ever hurt, and compelled them to return en-mass to forgive her in one massive pile-on loving embrace. Ba'al was completely defeated by their kindness; wept for joy, and capitulated into their loving embrace. Whereupon, the disembodied spirits killed the goddess Ba'al. And for once, done, and forever more, she remained so. Amen.

Ba'al complained bitterly of this trickery at her reincarnation hearing, but Stan only smiled and refused to issue her a new body, citing a lack of supplies.

Except, that it never really works that way with gods. But, that is another story, please see coming additional volumes of this narrative, such as Book III; *The Mists of the Abyss*, in which the Scions save humanity from the Faerie. Again.

But, for the first time in that universe. Again, another story.

The London Station, remember the London Station? The London Station was built upon the same grand design as was the Москва Station in Moscow, Terra, commissioned by Uncle Joe prior to the onset of the Great Patriotic War. The floor was smooth rectangular blocks of marble that were so highly polished that they reflected the true appearance of anything that gazed into them. Octagon marble columns stretched on either side of the long corridor as foundations for the arched buttress topped with flaring crown moulding. The long straight tunnel was lit by huge candelas, interspersed with marble mosaics of historical, universal, and biblical interest.

Mick had only ever once gazed into his true reflection as shown by the floor once, during his first visit to the London Station's grand opening. The Angel saw his own flowing blond hair and radiant face bleakly looking back at him, dressed in a long flowing white robe that was stained with blood and gore. The reflected Angel held an automatic pistol in one hand

and a skinned Human skull in the other. Behind the reflection, black mists swirled that resembled Demons, Hellspawn, and Nightmares all dressed in military uniforms and battle gear that spanned the ages of Humanity's existence.

The reflection had been so accurate that Mick had had to look at his own hands to assure himself that he wasn't holding anything. The Angel had even looked around himself to make sure that he wasn't surrounded by Demons, Hellspawn, and Nightmares, but could see no one. Later, much later, he realized that his being alone then was odd. But so many odd things had happened to him during his Angelic existence that all he did was shrug and move on.

Mick had made sure that he never looked directly at the floor again. Nobody likes seeing so much truth all at once.

Mick sat down for a moment upon one of the mahogany benches recessed back under the arches. It was a ritual he practiced every time he came here, or to any other underground tube station; the ritual of remembrance. The Angel had found meditative remembrance necessary after the first hundred years among humans. If you didn't practice memory, it faded and eventually disappeared.

What, what, what to remember?

Certainly not Heaven. That was all white robes, golden streets, Devil's Food Cake, and rinse, repeat.

The Final Match? No, too many died that day. Even Stan was sick come the end.

The Old Woman?

The Old Woman is, in actuality, the mother of the Immortals.

Please note; Immortals are immortal, but not all immortals are Immortal. So don't confuse them with ordinary vanilla flavoured immortal creatures that happen to have immortality but can be killed. The

127

Immortals are also indestructability, which is a much rarer quality.

And the Old Woman is the mother of all of them, as in the biological matriarch, grandsire, great grandsire; you get the point, of all of the Immortals. Not much is known about the Immortals and indeed, many an Angel will tell you that the Immortals are a Faerie-tale and don't exist. Granted, many a Demon will tell you the same thing, but that's because the Demons are gigantic fuck-all-liars. The only thing that is really known about the Immortals is that they more closely resemble Humans than Angels, and that for an Immortal to reproduce an Immortal, it must mate with another Immortal. And yes, a few seconds of serious thought about that should leave the reader feeling slightly icky.

There is only one known instance of a mortal achieving the immortality of an Immortal, and that is the case of one Bowerick Wowbagger, better known as Wowbagger, the Infinitely Prolonged. It is not clear how Wowbagger achieved this state of indestructability, although the Metatron has theorized that "The Creator is a funny Guy sometimes." Stan has claimed responsibility for the account on many occasions claiming that Wowbagger welched on their deal, but has always declined to specify the terms of the arrangement. Wowbagger himself has only ever admitted to being drunk at the time, plus some clearly bunkus nonsense about an irrational particle accelerator and rubber band.

Just how the Old Woman managed to conceive the first Immortal child remains a secret of History, and History has always declined to comment on the subject, citing the Old Woman's right to privacy. History can be like that, the ornery old hen.

The first time that Mick was absolutely certain that he had met the Old Woman was on the Chicago El, traveling back from Versailles, Christmas Day, 1919.

Of course strictly speaking, the Chicago El, or Elevated Railroad, was not founded until the unification of several competing railroad lines in 1924. But, really, just saying 'EL' is so much simpler than 'while riding on one of the railroad lines that was actually operating in 1919, and oh by the way, nobody remembers who in the Hell they were, and have you ever tried to look-up the name of a company that has been discorporate for some 14,272,092 years, and you don't have an expense account or graduate students to sick on the research? No? Well let me tell you buddy, it ain't bloody easy. Like really, nobody should care about a detail like that. But oh no, you write 34,395 great words and what do people do? Send hate-mail saying, 'In Chapter 5 you said that the El was in operation in 1919. Well dumbass, the El wasn't founded in until 1924...' etc., etc., etc.

Are you in the Army? the Old Woman had asked the Angel Mick.

Mick hadn't even noticed that she was there, sitting next to him. He looked at his black boots, brown trousers, duffle bag, Captain's insignia, his left hand that would have been missing had he not been an Angel. Then he nodded.

I wish you guys were unemployed, the Old Woman said.

Mick nodded again.

The El lumbered on.

A new mother settled her orphaned son.

A young girl-child asked its father; *Why do the men fight?* She had been looking at Mick when she asked her father, and hadn't looked away when Mick glared at her.

Be like one of these, the Angel heard in the dark space between his ears.

Why did you go to the war? The Old Woman asked.

129

Mick reached down and flipped the top of his bag away. He withdrew a small, battered, and blood stained copy of the *King James Bible*, and handed it over to the Old Woman.

No thanks, she said folding her hands under her arms. *I was framed in that.*

Mick shrugged.

A whistle blew.

The train came to a gradual halt.

Steam released and the engine cooled.

People shuffled out.

The Old Woman stood.

You must be the best Angel ever. Always doing what you're told.

Mick blinked and looked around himself, but she was gone.

Mick blinked and looked around himself, and there she was.

What's the difference between a terrorist and a freedom fighter? The Old Woman had asked.

Mick grinned.

I don't know, the Angel replied.

Which end of the Goddamn gun you're standing on.

It had taken Mick centuries to understand what that Old Woman had meant, and when Mick did finally figure it out, the daft old daughter of a bitch had been dead too long to tell off. Besides, the old dodger had gotten into Heaven somehow and you just didn't tell people off in Heaven, no matter what you saw in the Hollywood movies. Mick had believed that the Old Woman was in Heaven because he knew that the Old Woman wasn't anywhere else. That was what he thought, until he met her the second time.

Besides, the Old Woman might have been dead, but that really did not slow her down much.

Nobody was sure, Mick certainly never was sure, just what had happened to the Old Woman to prolong her life and the lives of her children.

The Old Woman knew, but since she didn't know she knew, the fact that she knew didn't amount to much. Not that she would care even if she knew she knew.

Hat knew and knew she knew, but just happened to be wrong. All of which only proved the old fortune cookie wisdom:

> "He that doesn't know and doesn't know that he doesn't know, doesn't know.
> He that doesn't know, but knows that he doesn't know, still doesn't know.
> He that knows, but doesn't know that he knows, still doesn't know.
> Only he that knows and knows that he knows, actually knows."
> --*The Act of Knowing*, from *The Little Book of Big Sayings*, by the Demon James

Bowerick Wowbagger the Infinitely Prolonged knew and knew he knew and knew he was right too. It had everything to do with the second rubber band. That and the fact that the Old Woman's mother also happened to have been a special friend of Wowbagger's back in the light jazz on the beach days before outliving the Hell out of everybody got to be too tedious for him. It was always a torment to Wowbagger that he sired a serine bastard superheroine that went on to birth a litter of serine bastards, who in turned pupped even more serine bastards. For several centuries after the Spacer Rebellion of 2805, Wowbagger amused himself by devising several ingenious albeit deathless methods for assassinating his own serine descendants. Wowbagger had a great deal of fun too until he exploded an ancient AN602 hydrogen Tsar Bomb under the same table where the

Demon Keith was wooing the coquettish schoolmarm Eliza Wharton. Keith was so pissed that even after the long wait to get a new body, the Demon returned unto Terra and forcibly transcended Wowbagger straight to Heaven; do not pass death, do not collect your resurrection chitty. Game over man, game over.

But all that just proves that the Creator has a sadistic sense of humour.

Several observers of humanity had speculated that the Old Woman had been Patient$_0$ of the Immortality Virus outbreak. Both Mick and Hat however, knew that the Old Woman was much older than that. It wasn't that Mick thought that the Old Woman hadn't had a hand in the Immortality Virus outbreak. Mick was certain that she had, Hat had once said as much once when she was drunk.

No, it was just that the Old Woman had always insisted that they had first met about five centuries before Mick remembered meeting her. She had always claimed they first met during the Sepoy Rebellion of 1857. It was a point that the Angel was still uneasy about; although the Old Woman had insisted, it was true.

Mick had, in company with a band of hired mercenary Pakhtuns, crept into the outer chambers of His Royal Highness Abu Zafar Sirajuddin Muhammad Bahadur Shah Zafar, also called ابوا ظفر جارس اُلدّين محمد ظفر شاه بُهادر, in order to put a sharp end to the rebellion before it really got underway. With his hand on the bed chamber door handle, the Angel of the Lord had turned to his men, looked into the face of an old woman, saw bright light, and woke up days later in a brothel in Jalandhar. The rebellion was well underway by then.

When Mick told the story to Sir Harry P. Flashman, VC, KCB, KCIE, the latter responded; "Well-done old boy, that got you well out of it. I's not so damned lucky. I had to fight my way out of it to the last. But I saved our flag, oh yes, saved her Imperial Majesty's honour I did."

132

What was it that the Old Woman always said? *Get that silly sheet off your head, this isn't an episode of Scooby Doo*? No wait, Mick thought, that was the transvestite comedian that the Demon Keith had made famous.

Mick had never seen the Old Woman in Heaven, not actually in Heaven, now that he came to think about it.

Mick shrugged and cleared his mind.

He remembered the Node Collapse Disaster that lead to the eventual construction of this station. It had happened shortly after humanity had discovered the Node Pathways for the third time.

Contrary to popular mythic history, humanity was not always the pawns of the gods, although the gods have always been the real life-sized action figures of the Creator, and mortals His' sims.

Anyway, humanity actually started out as near demi-gods with more power than the run of the mill gods, just below the Archangels in power, and well above ordinary Angels and most of the Demons. It was only through a carefully crafted campaign of religious education that humanity learned to first believe that it was dirty, second that it was powerless, and third that it was the obvious desire of the Creator that man should live in eternal subjugation to those masters that were more rich and powerful than the rest of it. Stan still considers compulsory RE to be his greatest achievement.

But, before all that happened, the ancient wise guy Avatar Holt discovered the Node Pathways for the first time by the simple expedient of falling into the entrance of the Node Pathway just south of the great lake called Michi Gami. Unfortunately, for Holt though, he got lost in the pathways, and was later, several centuries later, discovered wandering aimlessly through the shadow lands that flank the pathways in every direction. Holt never recovered his mental capabilities, and eventually died of Swine Flu. Later a

133

rather odd man put a pub on top of that Node Pathways entrance and did a rather brisk business, as he never minded what his customers looked like as long as they didn't tear the place up.

But a few people learned two significant facts; one does not age while in the Node Pathways and also that wondering off the Node Pathways into the darkness is unhealthy. In the darkness, one simply continues to exist. Never changing, never dying. Just slowly going cuckoo.

The second time humanity discovered the Node Pathways was when Amelia Earhart came flying out of a clear blue sky about 70 kilometres southeast of Tonopah, Nevada on the 10th of September, 1993. By tracing her fly path directly backward, the US Air Force discovered a temporary entrance to the Node Pathways. But after losing two MQ-1 Predator drones, one Boeing X-32 plane, and two Sikorsky HH-60 Pave Hawk helicopters into the Node Pathways, the US Air Force decided to simply observe the phenomenon until it disappeared about a week later.

Mick stood and stretched. A few hours had passed while he sat in his contemplative revelry. A faint smile passed his face as he saw that the TripleA terminate was still underway, and it had been for years if Mick was any judge. Giant Gas Ball Coffee cups were littered around the players, along with chip bags and soda cans.

Mick had often wondered about how his own memory worked.

It wasn't chronologically ordered, of that the Angel was certain. His memory was more closely organized on an association basis, where all things about War were filed now in the A-bin, under Avoid, and all things Medical were filed in the NMB-bin under Not My Business. Love, Romance, and Kids were all filed indiscriminately in the GGS-bin, under Gross Girl Stuff. It was like a Cicero Memory Palace with too many rooms and no lights.

Mick stopped his wondering in front of a bronzed war memorial dedicated to the Spacer Rebellion of 2805, in which the former planetary colonies of Terra all declared war upon Terra, and in most cases, on each other too. The Spacer Rebellion was relatively short and astonishingly low in casualties, due to the great lengths of time then required for travelling between the stars, at that time in Human history. The event is generally considered the onset of the Spacer Epic, which lasted until 5468 with the discovery of Space Folding as a by-product of the Herbert Effect.

The Herbert Effect, also loosely referred to as Space Folding, is the process by which vast stretches of space are covered at a near instantaneous speed. While the Herbert Effect Theory postulates no upper limit for the distance that can be crossed, the actual functional limit of the Herbert Effect Space Folding Drive Mark 7 is a mere 7 billion light years at a single go. The Camulodunum System for example was some 242 billion light years from the Sol System, so using the Mark 7 HESF Drive there would have been a required 35 jumps to make the journey. Since each jump took approximately 1 standard Terran minute, the journey would effectively take about an hour, including boarding and unload time. All things being equal, it was considered a quick ride, unless of course you happened to be someone like the Metatron, whom just willed himself to be wherever it was that he wanted to be.

This just goes to show that no matter how clever you are, some twerp bugger of a natural prodigy will come along and make you look foolish. Angels are good at that.

Mick finally found what he had wanted all along, about a kilometre down the central station corridor, wedged in between a Frost's burger joint and a Coyote Video Store. The Angel paused for a moment to critically inspect the frosted letters of the store window; *Beta is Back!!!*

135

With a deep sigh for the long-gone better days of television entertainment, Mick turned his attention to what he was really looking for. The sign read:

MacGuffin's News
est. 1605 Anno Domini
The Really Old Firm

The lead article above the fold read; *The Gravitational Wormhole Initiator: Scientists Conclude that Time Travel is Just a Waste of Time; Right or Wrong, You Decide.*

The Angel grunted.

"What?" asked a short, blond haired man that wore an apron that said; *Hi, my name is Johann. How can I help you?*

"Time travel is rot," the Angel said. "Honestly Mr. Carolus, I don't know why you bother with this stuff."

"It moves in the Demon market," Johann, lately identified as Mr. Carolus said. "Some of the underground elements want to go back to the Big Bang and jump the Creator when He's not looking."

"Do you think that would work?"

"Hell's no," Johann Carolus said. "Trying to rebel against Ineffability is almost as pointless as playing poker with the Son."

"Then why haven't you gone onto Heaven?" the Angel asked.

The newsman shrugged. "Why haven't you?"

"That's easy," he said scanning the titles on the racks. "If I hear *Amazing Grace* once more this century, I'm going to go over to the other side."

"It's *Onward Christian Soldiers* for me," Johann Carolus said. "That song has always given me the creeps. Let ye who is blameless cast the first stone, one-shot-one-kill-mutter-fucker!"

Mick picked up and flipped through the final issue of *Rotten Tomatoes Magazine*, and paused arriving at the review of the last-really-really-really-the-last-as-in-the-final episode of "The Simpsons."

"The Simpsons," like many other wildly successfully television series, outlived, rather literally in this case, its Creators. With more than 999,863 episodes, spanning the length of 370 centuries, "The Simpsons," along with their spinoff series Maggie in the Middle, Bart's Beat, Snowball's Revenge, Ms. Albright's Nursery, Bill and Marty's Happy Hour, and Disco Stu's Soul Train Revisited, became the primary social creation engine for Terra. This goes a long way to explain why the Spacer Rebellion occurred in the first place. And like most good shows, "The Simpsons" WAS cancelled before their prime had passed.

"Ah, they don't make 'em like that anymore," the newsman said. "Oh to have met Kent Brockman."

"No," Mick agreed. "They don't make 'em at all anymore. And Harry Shearer wasn't all that. I think he did his best work in *Abbott and Costello Go to Mars*. It was pretty much all downhill after that."

"You ever thought about doing another movie?" Johann Carolus asked.

The Angel carefully refrained from looking at the newsman.

"I think you should do a war movie," Johann Carolus mused. "You know something classical, Greek maybe- you know, dawn of time stuff. *Three Cherry Trees* maybe?"

"That would be Chinese then, not Greek," Mick said.

"Nuts then," Johann Carolus said. "I never could stand those foreign buggers. Mind you, most lovely women God ever made were Chinese."

"Right," Mick said after deciding to ignore the contradiction in the newsman's statements. "*Three Cherry Trees*?"

"You've never read it?" Johann Carolus asked, genuine amazement spreading across his face.

"No," the Angel said. "Should I have?"

"Oh gods yes," Johann Carolus said, "It's like that book by Nabokov on crack. This guy clones his wife ND his first horn-dog love and then raises them up to be the *perfect* wives; Angels in the light, barefoot in the kitchen, and total sluts in the dark. I've got a copy around here somewhere."

The Angel waved him off.

"Okay. But you really should read it. It's a bloody Post Post Modern classic of moral relativism."

"Oh," Mick said.

"Yeah," Johann Carolus agreed. "And considering it was written by the Demon James, most people consider it to be non-fiction. For the love of the Creator, I thought that your Committee on Unheavenly Affairs would have been all over that."

"Why do you want to do a movie?" the Angel asked, dodging any further conversation concerning the Demon James, a guy who made Schizophrenics look savvy and Sociopaths look empathetic.

"Criticism," Johann Carolus said without pause.

"What?" the Angel said taking his turn to express genuine amazement. "Why in the Hell would you want any of that rubbish?"

"Call it what you will, it sells," Johann Carolus said in that infuriatingly calm tone that radiated the same sense smugness as an English Professor has when about to monologue on his favourite novel. "Take movie reviews, right, that's criticism-light. But man, you get someone that disagrees and they write in to complain about what was said about their last favourite movie and before you know it, you got an old-fashioned snail-mail flame-war going on. Hell, the last time Amy, President of Hell, got a letter published; he bought 700 copies off me and passed them out to all his banking cronies. People put more love and passion into movie and TV criticism than anything else under the Creator's many suns."

Carolus was right. The Angel knew it too. That was why he had gone to Hollywood in the first place to have an impact. People never cared as much about religious or secular leaders as they cared about a mind-fucked starlet.

Mick looked up from the magazine and stared at the old incarnation of something better best forgotten.

"What are you anyway?" the Angel asked.

"An Immortal," Johann Carolus said. "One of the chosen few, a natural serene bastard. Bastard bad-luck if you ask me."

"Tell me something, the Old Woman, is she an Immortal? One of the original ones I mean, not one that got it off the Immortality Virus."

"Well, sort of," Johann Carolus said cautiously.

"It is not your fate to know that, Angel," said a deep throaty female voice that sounded rather like extremely expensive cancer.

Mick turned to see a medium height woman, with dirty blond hair, green eyes, and a tight pink t-shirt on. The cryptic inscription on the shirt read:

62 6f 6f 62 73 21
Ym9vYnMh
98 111 111 98 115 33

"Ah, Fate," the Angel said grimly, remembering the last time he had seen her. It hadn't been a good visit.

"Always nice to see you Mictlantecuhtli," Fate said.

"Hi-ya, Boo Boo," Johann Carolus said. "How's tricks?"

"Suck, totally suck," Fate complained, "I always know how they're going to work out. Once, just once, I'd like to be surprised by something."

"Will this Angel ever find love?" Johann Carolus asked.

"Nope."

"You got any comment on the new bomber stud taking the Triple Crown?"

"Now, now, you know I never comment on that sort of thing," Fate said airily.

"Yes, but, if you-"

"Mick, Mick, Micky-Mic-Mic-Mick." Fate purred as she took the Angel by the lapels of his trench coat and pulled herself close into him.

The Angel looked down upon the black bold lettering of Ym9vYnMh, coughed, and rearranged the universe so that he was on the other side of the newsstand.

Johann Carolus chuckled.

Fate shrugged.

"Have it your own way I'm sure," she said making such a transparent pouty-face that even toddlers would have laughed at her.

"What am I not supposed to know?" Mick said, wishing that he didn't know what her shirt meant.

"About the Old Woman, for one thing," Fate said running her hand over an open box of Bazooka Bubble-gum. She paused and picked up an individually wrapped piece of gum and twirled it in her nimble fingers. "Hmm, What did the dolphin say when he bumped into the whale?"

"S'cuse me, pardon me, not plankton--not plankton, won't digest well, sorry, sorry, and sorry?" Johann Carolus asked.

Fate laughed. It was a warm sharp sound that felt like sunlight exploding in your nose.

"I- didn't- do it- on- porpoise," she gasped.

"That's a real knee slapper and no mistake," Johann Carolus said tapping his left elbow with his right hand.

The Angel sighed audibly and shifting his weight in a manner that suggested that he was, right then, the most put upon creature in the entire universe.

Mick wasn't the most put upon at the moment. It was most likely that it was Hat, who was at that very moment attempting to chair the first All Scions staff meeting to be held in centuries. It wasn't going well and Daren Matthews, Scion of Papa Legba, had just knocked over her coffee by banging his fist on the table. Hat was just then, considering genocide against all her own kind.

"The prophecy, mademoiselle, if you don't mind," Mick said crisply.

"Oh all right," Fate said tossing the wrapped gum back into the box. "Really, I don't know, I just don't know why I bother with you lot, it's not like you're going to listen. Damned Angels never do. At least the blessed Demons listen. But not Angels, oh no, not them. Never mind all the times I've been right. This time it'll be different. The bubble won't burst, we can go on like this forever, and the poor people in the inner city won't take up arms and slay their greedy gluttonous overlords. Yeah, yeah, yeah. Never mind the prophecy of Fate from the only genuine oracle in the universe-"

"Today, please," the Angel said.

"You *Sir*, Angel, *Sir*," Fate said with an auditable chill in her voice that made Johann Carolus' neck hair contract, "It will be your fault, at the End."

The Angel sighed.

"And the prophecy please?"

"It will be your fault, at the End," Fate calmly repeated in that special way that screamed; *pay attention this time you daft idiot.*

"What? What for?"

"Oh, pretty much everything," Fate said. "Except those bits that are the Demon's fault. Or the bits that are, will be, the collective fault of the Scions. Oh yeah, and the bits that are-" Fate broke off with a grin.

"Yes?" the Angel demanded angrily.

"Sorry, not authorized to tell you that," Fate said curling her left finger in her hair and batting her eyelashes at the Angel. "Buy me dinner first. I always talk in bed."

"Will you just go away?" the Angel asked, turning his back on Fate.

"Oh, I wish I could, I really, really, really wish I could," she mused. "But mine is to suffer the slings and arrows-"

"Of time?" Johann Carolus asked.

"Hmm," Fate hummed, and concluded, "No. Self-righteous Angelic-pig-headed stubbornness."

"Tell ya what, Boo Boo," Johann Carolus said. "Why not tell me. Mick's right there and he's not going to shove off anytime soon. Not after he finds out I've got old vintage 35 mm black and white that I've tucked away for him."

"WHAT?"

"See, told ya."

Fate grinned.

"Of who, of what, where?" the Angel asked.

Johann Carolus looked from the Angel to the Personification and back again.

"You going to listen to the young lady or what?"

"Fine, fine, fine," Mick said, and turned his full attention to Fate.

"It'll be your fault, at the end," she said. "All of it."

"Yes, and?" Mick asked.

"That's pretty much it," Fate said. "That and don't tell the next Gatekeeper about the key, but that bit's an order, not prophecy."

"Don't tell him what about the key?"

"That it's in his hand."

"Oh, sure, sure, no worries, anything else?" the Angel asked impatiently.

Fate shook her head.

"You will be an even littler man in the next universe than you are a fallen Angel now," Fate said. "You'll be fallen like that Márquez Angel, not, you know, Fallen like Stan sort of Fallen."

"Nothing new there," Johann Carolus said.

"Okay, thanks sister," Mick said. "Now Johann, what you got for me?" the Angel continued, firmly placing Fate outside of his attention and memory.

Johann Carolus showed the Angel as Fate shrugged and faded into the background.

Mick flipped through the titles; *Броненосец Потёмкин*, *The Empire Strikes Back*, *Citizen Kane*, *King Lear*, *Schindler's List*, and *Casablanca* in the original director's cut. Also, the Angel found; *Xenophōn's Complete Histories, Abridged*, and the original 1972 *Poseidon Adventure*.

"I'll take all of them, plus a Pre-Armagedōn pack of smokes," the Angel said.

"Ain't got those," Johann Carolus said. "I got these crummy fags from the Lone Star Planet. I've never been one for super-tobacco though. Stuff just chokes me up.

143

"Sure, sure, whatever," Mick said. "Put 'em in plain wrapping. You got a 35 mm projector?"

"Can't help you there," Johann Carolus said.

"Damn."

"My feelings entirely." Johann Carolus said. "Tell ya what though, have a copy of this instead."

"Will you hold the movies for me, just for a couple of hours?" the Angel asked.

Johann Carolus frowned and then nodded.

"I'm sure I have a cardboard box around here somewhere," he said.

The Angel looked down at the proffered magazine. *A Collection of Unbeatable Mental Crossword Puzzles, Beta Edition.*

"What is that?"

"Something Shax sent along a few days ago," Johann Carolus said with a shrug. "Not your thing?"

"No, definitely not," the Angel agreed handing the book back. "All right, I'm off."

Johann Carolus watched him walk off down the tube station main corridor. Once the Angel was well out of sight, Johann Carolus closed up the newsstand, hopefully for the last time, and let himself into the Coyote Video Store.

Johann Carolus had really come to hate the news business in the last couple of million years and had jumped at Basil Berry's invitation to "stir things up a bit."

Johann Carolus headed back to the furthest corner of his store and passed through a beaded curtain into a room that, well, wasn't family friendly, although some of the depicted acts could get you in the family way. The walls, the racks, the shelves, and indeed every surface of the room was covered in pornographic images of young girls doing things that even the most drug dependent mother wouldn't have wanted her daughters doing.

And in the center of the room stood a real life and furious tall blond Nordic woman dressed in what centuries ago would have been called a power suit. She stood glaring at another man, dressed all in black, who was flipping through a magazine titled *Not Even Close to Legal*.

"The end is nigh," Johann Carolus said.

"This is who we are," the man replied.

"Why is *he* here?" the woman demanded pointing an accusing finger at the man flipping through the magazine.

"I always thought 'Recalled to life,' would be a better response," the man in black said.

"Where'd you get that?" Johann Carolus ask.

"The bastard Rahab, Patton's half-sister," the man in black said. "Did you know she's still alive?"

"Really? No, I didn't know." Johann Carolus said. "She's mortal?"

The man in black shrugged.

"What! Is! He! Doing! Here?" Ms. Carter managed in five increasingly louder screams.

"Now-now, Ms. Carter," Johann Carolus said in an overtly patronizing voice. "Fornicó has just as much right to be here as-"

"Don't give me that Ms. Carter crap," Ms. Carter snapped. "I thought we agreed that he wasn't *supposed* to be here."

"No, Ms. Carter," Johann Carolus said in the wearied tones of one that had been over this argument repeatedly. "You agreed and I just stopped arguing with you. That's not actual agreement. You do that a lot."

"That's true," Fornícó agreed. "But she does invite it you know, always sticking her nose in things that don't concern her."

And that was true too. According to the *Prognosticated Peerage*:

> **Joanne Carter**: called Ms. Carter: One of the natural Immortals, who fancies herself the Patron Saint of Reporters. She was discovered by Sešat in the city of Carthage in 146 BC. Ms. Carter appears throughout history in minor roles, making her first major contribution to the course of history with her work in the founding of the Continuation of Our Weekly News first published in London in 1623, and then her move to the Oxford Gazette now the London Gazette first published in 1665. Ms. Carter held various news and information roles, until she went to work for the newly founded British Secret Service Bureau in 1909 which was later reorganized as the British Intelligence Services in anticipation of the Great War. Ms. Carter remained with British Intelligence Services until the 7th of May 1946, after which she held several major editorial and management roles in various English-speaking news agencies throughout the world. She is considered to be one of the most notorious undercover reporters of all time.

On the other hand, one could just ask Ms. Carter, she'll tell ya all about Ms. Carter, it's her favourite subject. Actually, don't bother asking. Just wait, she'll tell you. Neither the disdain of Fornícó nor anyone else has ever stood in Ms. Carter's relentless self-promotion.

Ms. Carter scowled at Johann Carolus.

"Now," Johann Carolus said smoothly, "the mark's got the punt, so let's all just settle in and wait."

"Must I wait *here*, with *him*?" Ms. Carter demanded.

Fornícó looked up, smiled, and showed Ms. Carter a magazine picture of a very short girl.

"No, no, no," Johann Carolus said snatching the magazine out of the man's hands and tossing it behind the counter. "I have set up another room, all for you. I've collected most of your original footage from the ABC, CNN, and the Gileadean News. It's all about you dear."

"Oh," Ms. Carter said with a soft in-take of breath. "Really?"

Johann Carolus nodded.

"Do you have my interview with Khadijeh Saqafi?"

"Yes, and the ones with Traudl Junge Humps and Harriet M. Welsch too."

"The one with Anna Howe?" Ms. Carter asked with obvious nervous anticipation. "That was my best work I think. I had to go into a serious deep cover for that one."

"Yes, original and unedited even," Johann Carolus said. "Plus I've got Georgia O'Keeffe, Lady Glencora, Eleanor Roosevelt, and Rosa Louise McCauley Parks."

"Oh- my- god-" Ms. Carter squeaked. "You're such a jewel."

After Johann Carolus had installed Ms. Carter in the next room and closed the adjoining door, he turned to Fornícó.

"You're such a jewel," he said. "Look at me, look at me, look at me, she's the worst of the whole family."

"Listen Fornícó," Johann Carolus said, "did you have to come here? Today I mean?"

The man shrugged.

147

"I've taken a very personal interest in Ms. Carter since she put me in jail," Fornícó said. "You might say I'm investigating her high-ness."

"You have to admit, they were a bit young," Johann Carolus said.

The man shrugged again.

"I remember once upon a time ago when an unmarried and un-mothered girl of that age was considered over the hill."

"Yeah and good riddance to influenza too," Johann Carolus said. "Look, all I'm saying is please don't cause any trouble right now. If this comes off, it will be the biggest deal since Armagedōn and it will just maybe put some life back in this old universe okay? And we *need* her, alright? She's got rapport with the Angel."

"Yeah, yeah, okay," Fornícó said, but in a way that left Johann Carolus completely unbelieving in his sincerity.

Chapter 6: V.I.P. Lounge

The V.I.P. Lounge, London Station, Zeta Orionis, in the Orion System.

Give, and it will be given to you: good measure, pressed down, shaken together, and running over will be put into your bosom. For with the same measure that you use, it will be measured back to you. --Luke 6:38, K.J.V.

And it came to pass that the Angel found not one, but two fellow journeymen.

Fate sat next to the Demon, Fruchtbarkeitskultus, called Keith, who was nursing his 106,109,101,115th bottle of Everclear since the end of Armagedōn, when the Angel walked into the bar, somewhere in the vicinity of Zeta Orionis.

Keith did not look up. He already knew who the Angel was.

The Angel, Mictlantecuhtli, called Mick, looked around the dingy bar at the scene of old broken down Demons, an intemperate Angel, a few minor and completely forgotten gods, and Peter Lorre.

Mick sighed. This wasn't how he had wanted it to be. This was sad and while the Angel had never himself been the most upbeat spirit in the world, he had been drawn to the light of happiness in the same ways that hornets are attracted to sweet jam.

The Angel didn't see Fate, as she had faded by the time he saw where the Demon Keith was. Plus the Mick's attention was taken up entirely by the sight of Peter Lorre convening the annual conference of the Comprehensive Research Investigational Thesis Inquisition Convocation Society.

Mick adjusted his khaki trench coat, pushed up his sunglasses on his nose, and walked towards the bar. The Angel completed the silver screen moment by pulling the matching khaki fedora down over his forehead.

Keith didn't look up when the Angel sat down on the bar stool next to him. Just because the Demon hadn't seen the Angel in a couple of million years wasn't any reason to notice him.

"You're a hard one to find, mate," Mick said giving Keith a jovial slap on the back.

"I'm not your mate," Keith said, and belched. Keith then coughed slightly and pulled a Blaberus craniifer roach from his throat.

By this point in the narrative, our three dear genteel readers, and everyone else too, should not be surprised to know that cockroaches survived the Apocalypse at Armagedōn. Nor should refined readers be surprised that roaches actually colonized the entire whole of the universe and without ever bothering to develop memory, language, or thumbs. In fact, cockroaches were the only alien species that humanity ever had any contact with, since the roaches were the only alien species the Creator ever created in this universe.

According to *The Complete History of the Roach*, by Gregor Samsa, the story goes something like this: In a galaxy right next door, just a few years before man was created, a fantastic volcanic eruption blew the planet Dictyoptera apart. The planet blew into trillions and trillions and trillions of much smaller rocks, rather like asteroids. And the roaches, the only sentient life forms that inhabited the planet, went off flying into space in billions and billions and billions of different directions. Most of the roaches from the time of the Great Space Spawning died, but not before they laid millions and millions and millions of eggs on every single rock that was carrying even one of them.

Over time, space dust collected on the eggs, which protected them upon their long journeys through the galaxies and upon re-entry into planetary atmospheres. Terra, being so relatively close to Dictyoptera geographically, received a disproportionate number of the alien species. This just goes to show you that it really is all about location, location, location.

Mick watched in fascinated horror as the roach ran down Keith's arm, onto the bar top, and into a bowl of peanuts.

"Peanuts?" Keith asked pushing the bowl towards the Angel.

"Uh, no thanks," Mick said. "Do you think I could get an espresso here?"

"You can get whatever you want here," Keith said.

Mick looked around for the bartender and realized that there was dust on the bottles behind the bar.

"Now you get it," the Demon said. "No Humans, remember? There was this big war, white hats verses the black hats, no take backs. We lost, you won, mortals completely obliterated everywhere in the universe, ineffable blah blah blah." The Demon took another pull from his Everclear bottle. "And you just try getting an immortal to go into service. Bloody waste of time even trying."

"Oh yes, I forgot," Mick said with effortless and equally false calm. He made the sign of an inverted pentagram in the air. A small cup of steaming hot Kopi Luwak espresso appeared on the bar in front of him.

The roach, covered in peanut dust, raised his head over the side of the bowl, its little tentacles probing the air.

"Espresso?" the Demon asked. "All of the universe to play with and you pull up an espresso?"

"Be not among winebibbers or gluttons; for the drunkard and the glutton shall come to poverty, drowsiness, and shall clothe men in rags." The Angel said primly.

151

"I just remembered why I don't like you," the Demon said with effortless and genuine calm.

Frowning, the Angel took a small brown paper bag from the front pocket of his trench coat and handed it over to Keith.

"What's this?" Keith said making no move what-so-ever to take the proffered bag.

"Call it a peace offering. For-"

"Not calling all these thousands of millions of billions of years? Are we in the trillions yet?"

"No."

"Feels like it."

"Yes," Mick said, his face showing as much discomfort as his faltering voice suggested. "Exactly, that. For not calling. I mean. For all these years."

"So much to do with organizing the Celestial Choir and all," Keith muttered. "I always thought that the Big Guy had more imagination than that. I mean really, you'd think that the same Guy that created the Heavens and the Terra and the Helix Nebula eyeball would have a better idea of what to do with all His chattel than have them sing to Him all the time."

Mick shrugged. "Always best not to speculate, I always say."

"You know what gets me the most?" the Demon asked shaking the Everclear bottle under the Angel's nose.

"Traffic wardens?"

"No," Mick said, "they get me second most. What really gets me the most is that in all this great big universe there never was any more sentient life than those lousy stinking Humans. I mean really. All this work," Mick added with grand waving gestures. "All this work, millions of years of work to make a sun, and another couple of millions to make a planet, and for what?"

"I really can't say," said the Angel.

"Exactly 777-sextillion Human beings, and a handful of immortals," the Demon growled, "That's what. And all of *them* related too. The biggest fuck fest of incest in history."

"Pardon?" the Angel said frowning.

"The Humans I mean," the Demon said. "All of them are incestuous. Humans are the only species capable of that particular crime come to that."

"I don't follow," the Angel said.

"The original immortals were all created individually," Keith said "And it doesn't really count for the animals which the Creator created by the hundred at a go. But all the Humans come from just one grandsire and one womb. Same line from two to the last of the 777-sextillion."

"Hmmm," the Angel hummed.

"Things that make you go hmmm," the Demon agreed.

Many post-apocalypse historians have made a great deal out of the fact that the number of Human beings that descended from Adam and Eve corresponded exactly to the number of stars in the universe. However, this coincidence has never been collaborated by any higher authority. When asked about it, the Metatron only replied, "Are you sure? My calculations don't add up that way at all."

Mick nodded at the Demon in the same way that college kids use to do to old men that went on about wars that were over and done before the kids were born.

"That's actually what I want to talk to you about," said the Angel.

"Incest? You want to talk about incest?"

"No," the Angel said and sighed. "Stop being a wilful dolt for a moment, please."

Keith left off his grumbling and looked at Mick for the first time. "Take off those glasses, you're the one that looks like a *dolt*," he said.

Mick pulled off the glasses and the fedora revealing radiant blue eyes and a mess of blond hair, which he shook out over his shoulders.

"You make me sick," Keith said.

Mick pushed the brown paper bag over to Keith.

Keith unceremoniously upended the bag, spilling its contents all over the counter. Keith smiled as his hand fell over a pack of vintage Camel Victory Blend cigarettes.

"Where did you get these?"

"Oh, I don't know," Mick said vaguely.

"You miracled them into existence, didn't you?" Keith said, his hand stroking the pack of 20 wrapped in honest wholehearted reverence.

"Well, yes, I did, sort of anyway. More like a minor time manipulation really."

"All right," Keith said, forcing himself to put the pack of twenty cancer sticks back down on the bar. "What's the catch?"

"Well," said the Angel. "I got them off of Johann Carolus, but they were Lone State Super Tobacco, and I know you don't like that brand so I convince them they really grew-up in South America and-"

"Not that catch," the Demon interrupted. "The other catch. The one that motivated an Angel to use magic. The catch that's going to muck up my dull boring and above all Angel-free eternity?"

"Peace offering?" Mick suggested.

"You tried that one already."

"No, really, peace offering."

Keith grunted. "First off, I haven't heard we're interested in peace anymore now than we were when the war started. Secondly, Metatron issued that General Amnesty a while back, so there's your ineffable mercy. Me, I just can't stand the choir. It's boring. So, I haven't bothered. I'm on the mailing list though. Don't see why the Celestial Choir needs to have a fundraiser, but there ya go, I get the mailer. Don't want the mailer, but I get the mailer. Do you guys have a no call list? I'd seriously like to kill the telemarketing calls."

"I have to admit," Mick said looking over both shoulders before he continued in a whisper, "I can't stand the Choir either. They never let anyone good play the organ."

"So I say again, what do you want?"

The Angel was silent for a long time. So long, in fact that the roach made his move, running down the side of the peanut bowl, and right up into the Kopi Luwak espresso. Unfortunately, the roach hadn't counted on the 75° C serving temperature.

"Have you ever thought about starting it all again?" Mick asked almost in a whisper.

"No," Keith said picking up the cigarettes. He hit the top of the pack three times against the base of his left palm and unwrapped them. He then placed one cigarette between his lips and lit it with the tip of his left middle finger.

"How cliché."

The Demon shrugged. "It's an expected thing. Can't be helped really. It was fated as soon as you miracled me vintage pre-Armagedōn fags. Nice spicy blend. My complements."

"I think existence has all gone a bit stale really," Mick said picking up his espresso. Looking down into the drink, he noticed the dead roach, and quickly replaced the cup on its saucer.

"Here, let me get that," Keith said scooping the roach out with two fingers. Mick cupped the wet insect in his hands and blew on it. The little bug, scalded bright red, then returned to its normal dark brown colour, hissed at the Angel, and fled up into Keith's sleeve.

"That's something that I've never understood about you," Mick said. "How can an Angel-"

"Damned Demon," Keith corrected.

"A previously Fallen Angel restored by Grace," Mick continued smoothly, "but Angel none the less for that, be so kind to animals?"

"Comes with the territory," Keith said with a shrug. "I was created as a Fertility Spirit, for back in the old days, before the mammals had gotten the whole sex thing worked out. I went around holding Sex-Ed lectures at the local community grove and clearing centers, until the fundamentalists came down on me for being anti-family. I said, 'What's so anti-family about family planning? Seems to me you need to think these days about obedience training. The natural order is completely out of hand, no respect anymore. And advanced hunting schools and all that will need a tax-deferment investment account. What are you teaching these little critters about the economic consequences of early spawning? You know, let the little bunny grow up into a full fledge jack before he has to commit to a 9 to 5 in Farmer Johnson's patch to feed the third brood this year?' They said, 'Oh no you don't, no using logic on us, we're immune to that shyt,' and so on and so on. I said, 'But that's what I'm supposed to do, creating things, healing things, helping things get knocked up, and I've got a sub-contract from the government, and I mean *the Government*.' But no, all of a sudden all the animals were *dirty* and people were *clean* even though they still looked dirty to me, and I was tossed out on my ear without so much as a thanks for a couple of million years of good service."

"I know, I know, same thing happened to me," Mick said. "I got sent to South America, you know, a minor P.R. job, right after the Son ascended to Heaven. I was just supposed to show myself and let the locals know that sooner or later, prophets were

156

supposed to start showing up to prepare the way for whatever was coming next. And this guy, king, chief, banking executive, or some other person more important than anyone else stands up and invites me to dinner at his place. So I accept and we go on over there and talk about, you know, the weather, and the crops, and his son who was off having an argument with the neighbouring kingdom about whether or not the basketball hoop should be turned up or sideways, and after about five minutes we got nothing else to talk about. I'm not Human, he's not an Angel, and we just really don't have anything to say. So when his daughter comes out with this lovely roasted wild boar, I joke, 'Oh, pork, tastes like Human.' And my host gets terrified and throws his daughter Mictecacihuatl at me, says take her, and runs out of the place never to be seen again. So I hang out and try to run the place for a while until the Committee Against False Idols pops around to get me on the *Pretending to Be God Clause-*"

"When someone asks you if you're God, you say?"

"Not now," the Angel said rudely.

The Demon shrugged.

"So I bunked off leaving Mictecacihuatl in charge," Mick continued in a peevish tone. "Funny, I never got around to going back. I wonder how it all worked out?"

"They formed a death cult," Keith said, smugness radiating off him like smoke curling off the tip of a cigarette.

"Oh my, I hope not," Mick said.

"Well, nice of you to stop by," Keith said getting up off his stool, "but I got things to do, people to not talk to, you know how it is. Ms. Carter was in here a while ago and I just love telling that starched-panties-twat sexist jokes. Nice seeing you."

157

"Wait," Mick said looking frantically around the bar. Absolutely no one was paying them any attention. Mick pulled another slim rectangular object wrapped haphazardly in a silk cloth from inside his trench coat, and handed it to Keith.

Keith looked inside the silk wrap. "Oh no, no, no. Not on your afterlife Angel."

"You don't even know what it is," the Angel complained.

"I do too," the Demon shot back. "It's only the bloody manual for getting the Big Guy to come down and drop a million tons of *You're-not-a-God* right on your head. Fuck that for a lark."

"You've read this book?" Mick asked, obviously disappointed. "I never even heard of it till yesterday."

"Read it? Freaking read it. Hells bells jinkies," Keith said. "I use'ta know her. That book's more trouble than Patton's Avorit manuscript on how two friends survived the Celestial Cold War."

"I never read that one. How did he-"

"They didn't."

"But this woman is different," the Angel whined. "I mean Patton was fruit cake of the first order. This Kin Arad woman has degrees and brains and sophistication."

"Patton wasn't a fruit cake, just inexperienced," the Demon complained. "And the more degrees anyone has just means they fuck-up more spectacularly than anybody else. Everybody always picks on Patton just because he visited another universe and wrote really crappy metaphors about his trip. Rahab's memoir is a much better read. Didn't Patton shoot himself into space like old Jago Jalo?"

"More like S. R. Hadden, but yeah, total looney toon," the Angel said and pushed the bundle slightly closer to the Demon. "Anyway, I'm not having that multi-universes argument again.

"I wonder if those nutters are still out there somewhere, drifting," Keith said, pushing the wrapped bundle back towards the Angel. "I use'ta hang out with Kin in *The City* in the '60s, when I was laying low draft-dodging. She used to bend my ear about Heaven, Hell, Mr. C., all the little gods. What's on the other side of black holes, and freak knows what else. I told her, 'Little sister, there ain't nothing on the other side of black holes but the answers to all Death's little mysteries.' She would hang out at N.Y.T.S. and J.T.S., bugging the unholy crap out of the faculty. She never took a single course at either place mind you, but I swear, she understood the C-note better than I did- do. And bam, she drops that bomb on the world!" Keith concluded, pointing an accusing finger at the silk bundle. "Only went and started one of the largest theological arguments that humanity ever had."

"Is that the New York Theological Seminary and the Jewish Theological Seminary" Mick asked.

"Yeah, that's them," Keith agreed. "Arad was their most famous non-student either ever had."

"Why then have I never heard of her?" Mick asked as he unwrapped *Continuous Creation, by* Kin Arad. "And how did you know it was this book?"

Keith shrugged. "That book's got an aura about a kilometer wide to the *I-don't-want-to-be-clobbered-by-God* types like me. And, you were off saving the world from imperial capitalism at the time."

"What?"

Keith looked around the bar in the wake of the Angel's outburst. Almost everyone was looking at them.

"I was fighting against the godless Communists, thank you," Mick said icily. "I was Chief American Strategic Advisor to the Diem government concerning the Rural Community Development Program and Strategic Hamlet Program, which was-"

"A complete fucking failure," Keith said and raised his bottle of Everclear to the Angel in a mock toast.

The Angel sat silently looking at his undrunk espresso. Something that looked very much like a roach floated in it.

The Demon continued; "Kick people out of their homes, take away their land, put them into concentration camps, yeah, that'll win hearts and minds every time."

"Nguyễn Ái Quốc was stealing everything as he came along, biggest robber in history," Mick said. "The hamlets actually helped prevent that."

"Bigger than Uncle Joe? He stole entire countries ya know, and not even just the ones he grew-up in."

"Knock it off."

"So you stole for Nguyễn Văn Thiệu, instead, is that it?"

"Nope," Mick said with a manic grin. "Look, I've got a place all picked out for the humanity reboot."

Keith looked again at the book. "We'll get into trouble for this, serious trouble. You know, false gods. The Big Guy can be a downright prat about that. I watched Him bitch-slap the Demon James once. Took decades to find all his teeth."

"No souls," Mick said getting to his feet. "If we don't give anyone any souls, then it's just moving molecules around, right? Think of it like a huge Pinocchio feast, Collodi style."

"No, definitely not," Keith said. "See you around the Cosmos. Better yet, I'll not see you around the Cosmos."

"It'll be just like T.V.," Mick said playing his last card.

It was a long shot, but both the Angel and the Demon had spent most of the history of humanity on Terra, and had been actively involved in cultural movements throughout history. They had instinctively gravitated to Hollywood after the founding of the Nestor Studios in 1911. They had moved seamlessly from Vaudeville to radio to films and finally to television. Later evolutions such as streaming media and live Simulated Reality Facilities were really just T.V. on steroids.

"More like an S.R.F. than T.V.," Keith mused. "Live-action so to speak. Giant planetary scale L.A.R.P., but a giant 1 to 1 scale model."

"No life, no problem," Mick said. "It's not given to the likes of us to create. Couldn't do it if we wanted to."

"I don't want any trouble," Keith said. "I've spent the last several thousand years trying to contract alcoholism just to avoid trouble. I just can't get the hang of it."

"It's the lack of metabolism," Mick agreed. "A real bugger that. No problems cross my heart." The Angels crossed his heart X-fashion.

"You haven't got a heart," Keith said. "Neither do I."

The Angel crossed the spot where his heart wasn't a second time and winked.

"Right," Keith said slowly. "Oh well, what the Hell? It's not as if I've got cable anymore. Let's go see this place."

Both the Angel and the Demon stood, turned, and stopped abruptly, confronted by the figure of an elderly black man standing just behind them.

It is very hard to sneak up on card-carrying members of the Celestial armies, even one with a dishonourable discharge. Neither the Angel, nor the Demon, concealed their surprise well.

161

Keith began to protest, but the old man held up one hand with a palm that resembled the cracked and shattered surface of an asteroid.

"I want to come with you," the old man said.

"Look," Mick said uncomfortably. "We're not really looking for any partners or anything."

"Nevertheless, you have both partnered with each other," the old man said.

Something bothered Keith about the old man; something that he couldn't quite put his mental finger on.

"No, really," Mick said. "We don't need, or want any help."

"You will, come the end," the old man said. "Not that you will pay any attention before then."

"I told you, we don't-"

"You will take me," the old man said.

"And who are you to give orders to one of His servants?" the Angel demanded.

The old man simply smiled.

"It's Chuku, isn't it?" Keith asked after finally arriving at what he just realized was his worst nightmare since the War at Armagedōn.

The old man nodded. "I prefer Chukwu, with the w-sound at the end," Chukwu the Creator Aspect said, "You will need my help."

Keith shot a look over to Mick as if to say 'Well, it's your party.'

The look Mick returned clearly said 'I knew we shouldn't have met here.'

"You don't even know what we are doing," Mick said.

"I have sat and listened these last few minutes," Chukwu said. "You are going to start everything all over again. You will need me to reboot humanity."

"Why?" Keith asked.

"It's my last job," Chukwu said.

"I thought all the Aspects were collected up," Mick said while giving the self-proclaimed Creator Aspect that long and steady look that had in bygone days reduced hardened Human criminals to soppy Human turncoats.

Chukwu, the Creator Aspect, said nothing.

Keith looked from one to another of them, tapped his toes, cleared his voice in a meaningful way, and finally got completely bored. It took about fifteen seconds.

"All right," Keith said. "Enough of this *my prick is better than your prick* stuff. I had enough of that crap when the Legions of Hell were all hanging out after losing at Armagedōn. I won't have it. Shake hands and let's get on with it before anyone else turns up to play spoilers too."

Chukwu put out his hand for the Angel.

Mick shook it, and for one brief instance had a vision of wondering through a storm, screaming at Heaven, with both Keith and Mōt chasing after him. As soon as the Angel let go of the Creator Aspect's hand, the vision was gone.

Keith clapped them both on the back. "Great," he said. "Just like the bad old days when everyone trusted each other and got along. One big happy family. Now, let's get."

Mick shrugged off his discomfort, made the interstellar sign for waving down a taxi - which consisted of waving used bank notes in the air, and the triumvirate was gone.

All that remained was one small roach, which already missed its own personal Demon. Life had been good with Keith, and now the roach would have to learn how to read in a hurry if it wanted to ensure its continued long life.

"Damn, no thumbs," the roach thought.

After a while, Basil Berry walked into the bar, and picked up three unopened bottles of Everclear, a bag of espresso beans, and the roach.

Chapter 7: Tafari

On the planet Tafari, in the Babirye Binary system, orbiting the Babirye Beta star.

Then the Creator said, "Let us make man in our image, after our likeness. And let them have dominion over the fish of the sea and over the birds of the heavens and over the livestock and over all the Earth and over every creeping thing that creeps on the Earth."   --Genesis 1:26

And it came to pass that the stage was set, the rehearsals began, and nobody but the Director noticed.

Creatures of the Celestial interstellar hierarchies, be they Immortal or just immortal, are not really part of the material universe in the same way that Humans, pigs, and dolphins are. So it was no inconvenience to them that the planet Tafari, third rock from the duel binary stars called Babirye, was a dust bowl.

"This is bloody inconvenient," Keith complained. "Why the Hell did you pick this spot Angel? You can't very well stage an epic drama in a place like this."

The planet Tafari, which will one day soon will become the foundation of Tafari City and hub to a large portion of the the Infinity Plane, was the third of twenty-seven planet-sized rocks orbiting the dual suns called Babirye, which were very close to the center of the universe. Tafari was mostly composed of grey dust, grey volcanic rock, and immensely large depressions that might have, millions of years ago, contained oceans. In short, it was the perfect place to build the central hub of a massive future-tech civilization.

"I thought that it would be nice," Mick said. "You know, humanity always thought that they were the center of everything. Well, Tafari is the actual center of the universe."

"And it turned out *they* were right too, Humans were the center of everything useful," Keith grumbled. "I thought it was a black hole at the center of the universe, but what do I know?"

"Well, this is the actual geographical center of the universe," Mick said, ignoring the Demon's inconvenient truth. "Well, the stars are, not the planet."

"No," Chukwu said. "The space between the Babirye twins is the center of this universe. Except for the black hole, which is where the Ishtar Gate is."

The Angel glared at Chukwu in bitter silence.

Keith wondered if that was the same gate as the one that was in Babylon.

"So, this dump is the center of the *inhabitable* universe?" Keith asked breaking the silence. "Well, could be worse," Keith continued with a careless shrug that almost concealed his carefully stepping between the Angel and the Creator Aspect's staring contest. Keith turned the Angel away from the contest, which he was losing. Keith hadn't seen Chukwu blink yet, and he'd been watching for it ever since he met the creature. Keith didn't like things that didn't blink. Even Demons blinked every few minutes.

"Where did you get this book anyway?" Keith asked flipping through the pages.

Chukwu sat down, crossed his legs, and began idly drawing with one finger in the grey dust.

"It's total claptrap. Seriously. I mean, listen to this," Keith said and started quoting from *Continuous Creation,* by Kin Arad. "*Finally, a planet is not a world. Planet? A ball of rock. World? A four-dimensional wonder. On a world, there must be mysterious mountains. Let there be bottomless lakes peopled with antique monsters. Let there be strange footprints in high snowfields, green ruins in endless jungles, bells beneath the sea; echo valleys and cities of gold. This is the yeast in the planetary crust, without which the imagination of men will not rise.*"

"Yeah, what's the problem?" Mick asked.

The Demon glared at the Angel for a very long moment while Chukwu continued drawing in the ash with his finger.

"You can't run a universe like that," Keith finally said. "Like I told ya, Kin Arad was a nutter."

"We don't need to run a universe," Mick said. "All we have to do is manage things here, on this planet. And I got the book from Hatshepsut."

Chukwu who had been forming small green planets out of the grey dust of the planet's surface looked up.

"What? That old insane Egyptian queen from the bad old days?" Keith asked in astonishment. "She's got to be deader than an Angel's conscience by now. How is that old biddie? I set her up in government service you know."

It should be noted here that Demons, like Angels are not exceptionally more intelligent than anything else, no matter how it seems to mere mortals. It is just that most of them have been hanging around for millions and millions and millions of years and have consequently gotten to know more than a few people. "People" of course is being used here in its most loose sense. It also helps that Angels and Demons are immune to brain degeneration or forgetting anything.

"That's nice," Mick said mildly. "And yes, they're all dead, that's the problem. And no, it wasn't from her. I got it from Hatshepsut Nefertari Djeserit Fukayna, last Scion of Sešat."

"Oh Hat," Keith said. "Why didn't you just say so? How is that slightly less old biddie?"

"Doing rather well, I guess," Mick said taking the book back from the Demon. "She's in charge of the Angelic Archives Department at the Elysion Library, and she's managed to find work for the rest of the Scion Tycoons too. She's more or less their official unofficial leader."

167

And that wasn't an easy job either considering how many Scions there were. In the latter days of the late 20th and early 21st centuries, there was a revival of the practices of immortals breeding with mortals and producing offspring, which are called Scions. Many theories abound as to why after thousands of years of not getting off with mortals, the gods suddenly and collectively took on mortal lust again. But the generally accepted answer is that it was due to boredom. You can only wait so long for the Apocalypse, and even the most diehard believers in the Creator among the gods were beginning to wonder when it was all going to end?

Another theory suggests that the small handful of the gods decided to increase their personal powers by conceiving children and then forcing the half-godlings to sacrifice themselves to their god-parent. The American gods fought the epic mini-gods war at Lookout Mountain following this principle. The war turned out badly for just about everyone; but still the idea is valid, if for no other reason than the evidence of the shadow war at Lookout Mountain.

The Scion Tycoons, like all other Scions, were all one part immortal and one part mortal, and their parents, on either side, generally ignored them. And it came to pass that a loose association of these half-Celestial beings formed the ancient order of the Scion Tycoons, which didn't do much besides organize *Save the Library* picnics and occasionally save the world until the invention of the internet.

Hat, who could pull virtually any book or scroll out of thin air, took to the internet as a duck takes to complaining about geese, and made a fortune in the Dot Com Bubble. Hat, whom made millions out of the bubble, was arrested, tried, and convicted on charges of insider trading, but her case was dismissed on appeal.

The appeals came from the highest levels of government and the judiciary branch, many of whom had received anonymous manilla envelopes; each containing twenty seven eight-by-ten colour glossy photographs with circles and arrows and a paragraph on the back of each one explaining what each one was and how it was to be used in the event that Hat ever had to spend one single second in prison. Hat was later quietly given a full pardon by the President of the United States, the PM at Number 10, and the President of the People's Republic.

"May I see that book?" Chukwu asked.

Mick shrugged and tossed Chukwu the book.

"Can we do a flat-world?" Keith asked. "I've always wanted to see a bunch of guys sail off the side of the world and explode in the vacuum. It'd be wicked mad fun."

"Na," Mick said with a sigh. "The Spindles did the flat-world thing already."

"Alright then, how about a trapezoid?" Keith asked throwing his hands up over his head to form a pointed edge.

"No."

"How about an icosahedron then?"

"What's the difference between a 20-sided cube and a sphere?" Mick asked.

"We can play dice with the 20-sided planet," Keith said making gestures as if he was throwing craps.

"I mean, after you put on the mountains and everything, it won't matter much, will it?" Mick asked. "Look the same, wouldn't it?"

Keith deflated.

"An Infinity Plane," Chukwu said. "An infinite flat world, a flat universe, infinitely expanding on the horizons of infinity, never beginning, never ending. Indestructible."

Keith looked at Mick.

Mick looked at Keith.

They both turned to look at Chukwu. They had both forgotten that Chukwu was there.

Chukwu sat cross-legged upon a patch of lush green grass that extended past his body for a couple of meters in every direction. Chukwu was shaping what appeared to be a large Bonsai tree, standing about a meter above the grass. The gnarled curls of the root system alone suggested that the tree was hundreds of years old already. The detail though suggested that the tree was in reality much larger but had been compressed in space. Kin Arad's book sat beside Chukwu on the grass.

Keith saw an absurdly tiny snow-white owl sitting on a Bonsai branch.

"What the Hell is that?" Mick asked.

"It's a Sequoia sempervirens," Chukwu said without looking up.

"Uh huh," Mick said.

"I always called them California Redwoods," Keith said removing his gaze from the small owl. "We had them all over Cali when I was there last. I hear they didn't fare so well in the Succession War of 2525."

Chukwu shrugged.

"What's an infinity plane?" Mick asked.

"Do you want math in your answer?"

"No."

"Think of your world being flat, at the base-line, but that it never ends," Chukwu said. "Think of it going on infinitely in all directions in a 3-dimensional space.

Mick thought about it for a moment and frowned.

Keith thought about it for a moment and smiled.

Mick thought, how would you get a sun to orbit an infinity plane? What would the sun go around if the planet extended in all directions? A star couldn't orbit infinity, could it? Would you just have a long line of suns moving along at intervals, like a solar Can-can line?

Keith thought about every video game he'd ever played that lined up armies of little digital men that marched against other little armies of cyber men. In every single one of those games, you eventually ended up running into a big black wall that you couldn't move past. Even games that were played on a "globe" where you could curl around the map from the Atlantic Ocean to the Pacific Ocean usually never let you go over the poles. If America were going to attack Russia for example with ICBMs, they wouldn't fly the missiles to Poland first. They'd just shoot them up over Canada and rain 'em down into the Motherland.

"I love it," Keith agreed.

"I hate it," Mick disagreed. "How would you get the stars to shine light upon the surface if they can't orbit the planet?"

"Oh, that's simple enough," Keith said. "You just line them up at the intervals you need, and there you go."

"And days."

"Hmm," Keith said. "Put a planet really close to the sun yeah, and have that orbit the sun. The shadow from the planets would create a night."

The Angel glared at the Demon.

"Wouldn't work," Mick said flatly. "Even Mercury takes 89 days to travel around the sun. It'd never work."

"Well, we can always do Around the Sun In 80 Days," Keith said.

"90," Mick corrected.

"Okay, make it a really large asteroid belt that," the Demon said. "You'd get the break you need at whatever intervals you needed for days and nights that way."

171

"No," the Angel said.

"Why?" asked Chukwu, returning to designing Tafari's first tree. "Just make it so that there is light. Was it not written that the Creator said 'Let there be light, and there was?' Let the mortals figure it out later. They are good at that figuring it out thing. And the best part is that they won't think that it can't be done, because it will have always been done that way all their lives."

"It just won't work," Mick said wearily.

Has that tree gotten bigger since I've been watching it? Keith wondered.

"Why not?" Chukwu persisted.

"Well, science, for one thing," Mick started.

"Astrophysics for another," Keith added, still eyeing the tree.

"So?" Chukwu asked forming a face in the bark of the base of the tree.

"Look, you just can't do that," Mick said. "The universe won't allow it-"

"Have you ever met a talking tree?" Chukwu asked.

"Not sober," Keith cut in ahead of the Angel's rising temper. "I got good and pissed before I went in to see the second *Lord of the Rings* movie. It was bloody brilliant until I realized I'd been out back for a couple of hours talking to trees in my yard."

Chukwu smiled.

"I remember that," he said.

The Demon frowned, but said nothing. He wasn't sure if Chukwu had meant that he'd seen the movie, or Keith being drunk that night. Either way, he didn't think he wanted to know.

"Science just won't have it," Mick said in a level tone designed for intimidating school-children and fundamentalists.

"Science," Chukwu said, "is merely a method of explanation. Do not confuse method with design, or explanation with truth. Humans had a rather messy and needlessly organic method for reproducing themselves, but that had virtually nothing to do with their method, or more precisely, their purpose. Neither one begets the other. In the same way, science explains the universe's methods of existence, but tells you nothing about why or where it came from."

"The Big Man twisted up this huge wad of bubble wrap and wham, here we were," the Demon said.

"That wasn't how it went," the Angel complained. "I remember-"

"You remember nothing," Chukwu said. "In the beginning, there was only the Metatron." The old man lapsed into silence as his hands slowly stopped running over the branches of the tree. Then he visibly shook himself and added, "And one very scared and confused man.

"Asteroids of Infinity," Keith exclaimed.

"What?" Mick asked, grateful for a chance to have something else to focus on besides the Creator Aspect, who was clearly insane.

"That's the game that didn't have borders. If you went off in any direction, you came right back to the other side. Top, bottom, diagonals, it never mattered."

"What?" the Angel asked, a hint of pleading crept into his voice. "I don't understand what you are on about."

"Think of it like this," Chukwu said using his right middle finger to dig a small lake next to Tafari's first California Redwood tree.

The grey dust slowly transformed itself into brown earth when it came into contact with the water.

"Instead of the traditional people on the outside of the sphere-"

"Icosahedron," Keith said.

"Three dimensional shape of your choice," Chukwu altered smoothly. "Have your people live on the inside of the three dimensional shape of your choice, and populate the hollow center with stars, and planets, and black holes. Essentially, put people on the ever-expanding physical boundary of the entire cosmos. Think of it as an ever-expanding Dyson Sphere with billions and billions of stars instead of just one."

"That's not how it really works," Mick complained.

"Are you sure?" Chukwu asked. "I don't think an Angel has ever even been to the end of this universe or any other universe. I don't think any of the immortals have ever been to the end of the universe either."

And it was true, none of them had. It wasn't allowed. He, Capital H, He, didn't allow that.

Mick had never really thought about the ban, or even why it was banned. It had never seemed to matter until now. It was just one of those odd things that the Creator said don't do, and he'd grown old not doing.

Even the Demons respected the ban.

Well, all of the Demons and the immortals, except the Demon James of course. Who, instead, occupied his time testing the Creator's patience in any way he could think of, including suggesting to Lilith that she might enjoy Adam's company and frequently traveling to the end of the universe and beyond.

"Have you been to the end of our universe Chukwu?" Mick asked.

Chukwu said nothing, only continued designing the face in the base of the tree.

"I said, have you ever been-"

"Put a nebula about 80 millions of kilometres up over The Infinity Plane," Chukwu said while drawing in

174

the ash. "Have the nebula pulse light down at regular intervals to the surface. Maybe you won't get as much darkness in your Infinity Plane night as you do on Terra, but that will hardly matter in the long view. And on an Infinity Plane, that would be a really long view."

Keith heard the capital letters, thrice, and knew that whatever the Angel said now wouldn't matter. The decision had been made, and whatever it was that the trickster spawn had wanted had just gone off the rails too.

Bloody Hell, the Demon thought, bloody fucking Hell.

"Now," the Creator Aspect continued, "we have our flat Infinity Plane here, semi-stationary moons about say 240,000 kilometres up from sea level, just let the nebula pulse light waves back to The Infinity Plane. You'd get irregularities sure, but it wouldn't be any more irregular than say seasonal variation or solar flares. Now working out seasons on an Infinity Plane, that would be tricky."

Damn, three times again, Keith thought. Once more and we'll have a trinity of thrices. No, no, no.

"Why not just put the nebula up at the Kármán Line?" Keith asked, stalling for time.

"The Kármán Line is only the distance from Terra's sea level to the Aurora and the Thermosphere," Chukwu said.

"Outer space?" Mick asked.

"More or less," Keith said absent-mindedly. "It's actually the upper-most layer of any planet's atmosphere, but the ultraviolet radiation would fry a human if they were to hang-out there. I think the Kármán Line on Mercury is ground level."

"Put the neb-web-thing out around Aphrodite," the Angel said.

"Say Venus," the Demon said, "Gaius won the contest, and you know it. And he who owns it, names it."

And for perhaps the first time in the entire novel, the Demon spoke absolute truth. Mick had bet the then Senator Gaius Julius the former planet Aphrodite against the Senator's retirement from politics that the Senator couldn't drink the Angel under the table. The Demon watched in bemused admiration as the future little god ordered 100 men to jump the Angel so the Senator could chop off the Angel's hand. As the Angel screamed Hell and damnation and his hand regenerated on its bloody stump, Senator Gaius Julius calmly drained the Angel's blood into a goblet of wine, crawled under a table, and drank. Thus, the Senator drank the Angel under a table.

"That little Matzah ball cheated."

Keith shrugged.

"Lunar lives around 240,000 kilometres above Terra," Chukwu continued as if nothing had happened. "And Venus lives 38 millions of kilometers from her friend Terra."

"But why even have planets at all?" Mick asked. "If this idea of yours is this flat world-"

"Flat Universe," Chukwu corrected.

"Flat thing," the Angel said, "why should there be planets at all? The new people won't need to bother with space, they'll never run out of resources, they'll just move on like legionary marabunta."

"Pardon?" Chukwu asked.

"Ravenous army ants," Keith translated. Or insane women, he added in the privacy of his own head. Was it actually private in here? Stop it; you'll end up talking to yourself if you go on like that. People will think you're a mental, or a writer, or something. The Demon took several deep controlled breaths to steady his nerves. It didn't work.

"Ah, I see," Chukwu said.

"Your new people might not make it out of the hunter-gather stage then, if they just keep moving on," Keith observed. "Never any lack of animals to hunt, you'll never need to bother with agriculture, no motive to evolve society, civilization, or-"

"Espresso beans" the Angel interjected sharply.

"Ah, yes, but no, I was thinking of a lack of movies," the Demon said.

"Is it not written that the imagination of men *must* rise?" Chukwu asked. "Has not this prophet of words not shown us the way?"

Keith turned away from Chukwu and looked over the ashen dunes for a long time, while the Angel counted backward from infinity. The Demon would have rather done several million other things than look at the Creator Aspect just then.

Keith watched as a golden ray of light crested the largest dune, raising highlights of purple and dark green that the Demon had not seen before.

And so it came to pass that the Demon Keith did squelch. Annoyed, the Demon looked down and saw water running around his shoes. The Demon moved to dryer ground, and it was ground, not ash.

"Okay, that'll do," Keith agreed. "We'll call it the Never Ending Nebby."

"A good story neither has a beginning, nor an ending," Chukwu said. "And look," he added pointing up at the sky, "Tafari planet already has seven moons of its own."

"Spoken like a true pulp-fiction writer," Keith said. "Man, would I have loved to have been your agent back in the day."

Chukwu smiled.

"It would never work," Mick complained, annoyed at himself for doing nothing besides

177

complaining. But the whole thing had gotten away from him now, and he knew it. "All the gravity and science and stuff wouldn't work on account of the world being flat; the whole thing would be about little jello-people. And who cares about jello-people?"

The Demon and the Creator Aspect carried on ignoring the Angel.

"Because we ain't," Mick continued rising his voice to drown out the chattering of the Creator Aspect and the Demon, "designing a new fracking universe. This is supposed to be a movie set, not a pretentious coffee shoppe conversation about how the *Creator totally could have done it this way if He'd had any imagination!*"

"No," Chukwu said to Keith ignoring outburst. "Space and Time all curve, no matter how flat anything seems. Give enough space and it will curve to make a gravity well. That bit's built in see, like numbers. You can't change that. But, you can have jello-people, if you like. Anything is possible. Take Kérberos for example, he shouldn't be able to walk with three brains controlling four legs, but-"

"Hold on a minute," Keith interrupted and turned to Mick. "What sort of story are we going to have here? On this world, in this new universe, I mean."

Mick frowned. He had not really thought about that. He had not really expected Keith to go along with the idea, and he certainly hadn't expected to be saddled with a rogue Creator Aspect. Mick didn't like Chukwu, and really wanted him to go away.

"All right," Keith said settling down into the ever spreading green surface on the dusty planet of Tafari. "Let's start with the basics, shall we? What kind of life are we talking about here?"

"People, I guess. Humans," said the Angel, kicking a clump of ash that had fused together after getting wet for the first time in millions of years. The Angel noted with interest how the clump drifted on long after it should have returned to the surface of the planet. "We need to fix the gravity here too," he mumbled.

"Well, I don't know if we can do living people," the Demon said. "Not genuine paid-up Humans."

"No Zombies," the Angel said abruptly. "Those things are an abomination unto the-"

"Right, no Zombies," the Demon agreed quickly. "Don't know what the Big Guy has against them, but okay, no Zombies. I guess we can do super natural people then?"

"No, I was given very clear instructions that," Mick began and then stopped.

"Instructions?" Keith asked. "We working for someone?"

"No," the Angel said primly. "I misspoke."

"Sure you did."

"I did," the Angel continued ignoring the leer on the Demon's face. "What I meant to say was that the instructions I have read in the books that Hat the youngest gave me were rather clear, and I would like to follow that template, thank you. So no super naturals."

"Okay," Keith said checking off one finger. "People, Humans, Human non-Zombies to be specific. What tech level? Are we talking about Merlin in Detroit; cowboys in space, merry men in Sherwood, or 20,000 fathoms under the dust bowl?"

"Why do we have to choose?" Mick asked.

"To live is to choose," Chukwu said wearily. "After all these years, even I understand that."

"How very Zen of you," Mick said bitterly.

After all these years, even I understand that? Keith wondered at that for a micro-second and than it was gone.

Chukwu looked up and grinned. "Is it not written that trees can't talk?"

"No, that's not written anywhere," Mick said, exasperation marching across his face in tiny little well-ordered formations.

"Wrong," Keith said. "It's in *Time's Gardening for Novices*, chapter 17, paragraph 3, verse 2. Says; "Trees can't talk, and stop asking the editor daft questions, and by the way, layoff the pot buddy."

Before Mick could respond, Chukwu bent down and lightly touched the nose of the tree. At the instant, the finger of the Creator Aspect left the tree, two knobby stumps opened to reveal deep jade green eyes. Barky lips parted slightly, allowing centuries of gas to escape in a long low wheeze that sounded like the weary sigh of a Professor that was about to explain to a student why cutting and pasting 10-pages from a website was still plagiarism, even if the student had listed the source website in the Works Cited.

"Nice," Keith said. "I've never been able to do that. I can only bring them back, or help them grow. I can't actually make anything by myself. Will you teach me that one?"

Chukwu shook his head.

"Damn," Keith said. "What I could do with that trick. Whole new fracking lines of organic herbal relaxation aids, new wines, an 8th colour, tea that doesn't taste like hot water strained through weeds. The profit margin would be dizzying. I always wanted to be the universe's first octillionaire."

Chukwu nodded, stood up, and swept the book up and into his pocket while the Angels were looking at Tafari's first sentient tree.

Keith noted with very mild surprise, the book was suddenly just that bit smaller and fit neatly into Chukwu's pocket. Yes, Keith thought, off the rails and heading for the next universe at speed. Better get back to that house and collect things before that third thrice hits.

180

"And it was said unto me," the tree said, "I shall make from you many seeds, and you shall be more numerous than the stars in the sky, and I shall make of you a great forest, and-"

The Angel stood, struck dumb by a metaphor, his mouth a gapping cliché O of surprise.

"Oh no, no, no," Keith said running over to Chukwu, but stopping just short of touching the Creator Aspect. "No talking trees, no way. Not here. That's just daft."

Chukwu laughed, turned, and walked away from both the Angel and the Demon, leaving little patches of moist brown soil behind him wherever he stepped.

Mick noticed that the Creator Aspect was not wearing or carrying shoes. Had he been wearing shoes in the bar? Mick couldn't remember.

Keith took a deep, audible breath, and turned away from the Creator Aspect to the tree.

"Okay, silly buggers it is then," Keith said in an uncharacteristically flat voice. "So tree, what's your name, tree?" the Demon added forcing a jovial and conversational tone into his voice.

"Hmmm," the tree hmmmed. "I seem to remember being called just a tree."

"All right, Just-a-tree," Keith said, "you're in-charge of trees, acorns, and forests, and so on. Go forth and reclaim the land."

"It will take a long time," Just-a-tree said.

"Time is the one thing we seem to have plenty of," Keith said. "A marked lack of common sense though, that I'll grant we don't have."

"How many," Just-a-tree wheezed.

"How many trees?"

"Yes."

"One, two, many, lots," the Demon said. "As many as possible. You'll have people along to deal with soon enough."

"Can I kill them?"

"Only if they have axes, no wait, make that only if they use axes or start fires," the Demon said standing up and brushing dirt, honest to Creator dirt, off his pants.

I'm talking to a fucking tree, the Demon thought. I wonder if I've fallen and I can't get up? Coma maybe? Never heard of a Demon in a coma. Doesn't mean it can't happen. Can it happen? Surely not—don't call me Shirley. Wha'choo talkin' 'bout, Willis? And Keith carried on with several pages of internal profanity that is not really necessary to relate here.

Just-a-tree closed his eyes, and began to hum in a soft deep tone that made the Demon feel young for the first time in, how long was it? A million years maybe?

How long has it been? Keith wondered, since I did anything fun? Saw a movie, or went swimming or something. I've just been sitting in the bar for about the last-

"A word Keith?" Mick said, interrupting the Demon's thoughts.

"Hmm? Oh, yes, what is it spoilsport?"

"Chukwu has got to go," Mick said. "I don't like him at all."

"What, this planet not big enough for the two of you?"

"No, it's not that," Mick said wishing that the Demon would stop being so dense. "Chukwu's a Creator Aspect. You know, an aspect of Him. You know, the *He* that is *Him*, Him."

"Yeah, so?"

"He's a spy, damn it," Mick shouted.

The words echoed oddly on the dusty planet.

Keith looked his old friend up and down. The Angel looked worried, agitated, and completely lacking in cool. Well, all right, nobody could look cool in a khaki trench raincoat.

"Tell me something Angel?" Keith said. "Just how long did you think you could keep any of this a secret?"

Mick looked around. Except for Just-a-tree, and a few patches of moist footprint-shaped bits of dirt, the entire planet looked like a monochromatic study in grey waves of ashen dunes. Mick half expected a large grey personal carrier to come over the horizon accompanied by any of the musical compositions of John Williams.

John Williams is one of a small handful of completely normal mortals that are mentioned in the *Prognosticated Peerage*:

> **John Williams**: Perhaps the most influential musical composer of all time, and certainly on the short-list for all-time best musical composer of the entire history of Humankind. Williams' vast set of accomplishments include such popular musical scores as the theme music for "Daddy-O" in 1958, "Goodbye, Mr. Chips" in 1969, "Fiddler on the Roof" in 1971, "The Poseidon Adventure" in 1972, "Empire of the Sun" in 1987, "Jurassic Park" in 1993, "Memoirs of a Geisha" in 2005, "War Horse" in 2011, and the film adaptation of "Sushi to Go," by Dr. Fukayna" in 2020. Williams' ability to invoke within the Human mind deep seated feelings of love, fear, compassion, and inspiration has been single-handedly responsible for glossing over the shortcomings of many an otherwise famed writer. If asked for an example of the sort of person that Heaven should have let at the Celestial organ, the Demon Keith would have undoubtedly mentioned John Williams right after Jimi Hendrix.

"You didn't think at all, did you?" Keith asked, poking Mick in the shoulder.

"No, not really," Mick admitted.

"All right," Keith said waving an exact copy of the Pyramid of Khufu into existence. "Glad we got that out of the way."

The Angel's jaw, only slightly recovered from before, dropped again. Even Celestial immortals, famously unflappable, aren't really prepared to see a million tons of stone appear out of nowhere. The local atmosphere pressure change causes the ears to pop for one thing.

"What?" Mick gasped. "I thought you said you couldn't create?"

"Life man, I can't create life. Things, no problem. I'm a regular Djinn out of ye-old-faithful magic lamp on things. Tempting with terribly terrific things is totally my treasure trove of trouble remit."

"How long have you been waiting to use that one?" Mick asked.

"Years man, years," the Demon grinned. "Sorry, alliterate almost always and- damn, never mind, got carried away again. Look, you go down there to the Pyramid of Khufu and have a good long think. I know you two were friends and all. Me, I'm going to hop back to my place and pick-up a few things."

Mick looked around. There was the Mastabas, and behind that the Funerary Temple of Khafre. Mick turned and was not surprised to see the Tomb of Hermon, the Western Cemetery, and even the late 21st century Ticket Office. The last of which the Angel rather thought spoiled the effect.

"Don't ya think you over did it a bit bringing the tourist ticket office?" Mick asked

Keith shrugged.

"That's what we do," he agreed. "Or, *over do*, if you like. No half-measures on our side. Give us what we want or we blow-up the economy. What the Hell do we care? Completely immune to starvation, disease, sleep depravation-"

"And just what do you need to pick-up at your place?" Mick asked eyeing the Demon, and half expecting him to sprout horns and a tail.

"Oh, just a few antiques I've been holding onto since the dawn of time," Keith said airily. The Demon failed to mention that he has also been steadily adding to his collection most days since the first sunrise. "Just a couple of old movie scripts, a few body parts, my complete collection of mammals, birds, fish, reptiles, amphibians, invertebrates, mystical creatures, and literary critics. I mean, shit, man, let's do this life thing and get on with it already."

Mick put an intense amount of conscious effort into controlling his expression. Not having hung around with Keith for eons upon eons had allowed Mick to get out of the habit of expecting the bizarre twists of conversation with the Demon.

"Literary critics?"

"Oh yes," Keith said tucking one arm under the opposite arm, and resting his chin on his free hand. "Nothing beats a literary critic for unprecedented dividends in evil amplification. The literary critic feels impelled- nay compelled- to comment on everything from literature to art to politics to sex to philosophy and all the time using such fuck-all polysyllabics that even Noah Webster is left scratching his head saying 'Well Hell, I really don't know either.' Your average literary critic is almost as bad as a good writing teacher for producing boring reading material."

In case you didn't know, Noah Webster, hated by schoolchildren everywhere, was a lexicographer, textbook publisher, English spelling reformer, political writer, editor, prolific author, and you guessed it- literary critic. His iconic work *A Compendious Dictionary of the English Language* in 1806, set the stage for the later publication of *An American*

Dictionary of the English Language, and finally simply *Webster's Dictionary*. With its emphasis on one singular spelling of any given word to the exclusion of all other possible forms of cultural context and pronunciation, Noah Webster did more to destroy regional dialects, vocabulary, and culture than three hundred years of radio, TV, and movies combined. Keith could not have been more proud of Noah if he had given birth to the rigid little bastard himself.

"That's utter nonsense," Mick said throwing his hands up in the air. "You're loony," he added tapping his forehead with his index finger.

"Watch it buster," Keith said. "I speak German sign language."

Mick stopped tapping his forehead and bit his thumbs instead.

"And let me ask you this, oh ye of little faith," Keith said as a big smile spread across his face. "What do you think the Admissions Consul at the Vienna Academy of Fine Arts would have done with Hitler's two applications had they known what was in store for them with him in political life instead of art school? Of course if Alois hadn't beaten his son unmercifully for wanting to be a Jewish-fagot-artist, maybe the Admissions Consul might not have had cause to scrawl "unfitness for painting" on young and tender Adolf's portfolio."

"I don't buy it," Mick said. "That's parents and academics, not critics."

"And just whom do you think taught them to be so narrow minded, hmm? Priests maybe? Critics in dresses, your average priest," Keith purred. "It wasn't me. They willingly gave up the responsibility for thinking to the critics, philosophers, and priests long before I started fragging them."

"Well, I don't buy that it would have been better," Mick said, shuddering at the recollection of even a few of the memories of that time. He had spent most of his time in Northern Central Europe working

186

with the various undergrounds trying to get as many people out of harms way as he could. It was the children; always the children, that made Mick grieve. He hardly cared about the mobs of adults, most of who cheered for anyone in boots that could march in a straight line. The mobs cheered louder if the jackboots brought bread and penicillin.

"Well, you're right about that," Keith said breaking the spell of Mick's reflection. "It would have been a lot worse, Hell of a-lot-worse. Had old Adolf not taken over, it would have been Wilhelm Frick instead in the Fuhrer Chancellery. Frick would have worked the Hebrews to death in the arms industry rather them burned them up. In fact, Frick died pissed that so much Hebrew labour was wasted, particularly the physicists. I can tell you, Frick never would have only invaded half of France, friendly Vichy government, or not, he wouldn't have stopped until he had the seaport and ship-building dockyards of Bastia, Marseille, and Nice. Frick would have not invaded Russia until after the Allies were defeated, and peace was signed with America, not that he would have declared war on America in the first place. It would have been a worse war in Russia, longer I mean and more dead, but a winnable one for the Germans and an extinction event for the Russians."

"How do you know that?" Mick asked.

"I went to law school with Frick in Heidelberg and we stayed in touch until he swung for the Allies," Keith said with a shrug. "That was when I came up with never-ending intellectual copyright and perpetual royalties. Now look, you run along in there," Keith, continued indicating the Great Pyramid. "Have a good hot bath or something. Relax, let your mind wander, and figure out what you want to do with this dump. I'll be back before you miss me."

"You're coming back?" Mick asked looking over towards the Great Pyramid.

"Wouldn't miss it for the all dust on Tafari," Keith said and vanished.

What a bastard, Mick thought.

Chapter 8: Fruchtbarkeitskultus

Somewhere on the planet Tau Boötis Ab, in the Tau Boötis system.

There shall not be found among you any one that maketh his son or his daughter to pass through the fire, or that useth divination, or an observer of times, or an enchanter, or a witch. Or a charmer, or a consulter with familiar spirits, or a wizard, or a necromancer. For all that do these things are an abomination.   --Deuteronomy 18:10-12, K.J.V.

And it came to pass that all of humanity entered into the drama.

The first thing that Keith noticed upon arriving in the center of his exquisitely hand-worked silver inlaid pentagram back home was that it was broken. This point was driven home hard because the Demon materialized 3 meters above it, and then fell face first into the stone floor the pentagram was carved into.

The second thing that Keith noticed was Basil Berry sitting on Keith's elephant hide couch, with his Scion feet up on the trunk of children's teeth.

And no, that wasn't a euphemism. The *Prognosticated Peerage* entry is as follows:

> **Trunk of Teeth**: also called the Trunk of Mankind: This special item was "liberated" by Keith soon after the end of humanity from the Elves of Candyland. The Trunk was not only covered in Human baby teeth, but it also contained at least one tooth from every Human being since Adam and Eve, up to the last several tens of thousands of souls that had not yet gotten their teeth in, much less lost them when the Battle at Armagedōn commenced and ended in Humanity's extinction. Keith never

gave a particular reason for why he did this, although, it is generally assumed that it was because he was a collector. An alternative hypothesis put out by Basil Berry was that Ernie, King of the Elves of Candyland, owed Keith some serious blood money and forked over the Trunk of Teeth in exchange for not having his face beat in with a baking tray. The trunk is the only known complete collection of human genetic material. All 777-sextillion souls, from start to finish, have a tooth in the trunk. Strangely, it could be easily moved by one healthy, albeit muscular, human being.

The third thing that Keith noticed was that the bloody grandsire of Fárbauti was reading the final draft version of *Continuous Creation*, by Kin Arad.

"This ain't half bad," Basil Berry said, "for fiction I mean. Just cobbled bits of the original, plus a planetoid worth of fluff. Reminds me of my dissertation on 'The Geo-political Significance of *The Diary of a Nobody*, by the Grossmith Brothers as Providing Non-significant Psychological Markers; Thereby Artificially Prolonging the Post Post Modern War Upon the Individualism of-'"

"What in the name of Holiness are you doing here?" Keith demanded. "Bless it all, you're supposed to be looking after the Scions."

"I'm not sure about this Prime Directive bit, it's rather harsh," Basil Berry continued smoothly turning the 13th century Carta Bombycina paper page in its archivist grade gravity-field binder, which encased each page in a field strong enough to endure being in a black hole for several hours. "But I really like this Spencerian manuscript, that's your best touch. Too bad we won't need it now."

"I never liked the original handwritten manuscript plan anyway," Keith said as he picked up his reading glasses up off the trunk and glanced over the page. Then he reread it.

"I see what you mean, but it's still bullshit," Keith admitted. "Still, nobody ever obeyed it. Non-interference my pointy tail. All of bloody life is an interference of some kind."

"They still have a lot of fans around you know," Basil Berry said. "It never does to irritate people."

"Really?" Keith asked taking off his reading glasses and pointing them like a knife at his godson. "I repeat, what are you doing here?"

Basil Berry shrugged.

"Things have changed."

Keith looked down at the pentagram. The silver was broken through in seven places- seven places! Completely ruined.

"Yeah? How?" the Demon growled.

"Hat wanted me to check-up on you," Basil Berry said returning to the page he had been reading. "Seems you're even slower now than you were back in the day about checking in."

"Yeah well, I've been working and not in a bloody library either, I'm doing field work again, or had you forgotten?" Keith said moving to re-examine the pentagram damage. "Bloody academics. Not worth a pinprick of soldier blood the lot of them. Will ya just look at that," he added fingering the inlay. "You just cannot get native silver work like this anymore. The damned monkey-pigs are all dead now. I had this made well over a million years ago by the Quetzallians."

"The who?"

"Quetzallians. First people, first Human people. Well, first worth talking too. They were Aussies, back before the island ever got misplaced. First war caused the Tanami Desert. Each war after that caused a new desert. Very passionate people the Quetzallians were.

Damn shame too. Terra was a really nice place before civilization landed on it."

"Oh," Basil Berry said. "Before my time."

"Yeah," Keith agreed. "I totally got you beat in the years department. The rest of the world was settled by the Wankers that ran away from the Quetzallian Empire."

"Why'd they run?"

"You ever lived in an empire?"

Basil Berry shook his head.

"Well, let's put it this way," the Demon said. "You either help build the empire, or you get enslaved by the empire, or you get exterminated by the empire. And no, it doesn't matter if you're born into the empire, or conquered by it. Those are the only terms. It's just like working for *Mr. C.* You're on *His* team, or you run like hounds as far away as you can get, and hope *He* forgets you ever existed."

Basil Berry flipped down the paper that he was reading to reveal a slim face with round thin silver-rimmed spectacles perched upon a pointed nose, accompanied by raven hair, pearly white teeth, and cool grey eyes.

"I see you're still going for the pimp-librarian look," Keith said.

"It's a gig," Basil Berry said with a shrug. "I spend most of my time catching up on my sleep and filing the Standard Oil photo collection."

"That still hanging over your head? Damn," Keith said. "And I thought I was under motivated."

"Interest waned when I lost the stipend money on a double king showing. How the Hell was I supposed to know the Son was going to draw an 11 card 21? That's just not natural."

"And that's why I never play cards with that Kid," Keith agreed. "That's how I ended up working for the East London Christian Mission. Militant charity work. I miss those days."

"Hmmm?" Basil Berry hmmmed in a disaffected bored fashion.

"Yeah, never go drinking with the Son either. Be warned"

"Oh?"

"Yeah, last time," Keith said, "I'd this nice 1907 Heidsieck buzz, Shipwrecked vintage, last freaking bottle in the universe, right, and that Kid starts going on about how it will be several million years before the statistical average of children killed by drunk drivers will be less than 1 per year. And all of it like it was my fault. Fuck- I don't even drive- never ever have."

"Killed the buzz?" Basil Berry asked with obvious sympathy.

"Totally," Keith agreed. "And then- and then- He miracles the bottle into water and starts going on about how water is the most precious element in the universe-"

"Compound."

"That's what I told Him, it's a bleeding compound, hydrogen *and* oxygen- but no, *that Kid* keeps going on about the miracle of H-two-fraken-O and how nothing ever would have lived without water because of some design flaw in the carbon bonds and I tried to tell him that his *Old Man* could have just saved everyone the trouble and gone in for stamp collecting- but no, oh no, the next thing I know I'm single-handedly responsible for women never having had orgasms and I've never even been out on a date!"

"Bravo," Basil Berry said giving Keith a sitting ovation. "But I thought you'd known plenty of silent women."

"Oh, I've done plenty of bestial things with women. I've just never bothered to date any of them," Keith said and stormed off.

Basil Berry knew about the Demon Keith's financial backing of American Charles Francis Jenkins' project to develop the moving pictures Phantoscope and the sensation that was caused by Keith's use of the first fully functioning prototype to "document" the physical attributes, techniques, and queer tendencies of inner-city Jezebels.

Like Keith said, he passionately loved woman. He just preferred them to be silent.

A door opened. Followed by the sound of a Demon going down steps, followed by the sound of a Demon falling down steps.

"Did I mention the laundry?" Basil Berry asked no one. Another crash and Basil Berry said; "Guess not."

"What in the name of Heaven and Tafari is all this crap?" the Demon screamed from the basement.

"My laundry," Basil Berry said.

Basil Berry listened for a while to the strings of profanity that riffled up from the basement. A long string of Latin curses, followed by a longer string of German curses, a spattering of Korean curses, and then finally Dragon curses all reached Basil Berry's ears, giving the Scion a mild headache.

Small Demons and dark Shades appeared in the living room- invoked by every one of the Dragon curses. The invocations faded almost as quickly as they appeared.

Dragon is the best language for cursing, Basil Berry thought. You really get that nice combination of emphatic pathos coupled with sheer bloody-minded cruelty. You just couldn't beat Dragon for really wrecking someone's day. German comes close, but it just doesn't have the diversity of verbs that Dragon does.

Basil Berry wondered where the Dragons were now. He hadn't seen one in a very long time, not since the Vampire Wars at least, and that had been back before Armagedōn. It was so hard to keep track of time these days. Everyone seemed to experience it differently. One of the Angels had once tried to explain to him that the different experiences of time had something to do with the universe slowly starting to collapse on itself, but the Scion had dismissed it as utter rubbish.

You see, there is only one thing that both the Angels and the Demons are adamant about and it is this: they say that the original humanity all came and went about a million years ago. That is fine as far as it goes, which isn't very far at all, considering the source. The problem with talking to either Angels or Demons about time, or Time, is that they always turn around and try to introduce you to her. It's only slightly less difficult for you to talk to Angels and Demons about time because they just can't be bothered with it.

Angels and Demons, when tasked to do so, can move through time like hot pokers and clichés move through pretty much anything they like. So when either an Angel or a Demon says "About a million years ago," the only thing you can be certain about is that whatever time period they are actually referring to is past tense only in their own very special experience of time. What they are talking about as already having happened may still be in the future from the prospective of the listener. Whatever event the Angels and Demons are referring to might still be a million years in your future, while having happened to the Celestial immortal just yesterday. Or, it shall will have happened on the yesterday that comes after tomorrow.

And that, among other reasons, goes a long way toward explaining why time travel movies should never go to series, or worse, to television syndication.

Basil Berry fumbled a small crystal sphere out of his jacket pocket, huffed on it, polished it, and said, "Hey chickie, you there?"

Hat's young profile with a bun roll of hair, and bright eyes looked back at him. Her skin was a smooth creamy olive complexion that hinted of both the desert and the roaming hordes of Visigoths. She nodded. The lose curls of her hard hair rustled around her ears.

"He's here," Basil Berry said.

The face in the crystal nodded a second time.

"He's down in the basement," Basil Berry continued, "so I'm not 100% on what he's doing, but I would wager he's going for the D.N.A. samples."

A smile spread across the face that bespoke of wisdom and mischief that far outstretched the visible years of her face.

"Did you add in everything?" Hat asked.

"Yip, sure did, Boss-lady," Basil Berry said. "All the ancient creatures and the hybrids too as per Gatekeeper orders. And just for fun, I mixed most of them up, mislabelled hundreds, and added them in random places. It'll be fun to watch, I'm sure."

The face in the sphere rolled its eyes. Very few people in history have ever made a proper eye roll, usually favouring instead an upper half circuit of the eye socket. Hat's eyes though, made the full orbit of her eye sockets.

"Of course you did," she said. "I'm sure everyone's added their own little touches."

"And you?"

"Well," she said. "I made some rather judicious edits to the manuscript before the final print. I added a section lifted out of *Myth-Nomers* about how prolonged lifespans allow for the development of civilization proficiencies in both technology and magic, and about how shorter lifespans prevent individuals and thus societies from developing actual proficiency in either art. I double-downed by saying that people with shorter lifespans were more likely to be wasteful of environmental resources as they figured they wouldn't be alive to see the results of their laying waste to all the trees."

"Damn girl," Basil Berry said, "that's evil."

There was a knock at Keith's front door.

"Got to go old one," Basil Berry said, dropped the sphere back into his inner jacket pocket, and pushed himself up off the couch.

The front door at Keith's place had always impressed Basil Berry. The main thing that the front door did was announce that a working-class-made-good Under-lord of Hell had his digs there. The second and more important thing that the door did was keep a living record of Keith's major contributions to the health and welfare of the universe. The main center panel showed Keith scampering around The Garden whispering in the ears of several mammals that all had stupid grins on their faces. God alone knew what he told them, but then again, God alone sent Keith out on the job.

Basil Berry slid the wooden panel that was Keith's head aside and looked out the peephole.

On the other side of the door, a pale unhealthily skinny man in torn jeans and a dirty red New York Jets t-shirt looked at a pair of living eyes that had appeared in the door. The girl did not look much better, except that her jeans were tighter and her blue, white, and red halter-top shirt was shorter. But whatever joy that might have brought was assumed in the mass of brown ginger dreadlocks that reached down past the middle of her back. Small welts dotted her arms.

A tall mostly white feathered bird, crowned with a head of black feathers, and a long golden beak sat upon the girl's shoulder pecking insects out of her hair.

Basil Berry sighed and swung the door open.

"Hey Saki, Blossom," Basil Berry said. "Keith's down in the dungeon bitching up a storm. And Raven too? What a surprise. "

"I ain't no damned thrush knocking," Raven said, riding in on his beast of burden. The raven looked odd compared to his fellow fowl, being completely white below the neck. Its head was of the normal jet-black colour, but the lower half of his beak, wings, front and back, and legs were all snow-white.

"What a lucky day," Basil Berry said. "Two junkies and Raven. What the Hells happened to you, bird brain?"

"Would you believe that I got me pigment scared out of me?"

"Nope."

"Nutz."

"Hey, Raven; say *Nevermore*," Basil Berry said.

"You know what n-e-v-e-r means kid?" the Raven asked.

"Yeah."

"Well, blow it out your ear then," the Raven said. "I ain't no Hollywood whore no more. Messenger to the gods I am and always have been. Got a badge with a gold crown on it and everything. Ye are charged as a Scion to aid me in whatever way that you can."

"Hey bird."

"Yeah?"

"Blow it out your ear," Basil Berry said.

Raven grunted.

"Seriously though," Basil Berry said, "what the Hell *did* happen to you? I mean, you used to be all black, yeah?"

"Kid, you really lack in the tact department, you know that," Raven said.

Basil Berry shrugged.

"And you shrug way too much," Raven continued. "It's bad for your posture."

Basil Berry shrugged again.

"There's totally this guy that like owes me money," Blossom said to Basil Berry, "and as soon as he pays me, I'll pay you, like totally pay you back with cosmic karma interest."

"Tapped out Blossom," Basil Berry said. "I crapped out back at the Big Casino in the Sky. That's why I'm bumming it here."

"Oh man, that's righteous," Saki said. "Can we flop here too? We're on the run from the Angel Brigade."

Basil Berry shrugged and thought when are you not? He said; "Don't see why not. Keith's in an uproar though, fair warning. Keep your hands off his stuff and all that."

"Oh man, he's such a major drain," Saki said. "Major karma black hole that guy."

"I heard from a girl that was like banging his sister that Keith's getting into some really heavy major shit again," Blossom said. "Like he's going to go all the way, you know, carry on the defiance and stuff, like *The War*'s not over."

"You know what I heard?" Basil Berry said stepping closer to Blossom and lowering his voice.

Blossom and Saki both shook their heads and leaned closer. Raven lifted off Blossom's shoulder and beaked it for the rafters.

"The rumour in Heaven is that Keith's on the Holy take, that he's the main reason Heaven won," Basil Berry said. "Keith's been in deep cover for so long, he's forgotten who he really is. Who he really works for."

"No way man," Saki said. "That totally happened to me, I got pinched, and had to turn Heaven's Evidence. Damn, I wonder what they got him on."

"Trinity worship," Basil Berry said with an air of one imparting a major state secret. "Trinity worship."

"Oh man, he's a left footer? No way man," Saki said.

"He does have an impressive incense collection," Blossom said. "And he was totally incensed that time I lit them up too. Completely irrational. I mean, what you going to do after a three week Rave? Everybody stank."

"Shush now bébé," Basil Berry said sliding one hand around Blossom's hips, "Keith man's down stairs. He'll hear."

Blossom giggled.

"You old flirt," she said. "You're just as bad as your father."

"Worse," Basil Berry said with a grin. "You can always have a second helping of me."

"Hey man," Saki interrupted, "you got anything to eat around here man?"

Basil Berry gestured towards the kitchen.

"Oh wait," Blossom said tossing off Basil Berry's non-gesturing but ever questing arm. "I've got that book you wanted in my bag."

Basil Berry chuckled as he took the Angel Mick's copy, the universe's only authentic copy, of *How to Putte Questiones to the Dark and Understand Its Answeres* from his agent's hand.

"You know what this is little sister?" Basil Berry asked.

Blossom shook her head.

"It's the answers to all Fate's little mysteries," Basil Berry said. "How you lay hands on it?"

"Mewes and Smith lifted it off the Angel and swopped it for your faux copy when pricky Micky was coming out of the Elysion Library Coffee Shoppe."

"Brilliant babes, bloody brilliant," Basil Berry said and pulled Blossom in for an unrighteous snuggle.

Chapter 9: The Ghost in the Skull

In Keith's basement Hermetic Preserve on the planet Tau Boötis Ab, in the Tau Boötis system.

And Saul disguised himself, and put on other raiment, and he went, and two men with him, and they came to the woman by night: and he said, I pray thee, divine unto me by the familiar spirit, and bring me him up, whom I shall name unto thee. And the woman said unto him, Behold, thou knowest what Saul hath done, how he hath cut off those that have familiar spirits, and the wizards, out of the land: wherefore then layest thou a snare for my life, to cause me to die? And Saul swore to her by the Lord, saying, As the Lord liveth, there shall no punishment happen to thee for this thing. --1 Samuel 28:8-10, K.J.V.

And it came to pass the last true untranscended mortal was reincarnated.

Look down now, and see Keith, Under Lord of Hell, Healer, and Teacher, picking himself up off his basement floor. A pair of cobalt blue satin shorts, with a B. B. monogram, sliding off his Demon back.

Keith listened with only passing annoyance to the sound of additional voices in his upstairs living room. He had invited Raven around, and odds were on that the old messenger-bird would have dug up some low-life incarnation of something better-best-forgotten to ride here on. It was an aspect of the bird's personality that Keith had always found endearing. Raven would gladly spend 7 days working out how to ride 7 city blocks, a distance he could have flapped in about 7 seconds, on someone else's shoulder, rather than actually expend the energy to travel by his own effort. That level of laziness was what made Raven ideal as a Messenger of the gods, most of whom were even less punctual with answers, advice, or concern than the actual Creator Himself.

What annoyed Keith more at the moment was the lack of dust in a few spots on the shelves that contained his collection. Rows upon scores of rows of shelves expanded in all directions away from the base of the stairs. And upon each shelf stood, in neat rows, 7 books. And in each book, preserved as a study in bio-diversity preservation, were several hundred slides with different samples of every species of creature that ever roamed, slithered, flew, or just existed on Terra.

Except the cockroaches, who were from Dictyoptera. But Keith catalogued and preserved them too.

Keith had complained several times over the course of the eternity to anyone that would listen that; "Mr. Big might have told Adam to name the damn things, but I'm the one that had to catalogue every bloody thing. Did I get a mention in the story? Fuck no, I didn't," and so on and on until even the politest of the Putti would tell the old whinging Demon to bugger off.

It was true that, strictly speaking, Keith hadn't had to tissue sample everything. But he'd started doing that around the time that the world had been destroyed the fourth time.

The story of Noah and the Flood was actually the fifth time that the Creator had gone in for the ctrl-alt-delete-Death-Ray end of the world scenario. Neither Keith nor Mick nor most of Heaven's Hosts had been around for the first three wipeouts, but the fourth had involved two Angels, a number of bottles of Kentucky's Finest, several Angelphile dinosaurs, and one Creator deity that had really just had it up to here with lizards that didn't listen. And like all old fathers everywhere, He just really went off the deep end.

Editor's Note: Our legal counsel has been informed by the Dinosaurs United Union that we must insert this note to publicly disavow their connection to any stories contained in any Holy or Unholy texts that might involve a certain city, two Angels, a number of bottles of Kentucky's Finest, and ensuing destruction. As they, the dinosaurs have painstakingly pointed out to this author by their tried and true method of holding an author down and roaring at them until they surrender, they, again the dinosaurs, had been dead for millions of years before that other thing with the city happened. Lastly, they, the Dinosaurs United Union, would like to point out that since Angels were involved in their, the dinosaurs destruction, and the end of humanity, and the end of the Arits, a pre-dinosaur sapient species of garden gnomes, that anyone with any sense should stay several light years away from any Angels, good or bad, which for their money, the Dinosaurs United Union again, doesn't amount to any difference at all. *End Editor's Note.*

Keith remembered the broken section of his silver pentagram. Could the kid have broken it, he wondered. Could Basil Berry have broken a protection rune that had once stood up to Mr. Lewis C. Furr himself? Keith very much doubted it.

Now, concerning Mr. Lewis C. Furr, sometimes called Stan: Your average Fallen Angel, aka Demon, is even more of a traditionalist than your average Neanderthal or Republican, the first being the actual tradition, and the second being an armchair revisionist who likes to remember only the bits that worked out for them and not the oppression suffered by everyone else. And so the Fallen go to great lengths, even now so long after Armagedōn, to avoid using the names of anyone in the celestial Spheres or Choirs by actual name. For, is it not written; "He that nameth a thing risks getting its attention"? Indeed, it is written in Murphy 27:242.

In order to understand how obsessive your average Demon is, you need to understand that there are three celestial Spheres. The First Sphere is made up of Seraphim, Cherubim and Putti, and Thrones and Ophanim, all of whom are lowly petty counsellors. The Second Sphere consists of the Dominions and Lordships, Virtues and Strongholds, and Powers and

Authorities, who are celestial governors. The Third Sphere, which is rather better known than the first two, consists of the Principalities and Rulers, Angels, and Archangels who are rulers, rather in the fashion of the old forgotten kings. All are bound in their rigid social pyramid under the Directorship of one Imperial Creator.

The Choirs are simply too numerous to make for enjoyable reading, so we shall simply sum up: There's not a sound made anywhere in nature that there's some little bugger in a choir robe banging a cymbal, or a drum, or playing a comb like it was an even more annoying Kazoo. The Choirs more or less run amuck doing whatever they will and enjoy the absolute protection of the Creator, who really enjoys annoying the Spheres far far too much.

And all that is why Keith doubted that his godson, Basil Berry, could have broken the demonic silver pentagram that had once stood up to the third most powerful creature in the whole universe. He certainly couldn't have broken it by himself. Besides, the twerp Scion had a key to the front door, and his own security pass phrase too, so why bother with the breaking and entering when he could just enter without breaking? Why go through all the trouble to break a protection rune that he could just walk through? And someone had been at his collection too and had broken his transportation pentagram that ensured his movement from any point in the universe to it, without the inconvenience of materializing 5 meters above the floor, or 5 meters below the floor, or a couple of light minutes away from the floor in the middle of a star.

So who had been at his collection? Keith wondered, annoyed at so many unanswered details floating around in the narrative.

Keith picked up a long stiletto knife off his workbench and carefully lifted up the book directly in front of the fingerprints in the dust. Living for millions of years surrounded by Demons, Angels, and dolphins had taught Keith that a completely unreasonable fear of everything and everyone was the healthiest approach to problems. He considered it a good day when bombs only exploded in his face. He had once seen the Creator unmake a fellow Demon, and the memory still occasionally woke him from a hundred year nap in a cold sweat.

"You know, this is why I never had kids," Keith said, peeking under the book.

"I had kids once," said a disembodied voice. "Well, a kid."

"You had a prince," Keith said, "doesn't count. Homicidal maniacs the lot of them. Besides, he never knew you to be his father, so it doesn't count."

"He was princely on his mother's side," said the voice. "And besides, my little prince often wrote to me. I was more of a father to him than his mother's husband. What did his so-called-father ever do for him besides get him killed?"

Keith shrugged.

"Well, that saved you his laundry, didn't it," Keith said kicking away a scattered pile of Basil Berry's clothing and then flicking the stiletto knife into the cobalt blue shorts. After threading the shorts, the knife, not having anything solid to stick in, sagged and fell to the floor with a clatter.

"Did you see anything?" Keith asked.

"Nope, sorry, nada. I was napping in my skull."

"Damn worthless watchman you are."

"And to what do we owe the visit, oh Master Name-taker-and-writer-downer of Hugely Important Trivia?" asked the voice that, despite its lack of body, seemed to be moving closer.

"Temporary relocation, taking the collection too, or most of it anyway," Keith said looking down the rows of shelves. "Well no, all of it I think." Not sure if I'll be back, Keith thought.

"Fancy, big move," the voice said. "It's been a long time down here and I'm bored with this place now. Even the mice have settled down and started raising banking cartels. Hardly what I call civilized behaviour, but hey, they're mice."

How to do it, how to move it all? Keith wondered.

Keith remembered an old cartoon he had seen once. There had been a guy, a wizard, with a pointy blue hat, and a young kid, and in order to move house, the old guy just magiced everything small and flew books, plates, knives, furniture, everything, into an old leather bound carryall bag. Or was it a carpetbag? Leather maybe? The kind doctors never carried in the 1950s. Ever since Keith had seen that cartoon, he had wanted a bag like that. He'd finally found one, well after the Apocalypse. Now where the Hell had he put it?

Keith began pulling things out of the nearest closet. Out went the golf clubs.

"Well, aren't you planning on telling me where we're going?" the voice said petulantly.

Out went the complete of *Time's Gardening for Novices: New 21st Century Edition*.

"Nope," Keith said.

"I could help, you know," the voice said.

"Shirley, you jest?" Keith said tossing a complete run of *Magic the Gathering* cards over his shoulders. The cards flew out of the box in a thousand different directions, landing mostly in Basil Berry's laundry. Three Alpha Black Lotus cards landed inside a pair of red satin thongs; settling on two rather dubious looking stains.

"Oh now that hurts, that just hurts," the voice said.

"Come on, say it," Keith said pausing to look at an original hand typed copy of the privately published forty-three page "little book." The name E. B. White was written in a large firm Copperplate script on the inside cover of the book.

The disembodied voice sighed the sigh of one long used to disappointment and nostalgia for bygone and presumed better days.

"And don't call me Shirley," it said.

"Good, good, thanks," Keith said. I'll have to take this, he thought, tucking the book under his arm. Mind numbing justifications of bad writing are hard to come by. Good for religious ambiguity though. I'll see to it that the first prophets get a complimentary copy.

"You're not paying attention," the voice said. "Off in dreamland again."

"Piss off Ghost," Keith said.

"Well, at least tell me what you're doing?"

"All right," Keith grumbled pulling out an aged Louis Vuitton bag.

"That has got to be the ugliest thing I've ever seen, and I've done time under a couple of graveyards," the disembodied Ghost voice said.

"Yeah, lovely ain't it?" Keith said. "A dozen virgins sacrificed themselves for one of these once upon a time ago. I mean look, Spring Urban Satchel line from 2008. World's finest Italian leather, only the finest urban charms, and-"

"Urban- charms? Are you nuts? That's a cigarette box glued to the bag there."

"Yes indeed and there's a Broadway Theatre ticket for *Cats*.

"It's always for *Cats*," the Ghost said groaned. "There's always a fucking cat innit. Scrawny pussbags give me the hebegebees."

"Yeah, me too," Keith agreed. "It's them being wired into so many gods that does it. Every pantheon, tribe, ethnicity, and time period had cat gods. Hell, Christianity was practically unique for not having a cat god. You just never knew which intelligence was looking at you- the god- or the bloody minded hairball from Hell."

"Ouuu- is that a used prophylactic stuck on that bag?" the Ghost asked.

"No, worse luck," Keith said. "Only the wrapper."

The bag, a purse really, was a Louie Vuitton original. It was valued - back in the days when anything had a value, at $150,000.00 American Dollars. Had its Creator actually known it existed, or had anyone else known for that matter, it would have been a priceless relic of power. But as far as most people ever knew, it had only ever existed as a Photoshopped prank by an unknown visual satire artist. Just because something is an imaginary satire prank, doesn't mean it's not real somewhere.

In a universe of infinitely expanding boundaries, there is an infinite probability that anything that can happen will happen. Eventually.

Keith reached into the bag, rummaged around for a moment, and pulled out a small fluffy white rabbit with a pink nose.

"All right now, you can have the run of my place while I'm gone," Keith said. "But no, and I seriously mean no, shitting on the floor. The roaches around here have had a faeces-free existence for millions of years now, and you might actually kill them."

The fluffy white rabbit with a pink nose twitched its whiskers at the Demons.

"You got a Moose in there?" the Ghost asked, not wanting to let the conversation drift too far out of him being the subject.

"You want a real Moose?"

"Yeah, a really big horned biped Moose," the Ghost said without grinning, because he couldn't. He would've if he could've, but since he couldn't, he didn't.

"Moose are quads you dope," Keith said reaching into the bag again.

"A lion would do too," the Ghost added helpfully.

Against all rational possibility, Keith pulled a small Bull Moose out of the bag.

What do Moose know about rational possibility anyway?

Keith waited in bemused humour as a stunted Ghost completely failed to comment on the appearance, and sudden growth of a Bull Moose. Keith dodged the antlers as they rocked past his head. Then Keith frowned.

For many thousands of years, millions maybe, the Ghost had haunted Keith's digs, usually in the basement. Keith had gotten used to the Ghost's aura like most people get used to the smell of their loved ones. But now it was gone, leaving only a chill behind in the psychic field of afterlife.

Keith turned slowly to face the Moose, and then looked up. And then looked up some more. This Moose was tall, even by Moose standards, and must have weighed every bit of two tons.

"Hello Wilber," the Moose said in a hollow, slightly deep upper Pennsylvania accent.

"Oh no, no, no- not on your life Ghost, get your ass out here right now - back to the skull with thee."

"But Wilber, it's cold in the skull," the Moose pleaded. "Don't make me do it Wilber. There's no cable or wireless or anything in there but my own thoughts. *Please*?"

"How the Hell did you get in there? And stop calling me Wilber," Keith said looking up into two of the largest puffing nostrils he had ever seen not attached to a Dragon.

"Through the ears, Wilber."

"That's it. Have it your way."

In one fluid motion, Keith dropped the bag and jumped straight up in front of the Moose's face. Grabbing both antlers with his powerful hands, the Demon slammed his forehead into the Moose's forehead.

The Moose's eyes crossed, its legs buckled, and it slowly rocked backward and forward until it settled onto the smooth stone floor, its massive head slumping down onto the cool stone floor.

"If that man wasn't gay, then I'm a dandelion," Keith said rubbing his forehead.

The fluffy white rabbit with a pink nose nuzzled itself against Keith's leg.

Keith bent down and picked it up. Upon closer inspection, it turned out to be a her and soon to be a mom too.

"Evil God almighty," Keith said. "It's bad enough you're a clichéd fertility symbol, but did ya have to come out of the void knocked up too?"

The fluffy white rabbit with a pink nose nuzzled into Keith's armpit.

Keith walked over to his subterranean tropical terrarium and gently lowered the pregnant bunny inside.

"Now, don't eat anything red in here," Keith said. "All the green stuff will be just fine-"

Keith stopped for a long moment, gazing at the large plants that he had tended encased in glass for the last several thousand years. He ran his fingers through a thick lush Columnea allenii bunch.

"For fuck's sake Keith, did you have to hit me that hard," said the Ghost from behind Keith's back.

Keith turned and saw the Moose, a nasty knot raised between its eyes, looking up at him.

"What did I tell you about black and white T.V. references?" Keith said. "I won't have it in my house. Not here. I don't have to put up with that kind of shit in my own castle."

"All right, all right," said the Moose in the normal voice of the Ghost. "Chill out man, take a load off, and find your center and all that funky Cally Yogi Jazz."

"Tafari is a dust bowl," Keith said looking longingly at his plants, memories of the virgin Brazilian rain forest flooding his memory.

"Tafari?" asked the Ghost-possessed Moose that rose unsteadily to its feet, wobbled a bit, and then settled back down on the floor. "I think I'll chill myself a bit longer. Damn it Legionary that hurt."

"Sorry," Keith said. "I've not been in a fight since Armagedōn. I forgot how easily mortal beings hurt."

"Me too," the spectre Moose agreed. "It's kind of fun in a 'if you don't do it often it won't become a problem' sort of way."

Keith stared gloomily at the plants, wondering why he had left the planetary choice up to the Angel. The location should have been specified in the email.

Blasted Angels, dumber than an ocean full of loaches and sea monkeys, Keith thought. Wouldn't give you a proper shilling for the lot of them.

"So why's Tafari got you so glum?" the Moose asked as he again rose to all four feet. Pausing for a moment, the Moose looked down between its own back legs and sighed with obvious relief. He was indeed a he-moose.

"The damn Angel went and picked the center of the universe," Keith complained. "Deadest bit of space in the entire place, saving an Angelic Committee Meeting for the Advancement of Angelic Moral Development. I mean okay, we can do *Lawrence of Arabia*, or maybe the whole epic Egypt thing, maybe get Ríagáin, Queen of the Damned to play Cleopatra.

But there's only one tree on Tafari now, and he's as dense as any plank, even by tree standards. The whole place is just grey, grey, and grey."

"Can't say as I've ever been there, but it does sound like a problem," said the Moose walking over to the terrarium and eyeing a large lush Adiantum Fritz Luthii plant. "Hey, do ya mind? I don't think this Moose has been eating properly."

"Help yourself," Keith said with a grunt. "It only took a couple of hundred years to grow up down here."

The Moose took a large chomping bite out of the middle of the plant and began to chew it meditatively.

"So," said the Moose between chews, green sludge seeping out of his mouth onto the floor. "What you going to feed people in this dust bowl?"

"Oh, they're not going to really be alive, so it won't matter."

"Right," said the Moose taking another chomp out of the much smaller Adiantum Fritz Luthii planet.

"Ya know Ghost?" Keith said forcing casualness into his tone that he really didn't feel. "The *only took a couple of hundred years to grow down here* comment was supposed to mean don't touch it, you stupid wonk."

"Sorry about that," said the Ghost rider Moose.

No wait, that doesn't work. That implies that the Moose is riding the Ghost. Moose riding Ghost? No. Moose with Ghost in? No. Moose. That's it; he's a bloody Moose now until otherwise notified.

"Here's the thing Demon," said the Moose nay Ghost, "you need to be reminded of a few things. Since we're friends-"

"We're not friends," Keith said sharply.

"*Riiight*," the Moose said, drawing out the I-sound. "I'll take pity on you as you've never actually

212

been alive," Moose continued ignoring the insult. Centuries of living with Keith had made the displaced Human Spirit more than a bit hard of hearing where insults were concerned.

Keith said nothing. What was there to say? He never having been alive--no Angel or Demon ever had been. He had feeling, sensations, but he had always suspected, deep down, that it was somehow different, more vivid when you were alive. Keith didn't eat if he didn't want to. Drinking never really gave him more than a jolly buzz, and then only if he put a lot of effort into thinking he had one. Keith had feeling, of a sort, physical sensations. But he had always suspected deep down that life was more vivid when you were actually alive, and could die, in the normal, traditional no reboot allowed way. And die without knowing what, if anything, would come next. Keith was always annoyed at the prospect of his own impending death, the final permanent one. But it never occurred to him that he should be scared of it.

"Living things need to eat," the Moose marched on, "cockroaches excepted of course. Although," he added drawing the word out into a sentence worth of sound, "your average roach will start to eat its own self out of sheer boredom if you wait long enough."

Keith sighed. You can say a lot with a good sigh. This one said, *Yeah, what's your point?* It was such a good sigh that the Moose went right on as if the question had been actually asked.

"My point is that a body has got to eat," the Moose said. "What are your people-"

"I never said anything about people," Keith interrupted sharply.

"Yeah, sure you didn't," the Moose said. "I'm sure you're going to make a brave new world out of moose, rabbits, and roaches. Nothing whatever with a Trunk of Teeth. So tell me, why'd you keep those teeth anyway? 777-sextillion teeth is waaay more than you need for comparative anatomy. I mean, is it really a totally complete set? My old ones too?"

Keith scowled.

"No, souls," the Demon said ignoring the questions. "Creatures without souls don't need to eat," he added in a tone so petulant that the Moose's fur stood on end just between his ears.

"Hey, did you know that Moose hair reacts to annoyance?" the Moose asked.

"Nope."

"Neither did I until just now," the Moose said. "Could be why I wanted to stomp your foot just then. Anyway, you want a bunch of Zombies then?"

"What the Hell do Zombies have to do with anything?" Keith exploded.

Well, not literally exploded. Keith's in this picture until the end of the third book.

It was more like the Demon exploded into a sphere of Demonic verbs so long that it coupled with flailing arms and that weird boggle-head thing that some people can do, but only makes them really look like a right tit. It would have been less effort to actually explode. That's really more like what Keith did. It was all displaced anger because his careful game had been wrecked by Chukwu's appearance in the London Station's V.I.P. Lounge.

"Bodies got to eat, soul or no soul," the Moose said with the air of a tenured political "science" Professor that's just decided to really fuck with her graduate students just for the sheer fun of it.

Of course, Ghosts know something that political "science" Professors don't, and that's the fact that Demons have seen war, and starvation, and Human depravity, and ten-year-old girls that will prostitute themselves for the price of a hot meal to calm the stomach pains and a stiff drink to forget the price of the dinner, and the Demons all to an Imp know that there is absolutely nothing that any mortal Professor can do to them that is worse than going back into the Army for a single Creator-forsaken-day. This is also why you find so many Demons out making history instead of sitting around commenting about how the history was made incorrectly, or how the real made history just won't work, never mind the inconvenient truth of the history still being made and stubbornly refusing to unmake itself to suit Professors.

"Only things like you that don't really have bodies per say," the Moose continued, "but rather are only physical manifestations don't have to eat. Your body is a construct of Divine Will, not biology. Biology has got to consume other biology to live, period, full stop, end of conversation. And if you don't like it, take it up with *Him*. Not my problem. Trust me; you really get to understand how a body works once you ain't got one to distract you from thinking all the time. You create a biological body and don't feed it and it's going to go all gooey and smelly on you in a matter of hours, maybe less. Of course, it won't be worth much of a damn after the first couple of minutes, a day maybe if it comes into being with a full tank of adenosine-5'-triphosphates."

What is there to say about adenosine-5'-triphosphates, aside from the fact that the Moose is just showing off that he used to watch the Discovery Channel as a young Ghost? Adenosine-5'-triphosphates is also called A.T.P. because even biochemists don't like saying fuck-all words like Adenosine-5'-triphosphates. A.T.P. is a multifunctional nucleotide that functions in cells as a coenzyme. And already you're in deeper trouble now because who knows or cares what a nucleotide is? Right, well, if you answered, "I do," then grab the nearest biology book, or a copy of *Gray's Anatomy* the book, not the T.V. show, and look it up for yourself.

The important thing to know about A.T.P. is that they are chemical energy that is essential for metabolism, which is essential for the thinking, growing, being alive processes of any organic body. Actually, it's absolutely you get it, like cannot be avoided essential for all life as Angels and Demons ever knew it. A.T.P.s were discovered by Karl Lohmann in 1929, understood by Fritz Albert Lipmann in 1941, and artificially synthesized by Alexander Todd in 1948. The latter point being the one that is about to be important and relevant to the actual course of this narrative history.

"I hadn't really thought about that," Keith admitted. "Do you think we could use a synthetic? You know, pump 'em up like a combustion motor with gasoline?"

"Might work," the Moose agreed. "Then again, maybe not. But the A.T.P. problem is why there have never been any real Zombies. Well, not the classical nightmare Zombies. You got the brain dead sort sure, but they are not much for anything other than a short life if it's not artificially prolonged and you won't get a decent day's work out of them. And you can just forget that one drop of blood makes another Zombie thing."

"I've seen those host shells," Keith said as he pulled on a pair of black leather gloves. "I went out the next day and got a durable medical power of attorney. Screw that living will crap," he added flexing his fingers inside the gloves. The smell of centuries old leather permeated through the room.

"What's a Demon need with a living will? You're immortal; your return ticket is prepunched."

Keith's hands began to take on a dull blue glow that slowly intensified to a deep blue cobalt hue.

"Yeah, the *me* part of me is immortal- the *me* part of *everybody* is immortal. But the body ain't," Keith explained while waving his hands about as if he was conducting a symphony orchestra the Demon's hands trailed metallic blue light tracers behind them in their flight. "It's like you said, we are constructs, not real biology. Our bodies can live for millions of years if taken care of. Metatron always boasts that he's in his original body, which only proves what a pantie-waist he really is, in my, oh so unhumble opinion. But you can get a body really fucked up with the right sort incendiary or nuke bomb and your body is toast, usually literally. My last body was cashed in at Hiroshima, on August 6th, 1945. That one I didn't mind. It was a bright light for me and then I'm standing in front of the Apostle Simone at the Pearly Gates saying, "Shit, I was watching that."

"Hmm," the Moose said. "I wonder what it's like to die."

Keith pumped his hands several times and watched the blue balls of energy crackle around his hands. The Demon felt energy flowing through his limbs, building at the base of his skull, ready to explode at his command.

Damn I've missed this, Keith thought.

"I said, I wonder what it's like to die?" the Moose prompted.

"Not all it's cracked up to be sometimes," Keith said. "The first time I bought it, I was sun surfing with Gabriel, Michael, Raphael, Raguel, Remiel, Saraqael, Uriel, and Diábolos and Stan. This was back in the Dinosaur Age, pre-mankind, pre-pit-fall, pre-Housed Divided. I went in for this double barrel of HEV and completely wiped out. I remember laying there, sizzling. Smelt of burnt hair and melting Styrofoam, and I thought my mind would explode it hurt some much. After I got a new body, I didn't even go out for a million years. Kept my ass right at home I did. If I hadn't been sent out on assignment by Mr. Big, I think I might still be right there sitting in the Heavenly Barracks doing nothing. I turned into a regular barracks rat I did. I didn't feel like that again until the Great Crash of 2020."

"You wiped out sun-surfing again?"

"No way mate, never done that since," Keith said. "America defaulted on its debt and sold itself to the billionaires for a flag, a body bag, and a swift kick in the ass, which they got from the Persians. Bottom completely fell out of the bond market and I actually had to get a job. Damn, I love these gloves."

The gloves were an item of magic focus which were given to the Demon Keith by the Archmage Harry Blackstone Copperfield Dresden in exchange for his help in defeating an Ancient Aztec Zombie-ghoul-god-thing that had popped up in Chicago shortly after the end of the Final Match at Armagedōn.

The Wizard Dresden, like most Human practitioners of the arts found himself cast-off as one of the Left Behinds who were to endure for a short time after the near-extinction event at Armagedōn. But that is another story. Please see future editions of these histories, particularly volumes *Left Behind, I'm Right But Have Nobody to Lord It Over, My Girlfriend is a Sunburst Cichlid*, and *Honey, I'm Dead, Why Do I Still Need to Take Out the Garbage?*.

What is important here is to know is that the gloves helped Keith to focus his power in terms of both volume and objective. Instead of most of the Demon's power radiating off his hands in all directions like a spherical star, the gloves forced the power to flow out of between 1 and 10 points, depending on what the wearer wanted done. Of course, one might question Dresden's wisdom in giving this particular artifact to a total nutter like Keith, but it was typical of Dresden's career that he would richly reward such a minor service with such a lavish gift, while at the same time completely forgetting to say thank you to his closest friends and allies. Keith of course never bothered to point out the character flaw.

"You still got a problem with your people though," the Moose said returning to the original topic, ignoring the Demon's excitement at practicing his Demonic arts again for the first time in several centuries.

"Not really, not if we can get the synthetic to work," Keith said just before throwing his arms out wide and slamming his hands together producing a loud thunder clap.

Everything in the basement seemed to jump. Or, more accurately, everything in the basement seemed to skip over the next two seconds.

Then, a great many things happened all at once.

The Louie Vuitton bag rose up off the table and floated over towards Keith. All of the urban detritus that had been stuck to the bag fell off of it, turning to dust before they hit the floor.

The large leather bound books, each binding housing dozens of different species tissue samples, rose up off the shelves and began to sped towards the open mouth of the now clean Louis Vuitton bag. As the books speed towards the bag from all directions, they began to shrink, smaller and smaller, until they could hardly be seen at all, dropping into the bag like individual grains of sand falling through the air on a breezy day.

The Moose stood watching the spectacle in silent admiration.

I want a beer, the Moose thought.

Keith stood conducting the bookish traffic like a mighty air traffic controller or an insane apprentice wizard mouse conducting a hurricane.

"Hey Moose," Keith called out above the roaring din of flying books.

"Yeah?"

"You want to be anything else besides a Moose?"

"Na, thanks for asking. A beer would be nice though."

"No worries," Keith said pulling out a slide from one of the lines of books. "This here is a blood stain of the Liger named Dantès. Famous cat, used to do all sorts of Hollywood work back in the day." He then waved a hand over his workbench, causing a shallow silver pail filled with water to appear, and beside that, a tall frosted mug of beer with a straw stuck in its dark head.

While the Liger may sound like a mystical creature, and we would not be surprised to find our readers at the point in the story assuming it to be so, we can assure you that it is or was quite real. The Liger is a hybrid cross between a male lion of the Panthera Leo type and a female tigress of the Panthera Tigris type. Why it won't work with a female lion and a male tiger is anybody's guess. But what you get is a cross breed between two species, which is pretty nifty, even if the name does entirely lack imagination.

The Moose lowered his head in order to dodge being bludgeoned by the legions of flying catalogue books and began to drink his beer.

"What you do is this," Keith said picking up a small scalpel from his workbench. "Scrape just the smallest part of the sample into a pail of water. It doesn't have to be silver pail mind you, that's just traditional. And then," the Demon added placing the scalpel and stain sample on the work bench, "you electrocute the whole thing!"

Sharp blue electricity shown from all eight of Keith's fingers, while an arch of dark black-purple power crackled between his thumbs. The eight lightning-electricity-bolts continuously crackled for a long second that seemed more like a long hour, but the water showed not the slightest reaction.

"Epic fail," the Moose said, licking beer head from his nose.

"Wait for it," Keith said.

The water in the silver pail clouded, first grey, then black. An odour, something between burning potpourri and snorted powdered limestone gusted through the room.

The Moose's jovial expression faded as first one green lidless eye appeared in the water, followed by a second one, and then teeth. The Moose did not really register the appearance of the rest of the body. All he saw were teeth, which were getting larger and larger.

"Holy Mary Shelley," the Moose breathed as he watched the water turn blood red in an instant. The empty beer smashed against the floor.

The Moose had the unpleasant sensation that the first face had been washed away by blood.

Then, the formation of small hard spheres like little marbles appearing to form in massive clumps directly after. The blood water rose-up in a sphere, encircling a quickly formed fertilized set of chromosomes. In speed, like an old CGI movie, there formed an embryo, suspended in an ethereal uterus of bloody fluid, and soon the beat-beat-beat of a heart. A long spinal column began to form around the beating heart, the nervous system spearing in all directions. The liver, kidneys, and intestines began to take shape, inside a thin ribcage. Two milky white eyes grew out of the thick skull, atop a body the sprouted four legs, and twenty straight toes. Thin lips parted below the eyes, to reveal two rows of razor sharp milk teeth. Eyelids formed over the eyes at the same time that a space of soft skin collapsed, popped, and formed a nose.

The body flipped first this way and then another, turned its large open eyes upon the Moose, which froze, locked in primal fear that had little to do with its Human mind or Moose body; for both the Human and the Moose were looking into the unborn eyes of an ancient predator that was just as happy to eat Moose flesh as anything else.

The Moose took several steps backward, noting with alarm that twenty long claws had begun to grow out of the paws.

The giant cat's face elongated into the shape of a tiger, but took on the soft white fur of the lion's face, spotted with a dark brown fur.

Solid bones began to replace the cartilage skeleton. A tongue lapped out, drinking in the amniotic fluid that swirled within the bloody sphere that hovered above the empty silver pail. Vocal cords appeared and began to flex in and out with a breathing rhythm. The Liger baby curled its nose under all four paws and began to grow larger and larger.

Finally, after the longest minute of the Ghost's eternity, the blood sphere burst, and a fully formed two-foot long, 50 pound, blood-soaked bébé Liger dropped onto the workbench, legs on every side of the shallow silver pail.

"And sod evolution," the Demon said with a hugely self-satisfied smirk. "I don't need no Hell blessed theory to tell me how to do this. I learned at the Creator's knee I did."

The Dantès clone stretched its long back, yawned, circled three times, flopped down, and started to purr before its eyes shut.

"You know, you should go see Lady Zhurong and Lady Jing," a very nervous Moose said. "I once saw them grow several thousand acres of Amazon jungle, in less time than that little miracle took. It happened a lot like that. Fucking scary fast."

"Hey, that's actually a good idea," Keith said. "Who knew you had it in you Moose?"

"Yeah, sure," the Moose said. "Just get me out of here, alright?"

"Sure, sure," Keith said picking up the sleeping Liger in one arm. "Where's your skull?"

"Over on the mantel," the Moose said without taking his eyes off the sleeping cat cub.

Keith walked over to the ornately carved mahogany mantel over the basement fireplace and opened a small jade green box with oriental ivory inlayed carvings of words. Keith opened the box and peeled back the still fresh smelling large green leaves to reveal a perfectly smooth Human skull with a complete set of teeth.

Keith picked up the skull, held it up to eye level and said, "Alas poor-"

"Don't you fucking dare," the Moose said with malicious.

"Spoil sport," Keith said and placed the skull back inside its container. He then covered the jade box lid and placed it generally within the confines of the Louis Vuitton bag.

"By the way," the Moose said walking over to the base of the stairs, "what are you guys going to do on Tafari? I'm all in for *Rosencrantz and Guildenstern are Zombies*."

"*King Lear*."

"Really?"

"Yeah, *King Lear*, it's always bloody fucking *King Lear*," Keith said. "No matter what Angels start out to do, it'll be bloody fucking *King Lear* in the end, no matter what. It's bloody ineffable."

"That's sad."

"Tell me about it. Still, it explains why the Big Guy only ever had one kid. Saves loads of trouble all around. No fucking probate court."

"So why bother?" the Moose asked.

Keith shrugged, and said; "It's in our nature. Angels, Demons, whatever. We're all dogs fighting with Lazurus for the table scraps."

"That's even sadder."

"The Creator is a comedian playing to an audience that is afraid to laugh."

"Oh, I know that one," Moose said with a grin. "Voltaire."

"Mencken."

"Are you positive?"

"Yeah," Keith said. "He got it off me. That guy was always stealing my best lines. Like, I said Stan

223

was the most dangerous Demon in Heaven because Stan was always the one that could think things out in cold brutal logic, without regard to the prevailing whims of the Metatron or mortals."

Moose glared at Keith.

"You ever been struck by lightening or anything?" the Moose asked.

"Not yet," Keith said. "Well, not since Thor sailed from Mithlond to Lindon looking for Arda. I miss that guy."

And there, in silence, a Demon, a Moose possessed by a human Ghost, and a rabbit, watched as Keith's massive collection of D.N.A. catalogues pack themselves into one small Louis Vuitton bag.

Chapter 10: Völundr

Starting on the planet Tau Boötis Ab, in the Tau Boötis system, and ending on Terra, in the Sol system, orbiting the Sol star.

And Nebuchadnezzar carried away all Jerusalem, and all the princes, and all the mighty men of valour, even ten thousand captives, and all the craftsmen and smiths: none remained, save the poorest sort of the people of the land. --2 Kings 24:14 K.J.V.

And it came to pass that a Raven learned that even immortals fear.

Keith was not surprised to find Basil Berry on his elephant hide couch making out with Blossom and Keith was even less surprised to see Saki in his kitchen eating Frosted Mini Wheats and drinking the universe's last bottle of Diva Vodka.

"Who the Hell let you in here?" Keith demanded as he snatched the bottle out of the Avatar's hand. "Oh for the love of Mr. Big - there's fracken backwash in there."

"Not me, man," Saki said through a mouth of Frosted Mini Wheats. "It was like that when I found it."

"You slothful son of an Angel," Keith growled through clenched teeth as he carefully placed the extra-dimensional Louis Vuitton bag that contained an extremely complete biological catalogue of every creature that had ever existed in the entire universe on his kitchen table, along with one extremely depleted bottle.

Then the Demon screamed, "Out! Get out! All of you - out now!"

"Right, let's split babes," Basil Berry said.

"Not you Beanie Baby," Keith screamed as he bounced a saltshaker off the back of Saki's fleeing head. "Want, a, word."

Basil Berry followed Keith into another room with a look of dread on his face as the Avatars of the Beat and Grunge generations fled.

"Hey bird," Saki said sticking his head back in Keith's front door to talk to Raven. "You got cab fare man?"

Raven looked himself up and down, white feathers, black feathers, and sharp bony talons.

"No pockets kid," Raven said.

"Oh yeah, right, sorry," Saki said and split before Keith really went mental.

Basil Berry sprinted out of the other room, followed by a Liger and a Moose, both of whom walked out into the cool evening night.

The Moose winked at Basil Berry as he went out.

"Right man, thanks for the grub, man," Saki yelled from across the front lawn.

"Hold on, hold on ya Avatar bastards," Basil Berry yelled out the front door. "We're taking the trunk with us."

Saki's head appeared from the middle of the doorframe and said; "It's is so time to slip these digs before the bust."

"Come on, I've got cab fare," Basil Berry said.

"Righteousness!"

And with that, one Scion and one seriously put out Avatar lugged the Trunk of Teeth out the Demon Keith's front door.

Keith came out of the other room and slammed the front door behind them.

After a long moment in which Keith glared at his broken pentagram, he turned and went to the kitchen. The Demon picked up the bottle of Diva Vodka, and fished out the wand, which contained small diamonds and red rubies.

"Weren't rubies her favourite?" Raven asked from the ceiling support beams.

"Um-hmmm," Keith confirmed.

"Well, 'tis better to have loved and lost-"

"Raven," Keith said in a distant tone.

"Yeah boss?"

"Do you want to live to see if there really will be a *next* universe?"

"So, I woke up 'tastes-like-chicken,'" Raven said quickly. "He said-"

Keith held up his left pointer finger.

Raven fell silent.

"She. She, as in, a she-Dragon that gives birth, has given birth to universes kind of *she*," Keith said.

"Yeah, yeah, sure," Raven said. "Whatever. Look, Dragons are like, you know, moody-"

"I'm just saying that she is a she," Keith said tucking the vodka wand into his coat pocket.

"Hey, what do you call a 6' 6" fighting-mad frog with the power of a Norse Thunder God?" Raven asked.

"Sir."

"No, you dope, not when you're a bloody three foot tall Raven," Raven screeched. "You call it any damned thing it wants to be called. Thor, god, master, Sir, *whatever* it wants, that's what you call it. And Trâgu refers to itself in the masculine."

"Alright, alright," Keith said. "What did the gender-confused say?"

"Wælcyrges, only like really loudly, like in all CAPS and **BOLD 𝕱𝕺𝕽𝕿** kind of loud."

"You, must, be, kidding, me?"

"No way mate, I'd sooner kid you about the Third Coming than Valhalla Girls," Raven said.

Keith scowled and stormed off into the kitchen.

Raven flew down to the table and perched upon an empty silver candlestick.

"You know, by rights you should have the skull lain out for me," he called into the kitchen.

Raven only heard the pop of a can, followed by a guzzling sound, and the smashing of a can for an answer.

Keith returned to the combination dining-living room carrying 5 cans of Pabst Blue Ribbon by the empty plastic ring where the sixth can had been. Keith belched, sat down at the table, popped a can, and slid it over to Raven who scratched it with a talon.

"You got any Weltenburger Kloster?" The Raven asked without any real hope for he was well acquainted with Keith's beer drinking habits. Alcohol had to be good, or at any rate, expensive, which the Demon often thought of as being the same thing. But beer, beer was to be bought by volume, not by taste.

Now, we understand that there is some difference of opinion on what constitutes good beer, and there is room for differences on this topic. But Weltenburger Kloster Beer is simply the best beer ever made on Terra and maybe in the whole of the universe too.

Yeah, yeah, yeah, we know, whatever YOU like is actually the best beer in the world. But trust us; Weltenburger Kloster really is the best. It was, and still is, even in these post-humanity days, brewed in Regensbugs, Bavaria, Germany, and has been, since the 7th century, in the Weltenburg Abby. And in all that time, brewing has only been interrupted twice. Once by that nutter Bonaparte after being routed in Russia. And the second time after the Final Match at Armagedōn. But then only until most of the radiation lifted, and then the Demons took over. Of course, Demon brew isn't up to standard really, them not having taste buds unless they remember to have them. But by then there was the only brewery left, so they won by default.

Keith shook his head and drew out a large book titled *Customs of the Ancient Ones: Be Mindful of Purpose or DIE!*, from the Louis Vuitton bag. Keith had also packed his small, but extremely precise library of books on the histories, customs, and social systems of all of the immortal clans, as they were all, like humanity, one rather large and dysfunctional family. The Demon even had a pamphlet on the Empires of Lilliput and Blefuscu. But the strangest volume Keith had was called *W.I.P.: The Journey of Professor Fen and Yigal Amir Through Hell.* Apparently, in that universe, Hell was ruled over by some sod called Old Harry who had a serious thing for war games. Keith thought it was rubbish.

Keith flipped through the pages of the book he had wanted until he found the custom that might pacify Lady Jing long enough for the old Demon to get a word in before having his body rearranged on the sub-atomic level. Because of offending the Ancient Jing, Keith had once spent a century as a Hippomane mancinella apple until a daft princess took a bite of him and died, thereby taking them both to the Afterlife. He started to scribble extremely detailed notes.

"You got a copy of the *Book of Nighthawk*?" Raven asked apropos of nothing.

"Doesn't exist," Keith said.

"Well?" asked the Raven after he drank down as much of the beer as he could reach with his beak.

"I'm not dealing with *it*, you deal with *it*," Keith said.

"Oh come on, she'd like to see-"

"No."

"Right, right, okay," Raven said. "Not like I've got anything better to do. Message for her?"

"No."

"Okay, okay, I can see you're a bit grumpy. I just thought, you know, after all this time and-"

Keith looked up from his book and made eye contact with the Raven.

Raven looked into eyes that were older than most of the stars he'd visited in his long life. The eyes contained, many things, mostly a lack of pity, which Raven knew to be a strange kind of love, demented, and twisted though it might appear. But today, there was something different.

"All that I have done," Keith started and then stopped.

"Yes, yes, that's good," Raven said. "You did for her, yes, and-"

"I did for myself," Keith said. "And occasionally for the Big Guy, but only when it was easier than not doing it His way."

"Do you want her in the new universe?" Raven asked breaking off eye contact and looking at his talons.

"It's not really my place to say who goes and who stays," Keith said. "I think that's the Gatekeeper's gig."

"Really? I thought you were the author?"

"What, of *Continuous Creation*?" Keith asked. "Not me mate, some other guy did that bit. An old English Knight. Was his idea anyway. I just lifted some copy-text off him and fleshed out a whole book from his excerpts."

"So, you're a ghost writer of imaginary books?"

"No, but I did have a Ghost editor."

230

"Interesting times."

"Interesting times," Keith agreed.

"You angling for the Gatekeepership?" Raven asked.

"Heavens, no," Keith said. "Now be off with you. Go deal with- with what the Dragon wants. I've got to see another Dragon ere long, and I can't muck this up."

"All right, but I'm taking the Bentley," Raven said.

"No," Keith said with an evil grin. "You can take the Thunderbird."

"Ha ha, so funny I forgot," Raven said, and took off for Keith's garage.

"Forgot what?"

"Don't know, I forgot."

"Barf-bags are under the seat," Keith called after the bird.

"Never needed them before," Raven lied.

Later, Raven flew into Keith's mammoth garage and watched over his shoulder as the automatic doors swiftly closed behind him. The messenger god carried in one curled claw a key ring with one large key and a ZZ Top logo.

The garage, like the rest of Keith's domicile on the planet Tau Boötis Ab, in the Tau Boötis system, was modelled directly upon the Elephanta Caves of Mumbai, India, carved directly into the rock of the mountain that it inhabited. Rows upon rows of cars were parked in doublewide spaces lined in bright yellow reflective paint.

According to *The Complete Guide to Shyt Worth Seeing In Our Universe*, by the gods Di-zang and Mani, it has often been speculated that the Elephanta Caves, like those of the Sigiriya, called Sinhalese or සීගිරිය or Lion's Rock caves, and the Puma Punku ruins in Tiahuanaco, and of course the

Great Pyramids in Giza were built by space aliens. This is obviously false, as we now know that the only extra-terrestrial creatures that the Creator ever made were the Roaches.

In other more fashionable universes that the Creator has not devoted to winning a bet with Stan, there are billions upon billions of space alien races. But for our lonely Terran based universe, it's just the Roaches and us. And Roaches have never, despite their longevity, cunning, and hardiness, gone in for building cave cities, fortresses, temples, or monuments to themselves although it should also be noted that they never stopped Humans from doing it for them.

It has also been speculated that the gods or the Demons used their Celestial powers to build these massive ancient constructions, and it must be conceded that many gods, Demons, and even a few Angels did at one time or another claim credit for such achievements. Nevertheless, these claims and theories prove invariably false.

This is due to the fact that only one god, a certain Mossling, ever directly inspired the construction of such a massive structure upon the Isle of Atlantis called Ἀτλαντὶς νῆσος by Plato. Plato faithfully recounts the already then ancient legend of the Isle of Atlantis in his two dialogues "Timaeus" and "Critias." But Plato's information was by dint of the decay of detail over the centuries rather inaccurate. In what may truly be referred to as the Creator's only direct violation of His Agreement of Non-Interference with Stan.

That agreement, that bet, is the reason why our universe has been so generally bereft of His direct intervention. Stan of course completely failed to see the obvious problem of not including a clause against interference from the Angels, Demons, Immortals, and all of the other non-Human creatures in the universe on the Creator's behalf. Prior to the 20th Century, in which Stan finally managed to facilitate the development of Abnormal Psychology, thus providing a medical and legal foundation necessary to impression prophets, and incidentally liberating the Catholic Church from the burden of governance by actual believers, the Metatron managed to derail most of Stan's more formidable plans to cause the extermination of the Human species. After the conclusion of World War I though, the Metatron was reduced to using the most ineffective of tools available, the grassroots advocacy group.

But in the case of Mossling, the Creator caused a small asteroid to strike Atlantis about half a second after the goddess Mossling sat upon her throne of amber and gold for the first time, and proclaimed herself Goddess of all of Terra. The Creator's point, subtle as ever, was not lost upon the remaining gods, goddesses, Demons, and Angels, who were all expert observers of natural history and knew damn good and well what harm an asteroid about the size of a toddler's soccer ball could do to an immortal body.

Even Stan was disinclined to mention this violation of the terms of the bet.

It is whispered that the doomed soul of Mossling still haunts Terra's ocean floors, but this is most certainly an exaggeration. What is known is that Mossling's immortal body was torn asunder and that the impact went through the goddess, the throne, the temple, and deep into the foundations of the island causing a flood and shift in the base of the island's foundation. All the persons, both mortal and immortal had plenty of time to evacuate the island, but Mossling's body was left behind to go down with the remains of her one-second "divine" Kingdom Upon Terra.

As any Demon will tell you, the moral of this story is; "It may be possible to kill the Creator, but whatever do you do, don't proclaim yourself as the new Creator until you're damn good and sure the real one is dead. Better yet, never make the proclamation at all and just take the myrrh and run."

Raven stopped for a moment and admired the original Benz Patent-Motorwagen. The three large wheels supported an old style leather covered wagon bench, first built in 1885. Raven remembered watching Bertha Benz make her world famous long distance drive in the contraption and had been very disappointed, was still disappointed, that she did not kill herself in it.

Bright overhead lights clicked on with an auditable humming noise as Raven made his way through the garage looking for the Thunderbird.

Further, into the massive cavern garage, Raven found the complete Italian series of Pagani Zonda sport-roadsters. Keith had acquired all 206 of the cars produced between 1999 and 2011, even the demolished one that the Prince of Wales killed himself in in 2166 in flagrant violation of the international ban on the use of the combustion engine. The incident had unleashed scandal after scandal, which eventually ended the tax-exempt status of the entire British monarchy.

Raven finally found the 1955 Ford Motor Company Thunderbird "T-Bird," that Keith had said he could take in lot number ß-313. Raven was mildly amused to see that the car was canary yellow.

After looking around and above the cars to see that no one was about, Raven settled down on the smooth stone floor, and then flopped onto his back.

"Hellpus changus to sapianous hunkous," Raven said in a whisper.

Immediately upon uttering the last word, Raven's wings and legs extended, while his torso and chest grew outwards in all directions. A deep blue light began to imitate from Raven's eyes, nose, and mouth, before it engulfed him. For a moment, his head remained the same shape and size, but after the blue light engulfed it, it simply began to enlarge, without changing its shape. As the wings began to form fingers and then thumbs, Raven's feathers, below his neck, fell to the floor of the park garage. His thin bony legs began to put on flesh, first the dark red colour of muscle, followed by the brown skin of a Native North

American Indian. The growing of flesh spread from his legs up to his torso, chest, and arms, but did not spread above his shoulders, which remained covered in the dark black feathers of his natural raven form. After about a minute, Raven lay skin naked and panting on the floor, covered in sweat, surrounded by raven feathers.

Raven's head flopped to one side, and he saw several hundred sets of wheels meticulously lined up.

What kind of a mind, Raven wondered, spends Eternity collecting cars? Actually, Raven concluded, Keith was collecting everything.

Eventually, Raven sat up, wiped the sweat from his face with the back of his hand, and began to carefully collect up all of his feathers. He would need them later as it was just embarrassing to be spotty.

In his mostly Human form, which he called his 'Haida Knock-off,' Raven stood 2.5 meters tall, in a dark brown male body, which rippled with highly developed muscles. His Raven head, although enlarged to a proportion consistent with his body, remained otherwise the same.

Thumbs, Raven thought, flexing both of his thumbs and inspecting the rest of his fingers. Give a species thumbs and all of a sudden, they are bloody lords of all creation. Still, Raven conceded, at least the monkeys used their thumbs to make cheeseburgers, and that was almost worth forgiving them everything else.

Raven climbed into the Thunderbird, roared the engine into life, and activated the Star-to-Star Navigational System.

According to legal briefs filed by Völundr's attorneys in the epic Patent Violation case of *Völundr v. Star-to-Star LLC*, the Star-to-Star Navigational System was the brain child of the ancient Chinese god Di-zang and the old, but not quite ancient Germanic god Mani after seeing the debut presentation of OnStar by then General Motors North America Operations President

Rick Wagoner at the Chicago Auto Show, in 1996 Anno Domini. The two gods were both heavily invested in the rescue, guide, and navigation businesses, and began to seriously brainstorm about how to co-opt the new technology to their own benefit. After further conversations with the Greek goddess Ananké who had a stake in fate, the three gods decided to set up the Star-to-Star Navigational System in anticipation of humanity's migration to the stars. It was eventually decided that the system would have one Node Highway between each star, black hole, and inhabitable planet, plus entrances and exits to all the major conjunctions of the Node Pathways.

The three gods called a grand counsel of guides, which was attended by Genii, Hermanubis, Hermaphróditos, Ikenga, Isten, Pusan, Thot, Turms, and We-to. There the idea was conceived to create the navigational system as a self-aware intelligence that would span the entire universe, and that would appear to have been constructed by some sort of extra-terrestrial species. Their plans worked perfectly, excepting that tiny little detail concerning humanity inflicting a mass extinction event upon itself. In the millions of years that followed, the Star-to-Star Navigational System was greatly utilized by the non-Angelic immortals.

The Star-to-Star Navigational System A.I. also went mildly insane, but only in that annoying cousin that is never going to grow up sort of way, which it has to be admitted, wasn't so different from its original personality.

"Good Morning Lord," sung a springy singsong voice that Raven thought was entirely too chipper by two-halves. "What is your final destination?"

"Gylfagin," Raven muttered. He had never seen the point of being nice to machines, especially this one. Particularly since it never seemed to make any difference.

"Yes Lord. Is that the 1ˢᵗ City of Gylfagin, the 2ⁿᵈ City of Gylfagin, the current City of Gylfagin, the Planet Gylfagin, the Solar System of Gylfagin, or the-"

"Take me to the Temple of Gylfagin on the Hnitborg Mountain near the City of Kvasir, on Terra, in the Sol system."

"And what time would you like to arrive there, Lord?"

"Now," Raven thoughtlessly said and immediately regretted it. "No WAIT!"

For one instant that nevertheless felt like years Raven experienced the sensation of having his body stretched over billions, yes billions, of kilometres. This was because for the smallest fraction of time, a frozen slice of time so small that only the Creator could notice it, Raven's body was stretched for billions, yes billions, of kilometres between Keith's museum garage and the nearest entrance ramp into the Node Highways. Given that, this was the space between the planet Tau Boötis Ab and the furthest edge of the Boötis system, a mere 5,894,156,087 kilometres, depending on the orbit positions of both the central star and the planet, Raven had always thought that the side effects were, on the whole, not that bad.

Even so, Raven used the barf bags.

Through a stream of tears, and a wad of mucus, Raven watched as the car gently oriented itself away from the nearest star, into the comparative darkness of deep space.

"Operating at now plus 7 seconds, Lord," the Star-to-Star Navigational System supplied. "Estimated time of arrival, now plus 27 seconds, Terra Prime Meridian time."

"Yeah, great, can we take it a bit slow-"

Raven broke off as he watched the entrance to the Node Highway open. It always started with three spherical orb lights blinking into existence. The colours were always the same; red, blue, and yellow. As the lights grew, each one began to orbit the other two, with the entire set spinning around a central axis. Bright primary coloured light emitted from the spheres, and as it mixed with the other colours, formed bright and vivid shades of purple, green, and orange. The coloured lights mixed and mixed until there appeared within the center a dark black sphere that steadily grew larger until it encompassed the entire field of vision.

Raven, who had never particularly cared for driving on land, as it had always struck him as being too much like work, hastened to put on his seat belt.

When the black sphere in the center of the extra-planetary lights grew to about 25 meters in diameter, the Star-to-Star Navigational System announced, "Hold on tight- but just remember, if we hit anything, you'll be the last to know."

"I'll damn well be the only one to know it," Raven complained and shut his eyes.

And then, it was over. Except of course for the feeling that one had left one's lunch several million light years behind.

The constellations had all changed. They hung around a blue-green and blackened planet, a familiar moon upon which were the preserved footprints of one of the first Human beings to walk there, beside a single American flag. Mankind returned, many times over, until even the little sovereign city-state of Monaco on the French Riviera launched its own cruise liner taking holidayers to the Moon. But for always and ever, or at least so far anyway, the footprints and American flag were preserved under a transparent case of diamond.

"Would Lord care for a drink while we make our descent to our destination?" the Star-to-Star Navigational System asked with manic overtones of unrestrained joy.

"No."

"I'm sure Lord knows best. Care for a game of Tic-tac-toe?"

"Global Thermonuclear War?"

"How about some nice light rock? I have the entire Bonnie Tyler discography, including the New Age remixes, and-"

"How about when we land I melt you down and turn you into Outsider Art? I'll call it *Stupid Computer Don't Know When to Shut-up*."

"I can see you're not feeling well," the Star-to-Star Navigational System chirped. "Are you feeling hot flashes, night sweats, irregular periods, loss of libido, vaginal dryness, or otherwise hormonal?"

"Computer," Raven said dryly.

"Yes Lord?"

"Shut-up."

"Yes Lord, can do Lord. Now, if you will look out the driver's side window, you will see the ruins of the space station Der Leute Frei Stationiert, literally the People's Free Station, which was home to the last mortal survivors of the global War at Armagedōn..."

Raven turned the voice off in his head, put the seat back, and closed his eyes. Re-entry into planetary atmosphere and gravitational pull from orbit was always best slept through in Raven's generally unhumble opinion.

The Star-to-Star Navigational System continued to drone on in its entirely too chipper voice about the radiation levels of the upper atmosphere, and the amount of toxic sludge in the oceans, and the slow refilling of the giant crater that had once been the Arabian Peninsula, which had been mostly removed from the land to the upper atmosphere due to several nuclear missiles seriously disrupting the equilibrium of millions of gallons of crude oil, and the oil 's close proximity to a major world fault line. The explosion of the first oil field set off the explosion of a second, and then a third. The shock shifted orbit of Terra, which froze almost everything else. It wasn't until about a million years after the Final Match that the last great ice age receded enough that the Angels, Demons, and gods could stop using their powers to keep their own personal bits of the Terra inhabitable. Now, only the roaches thrived.

The Thunderbird gently settled upon a clear glade of grass near the base of the mountain upon which the Temple of Gylfagin sat like a splined crown. The jolt woke Raven, who sat up and rubbed his eyes.

Here, trees grew green, surrounded by colourful flowers, and a large area of cultivated gardens. And all under a dark haze occasionally illuminated by bright orange and purple lightning bolts.

Raven wondered which creature was keeping this area free of the toxic atmosphere of the rest of Terra. Given that the free zone seemed to include the entire area of the Hnitborg Mountain, and the ruins of the City of Kvasir, it was most likely a half dozen or more semi or entirely immortal beings.

Raven tucked the key into the sun visor, rolled the windows down slightly, and changed back into his normal bird form.

"Well, I do declare," said the Star-to-Star Navigational System. "That scenery just ain't something you see every day."

"Shut-up," Raven said.

Raven stood for a moment and stretched his wings while simultaneously taking deep gulps of fresh air. He was entranced by the contrast between the bubble of sunshine that the temple was in, coupled with the smell of orange blossoms which never should have been in this part of the world and the raging hellish storm that went on outside the bubble. But, the horizon of dark purple storm clouds and cobalt blue lightning bolts made Raven a bit air sick. He looked for a convenient landing place below to take a breather, and was highly gratified at what he found.

Raven landed on one of the rusted iron benches that lined the outside of the Deoradháin Café and looked into the café.

Miyako Astor sat just inside the window on the other side of Raven's perch. The Faerie sat reading a copy of *The Monk: A Romance*, by Matthew Gregory, while smoking a cigarette with the same vengeance that the Archangels used to smite mortals. Besides an overflowed ashtray sat a copy of *The Discovery of Jeanne Baret: A Story of Science, the High Seas, and the First Woman to Circumnavigate the Globe*, by Glynis Ridley with an Elysion Library "Let's Read" bookmark with a bookworm reading a book sticking out of the middle of the book.

Raven wondered how long the Faerie had been incarcerated in the café. It had happened sometime prior to the birth of the Son. But Raven, like most Post-Armagedōn immortals, had no idea how many years had passed since then.

It must be a little slice of Hell knowing that you're trapped in a box, Raven thought, and knowing that you can't even look out the window. Raven remembered that Miyako Astor had once told him that all he could see through the windows or off the back loading dock was massive storms that resembled a nebula vomiting up a planetoid.

Raven had always thought that was a bit harsh on the part of the Creator. He himself had been inside the Deoradháin Café thousands of times in thousands of places throughout this magnificent universe and seen some fantastic sights. He had seen a Spacer medical transport blown into millions of bright orange pieces of metal set against the ascending Whirlpool Galaxy. Raven had been in the Deoradháin Café when it had been posing as the Broken Wagon Wheel Watering Well during the Zita Revolt against the 3rd Faerie Emperor. And Raven had watched from the windows of the Deoradháin Café parked in space as humanity discovered the Minnesänger space shuttle crush on the Moon of Callisto, which led to the discovery of the Great Poseidon mother ship deep within the ammonia and methane ices of Neptune.

According to *Lies My Demon Told Me*, by noted Demonologist Eric Thursley, the story about humanity discovering the Minnesänger space shuttle crush on the Moon of Callisto, and the subsequent discovery of the Great Poseidon mother ship deep within the ammonia and methane ices of Neptune did not actually occur in the Terra universe. The fact that all of the planets in the solar system, as well as the star Sol, and even the asteroid belts were identical to those found in our own home-planet solar system is apparently just an astronomically impossible coincidence that did actually occur. Thursley is unclear about which universe the Minnesänger space shuttle discovery did occur in, and downright evasive on how anyone in our universe could have known about it. But the fact remains that Thursley stubbornly maintains that the Minnesänger space shuttle was not discovered by humanity, as we know it. It just happened to be discovered by a humanity that was in almost every detail identical to ours - just with a wildly different history.

Strange, but true.

Raven wondered for a brief moment if Miyako Astor was happy and very much doubted that the Faerie was. Raven had once before seen Miyako Astor like this from outside the café window some few years before the Final Match at Armagedōn. Miyako Astor had sat for a very long time just staring at the window that he could not see through, surrounded by an empty café. The Faerie looked utterly miserable just then, and Raven was not at all surprised that it cost the Faerie a visible effort to put on his happy restaurateur persona after a band of Humans wandered into the café. Raven had decided to give breakfast a miss that day and continued on his way.

Raven did the same today, and flew on towards the bottom of the stairs at the base of the mountain.

Raven found the Nordic Smith Völundr sitting on the lower steps, carved into the mountain, that lead up to the Temple of Gylfagin. The man was short, stocky, and wore a thick brownish red beard that was meticulously braided into several strands. His hands were thick, and most unusually for a god, were covered in a network of scars; callouses, and purple bruises. He sat comfortably reclining in the sunshine smoking a pipe, and occasionally blowing smoke rings that were completely uninteresting. In fact, the rings were so plain, so grey, and so quickly destroyed by the mild breeze that Raven found himself staring at them in sheer astonishment at their normality in a place so otherwise laden with minor-deity magic.

Raven landed beside Völundr.

"Good morning," Völundr said conversationally. "Or, maybe good afternoon, or evening. It's so hard to tell what time it is in these artificial atmosphere bubbles."

"I thought that the radiation had receded on Terra now?" asked the Raven.

Völundr shrugged, which is an ineffective gesture when one is leaning back on steps.

"It mostly has," he said. "You can walk freely in the blackened waves of grain now, and in the ash-basket of the Ukraine, or visit the ruins of the Forbidden City without much trouble, although I wouldn't recommend dress shoes. But here it's still a bit too thick for comfort."

"Why's that?" asked the Raven.

"You know that old Indo-Pakistani thing. The Hindus hate the Sikhs, the Sikhs hate the Muslims, the Muslims hate the Christians, and the Christians hate everything and everybody - including each other. Well, the net result was more nuclear weapons were exploded here than anywhere else."

Raven turned his head a full 90 degrees and looked at Völundr with a critical eye. Ravens are very good at this, and have been known to intimidate hawks with the tactic, mainly because it puts the hawk's blood-crazed mind into a tail-spin out of surprise that anything is standing up to it.

"Völundr, that doesn't make a damn bit of sense man," Raven complained. "Gylfagin, Hnitborg Mountain, and Kvasir are all of the Nordic Pantheon. Why would it matter where what happened way down south?"

"When the shooting started, many of the old world gods wound up here," Völundr said. "Particularly the ones in heavily populated areas that were being exterminated the fastest, like Pakistan and India. The gods all fled here, and the radiation followed them through some sort of psychic link. Search me why, I never asked."

"Americans," Raven said levelly.

Völundr raised an eyebrow, and then settled his face back into its normal furrow.

"Yeah?" he asked.

"There was a strong element of Nordic and Celtic hero worship in America," Raven said. "A lot of them were the out-doorsy types, and they fared better in the nuke war. Lived, oh, two weeks longer than the urbanites. The total cloud cover from the fallout got everyone in the end; even the ones in those top-grade military bunkers for the politicos."

"That's so," Völundr agreed. "They went in for just about everything over there. I visited there once, America I mean, before the Final Match. I stayed in the Chelsea Hotel and went to the Met. Had a wonderful time with this southern dame. She was an art teacher, showed me all sorts of things about pottery glazes, and ceramics. Did you know those monkeys made electric kilns? And here I was for the last million years doing it the hard way. I also toured the steel works in Detroit, and learned that there were these huge furnaces for electric phosphate smelting. Did you know that? I didn't-"

"Very interesting," Raven said, cutting Völundr off before he settled into a long lecture on the methods of pre-Final Match metallurgy as contrived by the human species. "By the way, I was planning on seeing you later, about the helmet."

"Oh, did it not work?" Völundr asked, his professional concern piqued.

Raven looked down at the white feathers of his body below his neck.

"Well yes, but then again, no," Raven said. "I'm not blind, and that is the main thing. But, I'm white feathered now. And you know what? It's the damnedest odd thing. When I change form, my white feathers turn black again. I can't understand it. But when I become myself again, bang, here they are, white again."

"Hurmp," Völundr hurmped. "Dragons. You can't trust those scaly buggers. Sorry, no clue white bird."

"Fat lot of help you are," Raven said. "Well, can you tell me where the Valkyrie are?"

Völundr nodded.

"Most of them are up, in the temple," he said with a lazy nod towards the top of the stairs.

Raven looked up and saw the 2,113 uneven steps cut out of the mountainside.

"Damn glad I can fly," Raven said. "Is Kára up there, and just what in the froggy balmy blue Hells are they doing up there anyway?"

"Am I my Kára's keeper?" Völundr asked.

"Yeah."

"I guess I am," Völundr agreed.

"What's she and the Valkyrie girls doing up there?" Raven asked.

"Waiting," Völundr said pushing himself up into a sitting position. "For me. And, I guess, for the 13 goddesses. I am waiting for them too and enjoying all this sunshine. It's nice, even if it is fake. You've arrived just in time for the goddesses' end game. Kára's the referee."

Völundr stood up, stretched his back and calf muscles.

"What end game?" Raven asked cautiously as he was rather certain he didn't want to know.

"The Dragon will rise from the East, and simultaneously eat the world and birth a new one," Völundr said. "No avoiding that one Friend. Apparently, that's why the Creator made the Dragons in the first place."

"Right," Raven said. "You know, I've never gone in for any of that mystical bull-shit."

Völundr raised an eyebrow.

"Seems an odd theological position for a god," Völundr said.

"When someone asks you if you're God, you say?"

"No!"

"Right," Raven agreed. "Saves trouble all around. So, I'm a Nature Spirit."

"Still a bird- brain," Völundr said.

"Hey, don't get me wrong," Raven protested, "I'm not in denial about the Creator, or the Son, or any of the prophets, or the whole unholy armada of immortals, or the Immortals. That's a damn unhealthy position to take. Besides, I know too damn many of them for that. I just have never gone in for the old stories, and some-called modern theology is worse. Except for Tillich, he's okay. Only mortal academic I ever knew that got a good line on what the Creator actually is."

"You are an old story," Völundr said ignoring the philo-theological bait.

Völundr had always held that there were more important things in life than understanding life, the universe, or anything. Take for instance Völundr's cousin, Yü the Great, the divine Smith, called 大禹 or Dà Yǔ, whom developed the first oven hot enough to melt iron, some 2000 years before the Europeans. And that was only a small part of Yü's career for he also built damns, dykes, irrigations systems, and wrote philosophy in his spare time. Yes, Völundr thought, there is a man to admire. The fact that he had accidently founded the Xia Dynasty was a minor flaw in Yü's career that Völundr was quite willing to overlook for he disliked politics almost as much as he disliked theology.

"Why you think I don't put any credit in any of the rest of those old stories?" the Raven said sarcastically. "It's hard to take that shyt seriously when you know how overblown your own propaganda is.

Völundr laughed.

"You know," he said, "the funny thing is, all one had to do to make some place East is to turn around and face West. And don't make a joke about wanting to know where she is. Everybody knows the Cardinal Direction Personifications are just an urban legend."

"Yeah, right, sure," Raven said. "I'll tell her that next time I see her. ' Hey babe,' I'll say, 'did you know that Völundr said you're just an urban legend?' I wonder how she'll take that."

"Whatever," Völundr said. "Have it your own way I'm sure. They still don't exist. I've been around longer than you and I've never meet them."

"Belief equals existence in this universe mate," Raven said. "I have it on good authority."

"Oh? The Creator told you so?" Völundr asked.

"Hell no!" Raven squawked. "My brain told me."

Völundr grunted.

Raven flapped his wings hard until he landed neatly on Völundr's shoulder.

"So, what's this con then?" Raven asked.

"13 goddesses are planning to escape to the next universe."

"No way."

"Ja way," Völundr said. "They've a pretty nifty plan for it too."

Raven listened in mounting horror and fascination as the little man's stocky legs climbed one-step after another, carefully avoiding tree roots and overgrowth.

"You know, that just might work," Raven said reluctantly. "Assuming anything gets out that is."

"Agreed," Völundr said. "Me, I'm not complaining. I've been here since almost the beginning. Since man decided, he wanted something better than a rock to club a tiger with. I'm all in now. A vacation sounds very nice. I want to go somewhere warm, with mixed drinks, and tan girls in short skirts."

"You dirty old man," Raven snorted.

"True, true," Völundr agreed. "I've never much like the idea of Valhalla. Did you know that they came up with nanobots at the end that could rearrange subatomic structures? Hat's research doctors were just on the edge of being able to send these little machines in to farm new tissue on the internal organs of Humans. Hat's people, the Royal Adelaide Hospital, and the Institut National des Sciences Appliquées were all in on it together. It would have been Immortality for Humans, and without the Immortality Virus. Hat was just about to finally win."

"Win?" Raven asked as he disinterestedly clawed a twig fragment out from under his right wing.

"Her battle against greed, hatred, and stupidity," Völundr said with a completely straight face that Raven immediately distrusted.

"Immortality cures greed, hatred, and stupidity?" Raven asked knowing he didn't want to have the answer.

"Yep," Völundr said permitting a slight smile to transgress across his face. "Hatter's idea is that if people were to live forever, they'd *have to* be nicer to each other. That they would think in the long-term because the long term would matter to them. That people would take time to figure out how biochemistry works so that they wouldn't mess up their own. And she thought that they would figure out history because they were going to be around for so much of it. Like starting with all that noise that the Creator made when He..."

Raven let his mind wander. He loved his occasional visits with Völundr because the stocky old man would ramble on about the entire history of engineering from the first picosecond to the present, often wandering back and forth along the whole timeline without the slightest regard for, or concern about, his audience. Raven loved that quality in a traveling companion. It gave him time to think.

Raven wondered what sort of a con Basil Berry and Keith were pulling, and just who was conning who. Raven didn't wonder about the why. With tricksters like Basil Berry and his Demon godfather, the why usually boiled down to 'Because I was bored.'

Basil Berry was a major variable though. It was almost impossible to know if the Scion was the con-artist, the shell, the marble, or on a million to one outside chance- just an innocent spectator, until it was all over but the explaining to the insurance companies. The two biggest problems with figuring out Basil Berry's strategy Raven knew were one, the kid almost never actually had a strategy, and two he'd change sides at the drop of a suggestion, threat, bribe, or whatever passed for humour in his math-ridden mind.

"And that's when Agnóstos Theós asked me if it could be done," Völundr said.

"Huh, what?" Raven said snapping out of his contemplation of which side of the cosmic chessboard he was on. Which was a pointless consideration from Raven's point of view. In Raven's experience, it was usually a 134,217,728-sided multi-dimensional board played in 7-dimensional space with between 1 and 134,217,728 players, ages 7 & up.

If one stopped to think about that sort of thing too long, one usually got stabbed in the back by one of those damn knights jumping over the pawns.

"That's when Agnóstos Theós asked me if the ring could be made," Völundr said.

"Ring? What ring?"

"The one I was just telling you about, bird-brain, weren't you listening?"

"Let's pretend I was," Raven said, "and you just tell me again."

"It was Sešat's idea originally," Völundr said. "A ring, any soul vessel really, that the goddesses can put themselves into. She originally wanted a gigantic space cruiser, like seriously huge, something that would take and maintain them safely for the travel into the new universe. Like Moses floating down the river in the papyrus basket when Meritamen found him. I talked her down to a ring."

"Oh, that old wives' tale about multiple universes?" Raven asked. "Give me a break. That crap only works in science fiction movies. There's only one universe, and we're in it buster. Be it ever so empty, there's no place like here."

Völundr shrugged.

"Suit yourself," Völundr said. "But that's what they wanted. I settled for a ring in the end. I thought it a fitting yonic symbol for thirteen goddesses."

"WHAT?" squawked the Raven. "Hells Bells you daft nutter. Have you gone absolutely fuck-bonkers?

You can't put a goddess into something, much less 13 of them."

"Oh, that's not true at all," Völundr said without the slightest sign of annoyance at the Raven's lack of belief in the project's success. "It is easy as anything to build a vessel that a soul can travel in. It operates on the same principles as those larger-on-the-inside flats that the Demon James used to build for his Yuppies, Guppies, and Cichlids. I've built stuff that has stood up to both Stan and the Metatron. Like Keith's demonic silver pentagram for example, labour on that one was a bitch. But that old lamp that Badroulbadour threw away did not contain a ğinn as the popular story gives out, but actually a god of desire that was enslaved to the lamp by Stan on account that the false god was racking up better recruiting stats than Stan was and the old boy's ego just can't stand that sort of thing."

"All true," Raven agreed. "Stan never has been able to take competition. But seriously, how in Hell's name did you make something like that?"

"Oh, it was easy," Völundr said. "The same why I made the lamp for Stan."

"You?" the Raven said not hiding his astonishment. "You made that damned thing? Do you have any idea how much misery that thing has caused?"

"Oh, it all worked out for Badroulbadour in the end, more or less," Völundr said with a shrug. "Mind you, Aladdin wasn't much of a catch. People impressed by the clothes, and the gold, and the royal titles never are. And the ones that will sell their dignity to impress others are the worst of all."

"Sod Badroulbadour," Raven said. "I mean the lamp. That damn thing has started wars, and tormented souls, and-"

"I didn't do any of that," Völundr said.

"But what you made did and-"

"I didn't tell them too," Völundr said calmly.

Watch out, Raven thought. Your about to walk straight into a wall of free will verses Ineffability verses 'I'm not responsible for those dead kids, I just gave the guy moonshine and laughed as he drove off in his truck drunk as a skunk.' You can't win this one.

Raven said nothing.

Völundr continued for exactly 100 steps before speaking again.

"The main thing was that the goddesses want to go into it," the Smith said reverting to his original discourse. "That was the main thing; they have to be able to enter into the soul entrapment of their own free will. It would have been much harder to force one into the ring, and forget about forcing 13 of them into the same ring. But, I started in the Annatar Forge and fashioned it out of Titanium. The old gals wanted moonlight silver, first unearthed by the light of a full moon in Autumn. I couldn't be bothered with all that ancient mystical jazz. Besides, if anything is going to survive a black hole, magically enhanced Titanium might have a chance, but I wouldn't care to stake my afterlife on it. Polished up, it looks the same as moonlight silver."

"Yeah, sure it does," Raven, complained. "If you've never seen moon silver, I guess you could fall for Titanium."

Völundr lapsed into silence for a while, and Raven left him that way. Raven felt that the old Smith was worried about this artefact that he had created, and Raven thought the best way to get details out of Völundr was to wait for the old man to work his way around to them. So Raven instead looked back down behind them and wasn't surprised to see that Völundr marched up more than half the stairs that led to the mountain Temple of Gylfagin.

"After I made the ring," Völundr started up again without warning, "each of the goddesses came to my forge and put almost all of themselves into the ring, save enough to keep their now mortal bodies alive and a spark of themselves inside the bodies for a fortnight."

"Why wait? Why not go right in the ring entirely, one at a time?" Raven asked, mystified by the whole idea. "Sounds like overly complicated Seppuku to me."

"Well, they all have to go at once, and that's just not possible, Völundr said. " So everyone is mostly inside, except Agnóstos Theós, she's to be last. She will embrace the others, and take them all in with her. Oh and tonight is the Paschal Full Moon."

Raven looked up at the sun shining evil black and purple clouds that blocked out all the stars.

"If you say so. How'd you got signed up for this insanity?"

"Sešat and Agnóstos Theós asked me, demanded really," Völundr said simply.

Raven wasn't impressed. "And?" he said.

"Well, I told them to bugger off at first," Völundr continued. "But then Brighid came by and asked me, followed by the moon goddess Chang'e. Jínn came by after that and did her usual 'Anything you could ever want I can give you routine.'"

"Lame," Raven said.

"Yeah," Völundr agreed. "Sedna and Shinatobe turned up then and stormed about my workshop for days. Then in turn, there came Mama Allpa, Kumari, Ninlil, Kohara, and Lilith. I told them all to get lost."

"Why?"

"Not a one of them ever said please."

"But you are involved now," Raven observed.

"Yeah," the grumpy old Smith agreed, "up to my eyeballs. Potnia Theron said please. That was all she said actually. Just showed up and said 'Please.' No act, no nothing. Just said please."

"Damn, that's impressive," Raven said.

"I hope it works," Völundr said.

"So what if it doesn't?" Raven joked. "Worse case, we lose a couple of goddesses. The universe is full of 'em."

"No," Völundr said with a heavy sigh. "Worst case scenario the magic botches and blows a hole in Gylfagin so big that it will crack Terra's Tectonic Plate, shift the orbit of Terra- again, and we all freeze to death. Worst-worst case is that we can start a chain reaction and just blow the whole planet apart. As much as the place resembles a free-market environmental policy advertisement, I still like the old rock. I don't really want to blow it up. For one thing, I'm not suicidal, and for another, I still got back order to get out."

"Don't you always?"

"Yeah," Völundr smirked. "That's why I always take payment in advance."

"Well," Raven said with an audible tremble in his voice, "if that second option happens, we can take comfort in it happening too fast to hurt."

"Oh, you think so?" Völundr asked.

Raven said nothing.

Chapter 11: 13 goddesses

On Terra, in the Sol system, orbiting the Sol star.

And it came to pass, when men began to multiply on the face of the earth, and daughters were born unto them, that the sons of God saw the daughters of men that they were fair; and they took them wives of all which they chose. And the Lord said, My spirit shall not always strive with man, for that he also is flesh: yet his days shall be an hundred and twenty years. There were giants in the earth in those days; and also after that, when the sons of God came in unto the daughters of men, and they bare children to them, the same became mighty men which were of old, men of renown. --Genesis 6:1-4, K.J.V.

And it came to pass that an agreement was brokered.

Völundr ascended the last uneven stone step leading up to the Temple of Gylfagin and stood atop a large plateau of smooth rectangular stones. Far below, the valley spread out like a small dab of green leafy butter in a frying pan of wasted black charred death. He stood for a moment; his back turned toward the temple, and contemplated the sight of the valley below.

Raven, looking the other way, saw the stone courtyard of the Temple of Gylfagin decorated with a central fountain, several benches, chairs carved of ancient stones all worn smooth by age, and one ancient tree. A few withered trees stood circling the courtyard blackened and naturally mummified, alongside a few lush seedlings that stood up to 3 meters.

Standing in groups of twos and threes were twelve goddesses, all dressed in a simple purple muslin gown with a white sash across her chest. There were thirteen goddess if you counted the other one.

Beyond them was the Temple of Gylfagin. The old pile of rocks, beautiful though they were, did not interest Raven half as much as the two immortals standing between Völundr and the main temple entrance.

The immortal standing closest to Völundr and Raven was not tall, barely 1.55 meters, but was slender like a river reed. Her hair was a thick black darkness, curly as snakes, and drawn back together in a long braided queue, which complimented her pale skin tone and purple-black Kimono. Her name was Kára, Warrior goddess of the Valkyrie and she was a natural Immortal. She looked every bit like the ambulatory clay fighter baked for a thousand years in the central African desert that she was. The Valkyrie wore black accented with dark tones of purple, her eyes were bright jade green, and she punctuated her words with precise sword-like gestures.

The other immortal was the ancient Egyptian goddess Sešat, the original Mistress of the House of Books, goddess of Wisdom, Knowledge, and Writing back in the bad old days, and goddess of Maths, Engineering, and Globalization since the Industrial Revolution, along with Electronics, Telecommunications, and Interstellar Travel since the discovery of the Herbert Effect and Space Folding. Sešat was also the mother of Dr. Hatshepsut Nefertari Djeserit Fukayna, M.D., D.D.M., D.V.M., N.D., Ph.d., A.A.A.S., B.M.E., C.A.P.A., C.C.E., C.Chem., H.S.D.I.P., M.A.B.T.S., M.A.S., M.S.S.W., Q.C., L.L.C., C.B.E., Lt. Col. MA.A.N.G., Retired, called Hat. For you would have to be "Mad as Hatter to lead Scions," as Scion Señor Sol used to say.

Sešat's ability to recall anything that ever had been written on papyrus and paper was one of the primary reasons why most of the gods, nature spirits, and other immortals never wrote anything down, even in code. Nevertheless, her ability was not invincible. Dangerously formidable though it was, it did not extend to writings upon cloth, silk, skin, stone, metal, or anything digital unless it was copied or printed onto papyrus or paper. Certain ingredients added to certain inks, particularly if they were coupled with certain protective magics also marred or completely eliminated Sešat's ability to read from the void. Also, certain Celestial creatures such as Angels, Demons, Watchers, and the Valkyrie were completely immune no matter how they composed their letters. Hence, Stan's practice of selling Honorary Demonships to Humans that had a particular need for secrecy, like the one he sold to Rían. Also, the blood of the Architeuthidae squid, Dragons, the very rare naturally undead or even rarer innocent mortal would also scramble the writing beyond comprehension for anyone except the original author.

Nevertheless, Sešat, or more particularly her agents, spent a great deal of time and money scanning and photocopying masses of data onto regular paper, and printing vaster amounts of data from computers. It was for this same purpose that Sešat founded the first paper-recycling mill in the world after her first meeting with the Chinese eunuch Cài Lún, also called 蔡倫, in the city of Luoyang in the year 101 B.C. concerning his recent invention of paper. The first appearance of paper-based knowledge had come as an unexpected shock to Sešat, and it took her a few years to track down its source. Since that time, she did more than anyone else in the whole of history did to spread the use of paper throughout the known universe. But it is easier to win distinctions like that when you are an immortal.

The second immortal Immortal, the Valkyrie Kára, was of both considerably more interest and concern to Raven.

There was no getting around it, even to a short-arse like Raven, who was tall for a bird and short of a man. The Immortal Warrior goddess of the Valkyrie, Kára, was short. She stood exactly 1.313 meters - if she hiccupped while standing on her tiptoes.

The Valkyrie stood still, a patient expression frozen on her face, listening to Sešat go on about only goddess knew what. The upper tips of the Kára's black wings moved just above the stylized shoulders of her onyx-black and purple Japanese Kimono that was trimmed in real moonlight silver. The Ouroboros Symbol, not any sort of copy, but the original Ouroboros Symbol of a Dragon eating its own tail made out of a substance that resembled black jade, but most certainly wasn't black jade, hung upon the Valkyrie's neck suspended by a string of star cores, which are like pearls, but are actually what's left after a black hole collapses. Solid rumour had it that the Ouroboros Symbol was the first thing that the Creator made way back in the mists of infinity, before He had gotten around in inventing either mists or time or even His own thoughts. If you think of a sedecillion, that's a 10 with 51 more zeros behind it. And that is a sedecillion of centillions, a centillion being another 10 with 303 more zeros behind it. If you think of sedecillion of centillion of years, you might just have an idea of how old the Dragon Ouroboros Symbol was. However old it was, Raven had never paid it any more mind than most humans paid mind or honour to the Ġgantija Temple on the Maltese island of Gozo. It was just something that was old, unfathomably old yes, but just old. It was just a symbol of the continuousness of creating that the Creator got such a kick out of.

But Tenebrarum Solis, the sun-darkened sword, the hilt of which was visible over the Kára's right shoulder, did interest Raven a great deal. The sword was not used as a symbol of power, a never truer symbol exists of a thing than the thing itself, but it was death itself. Not the Death, with a capital D, but just simple death itself, the thing, the act of ceasing to be anymore. And there were two ceremonial Bronze Arslantepe daggers tucked into the belt of Kára's Kimono too. The Bronze Arslantepe daggers were the same thing as their bigger brother, only shorter.

Little death, big death, little death, Raven thought. One death, two death, three death, more death? Hop on death. Debbie does death. I do not want your green eggs and death, Raven concluded.

Raven also knew that the old Warrior adored modern weaponry, and that there would be Stan-only-knew-what tucked into wouldn't-you-be-lucky-to-find-out-where on the Valkyrie's body. And that knowledge mildly frightened the old nature spirit. Simply knowing that at any time, the one woman could end everything for him, or anyone else, sans Death itself and the Creator that made her and her father. Kára's third place ranking in the cosmic ass-wiping department was not a position that someone like Raven, who was many tens of thousands of ranks further down that ass-wiping leaderboard, took lightly.

Take for example the note in *Arms, Armament, and Death: A Mortal's Guide to Shyt You Shouldn't Touch*, by Sūn Bìn, also called 孙膑. The Tenebrarum Solis is a sun-darkened sword, which is a blade that has been forged in the very center of a blue hyper-giant star such as the star Eta Carinae located in the Carina system. Both the nebulæ Homunculus and Eta Carinae are located in that system, and are well worth the travel time to see. But those not immune to serious bodily damage should view the sites with serious caution, as the blue star Eta Carinae is nearly 200 times more massive than the star Sol, which warms the garden called Terra. The star Eta Carinae's surface temperature averages some 40,000° Kelvin, which converts to an average of 39,725° Celsius or 71,540° Fahrenheit. Either way, it's more than enough to toast s'mores at 40 lights years. So it is difficult to imagine who, or whom, or even why, anything would use the core of a fireball of that magnitude to make a sword. The merest touch from the blade, even an accidental brushing of the blade's fuller, will cause the victim's death. Even the Metatron has been known to eye the sword with mistrust.

And that was the sort of toy that Kára carried around on her back.

Interestingly enough, Sūn Bìn mentions in a different section of the book that the Bronze Arslantepe daggers are considered by mortal authorities to be the oldest known "swords" in history. The book goes into

259

detail about why this is utterly ridiculous citing the Angels with flaming swords in Genesis which predated humanity but a few dozen years, and the Kusanagi-no-Tsurugi which is to Japan as Excalibur is to Britain, and the Ama-no-Murakumo-no-Tsurugi Sword of the Gathering Clouds of Heaven, and of course the Vorpal Sword used of old to dispatch from the world that annoying little rhyming Jabberwocky, all of which predate the Bronze Arslantepe daggers that Kára carried. The Valkyrie just liked the Bronze Arslantepe daggers is all and modified them to suit her professional needs.

Raven knew that as long as the Valkyrie remained humanoid and female, and maintained the same relative mass, that they could appear in whatever shape they wished. It was in their nature to appear to the mortals that believed in them in whatever forms mortals would find most comforting. Not that they ever bothered for immortals when they finally bit the proverbial "big one." An Immortal was lucky if even one of the Valkyrie turned up, much less Kára.

Raven allowed himself a brief moment to speculate about the Angel of Death motif that Kára seemed to be kitted out for. The dark silk fabric enhanced the paleness of Kára's skin tone, and he noted approvingly, she had laced her hair with a woven thread of moonlight silver.

Oh my dear apostasy, Raven thought. Yes, my Demon friend, I get it.

Raven kept his eyes fixed upon Kára by rotating his own head as Völundr turned around, noticed the two women, and set off to greet them.

Kára turned to them and made the formal greeting of her kind.

"What do you fear?"

"An inadequate life," Raven responded promptly. He knew trouble when he saw it.

The Valkyrie nodded.

Völundr looked up into the sky, past the bubble of pleasant sunshine and orange-blossomed scented breeze. He took a deep breath, pleased to feel the cold crisp mountain air inside of his battered leather boot-covered toes.

Völundr stroked his beard with one hand, while retrieving his pipe and tobacco pouch with the other.

"The fucking idiots that dreamed up the bomb and the even dumber bastards that exploded them, and the insane maniacs that eviscerated the E.P.A., O.S.H.A., and the Creator dammed economist bastards that convinced everyone that war is good for the economy. God forsaken war is horrible for the economy; corpses don't buy anything, they're fucking famous for it. One tin soldiers the whole fucking lot of them. I mean seriously, what's a corpse need with a refrigerator? Living breathing people put corpses in a refrigerator, but that's for the comfort of the living breathing nose, not the corpse nose."

Völundr fell silent again, took a deep breath, and began to fill his pipe.

"Is that all?" Kára asked.

"Well, I could tell you about faux patriot armchair cowards that get elected to office by race-baiting whatever today's enemy of the people is, but ignore those same voters every time there's an 9.9 magnitude earthquake or category 7 hurricane? I got loads to say about cowards and the idiots that put cowards in positions of power," the old Smith said packing his tobacco with his dirt-encrusted thumbnail. "You know the ones that never served a day in uniform - not even in the Girl Guides - but want your children to go fight their little war of pre-emptive defence. You want that rant too?"

"Creator have mercy," Kára said with a smile.

"They don't fucking deserve any," Völundr said folding his arms across his chest.

"Come here you old grumpy fuss," Sešat said and swooped down on the old Smith, sending Raven flapping away for his life. Sešat lifted the old Smith off his feet and hugged him.

"All right, all right," Völundr chocked. "Please put me down."

Raven settled down on Kára's left shoulder.

"Bird," Kára said with more than the clichéd hint of malice in her voice, "if you foul my Kimono, I will bake you into a black bird mincemeat pie with my own hands, sixpence, or no."

Raven gulped.

"Hi ya luv, nice to see you too, it's been, what, a wee-"

"One thousand two hundred forty-two years, three hundred thirteen days, and almost two hours."

"Glad you're finally coming to grips with your precision issues," Raven said. "How you been?"

"It was great until you showed up," the Valkyrie said. "What's the low-life ex-husband of mine want?"

"Who?"

"Don't play Dodo-brain with me, you're his only mate, and you know it," Kára said showing a genuinely pleasant smile on her face that scared Raven more than her heart-felt snarls ever had.

The woman really is bat-shit crazy, Raven thought.

"I'd enjoy listening to you talking to the Son," Kára continued, "You know, my delivering you from my hand to His hand. How's your soul? Been to confession lately? Feel like testing me today Bungee? Metal to beak at twenty paces? You know the Old Boy meant all that stuff about 'Blessed are the pure in heart, for they shall see God.' To be taken rather literally."

"Ah well, you know how it is," Raven said. "Creator created Raven and Creator saw that Raven was good. *Not my fault He didn't stick around to keep an eye on me.* I need looking after I do. Fell in with hawks from the wrong side of Sherwood, no ma, no da, no nobody besides Bennie and the Jets and you know that ain't' healthy."

"I had almost forgotten what heaping loads of steamers you dish out," Kára said.

"You just wait till I get my breath," Raven said and took a deep breath. "Taught Kenneth Williams everything I did."

"And we may never forgive you for that," Sešat said. "I do miss him though."

"Besides little dee death," Raven said to Kára, "Sonny Boy didn't say that *only* the pure of heart would get into the Kingdom. He just said that the pure of heart could see his Dad. I'm cool with never seeing Him. Heard Him once. I had to get treatment for P.T.E.D."

"Pardon?" Kára asked.

"Post trauma ear detachment," Raven said. "My ears ain't never been the same."

"You little greasy pip-squeak, I'm goanna fry you in duck lard and-"

"Lighten-up sweets," Raven said. "This Emo thing you've got going on is really giving me the giggles. Ittt'sss sooo hard to take you seriously when you talk like that."

There was silence for a long moment. It went on long enough for Raven to look at Völundr and see the look of genuine concern on his face.

Opps, Raven thought.

And then, Kára erupted in laughter, and Raven took flight again, motivated by pure fear, straight for the temple roof.

"Okay bird," the Valkyrie Kára finally managed. "What do you want?"

"The Dragon," Raven said, cautiously circling back. "The Dragon's not taking messages today and you can't have a proper paid-up prophesied end of the universe without the message getting to him-"

"Her," Kára corrected. "Dragon is her, a she, not a he. As in a she that gives birth to universes kind of she."

"Oh, for fuck's sake, not you too?" Raven protested. "Deep Fried Demon-brains got on that same rant too, and like I told him, when you're just a little bird like me, ancestor to dinosaurs or no, you don't go around correcting gender confused Dragons about how they refer to themselves. He thinks of himself as a he, and that's good enough for me, as-" Raven abruptly fell silent, realizing his mistake.

"Okay bird-brain, let's try this again," Kára said, non-metaphorical ice crystals forming around her words, coupled by the very real dark bloody-purple shades that now laced her Kimono. "What does that bastard have to say to me?"

"Hi there, how are ya? It's been a long time?"

Kára stared at Raven.

"Seems like we've come a long way?" Raven faltered.

Kára continued to stare right through Raven's skull.

"My, don't we learn so slow," Völundr added helpfully.

"But we learn so slow," Sešat corrected.

"That's it," Völundr agreed. "My, but we learn so slow," he said while tapping the air with is forefingers.

The goddess Sešat began strumming nothing.

Kára fumed and Raven began considering escape options.

About 1 second, Raven thought. 1 second before she's holding a projectile weapon. God I wish I had someone to pray to.

"And why must *they* grow up so fast?" Sešat sang in an entirely off-putting acapella. "I was just coming to grips with humanity," she added wistfully. "I was really getting somewhere with the whole improvement of the species community thing that my daughters were always on at me about."

"And gods, they come and they go," Völundr carried on with a wave a hand around the courtyard.

Sešat sighed, and said, "So true. So many phantom faces at the window, so many shadows on the floor, where my friends are no more."

"Lost enemies too," Raven added with a light tone that completely failed to lift Sešat's spirits or lighten Kára's glare.

"I've always wondered," Sešat said, "if the Creator would, or has, let us into Parádeisos? You can't call up a god on a Ouija Board and ask you know."

"No, I didn't know," Völundr agreed. "Can't recall ever trying. I usually want to get away from you buggers, not encourage you lot."

"That's it?" Kára demanded. "Lyrics from a fuckin' country rock band? Like I'm going to line up the Valkyrie for that bastard Demon and his gods dammed ego?" Kára glanced at Sešat, and added, "Sorry about that," in tones that suggested everything but the existence of regret.

Sešat shrugged. "I'm sure one of us has."

"What?"

"Nothing, nothing," Sešat said with a wave of her hand, "don't mind me. Do carry on."

"Were you expecting Robert Smith's *Love Song* instead?" Raven asked.

"It would have been a nice fucking touch," Kára said in such a low and menacing tone that Raven felt his heart stop. It would have been an inconvenience had he actually been using it.

"Warrior goddess," Völundr said in that most calm and flat tone that only engineers and their gods can manage, "while anger becomes your profession, it is lethal in mine. Please forgive the trickster messenger his foul jest."

I don't get paid enough for this shit, Raven thought. Besides, Sešat was doing a bloody musical. Why do I get all the grief?

"Well?" Kára prompted again in a much more normal tone.

"Well, the thing is, the truth of it is ya might say," Raven said.

"Out with it Kentucky Fried Crow," Kára demanded again and this time Raven could see the blood vessels in her head pulsing with intensity.

"Promise me first you'll go see Dragon," Raven said.

"Fine, after this," Kára said.

"Well, Keith, he" Raven started.

"Go on, go on," Sešat said encouragingly.

"He didn't really say anything," Raven squeaked like a Finch hatchling and took for the air.

He needn't have bothered.

Kára just stood there.

After circling seven times, Raven landed on Sešat's left shoulder. He turned to look at the old goddess and found her staring him eyeball to eyeball; one eye closed, the other bulging, just like a raven would.

Raven coughed, covering his beak with one wing and muttered, "Bitch," under his breath.

266

Sešat smiled and then laughed without making a sound, her entire body heaving.

Abruptly, Kára turned and stormed off towards the Temple of Gylfagin.

"That went well," Raven said.

"Raven, dear Raven," Sešat said. "Won't you tell Fruchtbarkeitskultus to just call our Kára? She's only mad because he won't call. He'd only have to eat a little bit of the proverbial cowpat. But I doubt it will amount to much, considering what he'd gain in peace, love, and eternal tranquillity."

"I've tried my lady, I've tried," Raven said. "I've been from Boston to L.A. and back again thrice over this one, with both of them, and neither is budgin'. Damn stupid both too. He's mad 'cause he screwed up and she won't let him apologize because she won't talk to him, or something like that. She thinks just the opposite, or something just as daft I'm sure. They need to just drop it and go have lunch or something. Life has moved on in so many ways. It's pure egotism on both sides if you ask me."

"I think you're being too hard on our Kára," Sešat said. "It was his fault. Cannot argue otherwise."

"Really?" Raven asked. "You remember that time he tried to stop drinking and she bought him a hip flask?"

"No," Sešat said.

"I do," Völundr said.

"Right, so if you start from fault, nobody will get anywhere, ever," Raven said. "I mean they *both* need to get over it. I mean you can hardly go anywhere fun without bumping into a Valhalla Girl these days. And all he does is sit around drinking and reading novels. I mean, it wasn't too bad when he ran that bookstore on Leigh Street in Bloomsbury. But after that, well, tedious is the word."

"Oh well," Sešat said. "Master Smith? Please, come this way. Everything has been prepared to your specifications."

Völundr nodded and followed Sešat towards the Temple of Gylfagin.

"What about Agnóstos Theós?" Völundr asked. "We can't start without her. My ring is pre-loaded with parts of all thirteen goddess, not just twelve, and most of the ring is held together by Agnóstos Theós' stubborn wilfulness," he added as he pulled on a pair of dark black gloves. "We can't start without her. It'd be suicide."

Raven wondered what Völundr's gloves were made of. They didn't just look black; they looked like they were holes in the fabric of space that just happened to be shaped like Völundr's fingers.

"What's up with those gloves," Raven asked. "They make your hands look like they don't exist."

Völundr looked down at his hands, or rather, where his hands were not. In a sense, Völundr thought, the bird was right. His hands didn't, strictly speaking, exist anymore, not in this universe anyway. Völundr had constructed them so that a piece of another universe bent inwards back onto itself over one hand, and a part of a third universe bent inwards upon itself over his other hand. This had the effect of placing Völundr's hands outside of the normal natural forces of things like gravity, time, and space, which control all universes. This was how he bent the elements of his creations to his will, as he did with the goddesses' vessel ring.

"Oh, nothing special," Völundr said. "Black magic. They help with the voluntary deaths."

"What's with the suicide theme?" Raven asked.

"It's been on my mind for a while now," Völundr said. "See, this thing either goes correctly at each stage or we blow most of the planet apart. An entrapment vessel to keep one soul a prisoner is sound theory; I've made hundreds of them. But a transport vessel that can be exited by the journeymen? And can carry 13 goddesses? That's never even been attempted before with mortals, much less goddesses, and who knows what influences on the process goddess suicide will have. I don't."

Raven was cut short in repost by the faint rustle of wind that spoke.

"I am here," said the voice that seemed to come from both everywhere, and nowhere, at the same time.

Of all the lame-ass shit that gods did, Raven disliked that voice thing the most.

"Yeah? Where?" Völundr asked.

"Come out, come out, wherever you are," Sešat said. "Our Master Smith likes to know where things-"

"Goddess," Raven corrected.

"Everything *and* everybody," Sešat continued, "is."

A form started to take shape, just between Völundr and Sešat. It was vaguely humanoid and female in shape, dressed like the other goddesses, and it flickered like a first generation Simulated Reality Animation, all spotty, slightly blurred, and out of focus. Raven had no doubt that he could simply fly right through it.

"Ah," Völundr said. "It is closer to time than I thought."

"Γεια σας κυρία," the Raven said. "That's about a third of my Greek by the way. Just so's you know."

A flickering Agnóstos Theós gazed at Raven for a while and Raven felt his feathers ruffle of their own accord, giving him the distinct impression that had the old goddess been at her peak, he would now be nothing much more than a hollow shell of instincts and fear.

"Greek? I think I lived with the Greeks once, for a while," Agnóstos Theós said. "But no, I am not Greek. I am much too old to simply be Greek. I do though love these airy dresses and there is something lovely and simplistic about open-air temples with columns. But no my dear bird, I am not Greek."

"Hello mother," Sešat said.

"Hello daughter," Agnóstos Theós said.

"Hi ya, Momma," Raven said.

"Hello baby bird," Agnóstos Theós said. "I would think you were an ill omen, if I believed in that sort of thing. How are you?"

"Oh, you know how it is in the Dragon taming business, always lively," Raven said. "And you? How are you?"

"Pre-transcendent."

"Opaque as usual," Sešat said. "Dad?"

Agnóstos Theós shrugged.

"No news is good news as the mortals use to say," Raven said.

Völundr looked around the courtyard and began ticking goddesses off on his fingers. Agnóstos Theós the Unknown and Sešat, one and two. Brighid the Triple Goddess of Multi-tasking, Chang'e of the Moon, and Jínn mother of the Djinn of Genie, three, four, and five. Kohara mother of all sea life, Kumari of Victory, and Liliththat the Rebellion, six, seven, and eight. Mama Allpa the Fertile, and Ninlil of the Garden, nine and ten. Potnia Theron the goddess formally known as Artemis, Sedna of the Sea, and Shinatobe of the Wind, eleven, twelve, and all.

Völundr like all immortals, and unlike mortals, knew that the number thirteen was a word of power, not bad luck. Mankind often invoked its power carelessly, and unable to control it, suffered, so they called it bad luck. But Völundr simply chose to avoid it, when he could. But today he couldn't.

"All are here now," Völundr said. "Let's go."

"You Völ, baby, I'd love to stay and all, but my work here's done," Raven said.

"Yes," Völundr said, "I told you, there is a good chance we'll blow Terra apart with this scheme. Life insurance up to date?"

"You can't live forever," Sešat said. "Or, so I am told."

"I intend to die trying," Raven said.

"Come on in, and watch the show," Völundr said. "It will either be long and dull as dog-doings, or short and terribly exciting."

"You got a warped sense of excitement," Raven said. "But put it like that and I can hardly refuse, can I?"

The main entrance to the Temple of Gylfagin darkened as it was blocked by a large humanoid figure. The female Demon stood 4 meters tall wearing the hair of a punk rocker, on the head and face of a crocodile, and the full body of an erect lioness, its main body covered in a hippopotamus hide leather suit, and human skin boots.

"Ammit the Tasteless," Raven sneered.

"Raven the Tasty," Ammit said. "How nice to see you."

"The pleasure is all yours," Raven said.

"Do come in," Ammit hissed. "I've been looking forward to tasting your tricky soul for eons and eons."

"Oh no, no, no," Raven cried, "I'm not going in there. Not for love or eggs. I don't want a front row seat for the end of my life. I don't what to be there when it happens."

"Where will you then?" Völundr asked, obviously amused. "You won't have time to get back to your car and escape."

"I don't intend to wait that long, not for you or anybody," Raven said. "I'm for the Deoradháin Café. I

271

can get there before you get to the deadly part. We once watched a super nova up close from in there, so I think it'll manage through Terra going bye-bye."

"Alright," Völundr said. "You fly and I'll buy, 'cause I can't fly."

"Agreed," Raven said and took flight. "See ya."

"See you later brood mate," Ammit said.

Not if I can help it, Raven thought as he beat his wings for all they were worth.

Later, deep down, where the roots of the Hnitborg Mountain become the Asthenosphere, where the forges of gods and the Dwarves of Dwarrowdelf burn, Völundr the god of Smiths, Agnóstos Theós, and twelve animated Terracotta Golem goddess gathered around the Master Smith Völundr's personal forge.

Each Terracotta Golem had been recovered, intact, from the tomb of the First Emperor of China, Ch'in Shih Huang, also called 秦始皇. As the famous Historian Sima Qian completely failed to note, the impressively short Master Smith Wáng Lǐ Chén, had built these twelve ambulatory Terracotta Golems as inner crypt guardians, to protect the mortal remains of the transcendent god Emperor from desecration by those that might survive the traps and the rivers of mercury. But as Chén and Völundr were cousins, and such guardians no longer served any serious purpose, humanity being extinct save in the watered-down form of Scions, the Terracotta Golems had been conscripted as vessels for twelve disembodied goddesses. Once possessed by the mostly dead goddesses, the Golems took on the shape and form of those same goddesses.

It would be wrong to say that Völundr had forged the ring. It was, in its first incarnation, too large for a simple forging. It had been constructed solely and singularly by Völundr's will. He had layered first tons of clay, then porcelain, then metal upon the ring construction. Then Völundr has fashioned thirteen mini-dimensions into what would become the interior of the ring.

The goddess Agnóstos Theós stood before her counterparts and took them one after another unto herself, their weakened souls merging with her soul. As each goddess became part of the unknown goddess, Agnóstos Theós became more substantial. Finally, she stood nearly corporeal before Völundr and nodded.

Come the end, Völundr drew a Morgul-knife and slew the goddess Agnóstos Theós, within the walls of the ring-shaped vessel, and drained the blood from the last Terran goddess, leaving the offal to Ammit. Völundr then mixed the blood of the eldest and last goddess with an oxidizing agent and that compound with metal enamelling to hermetically seal the surface of the ring.

Völundr polished off the last bottle of Chateau Margaux '09 in the universe and whistled while he worked. It seemed fitting.

Chapter 12: Grape Vine

Various locations within the light sphere of the Helix Nebula.

These six things doth the Lord hate: yea, seven are an abomination unto him: A proud look, a lying tongue, and hands that shed innocent blood, An heart that deviseth wicked imaginations, feet that be swift in running to mischief, A false witness that speaketh lies, and he that soweth discord among brethren. --Proverbs 6:16-19, K.J.V.

And it came to pass that Blossom made Saki promise not to tell anyone, but Basil Berry made Saki promise to round up the usual suspects. So Saki compromised between the two solemn oaths, and just told the broken down old god Baʿal.

And Baʿal pretty much told everyone else.

Baʿal found the Demons Agares and Gusoin in Paris, the real one, not the half dozen other ones in America, New America, or New Texas, trying to teach the roaches French. They agreed to join in and brought with them thirty-six legions of Hellions.

Baʿal found two more Demons called Marbas and Pruflas hanging out in an ancient abandoned refugee hospital in Libya, working on a cure for Zombieism. They agreed to join in and brought with them thirty-two legions of Hellions.

Baʿal found Amon posing for a *Demon in Sacre Bleu*, by the recently turned Parisian painter Barbatos, and Baʿal steadfastly declined to comment on what they were *actually* doing. They agreed to join in and brought with them seventy legions of Hellions.

274

Ipos and Leraie turned up snorkelling in the wreck of the Titanic. Ba'al ran them over in a blue Renault AX Limousine, which Ba'al complained, "Really needed to have its power steering adjusted." Ipos and Leraie agreed to join and brought with them sixty-six legions of Hellions.

Ba'al found the Demons Vapula penning the final word on the *Literary Merits of Stephen King, a Final Reflection*. Amy, President of Hell was camped out on Vapula's couch complaining about his children and lamenting the lack of moral fibre about the place since all the monkey-pigs went away.

"Seriously," Amy said to Ba'al, "how is one supposed to keep up an evolution of political philosophy whilst no one is about to take notice? Creator damn it, I miss political "science" Professors. I use to so love watching them flap their gums on and on about the next election, and not a one of them having the sense that the Creator gave a Demon blessed herring fish."

"Oh, I don't know," Ba'al said. "They did some good here and there."

"Yeah," Amy, President of Hell chuckled. "I remember my favourite referring to the second Iraq War as a "bad policy decision." Over two million people killed in that war and another million or more in the occupation, and it was dismissed as an 'Oops- my bad.' I mean, you just can't pay for that sort of ethical hypocrisy."

Ba'al listened politely, feigned interest at the appropriate points, and then sealed the deal.

Vapula and Amy, President of Hell agreed to join and brought with them seventy-two legions of Hellions.

Vapula mentioned the Tafari Film Project to his goddaughter the Scion Yente, who happened to mention it to the Scion Qdot, who mentioned it to the unofficial official leader of the Scions Hat, who called an Elysion Library all-staff staff meeting. At the first gathering of Scions in centuries, guest notables included the Valkyrie Kára, Amy, President of Hell, and the Angel Uri'el. And before this august assemblage, Hat said that there would soon be casting auditions for the first film to be made in millions of years. Interested persons should apply to the Empire Studio Company, now located on the planet Tafari that orbited the dual binary suns Babirye, in the Babirye Star System, at the center of the universe.

The minor fact that the Empire Studio Company Board of Directors hadn't actually been established yet didn't seem to bother anyone. It certainly didn't bother Basil Berry who made up the name without consulting anyone. The entire point of rumour mongering wasn't to spread a lie, but to turn a lie into the truth.

After the meeting, Qdot asked the Scion Mayghin if her mother, Lady Zhurong, might like to come along just for laughs. Mayghin didn't think so, but she thought a trip back home to Ryuunosuke Castle might be worth the trouble. After all, Mayghin had stored her best gear at her mother's place.

Even later, Ba'al found the Demons Naberius; Glasya Labolas, Beleth, Sitri, Paimon, Belial, and Bune sitting atop Mount Zion, chanting, and working on their inner Katra and taking turns being high priestess T'Lar.

At the end of her travels, Ba'al found the last of the royal Demons Buer, Botis, Bathin, Purson, Abigor, Valefor, Morax, Zepar, and Peter Lorre in a bar somewhere in the vicinity of Zeta Orionis. Everyone, save Archduke Peter Lorre Archduke von Erzherzog, joined in and began the trek to Tafari.

And then the rumour went viral.

Forneus, Ronove, Berith, Astaroth, Foras, Furfur, Marchosias, Malphas, Vepar, Sabnacke, Sidonay, Gaap, Crocell, Forcus, Murmur, Caim, Raum,

Halphas, Focalor, Vine, Bifrons, Gamigin, Zagan, Orias, Valac, Gromory, Decarabia, Amduscias, Andras, Andrealphus, Ose, Aym, Orobas, Cimeries, Flauros, Balam, Allocer, Saleos, Vuall, Haagenti, Phoenix, Stolas, Uri'el, and Fornícó all got cc'ed on the second email to have been sent in millions of years.

Most of the Demons were surprised they still had data coverage.

Uri'el sent a text message to Gabriel, Michael, Raphael, Raguel, Remiel, and Saraqael.

Saraqael posted a message on the news group dedicated to the Advancement of Angelic Moral Development.

After that, everybody knew what was up, even the people who didn't want to know knew, like the Seven Valkyries of the Personal Apocalypse, Eir, Guðr, Hervör Alvitr, Þögn, Randgríðr, Sigrún, and Kára. Well, okay, six of the seven did want to know, but that has hardly the official position of the Seven Valkyries of the Personal Apocalypse. But they managed to persuade Kára to call a meeting of the Intergalactic Medical Association of Sentient Beings in order to disseminate the movie dope.

The I.M.A.S.B. represented the medical and biological best interests of all sentient being in the known universe, except those sentient beings found within the territorial confines of the United States, her territories and protectorates, and New Texas, all of which were still practicing the freedom to die of treatable cancers, and cared not about the socialist tendencies of the Valkyrie or their non-profit puppets. The Valkyrie Kára, being the longest reigning President called the I.M.A.S.B. Stakeholder Meeting, and told everyone the same thing Hat had told her library meeting.

After the I.M.A.S.B. meeting, the Directors and Valkyries broke up into little groups of twos or threes and gossiped about Kára's interview with Raven, what films they wanted made, and who would receive the awards for best actress. The fact that cast auditions hadn't even been announced yet never occurred to anyone as a problem.

As Sigrún put it, "Kára hates Keith's guts so much that her still being in love with him is the only reason that makes any sense. So we walk softly and say nothing."

Kára for her part tried desperately to ignore them all. It didn't work.

Nobody had any idea where Shax was, and nobody cared when Basil Berry didn't turn up at either meeting, which he had said he would do.

And nobody, absolutely nobody, thought about telling the Dragon.

Chapter 13: Mictlantecuhtli

On the planet Tafari, in the Babirye Binary system, orbiting the Babirye Beta star.

He is proud, knowing nothing, but doting about questions and strifes of words, whereof cometh envy, strife, railings, evil surmisings, Perverse disputings of men of corrupt minds, and destitute of the truth, supposing that gain is godliness: from such withdraw thyself. --1 Timothy 6:4-5, K.J.V.

And it came to pass that the Angel was foretold his future, again.

Unlike Demons, whom all categorically built many castles of one variety or another over millions and millions and millions of years to house their hordes, Angels had only one home, officially speaking anyway. And since Mick had not been *home* for about a million years, he shrugged, and headed for the Pyramid of Khufu. It was just as good a place to wait for Keith's return as any other was, and Mick couldn't think of anything better to do.

As Mick approached the pyramid, he realized that for all its incredible accuracy, it was not an exact copy of the pyramid, as the Angel had previously believed. Or, at least, it was not an exact copy from the last few centuries of mankind's existence upon Terra. The last time Mick saw the Pyramid of Khufu, the radiation hadn't cleared up enough to get a good view of the hole in the ground that was left behind after the nuclear warhead landed on it.

The stones that made up the base of the pyramid, as well as the stones as high up the north side that Mick could see were as smooth and regular as they day they were set into the desert sand. Gone were the centuries of uneven weather damage. Gone were the many thousands of chips and cracks that the centuries of tourism had wrought on the pyramid. Gone were the worn stones that had been slapped down by millions and millions of footfalls.

But those were not the only differences, just the obvious ones. The original triangular North Entrance to the pyramid stood unsealed, uncovered over by the large exterior stones. The original limestone polished smooth stones gleamed, reflecting the starlight cast by the far away stars. Set deep into the limestone were two closed metal double doors. Mick was not surprised to see several subtle shades of black, swirling in under or around the surface of the metal substance.

Several meters below stood the not so original Robbers' Entrance that led to the even more cleverly named Robbers' Tunnel. What the thieves were looking for or what they removed from the pyramid is now known only to them and to the Mistress of the House of Books, Mick, and the Valkyrie Kára. The order to dig the Robber's Entrance and Tunnel was given in the early 9th century by men in the employ of Abdullah Al Mamun to men in his employment.

What Mick was certain of was that Abdullah Al Mamun's men had not left their entrance covered by a large round blood red door with the words **SERVICE ENTRANCE** written in large black block letters across its middle.

Mick ignored the blood red door, and climbed the thirteen stairs of new smooth stone to the level of the original North Entrance

Mick looked up at the engraving over the triangular-arched double doors near base of the replica of the Pyramid of Khufu.

Casa Villanueva

Mick groaned.

That was so like Keith. If there were a bad phunny-pun to be made, Keith would find it, even if he had to spend millions of clicks on the iNet to ferret it out.

Another anachronism Mick noted was that the triangular arched double doors at the base of the pyramid slide seamlessly apart as Mick approached them. Inside, the Angel saw smooth sandstone walls of the narrow tunnel of the inner pyramid, which again looked better than they ever had in Mick's memory

Figures, Mick thought. Let Keith get an idea in his head and it just won't ever leave again no matter how anachronistic. Damned lucky idiot.

It is written in the biographical notes penned by Ríagáin, Queen of the Damned, for the epic historical work, *How I Destroyed Mortality through TV, Movies, and Simulated Reality Facilities*, by the Demon Fruchtbarkeitskultus, Ph.D., that the first major activities of the careers of Mick and Keith in Prime Time Television had serious consequences for all mortals.

According to Ríagáin, Keith found work with the original overly inspired author Robert Wesley in the development of Wesley's *Star March* series. Keith justified his efforts by saying that an inspired reliance on technology like self-opening doors and space ships and a firm belief in alien species like roaches and compassionate conservatives would make mankind question the role of the Creator in the universe. Keith specifically suggested tossing in a hot black chick, a Japanese man, and a Russian in the crew thinking to stir racial hatred, desires for revenge on the former warmongering imperialists, and anti-Communist hysteria.

Trouble was, *Star March* actually inspired anti-war protests by showing the benefits of a United Terran government, scientific research into how the Creator actually created, spurred integration in the United States by showing white men just how sexy competent black chicks in Navy Officer's dress uniforms were, and caused a general insurgence of non-Caucasian actors getting work in Hollywood which basically cracked the foundations of American mental isolationism. For it is hard to hate that which you lust after.

Some readers might think they recognize this allusion and they probably do. Thing is, we just don't want to pay the royalties on it. Cue the "Oh my."

And it came to pass that Keith contributed significantly to a calming of Human angst, which allowed the Creator to move in, inspire, and generally move the whole rotten stinking species one inch closer to perfection. Keith considered his involvement with the project to be akin to a union organizer collaborating with U.S. Senator Joseph Raymond McCarthy.

The Demon never spoke about it.

Ríagáin, Queen of the Damned, went on to pen that the Angel Mick on the other hand had a similar failure through success. Like Keith's undesired success with *Star March*, Mick had a similar failure in his efforts to help found CBN, the Christian Broadcast Network. Mick's idea had been to simply explain over and over again that the Creator loved everyone and everything and that was really all there was to it. Let it sound as weird and contradictory as it may be, loving both children and war, but that was the way it really was. Instead, what Mick got was a long running monologue of a maniacal man, his harlot wife, and a crew of unrepentant thieves. But people sent them money, oh, yes, pension check after pension check. People believed that the maniacal man and his harlot wife spoke with, and for, the Creator Himself. They believed, even after Keith's new show, *The Shyt Rich People Own*, showed the 13-foot tall 18-Karat gold calf that was in the lobby of the CBN studios.

See, the Demon learned. Outright greed is the best lever that evil has ever had. So, instead of spreading love and spiritual grooviness, the CBN blamed everything on the pagans; the abortionists, the Feminists, the gays, the lesbians, the terrorists, "the lazy people" which is code for non-whites. And never once, not once ever taking responsibility for anything themselves.

And there was no end to the 'everything' that all those other groups were guilty of. When the truth was simply that the Creator really wanted everyone to sort out their own problems and to leave Him alone. That was the whole point of Free Will. Sort it out yourselves, with *your* own hands, *your* own minds, and on *your* own responsibility. Don't wait around saying, 'Oh, it's all in the Creator's hands,' or 'The Creator will solve that if you just have faith and pray hard enough.'

Besides, Faith had been MIA for centuries in any case. She was last seen in company with Poverty, Hunger, and Terror.

The only other thing that Mick knew that the Creator wanted, besides personal responsibility on the part of each and every mortal being, was to chase dolphins in the surf on long, eternally long, holidays. What Mick and CBN actually accomplished was to administer, to large portions of the English and Spanish speaking worlds, a vaccine against Judaism, Christianity, Islam, and the Creator.

Mick took the long view of his involvement with CBN by blaming it on the Ineffability of the Creator's Plan.

See, even Angels take that lame excuse every now and then.

But back to the plot:

In most respects, the interior of the Pyramid of Khufu that Keith had brought into existence on Tafari, was identical to the actual pyramid on Terra. Or, at least, how the pyramid had been when Pharaoh Khufu of the 4th Dynasty had seen it, long before the nuclear bombs fell during the opening mortal round of the War at Armagedōn.

In many respects, the Pyramid of Khufu resembled the homes of most Demons; massive, overwhelming, and with style that did not so much impress as smack one in the face. Mick did not notice the similarities for the simple reason that he had never once been in Keith's place, or the home of any other Demon for that matter, and no Demon had ever once seen Mick's flat in the Bronx. Mick, like all Angels, much preferred, like some 17th century noblemen courting a young lady, to steadfastly stand on the landing, rather than disgrace himself by intruding. Keith for his part loved to watch the Angel stand in the rain and often took more than his sweet time in answering the door.

Beyond the double doors, the Angel moved into the pyramid's Descending Passageway. The long corridor led down at a sharp angle and continued in the original smooth evenly placed stones. When Mick first stepped into the passage he bent his head and shoulders down, for he had visited the Pyramid of Khufu several hundred times, including during its original construction and men had been shorter then. But, the Angel stood up when he realized that Keith had, naturally, readjusted the tunnel to 3 meters in height.

The interior of the original Pyramid of Khufu was worn down, almost to extinction, by the time that Armagedōn came around. The main problem was that Pharaoh Khufu's Vizier Hemon never intended the interior of Khufu's pyramid to be trampled over by just short of a billion people. But the man had never really had what one might call foresight.

The hereditary Prince Vizier Hemiunu, Sealer of the King of Egypt; and Grandson of Sneferu; and Son of Prince Nefermaat and Itet, Nephew and Cousin of Pharaoh Khufu of the Old Kingdom, was an interesting character. Vizier Hemiunu also held the political posts of Son of Pharaoh Body, Chief Justice, and Head of the House of Thoth. Hemiunu was also an accomplished architect as well as mathematician, accountant, juggler, and devirginator. Hemiunu is believed to be the architect of the Great Pyramid of Giza, in Egypt. While the circumstances of Hemiunu death are unclear, it is believed that a Big Brother gang is responsible for feeding his body to the god Sobek's sacred crocodiles; after being drug first by the heals and then drug by the arms after the heels both fell off, behind a camel from the Great Pyramid to the base of the River Nile. Or, as the press had it at the time,

Hemiunu had a completely and totally natural heart attack.

Mick extended his arms parallel with his shoulders and felt the cool stone beneath his eight fingers. Neither the words smooth, nor polished, would do justice to the slick feeling beneath his fingertips as he slowly walked, his fingers gliding. But his hands easily touched both sides, so only the height, and the feel of the stone's surface in the tunnel had been changed.

Mick wondered ideally as he made his way to the intersection of the Ascending and Descending Passages in the Pyramid of Khufu, if Keith had merely change the height of the tunnel, or if the damned Demon had changed the reality around the pyramid too. The Angel hoped it was the former. It hadn't gone so well the last time the Demon had tried to rearrange the Creator's reality.

"Creator surrounds us," Mick said aloud. "I hope that damned idiot hasn't gone mucking about with the value of π again."

The crater that was left behind from Keith's little experiment in 'nice neat maths' eventually became Lake Baikal, also called Ozero Baykal, once the ground cooled off over the next several hundred years. It wasn't that Mick didn't like Lake Baikal, he rather enjoyed the place, and always stayed at Janna's Bed and Breakfast just off Kirov Square in Irkutsk, located in south central Russia, just north of middle Mongolia, because the rooms were tidy, and the mistress of the house was kind, helpful, and spoke better English than the Angel spoke Russian. Mick had always maintained that the crisp mountain peaks, and scenery that had not seen war on its soil since the passing of Genghis Khan, was almost worth the havoc that Keith wrought in global climate change. After all, what's a million year long winter when you have eternity to hang it in?

Mick shook off the old memories, and decided to first make his way to the King's Chamber, in order to pay his respects to the replica of the long gone old man's burial chamber. Mick of course knew that Khufu had never been entombed here, but that was entirely beside the point.

Old Pharaoh Khufu had run afoul of one of the worst of the Demons that had been bound to Terra for the entirety of the regime of Time. Dedi was its name, and whatever its sins were, Dedi was a damned nasty Demon, even by the notoriously high standards of Hell. Khufu had found the Demon inhabiting the body of some withered old scribe, while visiting the Phoenician city called, Byblos or **Βύβλος**. Whatever was left of the mind of the poor mortal Scribe that Dedi possessed was never known. But Dedi convinced Khufu to take him on as a personal soothsayer. All the lies that the ancient Demon poured into the old Pharaoh's ears resulted in Khufu becoming entangled in darkness, his mortal heart becoming twisted by the pursuit of fame, immortality, and the lusting after total control of all his subjects.

Mick remembered hearing similar stories coming to him in at the Court of the Yellow Emperor Gōngsūn, called 公孫. One tale, which Mick had always hoped was false, spoke of Dedi teaching Gōngsūn how to cause men's head to fall off and the wombs of woman to implode. What Mick was certain of though is that under Dedi's influence, Khufu became the first Pharaoh to be "removed" with cause, by an agreement of the key military and religious leaders of the kingdom. The act was to set in motion the deadly cycle of events that would plague Egypt until the last days of mankind.

For the prophet Micah had spoken truly, when he wrote, "But Terra will be desolate because of its inhabitants and the fruit of their deeds."

Mick had always liked the dramatic old bastard Micah's original penning of: "And the people of the book were all stupid and stiff necked and warred upon each other relentlessly, proving nothing, winning nothing, and in the end- everyone was dead."

No wonder the Hebrew priests had kept the raving old lunatic in chains and rewrote everything, Mick thought.

In the pyramid, the Angel slowed and turned sharply to the left to join with the Ascending Passage. An odd lighting effect gave the soft orange light that would be identical to that of a torch reflecting off the sand stonewalls, except that the lighting was regular throughout the length of the corridor instead of the flickering dancing that an actual torch would produce. And no torches were in evidence anywhere along the passage. Mick thought it was a nice touch.

Mick followed the Ascending Passage past the side tunnel that led to the Middle Chamber, and into the Grand Gallery, a passage not much wider than those that Mick had been in, but much taller.

Mick continued up the Ascending Passage until he came to the Grand Gallery, where he stopped in his tracks.

In the original Pyramid of Khufu, Mick knew that these walls were of smooth stone, and that they were, like the rest of the pyramid, devoid of paintings or markings of any kind. Over the centuries, grave robbers and tourists had left thousands of marks of graffiti, and archaeologists of almost every generation had destroyed a bit more of the ancient structure. But that was nothing compared to what the Angel now saw in this Grand Gallery now.

Later, when Mick reflected upon that moment, reflected upon what he saw, it was to become the worst moment of his entire long life. This moment, surrounded by signs and prognostication, that the Angel felt he should have quit, should have just left, and never come back. But Mick was ever immune to the wondrous awe-inspiring nature of reality, and instead only got pissed off.

Gone were the large blocks of mason cut stone, set so closely together that only an Angel hair or Demon's breath could pass between the seams. And in their place, were seven murals. The murals looked to Mick to be air brushed, using the late 23rd Century style common to the skin painting that replaced tattoos. But, whatever it was, the Angel Mick was sure of this; it was that he, himself, had never featured in any painting in Ancient Egypt, much less in-stylized hieroglyphic murals on the inner walls of the most famous pyramid on Terra.

All the characters of the first painting had that odd two-dimensional aspect of the Ancient Egyptian paintings, that particularly flat and elongated face, and arms either straight or bent at the elbows at odd uncomfortable looking angles.

In the first mural, Mick saw himself, standing atop a low wall of some kind. He stood in a stately pose, addressing a large number of immortal creatures; Angels, Demons, Hellspawn, and a bear. The Angel picked out faces that he knew. Keith sat on the wall smoking a cigarette, while Mōt, the adopted Scion of Death and god of Near-death Experiences, speaking to the Scion Hat. The Scion Hat was dressed in her mother's traditional ceremonial robes.

It was the oddest thing because Mick had known all of the Scions of Sešat at in their own time, and never had any of them ever dawned the traditional garments of the false idol that they called a mother. After a long moment studying the imagery, he turned to the next scene.

Mick walked slowly past the second mural, scanning it for detail, until he came abruptly to the end, and returned, scanning it again in reverse. This second scene disturbed the Angel more than the first, if that were possible.

This scene was not as stylized in the Ancient Egyptian method as was the first. But it was stylized in a period that Mick could not pick out.

Against a background of forest, parted by a river flanked on either side by mountains, sat Chukwu, surrounded by animals. Chukwu sat flanked by an ox and a lion behind, a tiger and cows to his left, a bear, a goat at his feet, and a leopard and lambs to his right. Two small mortal children, a boy and a girl, sat before them all, playing some sort of skipping game that clashed with the hyperrealism of the rest of the image. Between the river and Chukwu's back, stood a group of what were clearly Angels and Demons, engaged in what appeared to be a battle. The Demons wheeled flaming swords, while the Angels lashed whips and clamped chains upon the fallen Demons.

The painting seemed very familiar to Mick, as if he had once seen it in the Brooklyn Museum, or maybe at the Met. The fact that the painting was wrong was obvious to the Angel, but that only made the image the more disconcerting, as if someone was trying to speak to him through a visual allusion.

Or would that be illusion? Mick wondered. Hell's bells, this is worse than parables by a couple of light years.

In the third mural, Mick recognized everyone depicted. On one side, dressed in a business suit, a mass of brown ginger dreadlocks on her head, stood the junkie Avatar from the Elysion Library Coffee Shoppe, and behind her stood the man she was travelling with. The other woman was the she-Demon Ríagáin, Queen of the Damned.

The evil black-hearted she-Demon was dressed in a black lace dress, cut down to her slender form all the way to her evenly tanned belly button. The dress collar rose off her shoulders, encircling her dark hair, producing the same effect as if she was being followed by a halo mirror of darkness. Behind her stood the Hellspawn Phu.

Ríagáin, Queen of the Damned, stood on the right, while the other one stood opposite her. They both stood face-to-face, shaking hands, while each held a knife behind her back in her other hand.

For the first time since he had resolved to go see Hat, Mick wondered if what he was doing was right. Not right as in, correct, proper, or even ethical. But right as in Keeping with His Plan. There was no circumstance under which Mick could imagine that the meeting of an immortal junkie, and Ríagáin, Queen of the Damned, could be a good thing.

Mick put the idea away and moved quickly onto the next mural. If an Angel ever started thinking like mortals, it was a short step to rebellion. Mick knew that nothing but damnation ever came from thinking for one's self. The Angel had seen the results too many times to start indulging in that horror now.

The next mural puzzled Mick, as he was again the center of attention, and he found himself with the distinct impression that the painting had just this second stopped moving. In the painting Mick was holding what looked to be a screenplay manuscript in one hand, which he was angrily waving at another immortal. Upon the cover of the script were seven hand-written titles, the first six of which were crossed out, so that they read:

~~Mise en Abyme~~
~~The Muder of Basil Berry~~
~~Mahābhārata~~
~~The Mouse-trap~~
~~And Than There Were None~~
~~The Complete Works of Uncle Willie~~
Xenophōn's Complete Histories

But the odd thing was that standing opposite the Angel, with his traditional enigmatic smile, was Mōt.

Mick hadn't seen Mōt in thousands upon thousands of years, and couldn't imagine what he might have ever been angry with the little man for.

Mick paused for a moment and remembered the encounter with Fate in the London Station. What had she said? *It will be your fault.* How could something be his fault when he didn't even know what was going on?

The Angel sighed deeply and moved on.

Here, in the middle of the seven scenes, Mick found himself again, this time with Keith, and Mōt. The painting was done not in the stylized Ancient Egyptian mode, but rather in the disturbing accuracy of Ultra-Photorealism.

The three immortals stood in the rain, cast against a bloody purple and black sky, highlighted by lightening. The clouds looked organic, and Mick felt that whomever, or whatever, had made this mural had simply taken storm clouds from the day that Adam and Eve had been expelled from the Garden in Dakota.

That day, Mick remembered, had been a very bad day. It wasn't so much that the Serpent had been trying to get Eve to eat the apple, as it was that the damned Demon was just simple and didn't understand why anybody cared. Either way though, privately, Mick thought banishment was a bit of an over-reaction. Totally in keeping with the Creator's temperament though. Just ask any Demon. But still a bit, just a teensy weensy bit, over the top.

In the painting, Mōt stood still, as the quiet man usually did, without visible effects upon him or his clothes from the storm.

Keith on the other hand, looked like he had just narrowly survived a Japanese game show. His shirt was covered in mud, and he looked like he had stepped in every peat bog between Hell's Jacuzzi and Heaven's swamp. In the painting, Mick had fallen to his knees, and shook one clenched fist above his head at the sky.

Mick reached up to touch himself in the painting, and found that the stone was warm to the touch, the paint slightly tacky to his touch.

He let his fingers glide across the length of the mural as he moved on, smearing colours into three brown streaks.

In the next painting, Mick found himself again, standing in the bombed out wreckage of the Deoradháin Café, his shoulders slumped, and his head hanging down, obscuring his face. The diner looked like Sinn Féin had gotten together with the alumni of the English 1st Battalion, Parachute Regiment to refight Domhnach na Fola.

The café had clearly lost.

"This is disgusting," Mick muttered. The sound echoed with dullness that the Angel found less than reassuring.

The seventh and the final painting showed Chukwu and the Metatron, standing side by side, against a background of darkness. The two immortals were looking down at what Mick took to be a giant pearl.

Mick only glanced briefly at it, shrugged, and moved on towards the King's Chamber.

"Take a bath he said," Mick muttered. "I'd bloody well like to know where. Nothing here but delusional graffiti."

Mick barely glanced at a small sign that read: KING'S CHAMBER, in neat block letters. Beneath, a small black arrow pointed up the corridor.

"Yeah, yeah, I know, thanks."

Stepping into the King's Chamber Mick saw the familiar large smooth stones that made up the floor, walls, and ceiling of the bare room. A quick glance around assured Mick that there were no rogue mural paintings on the granite walls. He was rather happy to see that the security cameras, electric lights, motion sensors, and all of the tourist graffiti were gone. What was there was the old sarcophagus, with its broken corner, which was far too big to have fit through the King's Chamber door. But the lid to the external sarcophagus, the internal sarcophagi, and mummy were all long gone. What was there had been long gone by the time Abdullah Al Mamun had forced his way in. And they had only been decoys anyway.

Mick grinned at the memory.

"Carefully, carefully, careful-"

Smash.

"All right then, you motherless swine herders. That's gravel now."

"Will ya look at that? Gold. Real gold."

"I don't think I've ever seen real gold before."

"And ya won't either, if you damn well drop anything again. Gods damn it, for half a copper, I'd gut you now."

"Ah, but you won't, 'cause you'd have to carry it out then."

"Damn right you big bull. But do that again, and I'll make an ox out of you."

Seven men lifted the internal sarcophagus out, the dull shine of gold and cobalt blue gems sparkling in the light of oil burning lamps.

"Open it up you bastards. The key is inside."

Seals snapped, glue ripped, wood broke, and the internal sarcophagi rose for a moment and then slammed at the speed of gravity against the granite floor.

Diamonds, emeralds, and ivory lay scattered over the mummy, whom rested upon a single slab of carved jade.

But what all the robbers reached for at the same time was the large iron key that rested on the mummy's chest.

"I have it, damn you all, I have it."

And they all cheered, and congratulated themselves.

Then, the mummy's right hand reached up and grabbed the wrist connected to the hand that held the key, while the mummy's left hand plucked the key away. In one deft movement, the mummy snapped the wrist, and flung the man away against the wall.

The remaining six men were all down the length of the Grand Gallery before the mummy limped his way out of the King's Chamber.

Mick had stood at the base of the Pyramid of Khufu as the robbers burst from the tomb's entrance, screaming, and praying to every god, they could remember. What most of them got was heat stroke, and the open arms of the Valkyrie Kára.

After the Angel had stopped laughing, he climbed the steps to the entrance, where he saw a tall slender black haired Angel unwrapping the bandages from his head and shoulders.

"Hello Uri'el," Mick said.

The Angel grunted, and tossed Mick an iron key.

"Thanks," Mick said.

"It's too damned hot for this nonsense," Uri'el complained kicking the last of the bandaging off his feet.

Mick watched as the naked form of the Angel ascended skyward, its mighty wings sending him higher and higher into the clouds.

Mick thought for a moment, and watched with grim satisfaction as the bandages caught fire, and burned.

Mick blinked the eons away, and withdrew the iron key from the inside of his 1950s style khaki trench raincoat, marched to the middle of the King's Chamber, placed the key on the floor, and then did something not done in that room for many millions of years.

The Angel danced the Hokey Cokey.

Whatever it is called, the Hokey Pokey in the United States and Canada, or the Hokey Tokey in Australia and New Zealand, on the Okey Cokey in Alabama, of the Cokey Cokey anywhere else, the dance is the same.

It starts with the right leg in, the right leg out, and then moves on to jive until you shake, shake, shake your sillies out, followed by turning yourself about and about and about until you fall down.

Most of us did this dance as children. Or, at least, made fun of someone else that did it. But you've never seen it done until you've seen it done by an Angel in a trench coat.

Officially speaking, there are three hundred thirteen verses, many of which are illegal to perform in public. Thankfully, the Angel stopped after the seventh verse because the block of floor that the key and the Angel stood upon began to descend into the darkness.

"Well shit," the Angel said aloud. "I guess Keith brought the real one from Terra after all. Bloody damned nitwit."

The floor descended past the Queen's Chamber, which the Angel briefly considered visiting, and then shrugged it off. With a loud thud, the stone lift came to a rest in the most northern corner of the Center Room.

Every pyramid had one, a Center Room, and Mick had always been amused that the Egyptologists had never tipped to it, despite the numerous clues. It had never mattered how many rooms were found to have been built around objects too large to have been placed inside after the fact, most Egyptologists persisted in believing that the pyramids were made for one, or perhaps two persons. Even after Dr. Kent R. Weeks excavated more than 150 chambers and tunnels in the subterranean Tomb for the Sons of Ramesses II in the Valley of the Kings, many Egyptologists persisted in the idea that the pyramids were themselves, devoid of further discovery. The fact that Dr. Weeks entered his new find through the wall of a known tomb didn't seem to bother anyone besides Weeks and his graduate students. Had those same self-satisfied Egyptologists that decried Weeks as a fool only known what lay buried beneath the sands of the Great Sahara Desert, called the الصحراء الكبرى, the

Aṣ-Ṣaḥrā´ al-Kubrā, and the Big Sand Box from Which all Other Sand Boxes are But a Little Dust Mites, they would have hung-up their collective fedora hats and settled in for a nice quiet retirement writing science fiction novels.

What lay beneath the Sahara were the many thousands of tombs, cities, and yes, pyramids, that Pharaoh Ka's people built all up and down the Nile.

In the center of the Center Room stood the Triangular Stones. The stones were three 6 foot high, 4 foot wide, granodiorite steles stood back to back at 60° angles to each other. Upon each of the igneous rocks, were carved the same message, a peace treaty, signed by three different rulers.

Selk, also called the Scorpion King, signed for the People of the Nile.

Grandson of the Yellow Emperor, Emperor Zhuanxu, also called 颛顼, 顓頊, Zhuānxū, and Gaoyang 高陽, signed for the People of the Chinese Empire.

And last, signed in the eldest written mortal language the Ardipithecus Runes, was the single word Leader, devoid of title, ancestry, or even proper noun name.

The Angel had enshrined the relic here, as a testament to the true length of homo sapien sapien history, and waited patiently for it too be found. It never was, despite his many attempts to point out its location to reputable historians.

Truth be told, not much was done by the Angel really. All the Angel Mick ever said, or did, about it was too log onto *serious history* sites under the UserID: iwuzthereb4uidiots777, and make a major nuisance of himself mocking the stupidity of official recorded history, and to suggest dig sites like the Center Chamber of the Pyramid of Khufu, or the mountains north of the Zuni-Cibola Complex last located in Zuni Pueblo, New Mexico, where the actual Seven Cities of

Gold were buried. And prior to the advent of the internet, the Angel sent scathing letters to publication editors and Professors, none of which were ever answered, and few were ever read through. Which is a pity as Howard Carter well knew.

Although Mick didn't know it, iwuzthereb4uidiots777 was taken very seriously by a number of historians and archaeologists, but only when they were young and bright-eyed grad students. All of whom later went on to discover things like Vikings in Kansas, the plague that swept through the Americas killing off about 90% of the indigenous population in the early 15th century, and the Great Poseidon Adventure Ship sunk deep into the atmosphere of Neptune. But for some odd reason, all these newly coined PhDs inexplicably forgot to mention the internet flame-thrower that led them to their historical paradigm shifting discoveries.

Mick walked over and ran his fingers over the carving of the Leader's name. The Angel had liked the old creature; that never joked, never had any vices, and always led every battle by charging at its front. For the word "Leader" in Ardipithecus meant simply "The guy that's lived through more battles than anyone else around here, and if you want to live through this one, shut your damned mouth and listen to what you're being told to do. This is me, the Leader saying this to you."

While a minimalistic language, Ardipithecus was exceedingly precise.

As Mick's fingers past over the Ardipithecus Ruins, his eyes settled upon something that he had never seen before. Written in the Lătĭŭm script, which predated the Latin by a score of centuries, was written at the bottom of the stone below the word Leader;

I, Chukwu, observed this.

"What the fracking balmy Hell is that?" Mick demanded angrily of the stone. "Who the Hell did that?"

The stones completely failed to answer.

After a long moment, Mick lifted himself up and over the stones, to stand in the center, and examined the back of the stones. There he found that which he was afraid would be there. Carved into the back of each stone, and upon the triangular bit of floor between them, in four different languages was a message, addressed specifically to the Angel Mictlantecuhtli. Egyptian Hieroglyphics was on the back of Selk, the Scorpion King's stone. Ancient, yet similar to Traditional Chinese, Chinese script was on the back of Emperor Zhuanxu's stone. Ardipithecus Runes were found on the back of the Leader's stone. And finally, the Lătĭŭm script upon the floor.

In each case, the message was the same, and ran thus:

My dear Angel Mictlantecuhtli, being the 33,550,336[th] being to be created in this universe;

Nice joke, I rather liked it. A shame it never came off. Still, the best lain plans of Angels and Demons and all that. I would have really enjoyed the rediscovery of the Lost City of Atlantis, had it ever happened. Just so, you know, it wasn't near Cadiz, Spain like you thought. It is sunken into the desert sands south Ouargla, Algeria. If you are wondering how that happened, the wind changed. Eventually, the Terra quaked, and the ocean became a sea. But it started with the wind changing.

So, listen up, because the wind is about to change again.

You, Mictlantecuhtli, are a jerk. I mean that sincerely, and with feeling. You are a jerk. What is worse, you have embraced it. So, if you don't mend your ways, you're going to end-up in timeout. A long, long, long timeout. The sort of long that will make an impression even on an immortal jerk like you.

298

So chill out and start treating others like you would like to be treated, for that is the whole of the Law. Give them the clothes off your back, feed them your own food, and love them better than you love yourself. Above all else Angel; get that through your thick head, you don't get to pick and choose who, you have to love them all- every single one.

May Peace be with you, Chukwu.

The Angel's mouth just hung open for a very long time until the rage overcame him, and he drew the Holy Swords Zulfiqar and Al-Dhulfiqar and attacked the Triangular Stones. The Holy Swords cut through the ancient Triangular Stone tablets and the floor of the Center Room like so much realpolitik cuts through political theory. The speed with which the Angel drove the blades reduced large fragments of stone to dust in a matter of seconds.

And then, the floor caved in.

Chapter 14: Deoradháin Café Redux

On Terra, in the Sol system, orbiting the Sol star, for the moment.

The wicked flee when no man pursueth: but the righteous are bold as a lion. --Proverbs 28:1, K.J.V.

And it came to pass that the uninvited crashed the party.

The first thing that Raven noticed when he flew into the front door of the Deoradháin Café was that the storm doors were closed.

The second thing that Raven noticed after hobbling past the storm doors was that the Demon James was playing *L'Histoire Sans Fin* on the jukebox.

The third thing that Raven noticed was Miyako Astor putting down a silver serving tray and beckoning him to get on.

"Not goanna end up on the menu, am I?" Raven asked as he wobbled onto the tray.

"Ah no," Miyako Astor said. "I have strict enlightened Angel-enforced guidelines about not serving anything that can talk, or think, or has a soul."

"Lucky me," Raven said. "What's up with D.J. Jazzy Tones over there?"

"I don't know, at least he's left off K.D. Lang," Miyako Astor said. "That wench is depressing. Voice of an Angel, but bloody depressing all the same. Makes me wish I could suicide."

"I'm sure the never ending joke is worse," Raven said. "He hasn't been ranting about infinity again, has he? God, my head hurts."

Miyako Astor shook his head. "Worse, eternity. I haven't seen him this moody since the last time he watched all the episodes of M*A*S*H back to back."

"Can't be worse than Stalingrad," Raven observed.

"Ah, that movie was pish," Miyako Astor said.

"No, I mean when we were there," Raven said. "I spent most of my time avoiding becoming stew. The Demon James was the Commissar in-charge of overseeing the logistics operations for supplying the front. Uncle Joe said the soldiers were the priority, but well, starving civilians are hard to ignore. D.J. *Kill 'em All* fed everyone he could."

"Yeah," Miyako Astor said in an uncharacteristically mild tone. "A couple of Ukrainian and Russian boys stumbled in here from Pavlov's House."

"How did they get here?" Raven asked. "I don't remember you coming anywhere near Stalingrad. I'd have been in here and off like a shot if you had."

"A wrinkle in time? I don't know," Miyako Astor said. "I never did figure out how they got here. Came in through the bathroom, of course. The Ukrainians were all for going back immediately. The Russians though, asked for водка, and they got drunk lickety-split. I brought them Syrniki cakes, with honey and red wine Kissel, fried potatoes, and bacon. As they passed out, I put them in the booths, wrapped up in woollen blankets. I left dozens of wrapped cakes out for them before turning in for the night. You know, they all went back; every last one of them went back to that graveyard. Took the vodka, cakes, and blankets of course, but what do I care about that?"

"They went back?" Raven asked.

"They went back," Miyako Astor confirmed.

"There was a lot of that sort of thing in that fight," Raven said. "I went completely off carrion for about two centuries after that one. Too many children."

"So what can I do for you?" Miyako Astor asked briskly discharging his mild reflectiveness for his happy Post Transhumanist publican glee. The Faerie placed the silver serving tray, and the raven upon it, on the counter.

"Well, I had planned to come in crying "We're goanna die- we're all goanna die, but I slammed into your storm door instead," Raven said.

"Sorry about that," Miyako Astor said with a grin and tone that not only suggested, but also advertised, that he wasn't.

"S'all right," Raven said hopping off the tray. "Gave me time to remembered a half dozen other times I said *we're all goanna die* and was wrong. So I think this time, I'll just keep my beak shut and see what happens."

"Been my plan for time out of mind," Miyako Astor agreed. "Tell you the truth though, I've given up hope."

"I thought that the greatest of those things was Hope?" Raven asked using a talon to dislodge a dust bunny that had gotten lodged under a feather.

"Na, the greatest is *love* don't ya know?" Miyako Astor said. "But don't forget you always hurt the ones you love."

"Moving on from Cliché Avenue," Raven said with a cough. "I'd like escargot, caviar, and the deepest unhealthiest fried calamari you got. Oh, and a Weltenburger Kloster, and bring the bloody straw this time. I swear, you get into one story with a fox and a bad dinner, and for years everybody tries the same gag."

"Salmon or sturgeon?" Miyako Astor asked while writing in his Piccadilly lined flip-top notebook.

"Yes, please," Raven said. "And remember, no eggs in anything."

"Right-o," Miyako Astor agreed, flipping his notebook closed. "And wasn't it a fox and a crane or stork or something in that story? I don't remember there being a raven in that one."

"Yeah, and it took me a full hundred years past that sop Æsop's death to pay off that contract," Raven said. "Æsop's daughter and her daughter hounded me all over Terra giving me daily updates on interest accrued and god knows what else. But it was worth it. Way more than what I paid Edgar."

"Oh, I don't know," Miyako Astor, mused. "It used to be a sign of an educated mind in Western culture to have that one and a bit of poetry and Latin memorized."

"True, but they didn't, and I cannot underscore this enough, they didn't think of the raven as being as dumb as a stork either," Raven said. "Sometimes not having something happen is way more important than anything that did happen."

Miyako Astor nodded and walked off to his kitchen.

Raven turned and surveyed the more than six dozen figures in the Deoradháin Café. He hadn't seen the place this busy for centuries. Not since the all Demon Cricket test match, that Amy, President of Hell, dreamed up as a solidarity gimmick. It didn't end well, and Amy had had to be reconstituted when enough of his ashes had finally settled down to ground and they could do the rituals over him.

The room was filled with all manner of immortal beings such as Angels, Demons, Hellspawn, Nightmares, Avatars, and even Faerie whose custom Miyako Astor had always actively discouraged.

The Watcher nay Demon called Shax sat at a booth with Basil Berry. The Scion sat wearing a pair of white cotton archivist gloves gingerly turning the aged pages of *How to Putte Questiones to the Dark and Understand its Answeres*. Raven sighed. Imaginary books, like imaginary numbers, are where the real danger lay for the universe. For both had the ability to reconcile the impossible as possible, and what's more, in a nice neat methodical sort of way too.

The Avatars Blossom and Saki sat at a table, upon which a white rabbit gleefully munched her way through a naked garden salad. A bull Moose stood beside the table chewing the remnants of a spinach salad meditatively like a cow with her cud. Blossom was talking in low animated tones, obviously trying to make Saki understand something he clearly didn't care about.

Ríagáin, Queen of the Damned, and the Angel Uri'el were playing a standard game with the aid of the

Chess People. Uri'el was down both his bishops, a knight, and had doubled up pawns, while Ríagáin was down her queen, and was playing out an extremely defensive castle strategy.

Joanne Carter and Johann Carolus were looking through old Carter press clippings across a table from Lord Voll who was reading a 1304201217.

Varney the Vampire sat with Lord Ruthven and Count Orlok on one side of a table opposite Wilfred Glendon, Larry Talbot, and Úlfr Bjálfason.

Raven could not make out their argument, but as no one was bleeding, yet, he guessed the strict neutrality of the Deoradháin Café was holding. No immortal wanted to get barred from the Deoradháin Café. Because Hell, sometimes everyone wants to go where everybody knows their name and they don't try to kill you too.

Miyako Astor returned with Raven's beer, and the bird, now perched on a large glass sugar dispenser, sipped his favourite brew while continuing to look around the café.

Fornícó sat beside Peter Lorrie at the bar, trading old black and white photos of Golden Age starlets. Fornícó was fawning over a glossy of Myrna Loy in a two-piece bathing suit.

Duke Belial, first of the four Crowned Princes of Hell, sat alone with a decanter of the last of the Glenavon Special Liqueur Whisky, its pale gold liquid sparkling through the sunlight crystal. Duke Belial sat staring out of the window back up at the Temple of Gylfagin. Raven tried to remember if Belial had ever been involved with any of the goddesses, but quickly gave up the effort. He most likely had been involved at one point or another with all of them throughout the course of history.

Mōt, god of Near-death Experiences, sat alone at the bar, thumbing through his planner. Raven had to restrain an impulse to try to steal the book again. It had always been pointless whenever he tried it before. Despite Mōt being as slender as a river reed, Raven had only ever seen one other Immortal be able to pick up the book. That had been Kára.

Cain the Cursed, restlessly pacing back and forth in the back of the Café, fighting, and making wild gestures at things that only he could see.

""Here ya go," Miyako Astor said placing Raven's order on the bar.

Raven inhaled the aroma of sautéed snails, sherry, and Gruyère cheese baked in a clay earthenware bowl that mingled with the scent of lightly buttered toasted bread rounds. The second plate had an alternating pattern of nacarat coloured salmon eggs and black sturgeon eggs, which sat delicately upon crème fraîche covered blintz cakes. Last, Raven looked longingly at the Shanghai style fried calamari served with peanuts, sesame seeds, bean sprouts, and red, green, and orange peppers.

Raven eyed the calamari. "I thought I said unhealthy."

Miyako Astor shrugged and picked up the calamari.

"No, no, no," Raven said flapping his wings. "I didn't say I wouldn't eat it."

Miyako Astor smiled and replaced the entrée on the counter before walking along the counter refilling drinks.

"Another beer please," Raven called to him.

Miyako Astor waved an ambiguous gesture back.

Raven flipped a snail up in the air, spread his beak wide, and shivered as the garlic cheesy goodness slid down his throat. He did it again to an even better effect. His belly warming, and mind relaxing, Raven looked around the second half of the café.

Gaius Plinius Secundus, the Semi-immortal from Enoch, not to be confused with his grandson Gaius Plinius Secundus III the Unready, or Gaius Plinius Secundus IV Fishmonger from Newest New York, but Gaius Plinius Secundus the Scrivener sat listening to Under-lord Mania and Amy, President of Hell talk about how they would operate the new Empire Studios Company, which was odd, as Raven hadn't known it existed up till then. Things seemed already to be progressing beyond Keith and Basil Berry's original plan.

The Archangel Chrétien was playing darts with a trio of Nymphs. Raven guessed by the way they were flirting with him that they obviously wanted something from him.

Völundr slid onto the stool next to Raven and began to bogart the bird's calamari.

"Where the Hell is the silver?" he asked.

"No fucking thumbs mate," Raven replied and flapped his wings, "fork's no use to me. Oh, and word to the wise, its silverware tonight mate."

"Oh," Völundr said and went on using the chopsticks the Creator provided all thumb-welding mammalians.

"Where we headed?" Völundr asked.

"Tafari, I think," Raven said. "That's what I'm hearing people say anyway."

"What's the point of going there? It's a dead place."

Raven cocked his head sideways and stared at Völundr. Völundr shrugged his response and continued eating.

"And what would you know about it Mr. You'll Never Get Me to Travel Faster Than Light 'Cause It Ain't Natural?"

"Just because I think its unnatural doesn't mean I haven't done it," Völundr said twirling an exceptionally large calamari around his stubby index finger. "If you think about it logically, my not liking it means that I've at least done it once."

"That's not true," Raven said. "I haven't died yet and I don't like the idea of doing it at all."

"You're not logical," Völundr said.

"And just what the froggy fucking Hell was sister Ammit doing up there?" Raven asked ignoring the jab.

"Body disposal," Völundr said. "You can't just leave dead goddesses lying about. It's unhygienic."

Raven grunted.

"By the way, did you notice the time distortion?"

"The what?"

"I thought not," Völundr said. "I think we were out of phase with normal time for a year or so during the ceremony up at the Temple of Gylfagin, some sort of local distortion."

"No, I didn't notice," Raven said who wouldn't have cared much even if he had noticed. "I'm not working on a schedule that I know of. How long was it?"

"Six, seven months, I think," Völundr said. "By the by, I told Kára she needed to officially wake-up the Dragon," Völundr said. "She needs to get on with it. I think the universe is collapsing; time and space are getting really flexible lately. Next thing you know light will start getting heavy and-"

"I told her that," Raven said with reckless disregard for Völundr's lecture. "Why the redundancy?"

Völundr shrugged. "It's in the prophecy that it's got to be her. Kára's ranked legionaries are beside the point as far as Dragon is concerned. Kára's got all the speaking lines. I wanted to make sure she understood it had to be her."

"Aye, lizard-breath just said Wælcyrge," Raven said scooping up a beak full of eggs.

"And that's why you failed you're A Levels," Völundr said with a grin. "You're the only god I know that knows fuck-all about mythology. The damn myth's titled *Kára and the Dragon*."

"So it is," Raven said. "I never thought of that."

"You never have been qualified for this job," Völundr said.

"Nobody ever told me you needed qualifications to be a god. Polytechnic covered everything I need to know. Well, that and cable. The things you learn on the History Channel. If they'd had that when I was in school, I'd have done better. I only got in the god line because I thought I was going to get summers and bank holidays off. I never figured it would be work. Fucking reincarnation."

"I doubt it. TV would have helped much, even then," Völundr said.

"So, you managed to not blow up Terra I see," Raven said. "You get them all stuffed in there okay?"

"Yes I did," Völundr said withdrawing a small black felt covered box and placing it on the counter top.

"You know, it takes a lot to put a bird like me off baked cheese snails, but I think that little box just did it."

"Right, pass 'em here," Völundr said, and then yelled, "silverware over here," in the general direction of Miyako Astor.

"Are there really thirteen goddesses in that box?" Raven asked, his gaze transfixed by the power he perceived pulsing from the box.

"Yip," Völundr said nodding, "and one major ring of power."

"What you going to do with it now?" Raven asked.

"Give it to Hat," Völundr said.

"Caw," Raven cawed. "That's an offal lot of power to give to a freaken Scion. You sure about that? Those kids aren't stable, none of them, and Hat's the worst of the lot."

"That's what the Gatekeeper told me to do with it and who am I to argue with him when he invokes the name of the Creator?"

"Oh, damn," Raven said. "The GK actual invoked the Big C.?"

"Yes," Völundr said.

Miyako Astor arrived with a set of silverware rolled in a cotton napkin.

"You want anything to drink with th-" Miyako Astor said started and stopped abruptly, a set of rolled silverware hovering above the black felt box. "And just what is that" the Faerie added, withdrawing his hand and stepping back from the counter.

"It's just a ring," Völundr said.

"Rrright," Miyako Astor said. "You know, I've lost count of the number of worlds that have been destroyed by rings made by the Ðwer□az?"

"Oh, I haven't," Raven said. "There's the West Country, Miðgarðr, Nibelungenlied, Paflagonia and Crim Tartary, the planet Oa-"

Völundr sighed loudly.

"There's more, you want I should go on?" Raven queried.

"No, that's fine," Völundr said.

"Really, it's no bother," Raven said. "There's only a couple three dozen more. No bother, really."

"Look, thing is," Völundr said leaning forward and speaking in a low tone, "I got orders from on-high to do this."

"*He, Him, Him, He, Him* on *High Guy*?" Raven asked with a raised eyebrow. "You said it was the Gatekeeper that said you were to do this."

Völundr nodded and said, "Thing is, he showed up after I agreed to make the ring. He wasn't interested in the ring at all; he was interested in what I did with it after the old girls were entombed in it."

"Sorry about your luck mate, that guy nailed His own Son to a tree ya know," Raven said. "Talk about tough love. A fucking tree, man, a fucking tree. Nails the size of my talons-"

"Hush," Völundr said to Raven.

Raven looked at Völundr; saw that he was looking at Miyako Astor, so Raven decided to look at the old Faerie for a while too.

Miyako Astor's gaze was enthralled to the felt covered box.

Raven turned to Völundr to see if he had seen it too. Völundr nodded, and Raven turned back to Miyako Astor, Prince of Sídhe, and saw for a second time that the second oldest extant Faerie had misplaced both his pupils.

"Ἀληκτώ, Μέγαιρα, Τισιφόνη," the old Faerie said and for a brief moment, every second of his thousands upon thousands of years shown upon his face.

"Undead murders what?" Raven said, "My Greek's the shits."

Völundr nodded grimly. "It is. How you've lived this long, I'll never know."

"Cowardice mainly," Raven said. "Never fight a fight you can flight from and live to croak another day."

"We are undying rage, the root of evil, and vengeance," Miyako Astor said, still staring at the box.

"What, all that balderdash out of those three words?" Raven asked.

"With a bit of poetic tossed in-"

"Lying you mean," Raven translated.

"I loved her," Miyako Astor said. "She died at Chernobyl."

"Who?" Raven asked.

"Diaochan," Miyako Astor said in a whisper. "They all died there."

"Hey Astor," Völundr said snapping his fingers under the Faerie's nose. "Basil Berry just went in your kitchen."

"What?" Miyako Astor said snapping back to the here and now, his pupils restored before his words were entirely uttered.

"Sorry," Völundr said. "I just wanted to make sure I got your attention back."

"Will you give this to Hat when she wonders in," Völundr asked Miyako Astor while pointing at the felt covered box.

"No, no I won't," Miyako Astor said flatly. "I don't want to have that thing anywhere near me."

Völundr started to object.

Miyako Astor held up one restraining hand. "I will do this though, and only this; you can leave it in the airing cupboard in the kitchen. I will not take responsibility for it, either overtly or by any sign or signal, nor will I be bound in any way to it, to you, or by word or deed be responsible for its destiny, or any of the consequences of its existence."

"Fucking Faeries," Raven said.

"I agree to those terms," Völundr said. "We'll just have to trust in *His* plan."

Raven put a wing over his eyes and shuddered. *Creator,* he thought, *I really don't mind You, but could Ya do something about Your followers? No? Damn. Thanks for the notice; I'm in no hurry for the coffee chat You suggested last year. I am, &c and all that etc., etc., fazizzle.*

Raven opened his eyes and realized that he hadn't been breathing for a while.

"But for the time being, put that away," Miyako Astor said to Völundr. "I don't need the kind of trouble those girls can cause here, not now, not now."

And then Raven saw him, Roswell, god of Absurdly Improvable Coincidences. The god was wearing a grey t-shirt with the slender head of a green face with big black eyes. Below the head was the caption; "I don't need to believe". Roswell was reading *The Book of American Secrets.*

Roswell looked up and turned towards Raven before Raven could look away. Roswell slowly raised his thumb and forefinger towards Raven and mouthed the word 'Bang.'

Raven looked away not wanting to encourage the old nut.

Völundr secreted the black felt covered box into one of his many pockets.

"So," Raven said in a desperate attempt to lighten the mood, "what the Hell is Kára's beef with Keith? I mean, how long is she going to hold a grudge? My people made peace with the chalkies, the Yanks and the Ruskies made peace, the Vietnamese made peace with each other, and Mandela made peace with everyone. Hell, even the Spacers made peace eventually. What's up with her still carrying the grudge this long?"

"Her big problem with him is that he makes people laugh," Völundr said.

"Pardon?" Miyako Astor asked.

"Pardon?" Raven asked.

"Granted all-inclusive," Völundr said.

"So," Raven said with a shrug. "Keith makes lots of people laugh, so do I, so do you, and you even sometimes mean to do it."

"Ha, ha," Völundr returned. "So funny I for-"

"Waiter, a bullet to the head, please," Raven said. "I'm trapped in a '70s time warp again."

Miyako Astor rolled his eyes.

Völundr said; "Did you hear the one where the two chemists walk into the bar, and one orders a H_2O, and the next guys says-"

"Yeah, yeah," Raven said. "Heavy water, got it. So yeah, okay, I get it. Keith's sense of humour is not as dry as yours, what's your point?"

"Here I am telling water jokes and you call me dry? That's some double standard bird-brains."

"All right, all right, drown me in the depths of your acumen," Raven said, and then continued in a wiry voice that people do when they've just decided to listen to all of dear old granddad's jokes again. "Why is laughter so important?"

"It's not the laughter itself," Völundr clarified. "It's the ability Keith has to make people laugh. He's one part Lewis Black, one part Kenneth Williams, and one part that actually listens to every single damn word you say. So it's his ability in the first instance to laugh at himself, the second how he can effortlessly make people laugh at everything, and last Keith remembers what you say to him, and she hates that."

"But Kára laughs all the time," Raven complained. "I don't get that chick."

"So?" Völundr asked and moved on quickly, "Kára herself never makes anyone laugh. She's an obsessive workaholic. I don't know what drives her, but it's deep-seated and anger is usually the only deep-seated issue. She is conscious of herself all the time, so she never lets go. Oh, she laughs a lot, but she never makes people laugh. She's jealous of that in him, and hates him for it. He's sincere all the time, he listens, takes all that, puts it in a blender, and makes you laugh anyway. Or at least, he used to do that. She's so damned worried about being taken seriously that she hardly stops to listen to people, even her clients, and only makes people laugh by accident. Plus, she's been mad at him so damned long that it's become part of who she is, and she knows if she gets within touching range of him he's just going to start telling her the purest non-sensual bollox that she won't be able to help liking him again. And Kára's afraid that if she let's go of the hate, she won't know who she is anymore."

"Love and hate are the same emotion with different vectors," Miyako Astor said.

"Yep," Völundr agreed.

"You know, I've never understood what the problem with those two was," Raven said.

"Pride," Völundr said, "simple pride. Neither one of them wants to admit that they ever loved anything that was imperfect, and neither one of them wants to admit that the other one changed, and grew, and became something different or better without the other."

"That and jealousy," Miyako Astor added. "Neither has ever been happy with what they have, so they both want what the other one has. She wants his people skills, and he wants her brains. But it's mainly pride."

"Pride," Völundr said, "that's it."

Raven waited for a long moment before he answered the short Smith.

"You know," Raven eventually said. "I think that you might be one of the most observant people I've ever met."

Völundr gave a slight bow.

"Why do you think I stick so closely to my work?" he asked. "Metal doesn't get emotional on you. Metal doesn't lie to you. Metal will cut your hand off if you're not careful, but metal never gets up in the middle of the night of its own accord and steals your family fortune and runs off with your brother that later ends up dead in a motel in the middle of nowhere Nevada. Metal doesn't hold grudges either. And the best part is that metal never ever has any spiritual angst about 'What is it all about, really, when you get right down to it? Are we here for a purpose? Have I made a significant contribution to the evolution of Human culture or have I just been a parasite on the capitalist culture of market consumerism? Na man-"

"Bird."

"Na, bird," shifted Völundr without the slightest pause, "metal never has any of that jazz to deal with at 3 AM after it's had too many wine coolers and can't sleep because it's wondering if it should have married that fantastic brunette that it was going out with in college, or that equally fantastic blond from graduate school with the twangy accent that just made your skull hurt even though she was otherwise the most perfect creation of God's womankind, or that Heavenly bit of Lebanese-Jew that-"

"Okay, okay, I get it," Raven said covering his non-existent ears with his wings. "Man, you really know how to hammer a metaphor to death, don't you?"

Völundr grinned.

"The hardest part is getting it on the anvil."

Miyako Astor refilled their drinks.

"Völundr is right, you know?" Miyako Astor said. "I get them in here all the time, although, not as much as I used to. There's nothing like a bummed out

Hellspawn who's trying to figure out his place in the new liberated 'What'd ya mean I have to do laundry too?' world that we live in these days. I think Demons have it the worst because they can just remake the universe to suit themselves. But they just cannot control people. It's hard to have all that power and still not get your way."

"You speak truth," Raven said.

"Hey, can I get an omelette with the whole garden tossed in?" Völundr asked.

"Make that a Hyper-vegan omelette with the whole garden tossed in," Raven said.

"Sure," Miyako Astor said.

Völundr looked puzzled.

"Being a bird," Raven said, "I've got this thing against people eating eggs."

Völundr nodded and began to tell Raven the full story of the forging of the ring of goddesses.

And not for the first time, Raven wondered why Völundr hadn't ever gotten around to blowing up the universe, much less Terra.

Chapter 15: Two Friends

Deep inside Mount Li, also called 骊山, Terra, in the Sol Solar System.

And the Creator said, "Let the Terra bring forth grass, the herb yielding seed, and the fruit tree yielding fruit after his kind, whose seed is in itself, upon the Terra"; and it was so. And the Terra brought forth grass and herb yielding seed after his kind, and the tree yielding fruit, whose seed was in itself, after his kind. --Genesis 1:11-12, K.J.V.

And it came to pass that the growth of the Tafari forests was assured, so that one day, there could be a Tafari City.

Keith appeared inside the red sapphire Circle of Life, in the inner citadel of Lady Zhurong's Ryuunosuke Castle and clutched his head in his hands. Reaching out past the circumference of the Circle of Life, which had been carved from the heart of what had once been the largest red sapphire in the universe. Keith grabbed the silver bucket that was always left there for just this reason and tossed his last three meals into it.

As much as Keith liked Ryuunosuke Castle once he got there, he had always felt that the actual getting there wasn't worth the trouble.

Of course, the Demon reflected, as bits of bacon ripped tiny holes in his throat, one could travel through the Dungeon Dimensions to and then down the entire length of the Abyss until one came to the Gates of Hell and from there simply take the moving walkway from Maleficent to Despair and onto Extremism.

No, Keith decided, wiping the remains of a bacon cheese Danish out of his mouth that was all a bit too much to avoid a bit of bodily purification. The red sapphire Circle of Life was much quicker, if less pleasant.

Keith stood up, straightened his *I like Ike* t-shirt, and looked around.

Beyond the Circle of Life, the mammoth subterranean cavern swelled with thousands of signs of Lady Jīng's presence in the castle. Everywhere the Demon looked the cavern was busting with green vegetation from all over the universe. The small leaves of the Desmodium Gyrans dancing planet quivered and swayed as Keith past. Several Aquilegia chaplinei, commonly called Chaplin's columbine, opened their large yellow blooms as the old fertility spirit approached. Not to be outdone, the patch of Talinum brachypodum, called Laguna flame flowers, turned a darker shade of violet, to greet Keith, who found it all immensely satisfying.

Small mountains held up the furthest edges of the cavern that formed a natural canopy over a central life zone, at the center of which rested the black foundation stones of Ryuunosuke Castle.

Keith looked from one flower to another. The Demon saw flowers from all over the Terra, arranged according to colour without the slightest regard to the plant's home climate, or the need for natural light. The sight would have been breath taking, if Keith had ever bothered to breathe.

Living things could not help but to grow when they were near either Lady Zhurong or Lady Jīng, and both of the Ancients had been living here since at least a million years before the end of humanity at Armagedōn. The cavern was a scientific bonanza and Keith found himself wishing, just for a moment that someone else was there to share his joy. The young Maria Sibylla Merian drawing her butterflies came to Keith's mind.

Keith was unclear on just who, or what the Ancients were, or even how many of them there were. It didn't help that all of the Ancients always gave wildly different accounts of what the Ancients were, and such accounts that often contradicted the speaker's own previous statements on the subject. Keith suspected that the Ancients were intentionally taking a piss on the whole world with that shtick. He figured they were just really old Avatars and left it at that. There were too many question marks all over the Creator's universe to be bothering about any particular point that didn't make sense.

The truth was that Ancients were mortals that the Creator had just decided to really fuck with. This is a point that not even the Angel Metatron understood, although he had long since sorted it out by dint of observation.

Stopping for a moment's reflection at the base of the antediluvian stone stairs that led in a winding path up to Ryuunosuke Castle, Keith decided that he had met eleven Ancients. Solid angelic rumour said there were twenty-seven Ancients in all.

There was Lady Jīng the embodiment of Essence and Form, and who lived here with Lady Zhurong in the Ryuunosuke Castle, and there was Lady Zhurong, a direct descendent of the fire god Zhu Rong and a she-Demon, embodied Honour. Lady Jìn was the embodiment of raw Power, and Lady Li who was the embodiment of Despair. All four of these Ancients were Chinese, although they were not, strictly speaking, either mortal or immortal.

Keith had long held the practice that whenever he encountered Lady Li, even for a second, he, a damned Demon of the first order of Hellions, would go and find the Holy Ghost and sing campfire spirituals over s'mores until he felt better. Lady Li was just that evil, and the Ghost was good like that, always making room around the fire, and never asking dumbass questions like, "So, have you had your holidays yet?"

Then there was Lady Dōtoku whom embodied the administration of Justice and Restraint, who was Japanese. There was the Korean Lady Kim who stood a four-foot nothing for Courage, and it was only the dimmest of Demons, or anything else for that matter, that ever-crossed Lady Kim. The last Demon that Keith knew to have done so was literally unmade.

Lady Aroha never seemed to be from anywhere, excepting wherever she happened to be. She was hard to pin down like that and just like Lady Li, Keith found he needed his brain reset after being around Lady Aroha. Watching a snuff film usually did the trick. In extreme cases, which were rare since Keith could usually feel Lady Aroha's presence from the next time zone, so he could avoid meeting her whenever possible.

Lady Nuha stood for Wisdom, and was the eldest of the Ancients that the Demon Keith knew anything about. She had always appeared Arabian to Keith, although many others had told him that Lady Nuha was Mayan or Aztec. Keith had once asked Lady Nuha if she were Arabian, Aztec, or Mayan. The Ancient had only smiled at him and asked what was the difference between the three? When Keith had started listing the differences between the three peoples, nations, and their roles in history, Lady Nuha had only laughed and changed the subject.

Lord Văn was Vietnamese and stood for Knowledge, Literature, and carried an anti-theory stick that he would club people with if he thought they were being too pompous. Keith had always made a point of keeping his big trap firmly shut whenever the man was around. Unless the Angel Mick was there, in which case Keith was always willing to take a mild beating for the sake of watching the Angel get handed his pride in a small take-away bag.

Lord Fornícó, whom was rumoured but never proven to have been the child of the Duke Belial, one of the Four Crown Princes of Hell, had been European at some point in the past. But Lord Fornícó, who was almost universally simply referred to as Fornícó, immigrated to the New World with the Roanoke Colony settlement. Years later, Fornícó would boast, "I just had to see how a 7:1 male to female ratio was going to work out for them. I was surprised that they ever made it to the New World in the first place. Seriously, seven badgers trying to get in the same hole that was the most entertaining journey I've ever made."

And there was the eleventh one. Keith knew her, at least, Keith thought of it as her. Every time he met her, he said to himself, "Damn, I've met this wench before. Better damn well remember her name this time." And just as soon as she was out of Keith's sight, he would forget about her as cleanly as a morning dream slipped out of your mind, leaving only the memory of a memory.

Keith crested the top of the steps and found himself confronted by the two Ancient Ladies that inhabited this subterranean botanic paradise. They sat cross-legged on a red and an Imperial Yellow cushion, with a two-foot high table set between them. Keith stopped, went down on one knee, and bowed deeply, first to the Ancient on the red cushion. He then stood, turned, and repeated the procedure to the Ancient sitting on the Imperial Yellow cushion.

The Ancient on the Imperial Yellow cushion nodded a head of wrinkles crowned by dark black hair at Keith and indicated that he should sit himself at her left side.

The most distinctive feature, among the many powerful features of Lady Zhurong of the Imperial Yellow cushion was this; two large grey eyes. It wasn't that the eyes were mostly white, with a ring of grey around a black pupil. It was that the eyes were grey all over. Lady Zhurong was completely blind.

Not that that gave Keith the slightest bit of comfort. It was rumoured that the old lizard could smell the colour of magic and hear the sound of the future.

If anything, Keith was more terrified of her blind then he ever would have been had she had the full-scale set of senses permitted other creatures in the universe.

Keith removed his shoes, bowed, and settled down onto the black cushion. Spread before him on the table was all the vestments of a traditional tea and they were oriented on his space.

Keith groaned inwardly. The rites of a formal tea with these Ancients were hardly a surprise, but still, he had been hoping to avoid it. The Demon reached into his jacket producing his glasses case and placed a small set of pince nez reading glasses upon his nose.

Lady Zhurong smiled at him as the Demon also withdrew a slim black-bound Piccadilly-lined flip-top notebook and studied his notes.

Right, I'll show you, ya old lizard, Keith thought.

Laying the notebook aside, Keith picked-up one of the two empty Yixing teapots and snapped the fingers of the other hand. He now held a cold Yixing teapot filled with water. Balancing the pot in his left hand, he began to draw energy up out of the mountain, through his waist, arm, and hand, which he drove into the bottom of the teapot. Keith than muttered the Calcifer spell, so that a small ball of fire appeared on his palm to heat the teapot. At the same time, he lifted up the Chahai tea pitcher and visually inspected the tea. For a further show of effort, he sniffed it and smiled.

Smells just like all the other bloody weed in the universe, Keith thought.

As Keith drew energy directly from the mountain and pulsed it into the pot, the water began to boil and steam. The Demon replaced it on the brewing tray's flat porcelain plate. Next, the Demon took the tea towel and teaspoon and cleared the spout. Keith then poured boiling water into the sterilization bowl and using a set of wooden tongs placed each one of the smooth clay teacups into the water.

Keith then paused and consulted his notes.

Bugger it, he thought; I forgot to pass the tea around for the old toads to smell.

Without looking up from his notes, Keith took the Chahai tea pitcher and passed it over to Lady Jing on the red cushion, who looked at the tea and scowled. The Demon calmly passed the pitcher on to Lady Zhurong of the Imperial Yellow cushion.

Keith saw in his peripheral vision that Lady Zhurong turned one dead grey eye to follow his hands, while keeping the other eye firmly fixed on his face.

Rinse three times, Keith read in his notes, and thought, ignore the creepy toad.

Keith took the tea back from Lady Zhurong when she extended one long arm and he pointedly ignored her extremely long fingernails. He then scooped three heaping spoons of tea into the second Yixing teapot, and filled the pot with boiling water from the first pot. The Demon then carefully poured the water out, using the spoon to keep the tea from slipping out the spout. He repeated the rinse three more times, all the while wondering what the point of this ritualism was. He didn't think there was one.

Keith then picked up the second Yixing teapot and cupping it in his hand as he did the first pot, pulled energy a second time from the mountain and forced it into the pot until the water boiled. Without placing the pot back on the porcelain plate, Keith fished the wooden bowls out of the sanitizing bath, flicked off the excess water, and filled the three cups with tea and waited.

After humming *Pregnant Women are Smug*, by Garfunkel and Oates once to himself, Keith tossed the tea into the grass.

Lady Zhurong on the Imperial Yellow cushion grunted.

Keith looked up at her and winked before filling up the teacups a second time. Rising up on his knees, Keith first placed a cup of tea in front of Lady Zhurong and then a cup of tea in front of Lady Jīng.

323

One last touch, Keith thought, allowing a grin to perish in his mental eyeball. He reached into his coat pocket and retrieved a small black media player. He listened in satisfaction as the distinctive guitar riffs of Angus Young ripped out into the cavern.

Lady Zhurong smiled, revealing row upon row of sharp pointed teeth.

When Bon Scott sung out, "Living easy, living free-" Keith felt the media player snap out of his hand. It happened so fast that he did not see it and barely felt it.

Lady Jīng calmly switched the player off before she closed her hand over the small piece of electronics. When she opened her hand a second time, a small black and white butterfly parted its wings, shivered slightly, and took off towards the treetops.

Keith glared at Lady Jīng, who simply reclined on her cushion without making the slightest effort to conceal her amusement at his expense.

Lady Zhurong picked up her tea, took a sip, and frowned.

"It tastes like burnt tree bark," she said.

"He is most impatient, even by devil standards," Lady Jīng agreed. "He did not wait for the tea to simmer."

Keith shrugged and knocked back his own tea in the same way he might have knocked back a shot of Wild Turkey, and screwed up his face.

"No, I think I've had better bark," Keith said.

Lady Zhurong laughed. It was the kind of deep full laugh that cheered one up no matter what. It was the kind of laugh that said, *Hey, life ain't so bad. Dead Hubby? Here, have a puppy. Now you just buck-up and try that life thing again.*

Lady Jīng clapped her hands three times and the entire tea set disappeared.

Keith, whom had been holding his teacup at the time, felt the first layer of his skin go too and winced.

She clapped her hands a second three times and an entirely unmolested tea set appeared.

Keith watched in mild admiration as Lady Jīng gracefully set about preparing a traditional Chinese tea. Every movement of her hands reminded Keith of the tiny dancers in the Mariinsky Ballet Company and the Central Ballet Troupe that seemed to just fly through the air.

"What brings you to our wilderness, young one?" Lady Zhurong said after a long while.

Keith, who had, as far as he knew, been created a few days after the universe, wondered for a moment at the term "young one," but then breezed right on past it. It was always best to ignore the idiosyncrasies of the Ancients, whom were either fully mortal or fully immortal.

"With much respect to the eldest of all Dra-" Keith began, but was cut off by Lady Zhurong.

"Dispense with ceremony," she said and Keith knew it wasn't a suggestion.

"He already has," Lady Jīng said. "I've had better tea made by that junkie whore Blossom."

"Well, actually," Keith began again. "I've come to see Lady Jīng."

"Oh?" said Lady Zhurong turning from Keith to Lady Jīng. "Have you?"

"Whatever it is, I don't want any," said Lady Jīng as she carefully laid one tealeaf after another into the Yixing teapot prior to the first rinse.

"My dear Lady," Keith said.

Lady Jīng's head snapped up, her eyes flashing the same shade of jade green that proceeded tornados.

"Young one," Lady Jing said crisply. "You have no right to address me as your "*dear lady.*"

Keith bowed his head. He might have been discouraged, if this wasn't how most conversations with Lady Jīng went for most people. Lady Jing had once turned the Angel Mick into a Dwarf Gecko for suggesting that the Ancients had been created by Stan instead of the Creator. So far, the Demon hadn't become a butterfly, so he figured things were going pretty well.

"I beg pardon Lady Jīng," the Demon said after a long calculated pause. "I have not come to sell you anything, or to ask anything other than for your company upon the planet Tafari."

Lady Jīng snorted and continued rinsing the tea.

Lady Zhurong laid her head on one side and inspected the Demon critically. He wore what might have been referred to in bygone centuries as business casual. Black pants, an unbuttoned dark blue button-down Oxford with rolled up sleeves over an *I Like Ike* t-shirt, and comfortable dress shoes that were in actuality well disguised cross trainers.

"And what sort of evil can you get up to in the center of the universe?" Lady Zhurong asked. "The center is a dead place. Even for our kind"

"Not much, just at present," Keith said. "But the place is a dust bowl and that's the problem."

"And you want me to come there and make for you an oasis?" Lady Jīng cut in sharply. "So you can lie around in a garden and wile away the passage of time?"

"In a manner of speaking," Keith said. "Actually, we are going to make a movie."

"Oh?" said Lady Zhurong.

Lady Jīng continued with the preparation of the tea as if she had not heard a word said.

326

"Yes," Keith said. "We have not really sorted out the details yet. But the general idea is to make a movie. A bit like in the old days, with film and-"

"Actors," Lady Jīng grunted.

"Ah, yes, and with actors," Lady Zhurong said, "and the lovely young ladies too. Something classical?"

Keith nodded.

"红楼梦" Lady Zhurong asked.

Keith shrugged. His universal translator had never worked properly.

"Xueqin's *Dream of the Red Chamber*?" Lady Jing translated.

"We've been thinking Shakespeare," Keith said.

"Oh, modern," Lady Zhurong said with a dismissive gesture. "Never saw the interest in him, myself."

Lady Jīng poured the tea and handed it around.

Keith could smell oranges, roses, and morning rain wafting up from his cup. Whatever weed Lady Jing was using, the Demon thought it sure as Hell smelled good.

Lady Jīng collected up the untested tea, carefully poured it out, and then refilled the cups.

"Lady Jīng," said Lady Zhurong after tasting her tea, "I do believe that you are the best this universe has ever had for making tea."

Lady Jīng nodded her agreement.

Keith rolled his eyes.

"So, you want me to come to the center, the dead place, and do what?" Lady Jīng asked, finally looking at Keith again.

"Just be there," Keith said. "Nature grows around you no matter what you do," he added, looking around the expanse of the cavern, covered on almost every surface with green vegetation and colourful flowers. "Nature grows around both of you."

Lady Zhurong nodded.

"This is true," Lady Jīng said. "But I cannot create from what is not there."

"Oh, that's no worry," Keith said taking a sip of his tea, "Chukwu is already there. He can do that bit. I just want him to hurry up a bit."

Had Keith been paying even the slightest attention to Lady Zhurong at that particular moment, he would have seen the momentary frown appear on her face.

"You know, Lady Jīng, this tea really is rather good," Keith said. "I'm a confirmed coffee and spirits man, but I could really get used to this tea. You ever thought of bottling it for sales?"

Lady Jīng sought the gaze of her friend Lady Zhurong, who in turn sought the sound of the Demon. The Demon finished his tea, and wiped his mouth with the napkin.

"So yeah," Keith continued, "we're going to make a movie out there on Tafari and I thought that you might like to come along and help with the scenery. You know, get yourself out of yourself, and shake up the routine a bit. I don't know about you two, but Eternity is really stretching beyond the tedium-event-threshold for me."

"Have you ever worked with Chukwu before?" asked Lady Jīng.

"No, not that I remember," Keith said, fishing the pack of vintage Camel Victory Blend cigarettes out of his pocket. "I've only ever seen him twice before now and never really talked with him about anything. Why do you ask?"

Lady Zhurong started to answer, thought better of it, and said nothing.

Lady Jīng looked at the Demon for a long time before answering.

Keith for his part lit the cigarette and waited. He knew that like Angels, for whom you had to ignore their sarcasm and their ego, with the Ancients, you had to wait and ignore their impudence. Of all the non-mortals in the universe, Keith had always considered the Ancients to be the oddest. They weren't gods, not as such, and they certainly were not Angels, Demons, or anything like the Nightmares or Hellspawn. The Ancients were, well, the embodiment of really old ideas. The Ancients were sort of like the Anthropomorphic Personifications in that respect; except that the Ancients were not a common experience of all of mortality like Time, Hate, and the Tooth Faerie were. The Ancients often were the outgrowth of a cultural identity, or perhaps, and Keith thought much more likely, that certain cultural identities were a consequence of close proximity to an Ancient. In this respect the Avatar comparison worked, except that an Avatar grew out of a massive mortal following, whereas an Ancient caused a massive following of mortals.

Lady Jīng for example was the embodiment of natural order, which had been embodied in the Oriental collective consciousness through formal gardening, rigid forms of etiquette, and a social hierarchy that you could, and the Chinese did, build skyscrapers on. Hence Keith's desire for her presence on Tafari. Keith knew that Lady Jīng had once spent a week in 1968 in California visiting relatives and had as a by-product of her visit sparked the Post World War Environmentalism movement in the Western Hemisphere. Or at least, had opened the eyes of the average American to the movement that had always been going on all over the world. Plus, and this was a faint hope, Keith thought that Lady Jīng being on Tafari would help to keep the many different factions of immortals from falling back on their old standby habit of warring on each other.

"No," Lady Jīng said, ripping Keith's hopes to shreds.

"Pardon?" Keith said, blinking back to reality.

"You heard me, devil," Lady Jīng said.

"First off, I'm not the Devil," Keith said. "I would not take that gig if you gave it to me. The hours suck great big spider-monkey balls. Second-"

"It does not matter what your second is," Lady Jīng said with a calm that was calculated to infuriate the Demon. "My answer will remain, *No*."

"Will you, at least, tell me, why?" Keith said without pretence at concealing his anger.

Lady Jīng looked at Lady Zhurong, who shrugged.

"He'll know soon enough," Lady Zhurong said. "Everything began at the center and so shall it end at that same center. The Creator likes things to circle like that."

"I doubt that he'll bother to understand," Lady Jīng returned. "In all this time the young one has never bothered to find out anything worth knowing."

"Pardon me, oh, just pardon me," Keith said with a mock wave of his hands. "I'm just twenty-seven billion two hundred forty-two years and three hundred thirteen days old, thank you. Never mind me."

"I never do," Lady Zhurong said.

"Liar," Lady Jīng added. "Demon, do you know why the Gentiles were finally admitted into Heaven?"

Keith shook his head.

"It's because Joshua bar Joseph didn't want to hurt the feelings of the lady at the well. She loved a Gentile you see. Loved him so much she committed adultery with him and she didn't want him to go to Hell. That's what she and the Son were talking about when the twelve sidekicks showed up. The Son didn't say because that nutcase Paul would have had her stoned."

"So?" Keith said, not really wanting the answer.

330

"So," Lady Jīng continued, "rather than hurt this one woman's feelings, Joshua freed trillions and trillions and trillions of souls from eternal torment. All for the sake of one whore's lover and that same whore's feelings."

"And you two?" Keith muttered. "Barely older than Terra, the two of you. What do you know about anything?"

Lady Zhurong leaned forward and wrapped one long thin hand around the wrist of Lady Jīng as it rose up in anger.

Lady Jīng looked down with fury at the hand, particularly the long fingernails of the hand, which wrapped them around her wrist.

Keith was impressed. He had never seen fingernails as long and straight as those of Lady Zhurong, and he certainly never saw fingernails wrap around anything as if they were just longer fingers.

"Demon Fruchtbarkeitskultus," Lady Zhurong said. "I have pity on you because I remember not believing either when I was told."

Much to Keith's own annoyance, he found himself sitting a bit straighter and considerably stiffer at the mention of his true name.

"Lady Jīng and I are two of the seven hundred twenty-nine beings that were not born of this universe," Lady Zhurong said slowly releasing Lady Jīng's wrist. "That is what an Ancient is - someone who was not born in this universe. We are indeed older than you, much, much older than you, child of this universe."

"O-kay," Keith said, drawing out the word and avoiding Lady Zhurong's gaze.

What the fuck does that mean? Keith added in the privacy of his own head. He withdrew another cigarette from the pack and gently ran in through his fingers several times.

"Perhaps the devil is learning?" Lady Jīng said to Lady Zhurong. "Maybe even thinking before it opens its mouth again."

"Care to break this one down for me?" Keith asked.

"Chukwu is the Gatekeeper and his Keepership is drawing to a close," Lady Jīng said before her companion could answer. "So, he will turn the keys and the Gate and the everything - everything over to the new Gatekeeper."

"Yeah and then what?" Keith asked.

"Go on holiday," Lady Jīng said and laughed. "An eternally long holiday."

"Somewhere where bread does not make one fat," Lady Zhurong agreed.

"And what does this Gatekeeper do?" Keith asked lighting his cigarette off his finger.

"Keep the Gates, stupid," Lady Jīng said, grinning a sort of toothy grin that only an old lady that had never so much as had a case of bad breath, much less dental problems, could grin. Her teeth all but gleamed.

"What like the Pearly Gates?" Keith asked.

"No, no, that's one of you guys that guards that one," Lady Jīng said with a dismissive gesture. "The Gatekeeper keeps the Gates between the universes. Keeps the parallel things parallel."

"Dimensions," Lady Zhurong added.

"Yes, those, keeps them running side by side, keeps those out of this one and ours out of theirs," Lady Jīng concluded.

"But you make a mistake, Lady Jīng," Lady Zhurong said. "Gates are for traveling between the universes, whereas Steps are for traveling between the parallel realities contained within the one singular universe."

Lady Jīng shrugged as if to say, 'What am I, a theoretical physicist?'

"Steps?" Keith asked.

"Like portable doors," Lady Zhurong said. "Patton found one, there, in the center of the frozen planet.

Keith looked bemused.

"The Ishtar Gate," Lady Jing said.

"No it's like, how did the Metatron say," Lady Zhurong said unfolding her legs. "We have one universe, which is like a great big bubble, and only a Gate leads to another bubble, leads to another great big bubble. But there are all these parallel time lines, parallel universes, within one universe, and you have the steps to go between the parallels. The parallel times, it is like many little bubbles inside the one great big bubble. All the little bubbles are part of, contained in, the one great big bubble. Something like that anyway. Talks in circles that Angel does."

"Yeah, I like that explanation better," Lady Jīng said. "What she said."

Keith looked from one to the other looking for a sign of the joke. Failing that, he took refuge in Demon humour.

"That's the biggest load of Sci-fi Channel nonsense I've ever heard," Keith said with a grin.

"Think of the Gatekeeper as a head gardener, or grounds keeper, or Grand Vassar, plus universal body guard and bouncer," Lady Zhurong said. "The Gatekeeper is responsible for all that tedious business of gravity and making sure that the many different realities do not get confused."

"Um, no," Keith said rather more firmly than he felt entirely necessary. A Demon, even after amnesty, could get a lot of flak for what he was about to say. "That's Creator business. No God but Him God."

"Yes, yes, yes," Lady Zhurong said with a wave of her hand. "I know all about Him. But, He out-sources, see? Very Republican like that. Makes all these universes and then gives them over to some unqualified dolt with aspirations of owning everything and then He goes off. Creating more universes, or whatever He does when He's not actually around annoying people."

"R-i-ght-" Keith said slowly. He was beginning to wonder if the last million years hadn't gone somewhere in the heads of these two old-ass Ancients. This was the sort of talk that got decent respectable Angels tossed out of Heaven. Keith had always rather prided himself on the fact that he walked out in solidarity with his fallen brothers and wasn't pitched out, like some Demons he could mention had been.

"Have you met my daughter?" Lady Zhurong asked.

"Ah, no, I don't think so. Not today anyway," Keith said.

"There she is, coming up behind you. And that Cynthia Q. Lyons too, by the smell of her," Lady Zhurong added as Keith turned around to look.

Keith saw two women sitting, crisscross applesauce, on two small Flying Carpets, soaring up over the trees.

The lead caropiolet, Mayghin, Scion of Lady Zhurong, sat on an antique Shang Dynasty Carpet with her back straight, eyes closed, and hands folded in her lap. She was a short slender woman, dressed in a red, yellow, and green silk kimono with a long white sash tied around her waist. Mayghin's curly red hair began to curl as her freckle-spotted face changed from a pale ashen pink to a hue somewhere between fresh ruddy blood and Tyrian purple.

Cynthia Q. Lyons, called Qdot, Scion of Artemis, was the second caropiolet. She reclined on an antique Trina Greek Carpet. Qdot was a dark brown complexioned woman of about medium height, with a large Disco era fro. She wore a one-piece green shell suit that more than showed off her ample breasts, and hips. Qdot sat slightly reclined on the Carpet, as if invisible pillows were propped behind her. She was watching a semi-transparent holo-vid of *Mrs. Brown's Boys*. A small red cloth bag and a red envelope sat on Qdot's lap.

The two Carpets landed a few meters away from the Demon and the Ancients.

Without opening her eyes, Mayghin said, "Hi ya Momma-bear."

Lady Zhurong snorted.

Keith watched in fascination as smoke curled out of Lady Zhurong's nostrils.

Qdot rose, stretched, popped all of her knuckles in one swift economic movement, and returned to her knees. After kowtowing three times, she spoke thus:

"Elder Zhurong, mother Artemis, bids you greetings and bids me to present you compliments and best wished for a long and prosperous life."

"Oh, your dear mother," Lady Jīng said. "Look here young Demon, she sends Yunnan Pu-erh tea." The Ancient picked up the red cloth bag and waved it at the Keith. "Why you not bring this, devil?"

Keith rolled his eyes and looked towards the ceiling of the cavern.

"Stupid custom," he said.

"Everyone's customs are stupid," Lady Jīng said leaning forward and whacking the Demon on the knee. "That doesn't mean you ignore them. Ignoring customs, that makes you Stupid. Also gives me a good excuse not to help you."

"So, if I bring you tea, will you help?"

"Not a chance," Lady Jīng said. "I don't like Chukwu. He's crazy and not in that fun let's all go for a fly on the back of a blind Dragon sort of fun crazy. He's

335

fucking get you killed just when you are turning a trillion and finally going to collect on your social security kind of crazy."

"Chukwu is another one of us," said Lady Zhurong. "We were with Chukwu, in Afghanistan, when he offended *Him* who Is."

"Another what?" Qdot asked.

"One of the seven hundred twenty-none people not from around here. What you call the Ancients," Lady Jīng said. "He is also the Gatekeeper."

"Here we go again," Mayghin said, her eyes fluttering beneath her closed eyes.

Keith slightly raised his eyebrows in the Scion's general direction.

"Yeah," Mayghin continued. "They got this idea that they're from some other dimension or universe or municipality or something. They've both been smoking the tea for millions of years if you ask me. By the way, we're in."

"In for what?" Keith asked carrying on Hell's finest traditions of calculated indifference and determined ignorance of the obvious.

"For your dramatic farce," Qdot said. "Hat told me all about it, and I told Mayghin, and the other Scion Tycoons, and we are in. All of us. Sounds like fun."

"Pity, she didn't mention it to me," Keith said critically examining his tea. He didn't much like what he read there either. 'Don't count on it' was never a good message.

"Oh, come off it scales," Qdot said. "I want to see my name in big lights."

"Leaves say *not a chance*," Keith said.

"Tell ya what serpent bait," Qdot mused, "what do you need?"

Keith jerked a thumb towards Lady Jīng.

336

Lady Jīng narrowed her glaring eyes and pursed her lips across the table at Qdot.

"I don't know," Qdot said. "She'll be a tuff one. She's harder to kill than bacteria, so threats won't. She's an Immortal, so waiting her out won't work. And she has just about anything anyone would want, so bribes won't work either."

Lady Jīng contrived to look even smugger then before, which was hard to do. It was the way the wrinkles got just slightly deeper at the same time her eyes got slightly brighter that did it.

"Did you try saying *please, pretty please, with a cherry on top*?" asked Mayghin. "It always worked for me when I was a girl."

Keith looked Lady Jīng up and down, weighting his chances of survival after embarking on such a course.

"Na," the Demon finally said. "I'd rather not risk all that paper work to get a new body. Besides, nobody's seen Stan in ages and he's got to sign off on all new bodies for our team."

As has already been mentioned, neither Angels nor Demons can be truly killed, except by the Creator, whom so far has never shown the slightest interest in actually doing so, favouring rather the limp-wristed "Don't make me pull over and get out of this car and whack you," method of Demon discipline. Even so, the filing of paperwork in Hell for a new body is reckoned to be the second worst experience in bureaucratic hum drumming. The first worst is of course doing the same thing in Heaven, where the Celestial Choir of humanity is piped in over Heavenly AM Radio, which can't actually be turned off - ever. At least the music in Hell is worth hearing.

Oddly enough, nobody had seen quite a few of the more important Angels and Demons around the universe for a long time. Not that anyone really had noticed that they were missing. Free-range Demons like Keith tended to avoid other Demons whenever possible on account of their never having been all that keen on destroying humanity in the first place. Oh, they had individual grudges against individual mortals, sure. Nobody, not even the Metatron himself could live in a universe for very long without coming to hate the little Johnny-come-lately fuckers eventually. But it was just that free-range Demons had, while not necessarily reconciling with Heaven, come to terms with humanity's right to exist.

And a few, like Keith, had even come to like the mortals, either in the very small quantities of decent intelligent people like you get at Professorial tenure parties, or in hysterically large quantities. Like the sort you get when you are in an arena full of girly teenyboppers going to their first boy band concert under the supervision of their elder sister that ditched them before they were even out of their subdivision. But the point is, the really big point is, that Stan, the Metatron, Diábolos, Gabriel, and a few other notables had not been seen skulking about the universe in several centuries. Had anyone actually put this all together, it would have most certainly given them an uncanny dire feeling that would have resulted in a good lie down, a hot tea, and a couple of casual 'I'll just work my way around to asking about them phone calls.'

Shame nobody ever did though. Jane Marple is never around when you need her.

"They know that Chukwu is nearing the end of his parole," Lady Zhurong said, "and mark my word lad, that'll be a game changer."

Lady Jīng nodded.

"He's been pretty pissed since Mortality nuked itself," Lady Zhurong continued. "Chukwu's been working on ideas to keep an extinction event from ever happening again."

"Mists of the Abyss is one of them," Lady Jīng said, "or something like that. He's got this notion that Mortality should be all spread out, all over the universe like that crazy Russian wrote, so that they can't ever wipe themselves all out again. Seems to me 13,242 billion years with the buggers didn't teach him much about their nature."

"Here- here, Lady Jīng," Qdot said. "You have any idea how many gods of war that those mortal kids dreamt up? Nearly thirty-seven thousands of them start to finish and only maybe a 1,000 goddesses of love."

"Isaac Asimov?" Keith asked.

"Yes, that's him," Lady Jing said. "All the best books were by crazy Russians."

"Did they ever have a god of love?" Lady Zhurong asked.

"No my Lady," Qdot said. "Not that I ever met or heard tale of."

"What about that Cupid boy?" Lady Zhurong asked.

"God of desire, Mum," Mayghin said. "He could sell ya a good love rap, but he'd always be gone in the morning and there's you sitting there in a mound of chocolate wrappers and stale sheets and-"

"Yes, yes dear, we all know you got issues there," said Lady Zhurong lightly. "It may have a been a while, but I still remember how you got here."

"Hatched I did," Mayghin said finally opening her eyes.

"Pity you weren't a boy," Lady Jīng said.

Keith had a sudden image of himself caught between the Ancient of natural order and a Dragonkin. He did not like the position at all.

"Hmm," the Demon hmmed to himself. Take your pick, death by being treed to death or death by being burned to death. Cake, please.

"A boy wouldn't be moping around here being all cold water," Lady Jīng said. "A boy would be out there conquering the *Universe* for his Mother."

339

"Yeah, yeah, Mum and I've been all through that," Mayghin said mildly. "She's not interested."

Lady Jīng looked at Lady Zhurong, who only shrugged.

"And you are going to go to this film festival?" Lady Zhurong asked before Lady Jīng could carry on.

"Yes, sounds like fun," Mayghin said. "As you mentioned, I've been moping a bit too long. Could use some fun, just like other overly serious types I could mention."

"This will be your own undoing," Lady Jīng said. "I bet you that you end-up buried alive. Chukwu likes that kind-"

Lady Zhurong leaned forward and laid a restraining hand upon Lady Jīng's shoulder.

"What will it matter now?" Lady Zhurong asked, indicating her daughter and the others. "They will all go to the new universe, just like the others before. This is how this it is done."

Lady Jīng gave a sigh and in that instant, Keith thought that she indeed did look older than the universe.

"We should have told them this a long time ago," Lady Jīng agreed.

"A long time ago and too many others as well," Lady Zhurong said. "This time it looks like there will be millions more souls in the great crossing. They will learn. It does not matter how if they understand."

"Or not," Lady Jīng said bitterly.

"Um, pardon me," Keith said.

Three sets of eyes and a keen set of nostrils turned towards Keith, who still sat cross-legged upon his black cushion.

Keith took off his reading glasses and rubbed his eyes before continuing.

"I cannot remember when I met either of you," the Demon said to the two Ancients. "It was that long ago. Lady Zhurong, I remember when your first daughter was born and I remember the thirteen since. I remember when the first Dragonkin was born and how nobody thought before that that it could happen."

Lady Zhurong nodded.

"It surprised me too," she said.

"And Lady Jīng," Keith continued, "I remember many things about you, of which I will not speak, knowing how private you are."

Lady Jīng nodded gravely.

"And in all that time, I've never known either of you to talk crackers," Keith said. "Cryptic, yes, almost always. Evasive, certainly. Stubborn," and here Keith looked directly at Lady Jīng, "without a doubt. But never crackers. So, if you don't mind, will ya kindly knock it the fuck off and just tell me what's what?"

Lady Jīng slowly rose to her feet, turned her back on the party, and began to walk further up the mountain towards Ryuunosuke Castle.

The company sat in respectful silence, until the form of Lady Jīng was lost to sight among the plants that her presence had created, nurtured, and loved. Nobody thought she was actually gone. They just couldn't see her anymore.

"Well, Mom?" Mayghin asked as she poured tea for everyone.

Lady Zhurong extended one long fingernail, call it a claw really, of her right index finger, and scratched just below her right ear.

"So long ago now," Lady Zhurong said allowing her grey eyes to gaze out into spaces well past her immediate company. "So long ago now that I don't really remember everything."

Mayghin and Keith exchanged glances.

"This is, my second universe," Lady Zhurong said.

Keith paused with his tea halfway to his lips, gave it a critical stare, and after a while placed it untested back upon the table.

"Not that I think we've only got one or anything," Keith said, "but how is it that happened?"

"I didn't notice when the universe changed," said Lady Zhurong with a shrug. "Lady Jīng insists that there was a change, but I never noticed. Everything pretty much stayed the same as far as I could see. I don't know."

"Lady Zhurong," Keith said very carefully. "I'm not inclined to disagree with you, but-"

"You think that's impossible?" Lady Zhurong said with such a note of absolute finality that Keith gave in completely.

"Well, in a word, yes," Keith said. "I'm fairly sure that the Creator would have mentioned-"

"Would He have?" Lady Zhurong asked turning her grey eyes upon Keith.

Keith found himself, against all his own notions of right and wrong and his own personal cynicism, inclined to agree.

"When did He mention Dragons to any mortal?"

"John's Revelation, Chapter 12," Keith said promptly.

Lady Zhurong reclined and managed an expression of pure smugness.

"One reference, in what, 4 or 5 thousand years? And even then, not a direct reference either," Lady Zhurong said. "No, I won't make up my mind about what is and what isn't because of what He said. Or more to the point, what some mortal said He said."

Keith was silent for a very long time. He idly watched as Mayghin poured more tea for the company.

He listened with less than half an ear as Qdot told Lady Zhurong about the current doings of the Olympian gods and some sorted double-cross between Qdot's half-sister Doris and the god Poseidon to overthrow Zeus, again. Then there was something from Mayghin about Xavier Xerses Smith having been caught in some sort of temporal-rift where he spent his time in an idyllic mountain camp next to a fresh-water lake stocked with every sort of organic food item that could be wished for. Apparently, it had almost driven him insane. When the Scion finally escaped, all anyone could get him to say was "Steak-burger, fries, and cherry-coke," over and over and over again.

"So how old is this universe?" Keith suddenly demanded.

"Nearly 7 Yōm," Lady Zhurong said, smoothly transitioning her attention back to the Demon. "When the 7th Yōm comes to its end, so will this universe. The life spans of all the universes are 7 Yōm. But not all Yōm are created equal."

"Yeah? And what happens to *this* universe at the end of the 7th Yōm?" asked Keith while glaring at the old lizard.

Lady Zhurong shrugged.

"How should I know?" she asked. "I was moved from the last one to this one without fuss. What do I know of the last one now? Or where is went? I fancy it became a black pearl and it sits enthroned upon the right ring finger of the Creator. But, I doubt it."

"One really large u-store-it garage?" Mayghin asked. "I wonder if we can loot it. What was the tech level there?"

"So, how does this Gatekeeper keep people from going back to the old universe then?" Keith asked cutting off the Scion's interjection.

Lady Zhurong shrugged again.

"Okay," Keith said taking a deep breath. "Let's try this another way then. If Chukwu is leaving-"

"Retiring," Lady Zhurong, corrected. "No one ever leaves, not really. We all get recycled, eventually and endlessly."

"Right, right, reincarnation, right, okay, whatever," Keith said. "If Chukwu is retiring and we're getting the boot out of this pad, then who's to be the next Gatekeeper then?"

"My bet is that it will be Miyako Astor," Lady Zhurong said.

Keith gave the impassive face of the Ancient the studied once over before bursting into laughter.

"You mean," Keith said, gasping for breath, "the old café manager?"

Lady Zhurong nodded.

"I can just imagine what a universe run by a Faerie Prince would be like," Keith said with tones of mirth dripping off his lips.

"Bloody murder," Qdot said.

"Wholesale death and slaughter," Mayghin agreed.

Lady Zhurong leaned her head to one side before saying, "Indifference. Complete and total indifference."

The Scions went silent, while the Demon gazed steadily into the old worms' blind eyes.

"I've always thought the Creator was indifferent to us," Keith finally said.

"I'm sure you have," Lady Zhurong replied. "But once you've actually felt indifference, you will know the difference between detached, and indifferent. When humanity committed suicide, the Creator was hurt. You could feel it everywhere, as if Gravity had caught cold chills. But no, the Faerie would not care, not even a little bit, not even for the creatures, he liked. He would not be sad, or happy, or anything. That universe will remain cold no matter what."

"Oh, I don't know," Keith began. "Old Miyako Astor isn't that bad."

"I have one question before you go," Lady Zhurong said. "Have you, any of you, ever stopped to consider what the effects of several millions of year's incarceration have had on that particular Faerie?"

It was Keith's turn to shrug.

"No," he said, "can't say I ever gave it the slightest thought."

"Perhaps it has taught him patience?" Qdot asked.

"Fat chance," Keith said. "Miyako Astor was once the most powerful Faerie in entire everything. I think it's only served to piss him off even more."

"The only thing that I am certain about in this world, or in any other world," said Lady Zhurong, "is that the Creator is, indeed, in-action, and in-jest, one damned hard Guy to read."

And if there was, anything that the assembled company could agree on, that was it. Whatever game the Creator was up to, it was His and His game alone, and he never told anyone the rules. Never.

"Tell ya what old devil that's not a devil, but a pretty good sport," Lady Zhurong said. "I'll gift my Scion with enough of my power for her to make your dead world grow. You won't get better than that."

Keith smiled, rose to his knees, and then kowtowed to the Ancient Dragon called Lady Zhurong.

Chapter 16: Somewhere on Tafari

On the planet Tafari, in the Babirye Binary system, orbiting the Babirye Beta star.

Oh that my words were now written! Oh that they were printed in a book! --Job 19:23, K.J.V.

And it came to pass that the next universe was created, and for a while, the gate between them stood wide open.

Chukwu sat in the middle of the first oasis that the planet Tafari had seen in millions and millions and millions of years, somewhere in Tafari's Great Grey Ashen Dune Sea. The Gatekeeper was thinking about *infinity*. Infinity and humanity's depressing tendency toward self-harm.

Chukwu had brought the oasis here from another planet in a nearby solar system, and in the middle of the oasis, stood the Ishtar Gate, made of blue marble tiles, decorated with gold dragons, lions, and other predator animals. Chukwu had decided that in the next universe, the Ishtar Gates and the new Node Pathways would operate in a similar manner, but only on the Infinity Plane itself, and not throughout the stars. Natural wormholes would do, if humanity ever got to the stars. Chukwu intended to see that they didn't

Chukwu had always been disappointed that humanity had never found out how to work the Ishtar Gate. When Terra was young, he had put the Ishtar Gate right in the middle of Terra's main land mass. But the Gate had been badly damaged in one of Stan's more energetic attempts to destroy humanity and Chukwu had never fixed it. In fact, it had taken nearly all of humanity's existence for Chukwu to figure out that the Gate was even broken. Chukwu had always wondered how humanity would have reacted to figuring out how to use the Ishtar Gate that would let them

346

travel through the dimensions. Now though, Chukwu's thinking was going in entirely different directions as he contemplated his last task, the construction of the next universe.

It would be an Infinity Plane; not just a planispheric shaped world, but also an infinitely extended world, a flat world expanding forever beyond the horizons. A world that would never have a beginning, never an ending, and no edges ever anywhere.

The Infinity Plane would be an entire universe in that the flat "world" would expand beyond the horizons of infinity. And upon that same flat world, there would be planetary-sized half spheres of impenetrable mists to encapsulate humanity from its planetary neighbours. Sort of like putting the entire Human species inside the bubbles of bubble wrap.

Yes, Chukwu mused, that would do for protectionism. A bit extreme perhaps, but pragmatically functional. An infinity of Adams and Eves and if any of their descendants saw fit to exterminate life in their half sphere, it wouldn't impact the other half spheres at all. The Creator liked things that ran in parallel after all.

Chukwu had been to the end of this universe once and it was an odd place, constantly moving just out of reach. If you stood still, the boundary of the universe stood still as well. But if you moved closer to the boundary, then the boundary moved further away from you. Even so, that boundary was several trillions of light years outside the orbit of the furthest star that Chukwu knew anything about. There had been, 777-sextillion stars, more or less in this universe.

The actual accurate number of stars is 777,000,000,000,101,313,242,027 Main Sequence Stars, which are the stars that are visible on the Hertzsprung-Russell Diagram. These cover the visible blue to red light spectrums and the sequences O, B, A, F, G, K and M. These are also the stars that produce the energy that comes from nuclear fusion by converting Hydrogen to Helium. While most stars are

Main Sequence Stars, not all of the stars in the Heavens are. Which is why, among other reasons, the Metatron won't vouch that the number of stars in this universe is the same as the number of souls that went through the universe. That and he's just one damned stubborn Angel. The other reason is that not everything that walked and talked had a soul, nor did everything that had a soul walk or talk.

How many other stars there were, nobody, not even the Metatron knew, and only a very small handful of extinct astrophysicists even cared enough to try to count them. Take the debate over whether or not Red Dwarf stars were actually stars. They are small, dim stars with relatively cool surface temperatures compared to their brighter neighbours, but they were at the heart of the now entirely irrelevant debate about what a "star" was.

Bugger it, Chukwu thought. Pluto is still a damn planet if you ask me. Silly Humans, changing the definition of terms just because they are in a discovery slump and have nothing better to write in their dissertation papers.

And for Chukwu's practical purposes, the ever-moving boundary of his universe counted as infinity, even if it wasn't really.

So what would an actual infinity look like? Chukwu wondered.

Chukwu began to whistle "This Little Light of Mine," while he thought about stars and bright starlight burning all around the Infinity Plane.

Take an object, say a sphere as an example, and make the center hollow, Chukwu thought. Now blow that hollow sphere up by an infinite proportion; and in order to make it an actual infinity, make it continually expanding. Not continually expanding like humanity had thought their universe was, that was just a trick of the light. But make the next universe actually expanding, adding new surface area to both the inside and the outside of the ever-expanding sphere.

The Jenolan people had once tried to build a Dyson Sphere. It hadn't worked, as Freeman had predicted it wouldn't. Eventually the Jenolans abandoned the relic without even managing to build 10% of it. But they hadn't been the Gatekeeper.

Chukwu conceded that Mick and Keith were right, to an extent. The logic of this universe's set of physical principles does not allow an Infinity Plane universe to exist. But Chukwu knew that was is only a minor inconvenience, not really a problem.

Now, Chukwu thought, take, and place your "world," on the inside surface of this ever-expanding universe. The natural sphere shape will conform to the natural curvature of the space-time-thing, whatever it was called.

Chukwu had never understood why it was important that this or the last universe conform to that natural law. He'd given up caring right around the time that he had figured out just how many maths there were in physics. Chukwu was not omniscient, only omnipotent within the confines of this universe, and he liked it that way. People were hard enough to deal with without knowing what they really thought about anything, and even then, Chukwu deeply suspected people weren't all that different, not really. Everywhere boys married girls because babies were on the way. Everywhere people pretended to be what they weren't and people denounced war, though they never really did much to stop the next one from happening.

But the natural curvature of the space-time-whatever it was called was important, and Chukwu accepted the time-space law, in the same way the he accepted gravity.

Gravity was there and Chukwu ignored it.

Chukwu ignored lots of things like Time: space, gravity, and health impacts of eating a quart of Peace, Love, and Chocolate every day. There had to be major perks to being omnipotent after all.

Chukwu turned to the page of *Continuous Creation*, by Kin Arad that the Angel Mick had torn, and placed the torn piece in its correct place. With a deep hum, Chukwu ran his right index finger over the torn edges of the paper, healing the tear through the passage that the Demon Keith had mocked.

Then, Chukwu read the passage again:

On a world, there must be mysterious mountains. Let there be bottomless lakes peopled with antique monsters. Let there be strange footprints in high snowfields, green ruins in endless jungles, bells beneath the sea, echo valleys and cities of gold. This is the yeast in the planetary crust, without which the imagination of men will not rise.

What an interesting instruction, Chukwu reflected, to intentionally put things in front of people that would cause them to imagine false things, false concepts, a completely false understanding of history and reality.

Then again, what was false?

The mortals believed, well, many of them believed, that the Creator personally came down and sparked each one of them into life. In a causality sort of way, that was true, but after the first two people, the Creator didn't seem to bother Himself much with how people begot more people. Some people believed that the Creator was terribly interested in their bedroom doings, but that was only vanity and ego on the part of people. And no worse than the idea that the Creator needed 72 hours to create the Terra, when in reality, it was already there just as soon as Mr. C. wanted it to be there, from the very moment that He thought of it. About 168 zeptoseconds usually did it in the Creator Aspect business, and Chukwu figured the Big Guy was way faster. So fast in-fact, Time simply reorganized herself whenever it suited Him and not the other way around.

168 zeptoseconds to create an infinity of parallel dimensions and everything therein. It was simply the neatest party trick Chukwu had ever seen. It still amazed him after all these years. Chukwu was rather proud of the Helix "Eye of God" Nebula that was still parked over in the Aquarius constellation. And he was still disappointed that nobody had ever worked out that the nebula looked exactly the same no matter what position in space you looked at it from.

But then again, Chukwu wasn't even sure it took even one zeptosecond for the Creator to do anything. The Metatron had once told Chukwu that the Big Guy actually operated an infinity of parallel dimensions in tandem.

"Everything that can be, will be, eventually," the Metatron had said.

Chukwu had always thought that Roger Waters had said it better; "Got thirteen channels of shit on the TV to choose from."

That was a point that Chukwu found remarkable. People could and did expect that the Creator could and did create matter, physics, time, and Himself out of thin air, but somehow still needed, or wanted, to use 168 hours to create a planet. Chukwu didn't think the Creator could have moved that slow even if he wanted to.

"Fucking metaphysics," Chukwu muttered. "Useless stuff."

So, what to put here, on Tafari, which would be the bedrock of the new infinite universe? Chukwu asked himself.

On the Tafari Infinity Plane, as Chukwu now privately called the ever changing landscape of Tafari, the lakes would be bottomless, and in their own way, so would the soil of the new world, and the sky endless. An infinity of sky going upwards forever, with billions and billions of stars above it, or more precisely 777-sextillion stars above.

351

One plane of planetary existence, stretching in all directions, yet conforming to the curvature of space, so that in the end, it would be the inside side of a cosmically large sphere. Of course, that would only matter in a conceptual way. No mortal creature would ever be able to cover the distance of space in a thousand lifetimes. And the Immortals would never be bothered about it at all.

Immortals?

Would Chukwu allow Immortals into the new universe? Did he have a choice? Chukwu doubted it. Both Immortals and immortal creatures crept in at the edges. Chukwu had never created any of them, but they turned up anyhow.

It was one thing to be in- charge of a universe, it was quite another to actually control anything in it. That was a power that Chukwu privately thought that the Creator either did not have, or had permanently turned off because it was boring and tedious to control everything. That was a point mortals usually missed, the distinction between power and control. Yes, the Creator had the power; he just didn't bother to control everything just because he could.

Chukwu had once tried to explain this thought to the Demon James. "It's like watching the same episode of *I Love Lucy* over and over and over again; millions and millions of times."

"No kidding," the Demon James said. "That used to happen to me all the time. Like every time I checked into a hotel after dark, I'd turn on the TV and there'd be Lucy and Ethel stuffing candy in their mouths, and bras, and whatever. Daytime TV was worse. It'd always be Oprah interviewing an author - and it was never me! I mean seriously, this one time she interviewed a guy that was like supposed to be a history writer, right, and he like made it all up. God bless it all, he was almost as bad as a freaken Republican presidential candidate."

"Yes, right," Chukwu had said sidestepping the Demon's incessant political ranting. "So imagine watching nothing but that one show of *I Love Lucy* over and over and over again for Eternity-"

"Do I get to see her tits?" the Demon James interrupted.

"What? Whose tits?"

"Lucy, man. Who would ever want to see Ethel's tits? Makes me limp just thinking about it."

"No, of course not. Now, just listen-"

"Damn. I read this book once where the TV asked this Scion if he wanted to see Lucy's tits, and..."

And not for the last time, Chukwu had wondered why he ever bothered talking to the Demon James. The Demon really did live on planet non sequitur, even if he did always insist it was a cultural reference of modern mythic proportions. What a weirdo that Demon was.

For a brief second, Chukwu considered bring the Demon James in on the development of the Infinity Plane universe. The Demon certainly liked going on about how the Creator could have "totally done it better if..."

And then Chukwu promptly rejected it on grounds of intellectual honesty. This was supposed to be Chukwu's work, as ordained by the Creator. He couldn't outsource this one. He'd have to see it through, to the end. Alone.

Then again, the Creator had put the Demon James in this universe and collaboration was not expressly forbidden.

No, Chukwu decided, down that road lay insanity.

This was Chukwu's very own work and would remain so, more or less.

The less is due to the fact that very few people ever get to create words these days, and even fewer of those words created words actually stick in a newly created language. So the words, the language we use shapes how we think, how we talk, and how we create conceptualizations like universes, worlds, and people. Therefore, the argument goes that you cannot be truly wholly independently creative because you use the word creations of another individual to express your own creation. And besides there was *Continuous Creation* and the Gatekeeper really liked that bit about bottomless lakes and cities of gold.

More simply put, any and all creations of any type are derivative of another form of creation. Just remember that whenever someone says, "Oh, that's just a knock off of *The Da Vinci Code*."

Take for example the word Zero. People had to first figure out that they had things, say pieces of dead roasted giant lizard leg, and that if you had say three pieces when you went to bed, and had one piece when you woke up in the morning, odds were that some silly bugger had nicked your other pieces of lizard leg whilst you were sleeping. That horrible feeling of hunger, not to mention the exhilarating feeling of wanting to bash that silly bugger's head it with your fists, lead to inspiration. Which would eventually lead to a complicated system of property rights, taxation, and lawyers. But you just try explaining lawyering to somebody that's never heard of a codified legal code when all he wants to do is go smash the face in of the silly bugger that was too dumb to wipe giant lizard leg grease off his face. And after you've found that fruitless, remember that you were supposed to explain the concept of Zero to him, not two missing pieces of lizard leg. So, all of that proves that in the end, we use the words and concepts of the people around us in this sort of communal way.

Unless it's got copyright, and then we call the theft parody, and move on quickly, just in case Disney actually got away with copyrighting the whole of Nordic mythology, Scions, and Christianity.

What, Chukwu wondered, had really fascinated him over the seemingly eternal centuries of mankind?

Their imagination, certainly, and not the least, the arrogance of confidence in technology. All technology failed and usually sooner rather than later, in Chukwu's experience. Most of nature failed too, but the difference was, nature didn't require people to make it all over again, nature only required time.

Chukwu picked up one of the books that Hat had given him after their long conversation and studied its cover critically. *Dimensions & Dæmons*, by E. G. Gygax, with contributions from D. Arneson, D. Kaye, B. Speer, S. Duncan, B. Blume, T. Kask, J. E. Holmes, R. A. Salvatore, M. Weis, T. Hickman, and M. Williams.

Flipping through the pages, Chukwu considered that some of the storylines were certainly interesting. But the art, the art was breathtaking, and by such a multiplicity of artists, that they had several dozen pages of credits at the end of the book. Such artistic talent had always amazed Chukwu, who could create stars and oceans and chocolate truffles by merely thinking about them, but who could not draw even the simplest landscape with either a focal point or a vanishing horizon. The fact that visual artists never got center dust-cover stage credits on books, even though it was usually the art that caught the passive attention of most customers just boggled Chukwu's mind.

Chukwu had spent many pleasant afternoons in old world Terra bookstores and museums just looking at art. He was particular of course, favouring realism but not photorealism, and the fantasy-sci-fi-fantastic-whatever-you-call-it styles of drawings and paintings over junk like Modernism, and blow Performance Art with a rail-gun. That was just people acting stupid and then only if you were lucky.

Fictional stories though, even actual history, came, and went often not even making an impression on Chukwu's conscious mind. But the pictures, the drawings, the art, all those things that he could create,

355

but not make with his own hands, stayed in his mind forever.

And this book, *Dimensions & Dæmons*, by all those people, compiled thousands upon thousands of his favourite works of art from all time.

Yes, yes, yes, Chukwu thought. I'll take all of them, except the Gremlins.

For reasons that historians of the Infinity Plane were never in the future able to establish satisfactorily, Chukwu hated Gremlins. It was not that Gremlins had ever existed in this universe, or the last, or even in the next one. At least, not to anyone's knowledge on either Terra, Tafari, the Infinity Plane, or wherever it was that the Great Poseidon Adventure Ship came from. But it was the concept of Gremlins that Chukwu hated. The Angel Mick once postulated that Chukwu's Gremlin hatred was due to trauma that Chukwu received during World War I, but it is generally accepted that Mick was talking out of his asshole when he said it. Like both politicians and Ministers, Mick felt he had to have an answer for everything.

So, that's settled, Chukwu thought to himself. Take everything, real, mythological, all of it. Ladi dadi everybody and everything, toss it all in.

But, how to protect humanity from itself in this next universe?

Chukwu didn't think Stan would be a major problem, or at least, no more so than any other Demon would be once the Chukwu v. Stan grudge match was finished.

Chukwu had seen one 99.99% successful mass-extinction event and loads of near misses in his time. Terra had been very inhospitable then for a very long time after the asteroid wiped out the dinosaurs. Chukwu was never sure just how long, but it was a long time, much longer then he thought was strictly necessary. But the planet survived and so did his little band of humans, even if not everything on the planet survived. Chukwu had to personally intervene to keep his small little pocket of humanity alive. And still, Chukwu wondered if he had done the right thing, keeping them alive. After that, Chukwu had paid a great deal more attention to the goings on in the Sol solar system, and knocked the occasional asteroid off its collision course with Terra.

It always irritated the piss out of Stan whenever Chukwu intervened like that.

At another point in history, Chukwu remembered, Terra had been scorched to a crisp by solar flares, reducing the planet to a barren waste dune, and again, Chukwu had had to personally see to it that humanity survived. And yet, water survived the solar flares that wiped out almost everything else on the planet's surface, and where there is water, there will eventually be life. Given a sufficiently lengthy stretch of time.

There had been other potential mass-extinction events, not all of which came close to their climax, but only diverted by a hair's breadth. There had been the genetically engineered super-Humans that escaped from Botany Bay and almost managed to conquer the world. There had been the Spacer Rebellion, in which the space colonies had dispatched war ships to Terra, armed with nuclear weapons. There had been the dirty bomb that would have exploded in Jerusalem, had not Chukwu jinxed the AΩ Divine Bomb's trigger switch. Everything except the truth was made out of the inscription on the bomb's casing that read; "And I will give power unto my two witnesses, and they shall prophesy a thousand two hundred and threescore days, clothed in sackcloth."

Chukwu had outlawed time travel right from the start for mortals, so that was no worry; not even Stan could trump that universal law. The immortal crowd never bothered much, and certainly never did anything that would lead to the destruction of the fabric of the space-time thing-a-ma-gigger.

Maths again, Chukwu thought and sighed. Bloody well hate maths. Science wouldn't be so bad without that bloody maths.

Then there had been the black hole that Stan had opened up in the Beta Centauri system and the Gamma-ray burst that Chukwu had had to turn off. Chukwu had always thought that Stan had gone way beyond in his efforts to get the YFZ Death Cult to build the Maunder Sporier Device to reverse Terra's magnetic field. Stan had gotten rather desperate towards the end, even going so far as to organizing robot unionization, robot strikes, robot uprisings, and even a robot civil war. Fundamental Laws of Robotics; what a joke that had turned out to be.

But in the end though, there was nothing that Chukwu could do about a Human on Human nuclear war. There were just too many of the buggers to keep track of.

The nuclear war at Armagedōn was attended by the Celestial armies of both Heaven and Hell, and became a mass-extinction event for the Human species, even those members not on Terra.

Stan just disappeared after it happened, and Chukwu had always believed that it was to ensure that the war spread into the galactic colonies, but he could never prove it. Chukwu also couldn't figure out how Stan did it either.

Even when Dictyoptera was blown apart, life, of a sort continued on, but not so with humanity. Unlike the cockroaches that spread into the universe riding on asteroids, humanity took up sides, then took up arms, and then took up war all over the universe. The result of which was that in dozens of world's nuclear winter still reigned, even now, millions of years after the wars all had ended.

Chukwu had always wondered if the Creator wasn't trying to make one of His extremely unsubtle points by letting the Human species kill itself. Stan failed to kill them and Chukwu failed to protect them.

Stan did not win and neither did Chukwu. Nobody won and everyone lost.

You didn't even need a planet for life, strictly speaking. Mind you, Chukwu had never taken to space flight, nor to the Node Pathways, or to Space Folding, or to any of the other ingenious ways that humanity or the gods had discovered for moving themselves from one place to another. So Chukwu had never once visited any of the space colonies. He regretted that now.

Chukwu often wondered these days if that had not been a tactical mistake in his governance of this universe. It had eventually and substantially limited his understanding of the Human experience.

Trains though, Chukwu liked trains. In the beginning, Chukwu had found trains to be the perfect answer to speed and comfort and safety, especially after they got their balance issues worked out. The later versions of speed-demon trains that went hundreds of kilometres in an hour were not to Chukwu's taste. The time it took Chukwu to travel wasn't really an issue. But pain, Chukwu could feel pain all right. And while he was an Immortal, that didn't mean he wouldn't feel like Hell's crapper while he put himself back together again.

And so Chukwu sat for a very long time, brooding on how to protect the next rerun of mortality from itself. How to populate the Infinity Plane with millions, billions, and trillions of people from the onset, and yet make sure that nuclear war did not ever destroy all of them again.

Chukwu sat drumming his fingers on the cover of *Continuous Creation*, by Kin Arad, now humming *Deep and Wide*, as the planet Tafari flattened itself, and began expanding in all directions transforming itself into a growing plane of infinitely expanding boundary.

Chapter 17: Red Door

From Tafari to Terra and back again.

At that time Merodachbaladan, the son of Baladan, King of Babylon, sent letters and a present to Hezekiah: for he had heard that he had been sick, and was recovered. And Hezekiah was glad of them, and showed them the house of his precious things, the silver, and the gold, and the spices, and the precious ointment, and all the house of his armour, and all that was found in his treasures: there was nothing in his house, nor in all his dominion, that Hezekiah showed them not. --Isaiah 39:1-2, K.J.V.

And so it came to pass that the Angel heard about the Gatekeeper from an amateur art curator.

The Angel landed in the center of the Subterranean Chamber of the Pyramid of Khufu, some 30 meters below the Giza Plateau upon which the original pyramid was built, or had been built. Mick wondered for a brief moment how much of the surrounding plateau the Demon Keith had brought along with this Pyramid of Khufu.

It didn't really matter.

This Subterranean Chamber, like the original, was unfinished. And it was a good thing that the Angel did not need to breathe, as even back on Terra, the rooms had been oxygen- starved. Here on Tafari it was only worse. Above lay some two million stone blocks, weighting some 3.5 tons each. The feeling of being in the room was, no way around it, heavy.

And dark. It was very dark.

There is a difference between the dark that we mortals, or even the immortal crowd, see at night, say when you sleep, and true darkness. Most people do not sleep in a crypt, covered over by over six million

360

tons of rock. So what they are really doing is just shielding their eyes from the lazy reflected light of the night. In true darkness, the pupils of the eye can grow to be as large as newly minted silver Liberty Coins, and it won't matter one wit. You will not see anything.

Mick lay still, listening to the sound of dust falling on him. Occasionally, a small rock would fall, making a dull thudding sound.

As soon as the Angel was certain the new vertical tunnel shaft was finished dusting him, he sat up, stood up, and sheathed the twin Holy Swords Zulfiqar and Al-Dhulfiqar.

Keith then dusted and straightened his trench coat, and withdrew his hPhone. He lazily waved his hand over the screen to activate the torch app. The Angel didn't really need it. But millions of years of pretending to be Human was a hard habit to break.

We are all, mortal or immortal, only a collection of our habits. This is why Controller Mustapha Mond worked so hard to instil the habit of emotional deafness and chemical dependence upon his people; and why priests, monks, nuns, and sensible atheists all require of themselves to practice daily acts of charity. Love and hate are habit forming. They are just like duty and responsibility in that habit-forming way.

The screen of the hand-held phone-computer-universal-GPS device instantly lit up with a bright light in equal portions of orange and white. The image of a burning wooden torch flickered on the screen.

As in other parts of the pyramid, Mick noticed that this room had been returned to its nearly original state. There were no graffiti marks upon these walls. The electrical cables laid down in the early 20th century were gone, as were the stairs leading that had been laid down over the smooth access tunnel that was the normal route out of the Subterranean Chamber back to the surface.

Mick, like most that had studied this portion of the Pyramid of Khufu, had never understood what the room was for, or why it was never completed. It had been originally intended to connect to the labyrinthine dungeon that the Demon James and his legions of Dæmons had spent hundreds of years building beneath necropolis on the Mokattam Hills.

Regardless, it was now a universal gateway, and over the centuries, the room had become a minor gate for the players in the Immortal Court. But the mortals that had originally built it had just left the room half-finished. The walls that were cut into the bedrock stone were not even smooth.

Mick turned his attention from contemplating why the inner walls of the Subterranean Chamber were, like the rest of the pyramid, bare, except those damned hieroglyphics murals in the Grand Gallery, and looked at the dead end corridor that lead to nowhere in the mortal world.

So the Angel was understandably surprised to see that there was now a large round blood red door at the end of the corridor with the word 𝕳𝖔𝖗𝖉𝖊 written in large black block letters across its middle.

Mick walked over to the door, which was where he had expected to find the secret passageway into the City of the Dead, where the Immortal Celestial Court resided in a vast underground complex dug into the living rock beneath the Pyramid of Khufu.

Mick approached the blood red door carefully.

Above the door, written in the common language of Dragons, was the inscription:

City of the Dead, New Necropolis, Terra

That was just how things should have been, except that there was now this red door standing in front of where the secret passageway should have been, and inscribed in Angelic Ruins upon the door Mick read:

Hell Hath No Fury Like Grubby Fingers Here

And Wipe Your Feet Before Entering

Now who, Mick wondered, would put a Portal Gate in front of the City of the Dead door? I haven't seen one of these Portal Gates in ages.

Mick knocked on the door, waited for about a minute, then opened the door, and stepped through. The Angel didn't wipe his feet.

And there it was, the feeling that one had left one's lunch several billions and billions of light years behind. And the Angel, like all immortals, knew instantly that he was back on Terra.

Mick steadied himself against the smooth smoke-grey marble wall that was on this side of the red door. The feeling of solid coolness flowed into Mick's fingers as his natural body heat flowed into the wall, to be dispersed throughout the stone.

As Mick slowly regained his balance, he looked around the large room.

Whatever Mick might have thought he would see, he had not expected rows and rows of wooden shelving, holding all manner of boxes, tubes, and barrels. The room reminded Mick instantly of two things.

The first was the liberation of Schloss Neuschwanstein Castle in Hohenschwangau, Bavaria, from the Nazis in 1944. More than 40 photo albums, all of which the Angel had seen, were captured. The photos documented the use of the romantic castle as a shipping depot for Nazi plunder from France as organized by the Einsatzstab Reichsleiter Rosenberg task force.

The second image that came to the Angel Mick was the closing scene of *The Raiders of the Lost Ark*, in which an unknown workman is seen boxing up the lost Ark of the Covenant, only to be hidden away in an unknown warehouse at an undisclosed location. Setting aside the fact that the whole movie was just daft, Mick had rather liked the idea of the Ghosts of ancient Hebrews destroying Nazi party officials and their soldiers. Although, Mick had always wondered what happened to the German Navy men, or the rest of the German Navy on the island. But that's movies for ya, plot holes that you swim submarines through.

The real truth was that the lost Ark of the Testimony, also called תִּירְבַּה אָרוֹן, was not lost at all. Mick knew precisely where he had left it.

The Angel Mictlantecuhtli had safely tucked away the holy relic in a safe out of the way site in what would one day become the French commune of Rennes-le-Château, in the Aude department of Languedoc. This occurred a few years after the Babylonians raised Jerusalem, grinding the Temple of Solomon into a fine powered dust. The stories that the Ark had been carried off by the Babylonians were true enough. But what was not recorded was that the Ark of the Creator was liberated in the dead of night by two Canaanites, one Roman, a Greek, three Philistines, and one Angel that just couldn't believe that nobody had invented urban night camo yet.

The tricky part had not been getting into the Babylonian royal horde, a simple, but large bribe took care of that. Two of the royal guards had even helped load the newly boxed up Ark into the wagon while two more held the gate open. Nor was the difficult part escaping from Babylon, the capital of the Babylonian Empire. No, the hard part was finding a ship's captain that would sail from Lagash, around the peninsula and into the Red Sea, and onto Suez, without asking any questions as to why Canaanites, Romans, Philistines, and an Aryan poster child were traveling together. Nobody ever cared what Greeks did.

Centuries later, Mick became both patron and irritating friend to the authors Jules Verne and Maurice Leblanc. With the aid and abetment of the two storytellers, the Angel carefully constructed rumours about all manner of things, including the Ark. Later still, the Angel paid Patrick Byrne, and many of his Freemason brothers, a large sum of money to spread the rumour that the Ark had decamped to the United States just prior to the outbreak of World War I. For a very short time, the rumours inspired a renewed search for the Ark, which the Angel Mick desperately wanted to succeed. Mick figured nothing could ignite a hotter religious fever than the discovery of the best old-time religious artefact ever made. But despite whatever Mick did, nothing ever worked. The searchers were dismissed as either cranks or zealots, which is a kinder way of saying crank.

Mick had even gone so far as to put the original Ark of the Covenant on a float and displayed it to the entire world in 1988 in Hanover during the Schützenfest Marksmen's Festival. People had complained that the gold, honest 18-karat gold looked fake. Had the Metatron not inexplicably shown up and taken the Angel Mick drinking, the anger the Angel would have unleashed on Hanover would have resembled Sodom and Gomorrah the last time that it was visited by Angels and their Harps of Destruction.

With the memory throwing up these and other images, Mick stepped into the next room, passing through an open passage between the storeroom and an even larger room beyond.

To say that the next room was large would miss a perfect opportunity to use the word *brobdingnagian*. The ceiling was well out of sight, and Mick felt air currents that resembled wind. Several stone columns rose ceiling-ward, presumably there was a ceiling somewhere up there.

Paintings covered every surface of the walls, and stood here and there, everywhere really, on easels.

"This has to be the most impressive collection I've seen outside of the St. Petersburg Hermitage Museum," Mick said to no one in particular.

The pseudo-Demon nay Watcher called Shax, who had been waiting for the Angel, looked up from his original 1669 monograph copy of *Bibliotheca*

Abscondita, by Sir Thomas Browne and said, "I don't know, Angel-hair. I think I've secured all of that collection. But what would I know?"

Mick spun around so quickly that he did a full one and half rotations and then slammed himself into the stone pillar that had been supporting the painting he was looking at. The pillar didn't care. The painting though, did care and would never be the same again.

As Mick gazed up, he realized that he was looking at the celling, and a great deal of the ceiling architecture of the Sistine Chapel. No, he decided, it was all there.

"Well, ain't you a bit jumpy," Shax observed as the Angel pulled himself back upright. "Come on over here and have a drink. I got Double Cross," added what appeared to be an overweight, balding man of no particular quality, dressed in a grey suit silk shirt. But the Angel saw what was really there.

"Of course I'm being double-crossed!" the Angel exclaimed. "I know it, I knew it, I knew it."

"Calm down Angelic pants, or you'll get your panties in a wad," Shax said while he poured two drinks. "Nobody's been double crossed. I'm just kickin' it here until the next universe arrives. And Double Cross is a whiskey-rum cocktail with two crosses in."

"This is what I get for working with a dammed Demon," Mick went on without heed to Shax's words. "Which one of you twerps is Judas this time?"

The accusation was technically inaccurate. As has already been mentioned, there was a general amnesty issued a few thousand years prior to the commencement of this story, so nobody is "damned" any more, not even national leaders that started wars for personal profit or for petty reasons like family pride.

But like Communists turned Capitalists and Capitalists turned Teabaggers, many of the Angels and Demons found it hard to give up the old ways of hating one another. This goes a long way to explain why one should never trust anyone over of the age of 30, particularly if that person is in a position to start a war that they themselves will never have to lead in battle. And especially if those same hypocritical bastards haven't been in the cross-haired sights of an enemy themselves.

"Oh tisk-tisk," Shax said, "Judas Iscariot was a Saint, don't ya know? He took his marching orders straight from the Son and that is that. Son's own fault really, tossing that pisser at the bankers in the Temple. Wealthy people know perfectly well that they're better than the poor. Stands to reason."

Mick looked at Shax's stupid grin and fell for it.

"Judas had no such instructions from the Son, end of conversation," Mick said.

Shax put down a tumble of whiskey and rum in front of the Angel, which the Angel refused.

"No, not really," Shax said mildly and picked-up a glass and started polishing it to a gleam with a bar towel. "Unlike you zealots, we pardoned, ever-redeemed Angels carry on reading, and thinking, and all sorts of devilishly liberal things like that. Tell me, have you even bothered to read the *Coptic Codex* that Judas' grandson stashed away in Beni Masah?"

"Where are we?" Mick asked changing the subject.

"Couple of hundred meters below Machu Picchu," Shax said. "The view used to be stunning. Pretty crap now with all the radiation and whatnot. Not a single tree for hundreds of kilometres."

"Nice place," Mick said with a faint effort to be polite.

"No, not bad," Shax admitted, forgoing the customary three times denial. "I've had digs here since about 5000 BC or so. After the end game at Armagedōn, I just didn't see the point in moving. So I put a Gate on the front door, and go where I want whenever I'm in the mood."

"Wasn't that when King Titicaca ruled?" Mick asked.

"Yes, when Titicaca first carved into the stone of the Machu Picchu summit," Shax said. "It was the first known case of mountain top removal. Took them forever to whack that thing down and flatten it out enough to put a city on top of it. The Machu Picchu that people remembered was built after I moved in under the village, back when people still remembered who Viracocha really was."

Mick raised his glass.

Shax did the same.

"Empty chairs at empty tables," they said together, drained their glasses, and slapped the tumblers on the bar top.

"What's really bugging you Mr. Michael Mouse?" Shax asked.

"Oh, I don't know," the Angel said. "Culture shock, PTSD, readjustment issues. Seven Rings of Hell, I don't know. I've never taken to peace very well I guess."

Shax refilled their glasses.

Mick scowled, but accepted the drink of amber whiskey that Shax handed over to him. The glass really did gleam in the oddly refracted light.

"I thought something was up," Shax, continued in the low modulated voice of the professional bartender. It was that same sort of voice pitch that might just as well served as sonar pitched to calculate how much coin the customer was carrying. "You are obviously still carrying on your hate, even of long dead mortals. I mean really, how long you going to hold onto that shit?"

"I've let go of all of that," Mick said.

"All?" Shax asked.

"I have nothing to say about the Euangelion Ioudas or his evil revelation book," Mick said.

It is a sad but true fact about the Angel that he just couldn't resist showing off his Latin, which truth be told, he always pronounced poorly, even when it was still a spoken language. But the point does bear a pause for consideration.

Euangelion Ioudas very roughly translates to 'Gospel of Judas from the village of Kerioth.' Okay, well done, most say. What's so interesting about that, eh? Well, the interesting point is that Judas Iscariot was the only Judaean disciple. It's pretty much akin to saying "Oh, that's the pulpier James from the West Bank" or "That's just the spick Jesus from Allen, South Dakota." Judas was the only poor Disciple among the 12, and was consequently as well loved, warmly received, and honoured as all poor people have through the entire course of mortal existence. Indeed, when immortal scholars consider the recorded actions of Judas Iscariot, their main question is why Judas didn't arrange to have the 11 remaining Disciples crucified while he and the Son made a run for the border.

"Well you would know," continued Shax in the same mild, almost bored tone, "had you bothered to read the *Coptic Codex* from Beni Masah, called the "Gospel of Judas" you would have seen that Judas was acting on the Son's orders the whole time. That's why they let him in to Heaven don't ya know?"

"They let everyone into Heaven come the end."

"True. But Judas deserved it and he got in without a lover in Newark, New Jersey. Shame you holy-panties couldn't see that."

"Yeah, like I'm gonna take theology lessons from a washed out Demon," Mick said. "Besides, I was there, I saw what happened."

"So was I," Shax said calmly pouring a third set of drinks. "Or, don't you remember that I had a better view than you did?"

Mick remembered.

It had begun that Friday, on the 16th of April 34 Anno Domini.

It had been a trying several months for the Angelic Armies as the Metatron had delivered his compulsory order of non-interference. He hadn't even said when the order would be lifted, much less why.

Well, there had been a *why*; Mick just hadn't liked it very much.

"This is nonsense," Mick had complained from the head of the crowd.

Several other Angels had muttered their agreement. No one else actually voiced what might have been called opposition to the Metatron's orders, not really dissent, per se. But they had, in a general low key sort of grumbling way, let everyone else know that the Soldiers of Heaven were quite ready to kick the unholy shit of our the Legions of Darkness if they were given half a chance.

The Metatron gazed on the assembled Angels in amused silence.

"We've been fighting for forever with both hands tied behind our backs," Mick complained on. "When in the name of holy righteousness are we going to be the white light that kills all of them?"

"Demons or humans?" the Metatron asked mildly.

"God knows his own - fuck the rest of 'em," Mick said.

A chorus of 'Yeahs' and 'Right on brother,' and 'Amen' and 'About time too' greeted Mick's declaration.

"I mean seriously Met, we're losing the war out there and this is what we've been preparing for all this time, the grand match," Mick soldiered on. "And, have you seen the sculptures these damned Greeks are making? Some of them are large enough for a woman to actually get on and-"

"Silence," the Metatron said. It wasn't said loudly. It was just said extremely firmly.

The crowd went silent.

Mick's jaw continued on for a while without sound before the Angel realized the pointlessness of it and stopped.

"This is the time of change," the Metatron said. "Big change and no one is going to be able to say that we did anything to influence things one way or another. The humans are going to get to sort this all out on their own."

Are the damned Demons going to be silenced too? Mick signed in ASL to the Metatron.

The Metatron glared at Mick and snapped his fingers.

Mick's body went rigid, causing the lesser Angel to fall to the ground in a catatonic state that would have done a master mime artist proud.

"Noooo," the Metatron sneered at the paralysed Angel, "they are not. They do not follow orders, that's a main definition of a Fall-en-ang-el. Damn it, I really don't like repeating myself."

The assembled host took several collective and synchronized steps back from the Metatron and their fallen Comrade Angel.

"I have spoken," the Metatron said. "To defy me, is to defy *Him*."

And with one last glare at Mick, the Metatron stalked off down the road towards Golgotha near Jerusalem.

The crowd dispersed in twos and threes except for Mick, who lay where he fell until sundown.

About a minute after the last ray of the sun set, the Angel's body relaxed, and slumped to the ground.

Mick groaned, rolled over onto his side, and sat up.

371

The Angel was just beginning to wonder what to do, when he saw the two figures in grey cloaks, leading an ass between them.

As they came closer, Mick recognized the two women as members of the Disciples of Bethany Magdalene. One had brown hair, the other blond, and that was about all the notice the Angel took of them.

It was the long forgotten Disciples of Bethany Magdalene that more than anything else served to promulgate the slander that both Mary of Bethany and Mary Magdalene were prostitutes. Nothing much could have been further from the truth.

In fact, both women advocated celibacy as a requirement for a woman to know the Creator, unlike Saint Paul who weakly said that celibacy was the 'best way, but for those who could not resist fornication, they should marry.'

But Mary of Bethany and Mary Magdalene countered by slyly asking, "How is it that if a man cannot serve two masters, then how could a woman do what a man cannot? How can a woman obey both her husband and her God?" When Peter, Paul, John, and Jude went unto the Son to complain, the Scion of the Creator only smiled at the men, and asked them when someone was going to get around to inventing Sūdoku?

But when the women Arsinoe; Joanna, Martha the sister of Lazarus, Mary Magdalene, Mary of Bethany, Mary Salome, Mary the mother of the Son, Miriamne sister of Phillip, and Susanna all came to the Son to complain of the men, the Son gave unto them a sermon concerning the great need of putting belief into action. The Son made no reservation concerning gender. Both men and women were called to good works because of their Faith. Of that, He was sure. And the women went away filled with wonder, and new hope for the usefulness of their lives unto the Creator.

And the Son said; "Verily, verily, that was close."

When the men returned and rebuked the Son, incidentally for the 1,000[th] time, the Son calmly informed them that that he had just remembered that Sūdoku was originally invented by a Chinese man in a Japanese tavern about twelve hundred years prior. And the Son asked the men if they knew where He, the Son, could find a Parisian newspaper?

The men went away astonished by such nonsense, whispering to themselves that the Son really should not be allowed to drink import wine. Saint Paul on the other hand, continued his mutterings against gossipy women; saying, "I'll get them, you just wait and see."

And it came to pass that four Marys and a Martha founded the first hospital for women while Arsinoe, Joanna, Martha, Miriamne, and Susanna went off to found the first women's teaching college. The hospital took in husbandless mothers, both pre and post confinement, and women who were unclean. While their medical knowledge was rudimentary, even by the standards of the time, the Disciples of Bethany Magdalene healed and comforted the women of Jerusalem without reference to time cards, union affiliation, citizenship, or ability to pay. And they had a comparatively amazing success ratio. Admittedly, this was due in the main to Martha being an OCD clean freak, and all of the Marys waging unrepentant species warfare on all manner of insects, pests, and perfumes.

But the women of the Disciples of Bethany Magdalene quickly earned a reputation as the "prostitute doctors," never mind the fact that many a highborn Hebrew, Roman, and Greek lady secreted themselves in by the back door for twice-annual check-ups, or the discreetly dispensed anti-itch cream.

In later years, many thousands upon thousands of Magdalene Houses were built, despite the fact that soon after the Crucifixion of the Son; the Disciples of Bethany Magdalene were all disbanded by force. Rumour had it that Saint Peter did it out of spite because one night he ordered Mary Magdalene to

"Shut up," to which she replied, "Make me," and verily, he could not.

The Angel had walked wordlessly back to town with the women, intending to take his shelter in the home of Saint Philip.

But, the Angel Mick never got there.

Just as they were all turning the corner into Philip's street, they all spied a woman, very near her time, squatting in the street.

As the two Disciples of Bethany Magdalene approached the woman, she said unto them, "Away from me good sisters, for I have no husband, and my dead lord's brother refused me in his bed, and so did my dead lord's father refuse me in his bed, so I can only give you the sin of unclean hands."

The Angel Mick folded his arms and nodded approvingly.

The two Disciples of Bethany Magdalene whispered soothing things to the woman large with child as they helped her up out of the mud.

"Thank you, oh thank you," the woman said, as the Disciples of Bethany Magdalene helped her up on the ass.

"Should stone the slut," the Angel muttered stepping well out of arms reach of the women, for while an Angel, he wasn't entirely stupid.

"Oh, it's not me, Angel," the woman said to the Mick, "my Demon is the slut."

Mick looked up in horror to see the blue-green eyes of the woman flash red, orange, and then solid black.

The Angel lunged for the pregnant woman.

The pregnant woman lunged at the brown haired Disciple of Bethany Magdalene, planted a wet kiss upon her mouth, slipped, and fell to the ground dead, her neck broken.

And that was when the Angel Mick met Gaius Plinius Secundus for the first time.

"Why are you putting a dead woman on your ass?" Gaius Plinius Secundus asked.

"Rough life kid, people die," the Angel said with a noncommittal shrug. "Now, go away kid, ya bother me," Mick added, confident the old one-line would work. Hell, it had worked on Cain.

"Do ya think the kid might have needed to talk to ya?" Mick remembered the Demon Keith asking him about Cain. "I mean Hell's Broken Bells Angel, you give the kid the brush off at a time when Cain's dad is out screwing Cain's sisters, and while his mom is out with Stan, and just after the Creator has shown up to the first barbeque in history which Able totally did not invite Cain to, and it never occurred to you that the kid might have just needed someone to listen to him complain about it all? Somebody to blow-off steam at?"

"And just what are you?" Gaius Plinius Secundus asked the Angel. "I don't think you're mortal."

Mick scowled at the memory of Keith's commentary about Cain and then scowled at the kid.

The kid just stood and stared at the Angel.

"Okay kid," Mick said, "what's on your mind? Unfaithful father? Mom out at all hours? Your brother just shown you up?"

"What?"

"When?"

"Location?"

The Angel sighed. Latin was just plain useless.

Mick gestured for the Disciples of Bethany Magdalene to go on, back to the hospital.

"Well?"

"I am an Angel of the God of Abraham, Isaac, and Jacob, the one true God, Creator of the Heavens and the Terra, and the sun-"

"I'm Gaius Plinius Secundus son of Gaius Plinius Celer and Marcella, and what the Hell are you?" Gaius Plinius Secundus said.

"I told you, I'm an Angel of the God of-"

"Yes, yes, I heard all that," Gaius Plinius Secundus said testily.

"All right, have it your way then, what's up ya twerp?"

But the Angel never heard what the twerp said because the screaming drowned everything out.

The Angel took off down the empty street and turned towards the Disciples of Bethany Magdalene Hospital, Gaius Plinius Secundus following right behind.

The Angel burst into the hospital, past the sick ward, down the hall, and into the confinement ward.

What the Angel found sickened even him.

The brown haired Disciple of Bethany Magdalene, the one that had been kissed by a Demon possessed woman not even half an hour before, calmly strode like Moses parting the sea, from one pregnant belly to another, cutting the bébés free. The fact that both bébé and mother quickly died didn't phase their killer at all.

Mick had raged, threw off his cloak, and expanded his wings wide. The Angel flew across the room, knocking the brown haired Disciple to the floor. Her knife hit the floor, sliding away from her.

Behind him, the young eyes of Gaius Plinius Secundus grew wide as he watched the brown haired woman roll back to her feet, and punch the Angel so hard that he flew backwards, landing on the last pregnant woman, breaking her water, back, and neck.

The Angel got up and looked for a moment at the dead mother's blood smeared on the back of his hand.

A deep laugh crackled out of the mouth of the brown haired Disciple of Bethany Magdalene.

Mick recognized the voice.

"I call you Shax," the Angel said. "Come forth now, out of her by your own will."

"Bugger off Twinkie," growled the lately identified voice of Shax.

"I command you now," Mick said, "come out now."

"Are you kidding me?" laughed the voice of Shax. "You've got the same control over me as the Son has over his own destiny."

"I call you Shax," the Angel said. "Come forth now, out of her by your own will."

"What- the- Hell- are you?" Gaius Plinius Secundu screamed at them.

"Cute kid," Shax said looking past the Angel. "Your body guard?"

"I am Gaius Plinius Secundus," Gaius Plinius Secundus said sticking his chin out at the Demon.

"Kid, get out of here," Mick said and pointed towards the door.

"Not until you tell me what you are," Gaius Plinius Secundus demanded.

"What?"

"What, you, are," Gaius Plinius Secundus screamed. "You're not a man; for all that you look like one. What are you?"

Mick gazed at the kid in amazement. Blood, gore, and stench all covered the ward, and this kid wanted to play "What's Waldo?"

377

"Fuckin' mortals," Mick and Shax said at the same time.

And that was when Shax sucker punched the Angel. It was a good punch, a Kid Dynamite hitting Jinx quality sucker punch.

The dark haired whore laughed loudly in the deep hollow voice of Shax.

"See ya in Heaven, Angel," Shax said, and popped out of the brown haired Disciple of Bethany Magdalene's body.

The woman's eyes glazed and she collapsed onto the floor, her breathing laboured, her hand clenched around the bloody knife, unspeakable humours soaked through her clothes.

The boy took one look at the woman's face and screamed, "Guards! Guards!"

Two Roman guards, followed by a Sargent of the Sanhedrin Temple Police, already alerted to the rampaging slaughter, appeared behind Gaius Plinius Secundus.

Too late, Mick remembered that it was now the Sabbath, the compulsory day of rest. It was an odd thought the Angel admitted, covered in the blood of a murdered woman, but that's reality for you. Just when it gets hopelessly dark, the brain latched on to something truly irrelevant.

"Oh shit," Mick said, as he lay dazed on the dirt floor of the house next to the dishevelled body of the brown haired Disciple, and listened to Gaius Plinius Secundus go on about Mick beating her to death.

Yes, Mick remembered all right. Funny how he never before spotted that the kid's name made out GPS. Like he was the tracking signal for the mortal authorities.

Shax was the reason Mick had missed the most important event in all of mortal history between the Expulsion from the Garden and the War at Armagedōn.

It had been almost six months before Mick was released from jail, and by then, everything was over. The Disciple of Bethany Magdalene was executed as a murderer the next morning.

Shax scoffed at the Angel's meditative silence.

"You know he set you up, right?" Shax asked.

Mick blinked and rubbed several millions of years out of his eyes.

"Who, Plinius? I doubt it," Mick said. "The rest of that guy's life was phenomenal. Inaccurate sure, but phenomenal none the less. I should have just called you the third time by the Will of the Creator."

"Yeah, you should have, but you didn't," Shax said in genuine good humour. "You've never been able to think worth a shit when you're under pressure. But, no you idiot," Shax added tapping his right index finger to his forehead. "The Metatron. He told me where to find you. I got 242 Silver Denarius for my service. Old school going rate for a specialist. The Metatron set you up. I was merely his willing tool."

In order to avoid confusion with the celebrated chronicles of the Wizard of Chicago, it must be pointed out here that the Demon Watcher Shax is actually talking about the Denarius currency, which was a silver coin that was originally valued at 10 asses, or silver pennies. Later on, inflation and false coining being what they are, the silver found in a silver coin hardly had more silver in it than Shax's own silver tongue. But in this instance, Shax asked for and received the Imperial Coin, which were all minted out of a nearly perfect silver bar, and not out of the souls of Fallen Angels, which was how Judas Iscariot was paid by the chief priests of Judea, one of which was the Demon Diábolos who placed the tainted coins into Judas' hands. It had been a bit of a trick on Diábolos' part as the Son had clearly given Judas instructions to denounce the Son freely and without compensation.

But Diábolos had played on the Judas' poverty and told him to feed the people, and so Judas was betrayed yet again.

Shax simply wanted the silver coin in order to melt it down and line the edges of Unholy Swords to sell to death cultists, and would have had no use for the Fallen in this particular instance. Actually, Shax never had any use for any of the Fallen at any point in the history of this universe, or any other for that matter.

"I don't believe you," Mick said.

"Listen here camper, I am a peer of the Under-realm and a General in the-"

Mick irrupted with gut-wrenching laughter.

A shadow passed over Shax's face, settling on his forehead like an evil halo of monochromatic despair.

"Peer of the," Mick gasped, "under-wear more like it." After which, Mick sat up, repeated the word underwear again, and fell back to indulging his laughter.

If the Angel wasn't drunk, he sure was putting up a good show, Shax thought.

"I am Shax- Duke of Hell- Commander of 30 Legions of Hellions!" Shax fumed.

This declaration only served to send Mick into such convulsions that he slid off the side of his stool in a manner that would have done Harpo Marx proud.

"Yeah?" Mick finally managed from somewhere near the carpet, "how many of them here?"

Shax tossed back the remainder of his drink, and poured himself another.

"You know?" he said, "This is a prime example of why nobody likes you, Micky Mick."

"I don't care," the Angel said.

"Look, did you see the Metatron's *Eternity and Possibility* pronouncement?" Shax asked with a studied indifference that normally would have alerted a sober Angel to be on its guard.

"You mean all that rot about "eventually" he was putting out on the *Oprah Show*?" Mick returned.

"Yeah, that," Shax agreed. "It all boils down to this: given an omniscient, omnipotent, and omnipresent Creator, then nothing, absolutely nothing is canonically impossible, and given that, it logically follows that anything that can possibly happen, will happen, eventually, just because it *can* happen."

"That's a load of bullshit," Mick said as he sploshed another drink into his tumbler. "Boring, played out non-sense too."

Shax shrugged, took the bottle, and wiped down the bar.

"Maybe it is," Shax said. "But it's true none the less for being played out bullshit. Think about Eternity right, I mean the long haul Eternity. I'm coming on my zillionth year of being sentient and whatever, and I'm so bloody tired of being around and being bored that I'm about to go in for rebellion again just in the hopes of getting blasted out of existence for the sake of some peace and quiet. So, think about how fucking bored He must be by now. Shit, man, how long you think before He starts to work on alternative universes and parallel dimensions and looking at questions like, 'So, what will Duritz's Mr. Jones do if I give him the ability to manipulate beautiful women and the forces of nature by the simple expedient of muttering a few words and waving his hands around.' Hell, you, Mr. Angelic-pants are so bored now, even on the short end of Eternity, that you're actually getting together with a bunch of untouchables to film a movie, which almost no one will ever see, and you're not even a billion yet."

Mick looked at the breathless Watcher in frank astonishment. "Obviously, Eternity is getting to you man. I'd check in at the retirement home for washed-out might-have-beens and get your head right, before He lops it off."

"Do you seriously think that His imagination is lamer then mine?" Shax demanded. "I mean seriously, His imagination should be infinitely more comprehensive than mine, and I can think of a billion things better and more entertaining than what has been in the last 3 universes."

"I don't think that-"

"Can I interject a question," asked a youngish looking man stepping out of the shadows behind the hearth. He wore a pair of faded blue jeans and a black t-shirt, and carried a cardboard box, which he placed on the bar.

Shax looked inside the box and then pushed it further down the bar away from the Angel.

"Fornícó, great, just fracking great," Mick said after turning around to see the speaker.

Fornícó nodded as he walked up to the bar and sat down at the bar, leaving a stool between him and the Angel.

Shax placed a tumbler of clear ginger coloured liquor in front of the newcomer, and started sorting through the contents of the box.

"Where the Hell did you come from?" Mick asked while still looking at the solid walls beside and behind the fireplace.

Many observers of the Angelic nature have openly speculated that it is absolutely impossible to surprise an Angel. The truth is, nothing could be further from the truth, or in fact, to employ another cliché, nothing could be easier. Angels always confuse their superior abilities with His superior knowledge, and are therefore always surprised when something unexpected happens. It is a curious circumstance of the Angelic mind that while they accept the fact that they and the Demons who are really only Angels with bad politics, can perform marvellous feats of miracle and magic, Angels just cannot seem to believe that anyone else in the entire realm of Creation can too. So both Angels and Demons are routinely surprised because of their arrogant assumptions about the capacity of non-Angels.

For instance, when the Seven Long Ranger Angels came to collect up the 3 Wrath gods, all seven of the Angels were blasted back to Heaven in a hand basket because they did not take seriously the reports that the 3 Wrath gods had stolen all of Stan's powers due to Stan's failure to read the really-really-really-excruciatingly small print in their contract that null and voided everything else in the 313 page document and directly ceded all of Stan's powers to the 3 Wrath gods for a period of 777 years. After being recycled into new bodies, the Seven Long Ranger Angels simply skipped ahead in the time line, while looping the Wrath gods through the same 7 minutes 58,381,560 times, and kicked the unholy shit out of the 3 Wrath gods about 5 minutes after their power-sucking arrangement with Stan ended. See, even old Angels can learn new tricks.

"I came from the lusts, desires, and intrigues of the shadows," Fornícó said with a smile. "Fireplaces are really good for me in that way. So many bastard sacrifices have been made to me in front of fireplaces, especially on shag carpet and-"

"Right," Shax said cutting Mick off before he said anything daft. "What was your question?"

"Do we all agree on the Bossman being omniscient, omnipotent, and omnipresent?" Fornícó asked.

"Yes," Mick said with emotion, "and omniarch, omnicompetent, and omniparient-"

Fornícó stopped listening when the Angel stood up. He knew that the Creator's Omni characteristics were these: Omniarch; a ruler of all things, Omnicompetent; able to judge or deal with all matters, Omnidirectional; sending or receiving signals in or from all directions, Omnifarious; of many or all varieties or forms, Omniferous; all-bearing; producing all kinds, Omnific; creating all things; having unlimited powers of creation, Omnified; universally present and prescient at all points in space at the same time, Omniform; having every form or shape, Omnigenous; consisting of all kinds, Omniparient; producing all things, Omnipatient; capable of enduring all things, and Omniety; that which is all-pervading or all-comprehensive; hence, the Deity-God-Creator-Guy *is* Infinity. And considerably more in that same line.

Hearing an Angel go over this familiar ground wasn't doing the little god immortal any good. It wasn't even amusing. It just was.

"Right Angel, kill the dictionary recital, okay?" Fornicó cut in and pushed the Angel back on his bar stool.

"Omnibenevolent," Shax added, "as we all know literally from the Latin means *omni* or "all," and *benevolent* meaning *good*. More loosely rendered as unlimited or infinite benevolence."

What Shax failed to add was that most sentient creatures would, if they ever bothered to think about it, consider Omnibenevolence to be an impossible trait for the Creator. For it had to be argued that allowing evil into the world undercut the benevolent angle. Or, not having the power to prevent evil would undercut the omniscience and omnipotence angle. Both philosophers and Theologians have spilled millions of metric tons of ink on the issue, making it all black as pitch, when the truth is that it's really a funny old world after all.

"No," Mick said rising to his feet again. "No, not one bit. Remember Noah? Man that was a bad day."

"Bossman is all things omni, except the one's Mick doesn't like" Fornicó conceded. "Bossman's so omni that you might as well call us Omnians. So, let's consider that for a moment."

"Consider what?" the Angel demanded crossly and picked up his drink.

Fornícó laughed and slapped Mick on the back, causing the fussy Angel to spill drink on his trench coat.

"That's what I love about you Micky," Fornícó exclaimed. "You wouldn't understand the meaning of Verificationism if somebody explained it to you. One Authority, One Word, one perspective, zero disagreement."

"I guess it never occurred to him that Mr. B. might have left some stuff out," Shax said.

"Now look here, I'm not going to stand around-" Mick started.

"Sit down," Fornícó said gently forcing Mick back down.

"-here," Mick continued, "and listen to you two blaspheme."

"Theorize," Fornícó corrected. "We're thinking out-loud. Think of it as learning about your enemy from within? You have a first-hand chance here to get inside the psychology of the rebellion, or what's left of it. 'Know how a man thinks and you know how to control him.' Just like dear old Ma always use to say."

"Fine, get on with it already," Mick complained. "And there was nothing dear about Ba'al."

"True," Fornícó agreed amiably. "So, omniscience is to like have the capacity to know the whole of infinity, and everything in it, without going nuts, and never, never, never be surprised by anything, right?"

"Right," Mick said nodding cautious agreement.

"This by necessity means that you not only know what is, but that you also know what is not, yes?"

"Yes," Mick agreed again.

"Okay, so omnipotence means all unlimited power, can do absolutely anything even logically impossible shyt like turning the world into a *Tiny Toons*

385

Adventure. Complete and total pure *Agency of Will*. Anything He chooses in accordance with His own nature, although this also means that He can change His nature and once done, His nature has always been so, thereby providing consistency, and since He is also omniscience everything, including any after the last minute changes are already incorporated into His grand plan because they were always there, even before they weren't there. See?"

"Uh, yeah," the Angel said who didn't. "Sure, why not?"

"So He could change the entire universe at any moment, and nobody would notice, because from our point of view, it will have always been that way," Fornícó said.

Mick pursed his lips.

"And so we come to omnipresence, being ubiquity basically," Fornícó continued. "Now, in the Eastern-theisms, that means that the Bossman is everywhere, all the fuck time, no matter what. Bossman holds everything together; like He's gravity or whatever that sticky stuff is that hold all those sub-atomic quarks together."

"May the Boss be with you," Shax said.

"And also with you," the Angel responded without conscious thought.

"Right, good one," Fornícó agreed. "And due to His being everywhere, that also means that He's in all Times, Eternal. Everywhere and Everywhen, including those whens that aren't actually anywhere, which makes that an actual when and an actual where because He is actually there, where there is no when. Do you see?"

"No," Mick said and held up a restraining hand to forestall further explanation. "And I'll thank you not to go on about it. If it makes sense to you, fine. I hope you can sell it to Him if you ever need too. But for the love all things Divine, do not haze me with shyt again."

"You know," Shax said with a faraway look of memory on his countenance, "I've never worked out if omnipresence meant that you were always everywhere at the same time, or just that you could be, if you wanted to be, but that you didn't necessarily have to be everywhere if you didn't want to."

"Ha, that's the joke of it,' Fornícó agreed. " They're both correct."

"Figures," Shax said. "The Creator likes that style of thing."

"Sounds boring, don't it?" Fornícó asked.

"What? Why?" Mick asked.

"Because," Fornícó said, "You- that's the generic you, not the Mick you- would already know everything, every possible outcome of anything. No suspense, no drama, no narrative tension, nothing. And it is because of that lack of surprise that the Bossman goes in for the 'everything that can happen, will happen, eventually model of universe management. It's like He's a great engineer of ocean-faring ships but has never Himself been swimming, much less been on a cruise. The only real joy for Him is in the doing, the creating, and putting it all into action.

"I know programmers like that," Shax said.

Fornícó nodded and continued "Yeah, He knows which horse to bet on, sure, but that doesn't mean He doesn't want to see the horse race."

"Or the war," Shax added.

"Or the war," Fornícó agreed. "I mean, mortals watched reruns of shows they saw before, didn't they? So yeah, Bossman has already seen everything, and that also logically means that He's also already seen everything that didn't happen, and means by inference that everything that didn't happen actually did happen because Bossman saw that it didn't happen here, but that it could have happened somewhere else because

He saw that it didn't happen there where it did happen because He saw it."

"Dude, you need to stop freebasing your corn flakes?" Mick asked. "I mean seriously, that is some of the lousiest coffee shop patter I've ever heard."

"Doesn't mean it ain't true," Fornícó said tossing back the rest of his drink. "I've heard wisdom out of worse places in my time. It all boils down to being omniscient, omnipotent, omnipresent, and imagination."

"And being the Creator," Shax added. "That bit is like, built in, so to speak."

"I don't get it," Mick complained.

"Okay, let me make this simple for you," Fornícó said. "If Bossman thinks of something, even you know, to discount that something He thought of, then it becomes real-*somewhere*-by virtue of the fact that He thought about it. Get it?"

"So you're saying," Mick struck out, "that there is no difference between the imagination of the *Divine* and our reality?"

"Yes, more or less, that's it," Fornícó said.

"What's the less-than?" Mick asked.

"Reality does not have agency," Shax explained. "Physical matter doesn't, ha- ha, matter. Put a bunch of matter in one place without agency and it will settle down to inertia real quick. Bossman is agency though, that's what keeps the stars flaring and the universe turning. "I Am that I Am," *He* said, and it t'was."

"So you two knuckle heads are saying that somewhere out there magic really exists and all that junk?" Mick asked.

"Oh for Heaven's sake Angel," Shax complained. "You've met gods and Scions before and Hellspawn too, of course magic is real, even here in this universe it is real. The fact that mortals can't do it doesn't mean squat."

"No, I mean for mortals, pure mortals," Mick clarified.

"Yes," Fornícó said. "I don't know why it's never worked for mortals here unless they had the backing of a celestial creature, even if they didn't know it. I've seen it work in other universes and the Demon James swears magic is as common as muck outside of this universe."

"I think the Gatekeeper forbade magic for mortals this go-around," Shax said with a shrug. "He was tasked with keeping them safer than the Creator did in the last universe."

"Who's the Gatekeeper?" Mick asked.

Fornícó laughed. "I've got to take a leak. Shax?"

Shax gestured down the hallway. "Last door on your left, the blue one."

Fornícó walked down the hallway whistling, *Tain't Nobody's Business If I Do.*

"Here's the deal Angel," Shax said, "this universe was given 1 trillion years, and that time's about run out."

"Well, that's a rather particular number," Mick said settling down.

"1 trillion years," Shax said again. "Humanity should have colonized all of the stars in that time, and instead, only a couple of dozen solar systems, and that was only because of the Node Pathways."

"Whatever man, the Creator never said anything about that. What a cow pie. I can't believe you believe that old wives tale. Rubbish."

"That's because He couldn't."

Mick gave Shax a look that went on for a very long time. Shax just got on with polishing bar glasses.

"There is nothing that the Creator cannot do. He is the God, the One, and only God," Mick finally said.

"Yeah, alright," Shax said. "Say He wouldn't, instead of He couldn't then. Big C. made a bet with Stanley about one particular person, and in order to preserve the experimental conditions of the bet, they both agreed to keep mum about it."

"Yeah, then how come you know about it?" the Angel demanded.

"Because I'm older than you, Angel, a lot older."

Mick scowled and finished his drink. It did not taste good anymore.

"I still think its crap," he said. "The Creator doesn't do things like that."

"Oh yeah?" Shax purred. "You ever read the *Book of Job* or the *Book of Nighthawk*?"

"Job, yes, Nighthawk, no, never even heard of it."

Shax looked upward with an expression of tried patience. "Do you see? Do you see what I have to deal with down here? Seriously, I think I've done my time by now, yeah. I mean a joke's a joke already."

"And just who are you talking to?" Mick asked, pushing his empty glass at the Demon.

"Oh, Nobody that's listening," Shax said, refilling the drink. "Now about "The Book of Job-"

"Yes, that was an extended metaphor and-"

"Yeah, right, sure, metaphor, right, the Angel isn't a literalist when he doesn't want to be, got it," Shax said, and quickly moved on to add, "*The Book of Nighthawk* is the same thing, only different."

"Right, okay, I'll play along, and what happened?" Mick asked.

"Well, sometime back in the last universe-"

"What last universe?" the Angel demanded.

390

"Look, are you going to let me tell you this story or are you going to interrupt?" Shax asked testily.

"Yeah, yeah, sure, carry on."

"Right, like I was saying," Shax continued, "sometime back in the last universe-"

"Before it ended."

"Knock it off, Angel. It never ended. It's still there. There's a million-million-million infinity of them."

Mick waved his hands in the same way a bullfighter does to indicate that the bull can go wherever he wants to go.

"Right, so Stanley conceived this outright hatred for Nighthawk, and got the Creator to give unto Nighthawk the administration of this entire universe, bearing in mind a few unconditional terms, and bet that said Nighthawk would or would not blaspheme under the pressure of being a minor deity."

"Yeah, right, okay, and?" Mick prompted while suppressing a yawn.

"Well, he hasn't. It's been about, oh, 999,999,999,997 years since then, and time is about up. Stan has given up on winning since Nighthawk gave up mucking about with people a couple of million years ago, and has just let things cruise on autopilot, just like the Big C. does in all His other universes."

"And who is this Nighthawk?" Mick asked. "Don't tell me, you don't know who he is either, do you?"

"Why yes, yes I do," Shax said with a grin. "But before you ask thrice, I can't tell you. He's been working under an assumed name for millions of years. It'd be rude to blow it."

The Angel laughed.

"Obviously, if you told me, you'd have to kill me," Mick said.

"I could you know," Shax picking up his three-handed battle bow from behind the bar with a sigh. "I miss my War Chicken."

"War Chicken?" Basil Berry asked.

Mick turned around and wasn't very surprised to see Basil Berry sitting calmly kicked back, propped on his arms, upon a trunk covered in teeth. After Fornícó had shown up, Mick had figured it was only a matter for time before the party went both metaphorically and literally to Hell.

"Yeah," Shax said. "She was a 7-foot tall 300 stone beast that could peck through 3 inches of battle grade steel."

"What happened to her?" Basil Berry asked thinking of 300 stone worth of chicken laminated in Black Eyed Sally's barbecue sauce.

Basil Berry had always thought that of all the Human endeavours lost as a result of the last War at Armagedōn, Black-eyed Sally's BBQ and Blues on Asylum Street in Hartford, Connecticut would top the list of most mourned by the immortal and semi-immortal crowd. It was certainly the most mourned by Basil Berry's belly.

Many Scions and most of the named Demons of the Clavis Salomonis frequented the excellent feed stop for BBQ, Blues, and banter. Though no formal agreements were ever drawn-up by the ranked legions of Heaven and Hell, it was generally considered neutral territory, a grey zone, and the height of bad manners to cause a ruckus while there.

"A bunch of bastard Angels ate her after Armagedōn," Shax said glaring at Mick.

"Hold on now, I resent being called a bastard," Mick complained, still glaring at Basil Berry.

"Oh yeah Angel, who's your momma? Erebus, Gaea, Nemesis?" Basil Berry asked.

"Well, um, that is, the thing of it is," Mick said.

"Sounds like a momma 'less bastard to me," Basil Berry agreed. "You should pretty much be able to snap your Mama's name right off the cuff, if'n you were the non-bastard type that is."

"I don't think you can be a bastard if you were never birthed," Mick complained.

"Well, blow it out your ear then," Basil Berry said, "you're a bastard, get over it."

Basil Berry walked over to the bar, poured himself a drink of the warm amber Double Cross and bolted it down.

"Glugggg."

"Yeah kid?" Shax asked while slowly filling a glass of cold water.

"Freallkougg," Basil Berry said ignoring the proffered water in favour of bolting a second shot.

"Oh really, you don't say?" Shax added, placing the glass of water in front of the Scion.

Basil Berry bolted the water.

"The young these days," Shax complained, "can't hold their liquor."

"What are you doing here?" Mick asked once the Scion stopped sputtering long enough to pour himself a third drink.

"Looking for you, Angie-baby," Basil Berry said poring himself a third portion of amber whiskey-rum. "Righteous bad manners of you not to be in the Khufu crypt when Keith said you'd be."

"Me?" the Angel asked in genuine astonishment.

"Yeah, you," Basil Berry said, this time slowly draining the whiskey-rum. "Keith gave me a message for you."

"Why?"

"Because Don Vito a'told me too 'a," the Scion slurred.

"Oh, for the hate of Hell," Mick said. "Can't he keep a secret for 10 seconds?"

"Nope," Shax said.

"Keith said," Basil Berry, now visibly unsteady, cut in. "I'm to tell you that he's worked out your labour problem, the scenery problem, and the casting problem. No Zombies required."

"What are you talking about?" Mick asked in complete bewilderment. "We don't have any problems here, labour or otherwise."

"Yeah, sure you don't," Shax said. "You got nothing but a washed-out Demon, your Angelic self, a knuckle-headed Scion, and me, and I won't help. Oh yeah, and you got a dust bowl of a planet, too. Not really anything to work with there. Hadn't really thought about your labour problem, I must admit."

"What's in the trunk?" Mick asked trying to change the subject.

"2 sextillion, 305 quadrillion, 843 trillion, 8 billion, 139 million, 952 thousand, 128 pretty girls," Basil Berry said. "That's one, two, many, lots, one million, two millions, many millions, lots millions, and lots billions, lots trillions, and that's a lot of lots having like a googolplex of lots. You could make a whole new multi-planetary civilization with that many slots."

"You thinking of starting a new *civilization*?" Mick asked, the bitter sarcasm washing over every word.

"Na man," Basil Berry said pouring himself another drink and swaying slightly on his bar stool. "Clan's already here. Don't need those Human slots. Just wanted 'em." The Scion used his free hand to steady his drink holding hand and then downed his drink. "We're all the pretty," the Scion said and forgot the end of the sentence.

"Pardon?" asked the Angel.

The Scion belched.

The Angel sighed.

"Already here," Basil Berry said again going for another drink and missing.

"Yes," Mick said uncertainly. "I see you, and Shax, and Fornícó. There's nobody else here. On Tafari, I mean."

"Nope," said Basil Berry using one hand to steady the other hand, which managed to grab the bottle.

Now where the Hell did that glass go? Basil Berry thought.

"Oh good," said the Angel.

"They're outside the Khufu thing-a-ma-giger," Basil Berry said. "Amy, President of Hell said something about putting up a skyscraper across the street."

"What-what-what?" the Angel exclaimed, panic running through his voice. "Who? How many? What? Where? Fudge-fudge-fudge!"

"Um," said Basil Berry who had just found his glass again. "Angels, Demons, Imps, Avatars, Messengers, Nightmares, Scions, Hellspawns, my mother-in-law-"

"What? What? How many?" Mick screeched jumping to his feet.

"Um, all of them, I think," Basil Berry said and double-fisted his empty glass to his mouth. He made a loud satisfied gulping sound. "Bloody fucking text messaging. Emails too. Haven't gotten so many emails in millions of years. I'll never get 'em all answered. Never. I won't even think- thought, didn't, think, fart." Basil Berry stopped, took a deep breath, and said, "Didn't even think that hPhone still worked. Who'd'a thunk it? Hasn't been charged in centuries."

Basil Berry sat bolt upright and looked sombrely at the Angel.

"You're the new President, CEO, and film guru of the Empire Studios," Basil Berry beamed. "Brand new skyscraper right down at the film corner of State and Main, New Terra. You've got full creative control, and," here the Scion swayed gently. "And," he began again, "and something else. Can't quite seem to put my drin' on it. Drink on it."

The Scion slumped again.

"Oh no, no, no," the Angel whined, turned, and ran for the Red Door portal.

Fornícó stepped out of the bathroom, laughed, and followed Mick out to into the basement of the Pyramid of Khufu.

"Have another drink lad," Shax said with a smug grin and poured Basil Berry a double. "That was nasty, really nasty. I don't mind telling you, it's a privilege to watch you work kid."

"Work?" Basil Berry mumbled. "Who's a fuking working? I'm drunk. Fugging good stuff Shackky-shack-sshazzz. Sober to bloody fuck pissed in 5 drinks."

Basil Berry then gently slid off the seat and collapsed on the floor.

"Isn't bloody-fuck a bit redundant?" Shax ask while scratching one long claw at a flaw in a tumbler.

"Na-vay mate," Basil Berry said whilst ineffectually pushing the floor away from him. "Ya see-me's ethnic Euro-trash, that got'z trapped in America. Got my thingamgiggies all, what'ch'a call 'em, confused."

"Dictionaries?" Shax suggested.

"Ya, them things, right, got the think methods of a Euro-bum, with a damn American accent, not bloody fucking fair, and all those extra Us and Es, and nothing to hang an umlaut on, and you can just forget a decent iota," Basil Berry mumbled as his body finally went limp. "I went to a swamp near this bar and that where I meet my Iota, my little trollop named iiiiiioooootaaa. Eyyyyie-I-oooo-ta."

Basil Berry began to snore.

Shax finished polishing the tumbler with his bar towel before he went over to the limp Basil Berry, picked him up, and put him belly side down on the couch. Shax also placed a large unlined garbage can right next to Basil Berry's head and hoped that when the sick came, the kid managed to not choke to death on it.

One-bit Human, one-bit semi-divine, and all bits confused, Shax thought. Worse than being all divine or all Human. Damn mules, every one of them.

"Well done kid, well done," Shax muttered.

Shax than clapped a fire into existence in the fireplace, and flipped off the lights with a wave of his hand.

Basil Berry snored.

Shax then went over to the cardboard box still sitting on the bar and withdrew 35 mm film copies of 1971 *King Lear* directed by Peter Brook starring Paul Scofield, the *Complete Histories of Xenophōn, Abridged*, filmed in 2009 by the Historian Bettany Hughes for the *Museum of Curiosity*, and the 1939 *Gone with the Wind*.

With the three canisters tucked under his arm, Shax went out into his storage room, and out the red door.

Shax turned to face the door, Tafari side, after closing it.

In the dusty silence of the Subterranean Chamber, Shax muttered a word, and the round red door folded along its diameter, then folded down its middle to form a quarter of the original circle. It repeated the folding until there the door was not much wider than an old-fashioned skinny necktie. Shax picked the door up, placed it around his neck, and tied it into a daft Double Windsor Knot.

Être Poursuivie.

Except that is not really the end.

The Murder of Basil Berry: Book II of the Complete Revelation of Mick and Keith, by James H. Peterson III, should be available in eBook format on the 15th of March, 2017, and in print format on the 1st of April of the same year.

And Then There Were None: Book III of the Complete Revelation of Mick and Keith, by James H. Peterson III, should be available in eBook format on the 15th of March, 2018, and in print format on the 1st of April of the same year.

You can find the author's blog at TheInfinityPlane.com.

Copyright Acknowledgement

It is with deepest gratitude for their help in securing appropriate permissions that the author publically thanks Laura Forker of The Random House Group, Josh Crosley of Transworld Publishers, Joanne Williamson of Transworld Publishers, Shea Esterling of Aberystwyth University, and most particularly to Colin Smythe.

www.ingramcontent.com/pod-product-compliance
Lightning Source LLC
Chambersburg PA
CBHW071151250626
47159CB00001B/66